SPIRITED

A GOTHIC REVERSE HAREM BULLY ROMANCE

STEFFANIE HOLMES

SPIRITED

Musician.
Heartbreaker.
Murderer.

Dorien Valencourt is in deep shit.
His cheeky grin and stormy eyes won't help him this time.

But I will.
I've found love in the darkness.
Three broken muses possess me,
Mind, body, and soul.
I won't give them up for anything,
Especially not for a witch with a blackened heart.

In a school ruled by shadows and secrets,
I'll shine a light in the darkest places.
We'll expose a long-buried violation,
And force a villain to confront her sins.

If only our secrets don't devour us all.

With Titus and Ivan at my side,
we'll free Dorien from his cage.
We'll drag these skeletons into the daylight.

The ghost of Manderley will have her revenge.

A dark mystery unfolds around musician Faye de Winter in the final book of this gripping gothic college reverse harem bully romance by USA TODAY best-selling author Steffanie Holmes. Warning: Proceed with caution – this tale of three spoiled rich boys with unsettling secrets and the girl who refuses to put up with their shit contains dark themes, a creepy house, a smoldering second-chance romance, college angst, cruel bullies and swoon-worthy sex.

Grab a free copy *Cabinet of Curiosities* – a Steffanie Holmes compendium of short stories and bonus scenes – when you sign up for updates with the Steffanie Holmes newsletter.

JOIN THE NEWSLETTER FOR UPDATES

Grab a free copy of *Cabinet of Curiosities* – a Steffanie Holmes compendium of short stories and bonus scenes – when you sign up for updates with the Steffanie Holmes newsletter.

www.steffanieholmes.com/newsletter

Every week in my newsletter I talk about the true-life hauntings, strange happenings, crumbling ruins, and creepy facts that inspire my stories. You'll also get newsletter-exclusive bonus scenes and updates. I love to talk to my readers, so come join us for some spooky fun :)

A NOTE ON DARK CONTENT

I wouldn't say that the Manderley Academy series is particularly dark by romance reader standards. Reading should be fun, so I want to make sure you don't get any surprises, and that's why I'm writing this wee note. If you're cool with anything and you don't want spoilers, then skip this note and dive in.

Keep reading if you like a bit of warning about what to expect in your romance novels.

- There is some bullying in the first book of Manderley Academy, but our heroine holds her own. No heroes in this series threaten or are involved in physical or sexual assault of the heroine.

- In *Spirited*, Faye fights off a sexual assault attempt, which may be triggering to some readers.

- You'll definitely stumble over a few dead bodies and some vengeful ghosts.

- Faye and her three muses Titus, Dories, and Ivan have a consensual sexual relationship which sometimes involves all of them together. This series also contains MM – meaning two of Faye's men are involved with each other. This is a reverse harem series, which means that our heroine does not choose one partner at the end of the story – she gets her happily ever after with them all.

If that's not your jam, that's totally cool. I suggest you pick up my Nevermore Bookshop Mysteries series – all of the mystery without the gore and trauma and violence.

Enjoy, you beautiful depraved human, you :) Steff

*To Niccolò, Johann, Wolfgang, and Franz –
the original Bad Boys of Baroque.*

"I know not how it was—but, with the first glimpse
of the building, a sense of insufferable gloom
pervaded my spirit."

– Edgar Allan Poe, *The Fall of the House of Usher*

"You want to see something wild?" Dorien Valencourt peered at me over his absinthe glass, all pouting, rich-boy lips and self-satisfied smirk.

I tilted my coke toward him and returned his smile with one of my own. "You're going to vault over a piano again?"

"I learned my lesson. White pianists don't jump." Dorien winced. I could see he remembered the day at our summer music program when he bet me he could vault over the baby grand and land on his feet. Instead, he nearly impaled his testicles on a cymbal stand and destroyed the hopes and dreams of a generation of Dorien fangirls. He cut a long gash on his inner thigh and paid up from an infirmary bed – I still remembered his cavalier grin and the crisp notes he peeled off and tossed at me like confetti.

That was two years ago. We'd remained friends, causing chaos together whenever we met up at recitals and music camps. It was impossible not to like Dorien, not to be swept up by the whirlwind of his personality. We lived on opposite ends of the country and I hadn't expected to see him again until college auditions at the end of the summer, but a week ago he'd randomly shown up on my doorstep, touting a Louis Vuitton suitcase and declaring he was spending the summer with me. As if I couldn't possibly have had any other plans apart from hanging out with him.

He was half right – I didn't have plans. My parents made plans for me. I was to tour the South with them as part of their ensemble – a perfect opportunity to get my name on the lips of their influential friends. But Dorien intervened with his rich-boy smile and the promise of an influential friend of my own and somehow, they agreed to leave me behind to hang out with him.

"Don't you rich boys spend your summers in Martha's Vineyard or Majorca?" I'd asked as he lugged his suitcase up to my second-floor bedroom. A shadow passed over his eyes, but it was gone before I could question it.

"You should be grateful I've decided to slum it with my pleb friend. I've saved you from a summer of dull recital rooms and cocktail sausages. Besides, I'm bored of my parents and their boring money. You'll take the fold-out, of course. I can't sleep on hard surfaces."

It was hard to stay annoyed at Hurricane Dorien bowling through my life, especially when he pointed out with an impish grin that spending the summer alone as two sixteen-year-olds in New Orleans would be infinitely better than tagging along after my parents.

He was true to his word. With Dorien at my side, my city came to life. It's funny how you can live in a place for sixteen years and not see it as special until you show it off to someone else. We spent our days walking along the banks of the Mississippi, keeping our eyes out for alligators, or buying cheap absinthe to guzzle beside the duck pond in Louis Armstrong Park (I didn't touch alcohol – my parents believed if Micah's friends hadn't been drinking, they might've saved him – but drunk Dorien was *hilarious*). We spent our nights sneaking into jazz clubs with the fake IDs Dorien purchased from a black market pancake shop on Bourbon Street (the shop was a hub for anything illegal in the city – guns, counterfeit money, secret poker games. The pancakes were also delicious).

We were in one of those jazz clubs now, enjoying our first drinks of the evening before the city rose from her slumber and breathed her first jasmine-scented greeting to the night. "Sure," I said. "Show me something wild."

Bob Dylan once said that everything in New Orleans was a good idea, but I wasn't sure even the Big Easy was ready for Dorien Valencourt.

Dorien pushed his chair back and stood up. I thought he was heading over to introduce himself to the group of girls at the bar who'd been eyeing us since they came in. They were college-aged – a good few years older than us – but with his arresting looks and my muscles, both Dorien and I could pass for twenty-year-olds. But he dodged around them and leaped onto the small stage in the corner. It was empty except for the polished piano in the center and some mic stands set up. A board behind the bar listed the three jazz ensembles that would play tonight – none of them were here yet. Live music in New Orleans didn't start until late. You had to give the city time to wake up and unfurl her wings.

The bartender waved an angry fist. "Hey, man. You're not allowed up there."

Ignoring him, Dorien mashed the piano with his fingers, launching into one of his wild, incomprehensible compositions.

And just like that, the bartender dropped his fist. And his jaw.

Dorien's music soared through the bar, reaching the ears of every patron and dragging their heads from their glasses to pay attention. Dorien played as only he could – dramatically, flamboyantly, with a passion and fervor that sucked the air from your lungs. Dorien bit his lip, his head bowed with focus as his fingers danced through the scales. The song soared and swooped, a breath of air that raised goosebumps along my arms.

Dorien had a gift.

I swallowed back the lump in my throat as I thought of

another person with the gift. A person who could write music that could tear your soul to pieces and stitch it back together in three-and-a-half minutes. A person who should have been in this bar with us but was instead six feet under.

The girls crowded the stage, grinding against Dorien as he played on. One of them tipped his head back and poured her drink down his throat. Dorien dragged her into his lap and laid a trail of sticky alcohol kisses along her neck, all the while playing perfectly. Because he's Dorien.

A crowd of people wandered in from the street, drawn by the music conjured from Dorien's dark heart. They gathered around the stage – captured, enraptured, blessed by the melody of a music god.

My chest ached, groaning under the weight of memories.

At the end of the piano, I noticed a Les Paul nestled into a stand, a line of effects pedals lined up along the stage, waiting for the evening's booked performance to take the stage. My fingers itched to pick up the guitar and join Dorien. My mind pricked at the spaces in his composition I could fill. His eyes met mine across the bar. Those slate-grey orbs didn't beg me, they *commanded*.

I dug my nails into the sticky wooden table.

It took everything I had to remain in the chair.

The weight on my chest held me frozen.

If word got back to my parents that I was playing electric guitar in a dimly lit club…it would destroy them all over again. I pictured them the night our doorbell rang. I bounded down the stairs, thinking it was Micah home from the concert. But it was the police, to tell us he'd never be home again. I remembered my mother's face crumpling like tissue paper wadded into a ball. My father beating his chest, crying to God to bring back his son.

I couldn't do that to them.

So I downed the rest of my coke and watched Dorien's passion burn through his fingers as jealousy raged inside me. The bastard had everything – money, talent, brash confidence. I wished I could taste that kind of freedom, but Micah had taken it with him to the grave.

When he finished the song, Dorien stood and took a deep bow. The crowd erupted into applause. Even the grumpy bartender whistled and hooted.

All except me. No way was I going to applaud the cocky bastard.

Dorien slid back into our booth with two of the girls hanging off his arms and that arrogant grin perfectly arranged. His cheeks and neck were smudged with lipstick. He dropped three napkins on the table between us. Each one had a phone number scrawled in crimson lipstick. "You should have joined me up there."

I flexed my arm muscles. "That stage isn't big enough for my guns and your ego."

Dorien unbound himself from his two admirers and leaned forward, slapping his hands on the table. The mirth in his eyes vanished. "This should be our lives, Titus. Playing in bars like this, being on the road, writing music that speaks to us. No rules, no obligations. Being in the real world, not trapped in stuffy concert halls and orchestra pits."

"You're being ridiculous."

"I'm not. I'm deadly serious. Let's do it, you and me. Let's make music on our own terms." Dorien's eyes flashed. I stared at him, for the first time seeing that the darkness behind them wasn't part of his act. Maybe Dorien wasn't here because he was bored and could do whatever the fuck he wanted.

Maybe the great Dorien Valencourt was running from something, too.

"You sound insane."

"You want to get out from under the thumb of your parents? This is how you do it. You need this just as much as I do."

"What exactly is the *this* you're proposing?"

"We form a band. We refine the songs I've been working on

and show them to the world. We take classical music away from stuffy halls and elitist wankers and give it back to the people. We make it cool again."

I closed my eyes, trying to shut out the insanity. I had auditions this year at Juilliard, the Royal Academy of Music, Conservatoire de Paris. I couldn't just drop everything for one of Dorien's crazy schemes. But instead of shutting him down, my mind twisted around the melody he'd just played, seeing the gaps, hearing the harmonies and layers I could add. I could *feel* the music humming in my veins, and I hadn't felt music like that since Micah taught me the riff to Black Sabbath's 'War Pigs.'

I opened my eyes. Dorien leaned in close, his shit-eating grin devouring his whole face.

"I knew you'd say yes." With the certainty of someone who'd never been told no in his life, Dorien accepted another cocktail from the bartender – the aptly-named hurricane, on the house as thanks for his performance – and took a long sip. "Now, we need a third. A violinist, I think. I've someone in mind. Have you met Ivan Nicolescu?"

"Elena Nicolescu's brother?" I met Elena at a music camp last summer. She was a waif from Romania who barely said a word to anyone, but was the greatest pianist I'd ever heard. I remembered she had a twin brother, white-haired and silent, with those same ice-cold eyes that bore holes in your skin. He played the violin. He was nothing special compared to his sister, but he had a certain sledgehammer style.

"That's the fellow. He *lives* at Manderley Academy, can you believe it?" Darkness passed through Dorien's eyes again, but it was gone before I could comment on it. "He must be a vampire. That's the only reason I can think someone would want to shut themselves away in that shithole."

"My parents made me apply." Both Dorien and I were attending auditions for the major college music programs at the end of the summer. Manderley was low on my list. Why would I want to go to a rundown old mansion in the mountains when I could study in Paris? Or London? *So* many metal bands played in London, and it was almost far enough away from my parents for me to be able to breathe.

Almost.

"If she offers you a place, don't take it." Dorien slurped his drink. "I studied at the Usher School in New York. Victor is a fine tutor, but Gizella Usher is a piece of work."

I could smell the syrupy licorice of Dorien's absinthe from across the table. My temples pounded. I didn't really want to go to any of the schools I was auditioning for. Four more years of playing cello sounded like hell on earth. But what choice did I have?

Dorien was offering that choice.

"My friend Gabriel has a band named Octavia's Ruin. They're heading out on tour in a month. The opening act just pulled out and they need someone to replace them. I played him some tapes I made and he said if I could find a band and put a set together in time, we can have the opening slot. If we want it. I know it's insane; that's what makes it fun. What do you say?"

I leaned back in my chair. It wasn't heavy metal. It wasn't the roaring guitars and pounding drums I craved, but it was *different*. It had heart and soul and feeling, and that was enough. Dorien left space in the music for me to make it my own. His song flowed through my head, and I *felt* rather than heard the rough edges where his genius met the hurricane of his soul. Instead of polishing all those edges off, we could create something raw and bold and beautiful.

I could make the cello heavy metal.

I could do my own thing, away from my parents, away from the pressure of replacing the perfect son they lost.

I slammed my fist down on the table. "I'm in."

*I*van flew down to New Orleans a week later. He was just as silent and terrifying as I remembered. But the moment he raised his bow and ripped through an improvisation that bowled me over with its quiet malevolence, I knew he was the violinist for us.

We recorded the album at Skulking Dog Studios, the same studio where my parents cut their first recording. The music flew from our fingers. Dorien joked that he sold his soul at a crossroads to give him the compositions, and I almost believed him. Every note, every motif, every phrase dripped with black magic.

Ivan spent every moment we weren't practicing or recording on his phone to his sister, talking to her in harsh, barked tones in his native Romanian.

One of the girls Dorien met at that bar turned out to be an amateur filmmaker. She took us to the Lafayette Cemetery one night and had us run around in black cloaks and pale face paint, then cut an arty video for our first song, 'A Graveside Story.' We released it online and Octavia's Ruin shared it with their fans and before we knew it, we were climbing the Spotify charts.

By the time my parents burst through the doors at the end of summer to take me to my auditions, Broken Muse amassed eighty thousand social media fans and we'd been booked on a ten-city European tour. I showed them the music video. Mom watched in stunned silence, tears streaking her cheeks.

Dad stormed from the room and slammed the door so hard it rattled the whole house.

I packed my cello and left with Dorien the next day. We blew off our auditions to play the nightclubs of Paris, Berlin, and London. We followed the Octavia's Ruin tour bus in a tiny van jammed with gear, partied every night until dawn, and slept on friends' couches, in roach-infested hostels, and in the van on the side of the road during a freak Polish thunderstorm.

Dorien was in his element – every night another crowd to

enchant, in every city a new girl or guy to warm his bed. But sometimes, if I watched him carefully from across the stage, if the moonlight through the van window caught his face before he fell asleep, I saw that darkness creep into his eyes.

We never spoke about it, but I knew that Dorien wasn't just chasing fame and riches and hot groupies – he was running from something so rotten that even on the other side of the globe, he couldn't escape its hold on him.

BRUTAL KILLING AT MUSIC SCHOOL

A young woman's life has been tragically cut short at the elite Manderley Academy. Police recovered the body of twenty-two-year-old Heather Danvers from her fiancé's room at the music school. Her head had been brutally bashed against a steel bedpost, and she was stabbed seven times.

Heather's fiancé, musician Dorien Valencourt, has been arrested and charged with her murder. Dorien is the genius behind the neo-classical rock band, Broken Muse, who shot to fame six years ago when their first single, 'A Graveside Story,' went viral.

This is the second death to occur at the music academy in the last year. A young girl, Clare Fairbanks, worked at the school as a maid. She was found at the bottom of the stairs with her neck broken. Her death was ruled accidental, but given that Clare was reported to be dating Dorien Valencourt and he was in the vicinity at the time of her death, her case has been reopened.

Sources close to the school believe Valencourt may have influenced another student, Faye de Winter, to commit this crime. De Winter has a history of violence – she once violently assaulted a man named Aaron Varney – and resented the impending marriage between Danvers and Valencourt. At this time, de Winter has not been charged with any crime, although she is being investigated as an accomplice. She is the daughter of famed musician Donovan de Winter, who disappeared mysteriously ten years ago and has never been found.

Authorities face a tough challenge untangling this sordid saga. All this reporter knows is that Manderley Academy has more skeletons in its closets than a gothic novel.

1

FAYE

"The *genius* behind Broken Muse?" Titus made a face as he tossed the paper onto the grave. "How dare he?"

"*That's* what you take from the article?" Ivan growled.

"That even from prison, Dorien finds a way to take credit for *all* our work? Damn right that's the message I'm taking from the article." Titus' usually kind features twisted with anger. Angry looked good on Titus – but then, so did every other emotion. The guy was a walking clit closet. "The bastard even suggested Faye beat up this Aaron guy because she's *under Dorien's influence.* I wonder who told them that? Someone who still believes the sun shines out his own arsehole, that's who. When our girl goes nuclear, it's for her own reasons, not because the bloody Bad Boy of Baroque told her to."

"I'd like to point out for posterity that I didn't actually beat up Aaron." I drew my hands up to my shoulders in a vain attempt to rub warmth back into my arms.

We were splayed out inside the Usher mausoleum at Manderley. The hexagonal stone structure offered little shelter from the wet, gross rain dribbling down outside – bitter wind pushed the damp through the grated windows and into the cracks in the stone cupola. Our breaths came out in furious puffs, like steam locomotives building up momentum as they crested a hill. Elena sat next to me on Victor Usher's empty sarcophagus, swinging her legs lazily and nodding her head to a song none of us could hear. Titus leaned against a wall of niches, and Ivan paced beneath a weeping angel statue.

Just being in this stone tomb made my skin crawl. Evil itself seeped through the walls. I wanted nothing more than to walk away from Manderley and the Usher family forever.

But that was impossible.

Heather's death changed everything. Not even Commissioner Walpole could save Madame Usher from the media scrutiny of a second body to be uncovered at the school in the space of a year – both of them connected to Dorien Valencourt. The school was swarming with the press. At first, she tried to keep them out, barring the gates and forcing Harrison to stand out in the snow with his rifle to scare them off. But they'd flown out with helicopters and hiked in through the forest trails, and so she changed tactics and welcomed them inside, giving them the run of the place and filling their heads with her chosen narrative as she allowed them to paw through Heather's things. She even allowed a paranormal investigation team to film a segment on the staircase, calling for Clare to show herself and identify Dorien as her killer.

I was learning all of this now from Ivan and Elena because Madame Usher kicked me out. After her insane effort to bring me to the academy in the first place, my dismissal was somewhat perfunctory – she simply had Harrison deliver me a letter informing me our contract was terminated, and I was to be off the property by the end of the day or she'd have me arrested for trespassing. Heather's death had thrown a chink in her perfect plan, and now she couldn't risk keeping me around.

I longed to confront her about it, to throw my mother's poisoning back in her face, but I didn't want to play my hand too soon. Instead, Titus and Ivan helped me pack my meager possessions. Madame Usher didn't leave the east wing as I lugged my case downstairs, and a wicked idea occurred to me.

I marched into the storage room and took the Becker violin – my father's violin – and waltzed out of the school with it. It was my legacy, after all. As Harrison drove me away, I looked back at the house and couldn't see Madame Usher's face at the windows, but I could feel her gaze boring into me, promising that she hadn't finished with me yet.

My fingers closed around the neck of the violin. *Is my father alive? What has she done to him? Why does he haunt Manderley, taunting me with these clues?*

I wondered what Clare – the real ghost of Manderley – thought about it all. I came here today intending to ask her.

I moved into Mom's hotel room in New York City, paid for until the end of the year by Natalie's kindness. I found a job in a music shop and would hopefully be able to scrape together enough money to keep paying Mom's medical bills.

When the lurid headlines about Heather's murder hit, Amos and Delphine arrived to pull Titus out of Manderley. They were living in New York City too, while they applied to other programs so he could complete his schooling. They didn't let him see me in case it reflected badly on his chances at Juilliard. Titus wasn't talking about it much in the stolen conversations we had late at night, but I gathered living with his parents again wasn't exactly pleasant. They still hadn't forgiven him for having the guitar.

Aroha's parents tried to remove her as well, but I heard her on the phone as I was packing telling them that she would be graduating no matter what. I guess with fewer of us around, she figured her chances of winning the Manderley Prize just shot up.

Elena stayed with her fiancé, which meant Ivan remained behind at Manderley also.

Just like that, we were scattered. Madame Usher achieved her ends – she destroyed Broken Muse. If only Heather didn't have to die to make it happen. I hated that bitchbadger, but she didn't deserve *that*.

That was why we were gathered today. Titus and I snuck back while his parents were out. We hiked four miles through the forest to escape the reporters and approach Manderley from the rear, then peeled off the forest path to meet Ivan and Elena at the mausoleum. It was clear from its neglect that Madame Usher never visited, so it seemed a safe place to plot our next move.

We brought them mobile phones so we could communicate in secret, and exchanged news from inside and outside the school. Titus showed Ivan some of the newspaper articles and tweets about the band. It was clear that no matter what the police charged him with, Dorien had already been found guilty by the world, and I was his puppet, dancing to the tune of the powerful men in my life.

"What do we do now?" Elena asked.

It was a good question. One I'd desperately been trying to figure out ever since I walked into Dorien's room and saw him bent over Heather, the bloody knife in his hand.

"I suppose it depends if we believe Dorien is innocent," Titus said.

Three pairs of eyes bore into me.

I stared down at the bag of supplies at my feet, watching my cold breath swirl around the stones. I didn't know what to believe.

I believed the evidence of my eyes. Dorien had the knife. He was the only one in the room. We didn't see anyone else enter or leave the house. He was being forced into a marriage against his will, and I knew better than anyone that when Dorien Valencourt was cornered, he could lash out with unimaginable cruelty.

Dorien begged me to believe in his innocence. He sounded distraught and genuine as they shoved him into the police car, but I'd been through this with Dorien before. Every time I believed things were different or opened myself up to him, he betrayed me. I thought I trusted myself with him, but that knife glinting in the dim light, the blood on his hands, Heather's lifeless body staring up at me…

But *then* I came back to all the unexplained phenomena at Manderley – the objects flying over the staircase the first time Madame kicked me out, the face in the attic window, my dad's book appearing, food going missing from the kitchen, and those times I felt like I was being watched. I remembered Clare's words scrawled on the wall in the pantry. THE WALLS ARE TALKING. I'd seen the portrait of my father hidden in the attic, and we found Victor Usher's empty grave and discovered Madame Usher's plot to poison my mother. I knew we were on the cusp of unraveling Madame Usher's secrets, and now Heather was dead and Dorien was behind bars and it all seemed too…convenient. Especially considering the story Madame Usher was spinning for the press.

I raised my head. "What do you guys think? Did he do it?"

They exchanged glances. No one spoke. No one knew what to say.

I slid off the sarcophagus and paced across the floor, shoving my gloved hands into my armpits again in a vain attempt to prevent my fingers from falling off. "Okay, we have to agree on this before we go forward. So let's go through what we know. All of us were downstairs except for Aroha, and she met us at the doorway when I found Heather's body. She couldn't have snuck out of the room without Dorien seeing her, and if he'd seen her he wouldn't lie to save her ass. So that means all of us, Aroha, the Valencourts, the Danvers, Madame Usher, Father Aaron, and Walpole couldn't possibly have done it. That leaves only Dorien and Harrison. The only way Harrison could have made his way upstairs to kill her is if there was some kind of secret passage leading from outside to Dorien's bedroom, which we're not ruling out. But I don't believe Harrison's the murderer. His beef is with Usher, not Heather, and he had that gun with him, so why stab her? Why not shoot her?"

"That leaves only Dorien." Ivan's voice dripped with disdain.

"If we consider the living, yes. But what about Clare's words? What about that portrait of my father and his violin? What about Victor Usher's grave being empty?" I wrung my hands. "I've seen too many horror films to ignore the signs."

Titus stepped toward me, his huge hands wrapping around my shoulders. "Faye, are you trying to convince us, or are you trying to convince yourself?"

I sagged against him, letting his warmth envelop me. Being held by Titus was all-consuming – he wrapped his body around me like a shield, and inside his embrace I felt stronger, invincible. "I don't know what to believe. Is Manderley haunted by the living or the dead? Maybe Clare's ghost killed Heather. But why? Heather wasn't anywhere near the staircase when Clare died. And what about my father? Or Victor Usher? How are they connected to this? And it doesn't change the fact that Dorien was upset about the arranged marriage. He had every reason to lash out at Heather. I've given him seven million chances and each time he's broken my heart. I don't want to use a ghost to excuse him."

I looked up at the carved cupola. A rogue spiderweb brushed my face, its gossamer threads like fingertips reaching for me. I bit back a scream as the air sung with tension – the feeling that something monumental was about to happen. I remembered the sensation from the last time I'd been at the mausoleum, the night Dorien and Heather knocked me out with chloroform and trapped me in a leather bag. I remembered the cold in my veins as Clare rose from the shadows and closed in on me. Her hands reached for my throat as she rasped, *Only you can save Manderley from the voice in the walls.*

My heart pounded. "Clare."

"What about her?" Titus murmured, burying his face into my shoulder.

"She broke all those antiques when Madame tried to kick you out," Elena said. "You think she killed Heather too?"

"She is dangerous." Ivan grabbed his sister's hand. "We shouldn't stay in the house with her."

"She's the key to all of this. I don't think she's trying to hurt us. I think she's trying to warn us, warn me. Maybe about Dorien, but I don't think so. The walls are talking, she said. I don't think she's responsible. She's a victim, too. This is the second death at Manderley that's been blamed on Dorien, the second death that's been carefully constructed so he's the only possible suspect. He got away once, but someone has made sure he can't escape this time. We need the truth – we need to know what happened from someone who saw the whole thing. Heather can't tell us what she saw in his room, and the only people who know what happened on that staircase are Clare and Dorien. We all know his version, but we should get hers. Clare seems willing to talk to me. I came here today because I need to do what I should have done ages ago. I need to *listen*."

"How do you listen to a ghost?" Ivan said. "With a seance?"

"Exactly."

I expected Titus to laugh, but no one thought this ghost thing was funny anymore. Not after we'd all seen the portraits and vases flying over the staircase and smashing to pieces. Not after Heather had been carried out of Manderley in a body bag.

"When should we do this seance?" Ivan asked.

"No time like the present." I opened my bag to reveal a stack of candles and other supplies. Elena pulled her own from her tote bag. Ivan glared at her, then at me, but she poked her tongue out at him.

"Faye asked me to collect a few things," she said. "If we told you, you would have forbidden it."

He growled low in his throat. He knew we were right. "How do you know how to talk to the dead?"

I shrugged as I lit the last candle. "I don't. I based this off seances I've seen in horror films."

Ivan snorted. "Because they always end so well."

Elena set about placing the candles around the mausoleum and lighting them. On Victor's tomb, I laid out a serving tray from the kitchen, with a glass upturned on top. I tacked a piece of paper onto the tray. On a semi-circle around the glass, I'd written the alphabet and numbers 0-9, as well as the words YES and NO, just like a spirit board I found on the internet.

"The candles keep blowing out," Elena pouted as she tipped another match from the box.

"Don't worry about them." I hadn't needed a candle to see Clare in the mausoleum last time. "Come here. Everyone join hands."

We sat cross-legged on the dais holding Victor's stone tomb. The wind whistled through the trees, blowing out several of the candles. On my left, Elena giggled. Titus squeezed my right hand so hard I heard my knuckle crack.

"Clare Fairbanks," I said, trying to project my voice, to pluck the tension in the air and snap it into the corporeal world. "You've been trying to give me a message for some time. I'm ready to listen."

I narrowed my eyes at the glass, trying to see it and only it and not Elena's gleeful face, but also trying to see beyond it, into the shadow realm Clare inhabited. Goosebumps rose along my arms, but whether they were from the cold or from a looming presence I couldn't tell.

"Clare, please talk to us. We want to listen to you."

Faye. Fayyyyyeeeeeee...

My heart pounded against my ribs. The more I focused on that glass, the harder it was to believe the crackling voice was just wind in the trees, or that the mist encircling the tomb was just our freezing puffs of breath—

Wait a second...

The mists swirled and dipped, and I saw that the miasma didn't come from our mouths at all, but seemed to rise from Victor's empty tomb. It coalesced together, taking form and substance. Titus stiffened as he noticed it too, his fingers crushing my hand.

Elena cried out as a face emerged from the mist. On her other side, Ivan hissed.

Clare.

She met my eyes. Her turned-up nose pointed to the crumbling carvings of Jesus stumbling under the weight of his cross. Her lips opened a crack, my name hissing from her mouth like air leaking from a balloon.

She's here. I'm not imagining it. Clare's really with us.

"Hello, Clare." I kept my voice calm, even though I wanted to bolt from the mausoleum and never look back. "I'm sorry I've been ignoring your warnings. I won't do that again. We're here to talk to you, to get the story straight from you. Can you speak to us?"

Fayyeeeeeeee...

The gaping hole of her mouth opened, and what poured out wasn't words, not really. She issued forth a sound like no other, a sound like footsteps creaking on old floorboards and shadows moving in a quiet room. It was everything she already told me but spoken in a cold, creeping death that invaded my bones and squeezed at my organs. Dread pushed at the corners of my mind as I heard her, as I finally saw her for who she was. The girl wronged. The girl who must be avenged.

Elena whimpered. She heard it too.

An involuntary shudder rippled through my body. Clare snapped her mouth shut and shook her head. *Okay, so she can't talk to us without resorting to ghost speak, which I don't think I ever want to hear again. Let's try something else.*

"Can you move the glass? Spell out a message for us?"

Clare stared down at the glass and shook her head. The corners of her mouth turned down. She looked sad.

"You can't move the glass?"

She shook her head again.

"You can't pick up objects?"

Clare shook her head so furiously it sent a wave of nausea through my body. My chest squeezed, thinking of the violin music I played alongside her for so many nights, and the objects flying around the house the first time Madame Usher tried to kick me out, or the clothes left out for me before the party. Clare had to be responsible for them, which meant she'd been able to move objects. So why couldn't she now?

Or was she lying to us? But could ghosts lie? Maybe her ability to move things comes and goes.

I wish I knew more about ghosts than just which ones topped Fangoria's *best haunts list.*

Titus squeezed my fingers, reminding me I had more important questions.

"We want to make sure whoever hurt you sees justice, but we need your help. Did Dorien do this to you?" I demanded. "Did he kill you?"

I forced my eyes to remain open as my stomach tied itself in knots. I didn't want to see the answer, didn't want to shatter my hopes into shards of ice.

Clare shook her head so hard her hair whipped around her face. She was certain. It wasn't Dorien. My shoulders sagged with relief. I longed to fling myself at her and hug her, but I didn't want to feel her slip through my fingers. I held onto my calm and tried another question.

"Was it Madame Usher? Was it Heather?"

Shake. Shake.

Someone else, then. Answers started to form in my head, but I wasn't quite ready to test them aloud.

"Who else is there?" Ivan demanded. Clare whirled around to face him, spreading her arms out toward the door of the tomb, toward me. *She's pointing to me.*

She's saying I have the answers already.

I hated that Clare was right. I'd been flirting around the outside of this for so long, and I had to face the truth of my father's portrait and the Becker violin, of missing bones and murdered girls.

But first…

"Did you see who killed Heather?" I curled my fingers into Titus' palm.

A nod this time. My heart hammered against my chest.

"Was it Dorien?"

The question hung in the air between us. Clare's mouth hung open, her jaw slack, the dark void of her mouth yawning wide, threatening to swallow me whole.

She snapped her jaw shut and shook her head.

I let out a breath I didn't realize I was holding. The relief felt like dropping my bowing arm after a difficult concerto. Dorien didn't kill Heather. He was innocent. That meant he was being set up, and we had to help him.

"Who killed her?" Ivan demanded.

Elena screamed as Clare whirled around. She pointed to the house, and then down at Victor Usher's empty tomb.

I swallowed.

"Was it Madam Usher?" I whispered, although I already knew the answer.

Clare shook her head. She gestured wildly, pointing to me, then back at the house, then at the tomb again. She mimed playing the violin.

"He's been hiding in the walls," I whispered. "He was there when you were alive, whispering to you, like a ghost."

Titus' fingers tightened around mine. Elena let out a choked noise.

"Faye?" Ivan barked out, his voice dark with fear.

I couldn't tear my eyes from Clare. She nodded. I had my answer. The answer I'd been dreading but knew deep down inside all along.

Someone else has been at Manderley with us this whole time.

And that someone is a murderer.

2

<hr>

FAYE

"Step this way."

The officer shoved open a steel door and led me down a urine-soaked hallway, past a double row of cell doors. Even though the inmates couldn't see out, they must've heard our footsteps, because they banged on the doors, rattled the hinges, and yelled and cried and shrieked. I squared my shoulders, wishing I could turn around and run from this nightmare.

The cop shoved his keys into the last cell in the row. The door swung open but it took a few tries for my leaden feet to shuffle forward. As I stepped inside, he caught my wrist in his hand, twisting it so I had no choice but to lean into him. His lip curled as he looked me over, nice and slow. His hot breath rasped against my cheek. "Fucking rich boy crims get all the good pussy."

I raised my hand to slap his stupid mouth, but he'd already slammed the cell door behind me. I sucked in a deep breath and looked around.

A concrete bench covered with a thin plastic mattress. A toilet and enamel basin hanging at a precarious angle from the wall. A stench of feces and desperation thick in the air, clinging to every pore. A narrow window high in the wall, covered with steel bars.

A beautiful, broken boy stood beneath it, his hands shoved deep in his pockets and a curtain of dark hair covering his face.

I sat down on the concrete bench.

Dorien leaned against the wall opposite, so fragile the gentlest breeze would blow him away. He leaned his head back, and his hair started to fall away from his face.

I stared at my hands. If I looked at him for another moment, I'd break.

"Hey, Sprite."

That voice. It fucking *undid* me. I dug my nails into my palm, but that only made me picture his fingers laced in mine as he and Ivan had me over the piano bench. I sucked in a shaking breath and diverted my gaze to the stained wall above his head. It was covered with scratched graffiti – nothing recognizable as words, just squiggles and cartoon dicks.

"Look at me, Sprite."

I shook my head.

"Please."

His voice cracked. I couldn't deny him. I'd always had trouble saying no to Dorien, especially when he was hurting. I shifted my chin, lowering my gaze to see him, to really *see* him.

Even in this hellish place he looked incredible – he hadn't been shaving, and the stubble on his chin and dangerous glint in his eyes made him appear worlds away from the polished performer who'd held my heart since I was a girl. Dim light from the window pierced the room, bathing his aristocratic face in dim light. The skin around his eye was bruised purple and swelling up. His normally cruel mouth twisted with misery.

"You're a sight for sore eyes." Dorien tried to flash that shit-eating grin of his, but the muscles wouldn't do the job. He leaned forward, his fingers grasping my knee. His presence stole all the air from the room, and I struggled for breath.

Sparks darted against my skin where he held me. It took all

my restraint to shove his hand off me and jerk away. "We don't have much time. I can't do this if you touch me."

"I can't help it. I miss you so fucking much."

I sucked in a breath, anything to give me a moment to collect myself, find my strength. My mother's words spun on repeat inside my skull. "Give him hell, *mi cielo.*"

"Sprite?"

"I'm still here." I gripped the edge of the concrete bench. "You don't have to keep saying my name."

"Sorry." He didn't sound sorry. "I just…I know what they're saying in the papers. When you didn't come, none of you, I thought…I thought she finally convinced you I'm evil."

He was right. We hadn't talked since the police dragged him away. He tried to call us, but Madame Usher refused to allow any calls through the house phone, and I told the concierge at the hotel not to allow his calls through to me. I'd had to go through his lawyer to arrange this visit.

"Dorien, what happened?"

"They're charging me with first-degree murder," he sighed. "My lawyer thinks that if I spill about Jacob's abuse, he'll be able to argue self-defense at a trial. But that will jeopardize Rochester's investigation. Rochester wants me to wait it out in here while he builds a case against Usher as well as Aaron, but I don't know if I can wait that long. I'm going insane, Sprite."

"Dorien, I can't—"

"I swear to you I didn't kill Heather."

"I'm not asking that." I stabbed my nail so deep I drew blood. "I'm asking you to tell me what happened that night. I need to know everything you saw."

"I waited in the hallway for a few moments before I went inside my room. I needed some time to figure out what I was going to say. Heather and I aren't so different. We both have siblings trapped in the Temple. I was going to ask her to help me. I thought I heard her talking or laughing inside, thumping my furniture around, but I might've imagined it. I was a bit of a mess." He laughed without mirth.

"I pushed open my bedroom door and…and Heather was lying on the floor with that knife sticking out of her chest." Dorien shuddered. "I'll never forget how she looked in all my life, her mouth hanging open like that. I see now it was stupid for me to touch the knife, but I thought…I was trying to save her. It wasn't supposed to be in her like that. I had to take it out, but then there was so much blood…"

His voice wavered, and he swallowed hard, his Adam's apple bobbing.

"The police say the knife was taken from the kitchen. My lawyer says it's my best defense – you were all at the bottom of the stairs, and you saw me head straight up to my room. No one saw me double back or stop to grab a knife. It's not much, probably not enough for reasonable doubt from a jury that will have already convicted me in the media. But it's something."

I let out a long breath. He was right. I definitely would have noticed. But there was a long period between Dorien heading upstairs and me racing up to see what happened, the time when he said he was outside his bedroom door. The police might argue it was time enough for him to have slipped out the window in Titus' room, shimmied down the tree, and come into the kitchen from the backdoor. Would it have been time enough for him to have grabbed a knife and got back upstairs without us hearing him?

Maybe. If he was fast.

"Please say you believe me." Dorien pressed his knuckles into his swelling eye. "I can't fucking survive in here if you don't believe me."

I think of Clare's adamance that Dorien had nothing to do with either death. I know what we decided in the mausoleum, but I hadn't been sure what I'd feel when I faced him again. Until now. I looked into those slate-grey eyes and saw the love and the hope shining there like a beacon in the darkness.

I dived into Dorien Valencourt, drowning myself in the depths of his anguish. I touched the edges of him, and I lifted off the weight of his betrayals that I'd been carrying for so long. He never smashed my violin. He wasn't keeping me awake with footsteps in the storage room, or trying to frighten me by stealing food from the kitchen. The thousand tiny cuts of his cruelty healed over with new, tougher skin. When I first came to Manderley, I thought Dorien was my bully. But he was one of the victims, and I had to save him.

I had my answer.

I nodded. "I believe you."

"Don't sound so sure."

"No, I do. I—" I closed my eyes. I needed a moment without his gaze on me, a moment to collect the maelstrom of emotions swirling inside me. "It's hard. We've been down this path before, you and me. You say things and then you do something else. And you might have noble intentions, but what I see is betrayal. When I saw you holding that knife, I slipped back into that same pattern. But when I search deep down, I do believe you. That leaves us with a terrifying truth – that someone else at Manderley killed Heather. Probably someone hiding in the walls."

"You think Clare did it?"

I shook my head, opening my eyes to meet those stony orbs once more. "I spoke to Clare. Well, not exactly. She can't speak and she can't pick up objects, but we had a seance and she informed me you were innocent."

Dorien smiled. "I'm glad my ex-girlfriend is still amenable to my charms."

I have never been able to resist Dorien's smile, and today is no different. How could the simple movement of muscle and skin and sinew sing such music in my veins? How could that flash of perfect teeth and the dimpling of his cheek vibrate in my memory long after we part? *Dorien.*

That smile had been my comfort and my torment in equal measure, but that was what it meant to be in love. The joy of our music was the tension that wove us together, the hard and the soft, the tremolo shuddering against an open string. Thunder approaching over a calm lake, stirring the waters to life. Without the torment, my heart couldn't beat for him.

My whole body ached to be his again, and I wasn't going to waste another moment. I threw myself at Dorien, catching him by surprise. He wobbled off-balance and the pair of us toppled onto the narrow mattress. Dorien caught me before I rolled off the edge and held me against him, pressing our chests together so I could feel his heart racing against his ribs.

"I won't let you go," he swore, his breath hot on my lips. His fingers tangled in my hair, drawing my head toward him.

I nuzzled his neck, a lump rising in my throat at the thought that soon I'd have to leave him in this gross room to meet a fate we couldn't predict. "I only have a little time."

"Every moment with you is a gift." Dorien's lips brushed mine, soft, searching. He kissed like a criminal stealing his way to safety, silent and stalking, slipping his tongue between my lips to search out answers. He tasted like Dorien – dark and wintery – but also nothing like Dorien at all. He tasted of shitty jail food and despair. His tongue stroked mine, and I fancied I could taste the coppery bite of blood.

I pulled back, tracing the lines of his face. I wishing I could sneak him out under my bra and carry him far away from this place. I'd probably suffocate him in my tits, but what a way to go. I hated how comfortable he was here, how resigned to his fate. Dorien had been in a prison his whole life. I would not let him die in one.

"I'll figure this out," I said. The words echoed in the concrete room.

"There's nothing to figure out. It was Usher," Dorien said. "Nothing in that house happens without her knowledge. All of this is her grand plan, and she's got the police in her pocket."

"Madame Usher has nine witnesses saying she was downstairs the whole time," I said. "Including me. We know she's ultimately behind this, but she didn't plunge the knife into Heather. She never gets her hands dirty. I know this sounds insane, but we think there might be someone else hiding at Manderley. Someone who's been sneaking around doing her bidding, making us crazy thinking a ghost is responsible. Someone who smashed up my violin, and who left my father's book and violin to torment me. Someone whose bones should be rotting in his grave."

"You think Victor Usher is still alive?" Dorien raised an eyebrow. Of course he was into this – it was like something out of a gothic novel.

I nodded. "I have no proof, but it makes perfect sense. At least, it makes more sense than the other option, which is that my father is still alive."

"Wait, hold on a second." Dorien's eyes crinkled at the edges. "What's this about your father?"

As quickly as I could, I went over everything I figured out about Manderley and the portrait of my father and his violin, before cycling back to Victor Usher. "There's someone else haunting Manderley besides Clare. That's what this is all about. That's Madame Usher's secret. It's either my dad or Victor, and I need to figure out which one it is. You said when Victor was sick, Madame Usher forbade any doctors to see him. We know she has knowledge of plants and poisons because of the birthwort she gave my mother. She probably fed him something from the poison garden to fake his death, and he's been hiding in her private wing all this time. It explains why his bones aren't in his tomb. I think he creeps around the house when we can't see him, and does things to frighten us, like smashing my violin. Clare says she didn't do that."

"But why?" Dorien asked. "Why fake his death? What does it achieve?"

I smiled sadly. "I was hoping you might have some idea."

"That's what she thought I knew," Dorien whistled through his teeth. "In Cauda Venenum."

"The words on the poison garden? What does that even mean?"

"It's Latin for the poison is in the tail—"

"I *know* what it means. But if I go to the police and say 'In Cauda Venenum,' they're going to lock me up in here beside you."

The corner of Dorien's mouth quirked up. "When she was threatening to have me arrested if I didn't stay away from you, I said those words to her and she relented. I was bluffing, but she didn't know that. She thought I knew that she faked Victor's death and I was going to go to the police."

I tapped his chin. "And that's why she's coming after you now. If she can put you away for Heather's murder, no one will believe if you tell an insane story about her keeping her dead husband locked up inside Manderley."

"Rochester is investigating her," Dorien squeezed my shoulders. "He's trying to connect her to the Temple and Father Aaron. So far he's got nothing, but if you tell him what you know, he might be able to help you. If you figure out what that means, you've got her. I know you can do that, Faye."

"Yeah." I kissed his lips. "It's all starting to make sense now."

Someone banged on the door. I started to pull away, but Dorien pressed his palm into my back, trapping me in place. He whispered against my lips. "What if it's not Victor? What if it's your dad?"

"Then I'll do what my mom should have done ten years ago and kill the bastard myself," I whispered back. The words trembled on my tongue. Dorien sighed against me as he pressed me into his chest. We both knew I was talking a big game. *If it's my dad...*

I couldn't face it.

If it's my dad, he let me believe he was dead. He let me cry a river of tears for him.

If it's my dad, he's spent ten years hiding with that witch instead of being here for me, for us.

If it's my dad, then he's part of her conspiracy to poison my mother.

If it's him, I will fall spectacularly apart, and I don't think even my broken muses could put me back together again.

BANG BANG BANG.

"Ms. de Winter, you need to come with us now," the officer barked.

Reluctantly, I slid out from beneath Dorien. He remained on the slab, his knees pulled to his chest, his arms still embracing the air as if he could still feel the ghost of my touch. As I slid out the door, my heart rattled like a marble in my chest, and the trailing notes of our song shattered into ash.

3

FAYE

hen I cracked the door to our hotel suite, delicious smells wafted from within, stunning my nostrils with their awesomeness. I threw the door open, my stomach growling.

Mom sat at the small table by the window, tearing the lids off takeout packages of Mexican food. My heroine. How did she always know exactly what I needed?

"How was Dorien?" she asked as I dropped down beside her and slid over a package of tamales. I peeled back the corn husk and shoved one in my mouth whole. The spicy beef burned my tongue as I chewed. But sound the fucktrumpets it tasted so good, and at least it took my mind off thinking about Victor and my father and Ivan and Elena still up at the house with a violent ghost in the walls.

I swallowed and reached for another. "About what you'd expect."

"Struggling without his silk shirts and Wagner recordings and an adoring audience hanging onto his every word?" She said it lightly, but there was a hint of motherly concern in her voice.

I picked up a shrimp taco, careful to keep my gaze steady as I met her eyes. I hadn't told her yet about my suspicions. I needed proof first, especially if it wasn't Victor in the walls. "He didn't kill Heather, Mom."

"If you believe that, then so do I. It doesn't mean I think that boy is good for you." Mom leaned forward to wipe a strand of hair from my eyes. "You've lived through too much heartache because of your father. I won't let you make the same mistakes I did."

Her voice wavered, her eyes pooling with tears. For the first time, I saw what she had endured as she watched me grow up without a father. It was always the two of us against the world, even when Dad was in the picture. To me, she was everything I needed, everything I ever wanted to be. But she thought she had failed me. And that sense of failure was what drove her to be her remarkable self.

I reached up to her hand, lacing her fingers in mine and bringing it back to the table. "Dad was the failure, not you. You're my strength. You're all I ever needed, so don't waste a minute wishing things could have been different. I never will. Besides, I'm the one who's supposed to be looking after you. So get your cute de Winter butt back in that bed and stop worrying about me."

"I'll never stop, *mi cielo*." Mom stabbed the last tamale with her fork and shoved it into her mouth as she moved with shuffling steps to the bed. She leaned back on her stack of pillows and chewed, a sheen of sweat on her forehead. The poison had done a number on her insides, and moving and laughing and living were painful for her now, but I had to hope Dr. Nelson could help her body once again reflect her spirit.

I polished off a pile of tacos with gusto and slid into bed beside her, touching the book splayed across her raised knees. "What are you reading?"

She flipped the cover so I could see it. "*Prose and Cons*, by Steffanie Holmes. It's this reverse harem murder mystery series, and one of the characters runs a death-faking business. It's fascinating. According to him, people fake their deaths for three main reasons – for financial gain, to be with a lover, and to escape violence or imprisonment. I already skipped ahead to the last chapter, so I know who the killer is, but it's a good read. Very steamy."

I laughed. That was just like Mom – even in her leisure activities like reading, she had to be the one in control. She didn't like surprises unless she was the one creating them for her clients.

I pulled out my phone and scrolled through my emails. Seven million messages from reporters, wanting to pay me for an exclusive interview to get the scoop on my sordid relationship with Dorien. I didn't have the stomach to see what the world was saying about me on social media, so I deleted the apps. Judging by the abusive emails from Broken Muse fans who found my private email address, it couldn't be anything good. Mom buried her face in her book. I gazed at the cover, thinking about what she said.

Why fake Victor Usher's death? It can't have been for love – the pair didn't have the greatest marriage if Madame Usher was screwing around with Dad. Elena said Victor would leave the house to hunt in the woods for days at a time and Madame Usher never seemed to mind. But what about financial reasons? Victor's family was rich – he probably had substantial life insurance.

Or what about to escape crime or violence? I could believe it. But I had no evidence, no way to prove it beyond random ideas and suppositions.

Or did I?

"I just need to make a phone call. I won't be long." I slid out of bed. Mom nodded, not looking up from her book as I crept into the hallway, pressing the phone to my ear as I dialed a number I wished I'd never have to dial again.

"Faye? I'm so happy to see your name pop up." Creepy Cory picked up on the second ring. I could hear chatter and music and glasses clinking in the background. He was at work. We were never supposed to answer our phones at work. I wondered if I should feel grateful he was risking his ass for me, but all it did was up the ick factor.

I can't wait until I don't need this guy anymore.

"Hi, Cory." I leaned against the wall, watching as the elevator doors slid open and shut on a businessman with a large briefcase. *Be strong. Remember that Ivan and Elena are still at Manderley. Every day that goes by puts them in danger.* "Remember last time we talked, you got me some money from Gizella Usher's accounts? I was wondering if you still have access to them?"

"Of course." I could hear the smugness in Cory's voice. "How much do you need?"

"No money. I just want you to have a look at the transactions – especially from twelve to twenty-four months ago. You're looking for big sums, like an insurance payout, or anything else unusual. Could you do that for me as a matter of urgency?"

"I'll get started tonight," he purred. "That is, unless you're coming over to show me how grateful you are."

"That's not happening."

"Come on, Faye. I've seen the papers. I know you're through with those boring musicians. You must be so upset with that girl being murdered. I can be your shoulder to cry on."

"I bet you're good at making girls cry." I couldn't help it.

My jab went right over Cory's head. I could practically hear him panting through the phone. "Are you still up at that school? Maybe I'll come and visit you—"

"Don't go near that school. It's dangerous." Cory was gross, but I didn't want him to become Madame Usher's next victim.

"Fine, fine. I know you're in New York City, anyway." My heart stuttered. *He shouldn't know that. There's no way he can know that.* Natalie has been careful to hide our location from the press. "You know we're meant to be together, Faye. That's why you keep calling me. And this time I'm not going to let your gorgeous ass get away from me."

He thought he sounded like a hot alpha male, but his words sent a chill down my spine.

"Call me when you have the information." I clicked off the phone and threw it across the hall, wishing I could wash his vile voice out of my ears. *Calling Cory was a mistake. I should have gone straight to Rochester.*

How does he know I'm in the city?

I glanced down the hallway to the elevators, my heart pounding as the bell dinged and the doors opened, revealing an empty car. *Stop it. You'll drive yourself crazy. You've already got enough to worry about. You can handle Creepy Cory.*

Sighing, I picked up my phone and headed back inside, crawling into bed with Mom as she surfed through channels until she found a horror movie. "You aren't hanging out with Titus tonight? I assume that's who you were talking to?"

I shook my head, not bothering to correct her. "He's got an audition first thing tomorrow. His parents won't let him out to play."

"He's a good man, *mi cielo.* He—" Mom broke down into a coughing fit, bringing me crashing back to reality. I wrapped my arms around her shoulders as her body convulsed.

"I'll call Dr. Nelson. We need to go to the hospital—"

Mom clasped her hand over mine, her eyes watering as she fought for control. "Don't do that. I'm fine. Dr. Nelson says this is normal. It's going to take time for me to heal, but I'll come out of this stronger than ever."

I hope so. I wrapped my arms around her, so beyond happy that she was awake and alive and with me again. *I could have lost her.*

I didn't want to think about what happened to her. If I dwelled on the poisoning too long, I felt my thin veneer of control slipping away and a violent rage bubbling up from the deepest, darkest parts of me. What Madame Usher did to her was *insidious*, and if my father was in any way involved, then…

Even if I found out the truth, I could never tell her. She would carry the guilt for his crime, and I wouldn't allow that to happen. She's spent her whole life taking care of me – now she needed me to protect her, to avenge her.

Mom hit PAUSE on the movie and turned to me with her big, brown eyes. "Will you play for me tonight?"

I'd had to leave my beautiful instrument Titus gave me at Manderley, because it was in the Red Room and Madame Usher barred the door with her body. I thought of the Becker hidden in my violin case under the bed, that vile inscription on the back. If Mom saw it, she would recognize it as his, and I'd have too much explaining to do.

I kissed her forehead. "I can't tonight. I'm too tired."

"Okay." She snuggled against my shoulder. A few minutes later, as the heroine was being chased through the forest by the serial killer, she let out an indelicate snore. I stared at the screen, my mind whirring and my father's instrument boring a hole through the bottom of the bed. I'd never kept secrets from my mother before, but how could I tell her it was possible that my father – the man who might've tried to kill her – was still alive?

4

IVAN

"I cannot believe it was really Clare," Elena whispered. She stretched out along the bench at the kitchen table while I chopped vegetables for *ghiveci*, a vegetable stew our mother used to cook for us. "You saw her, too. You weren't just pretending?"

Now that Faye was gone, Madame ordered Elena and me back into the kitchen. With only three students remaining at Manderley, plus Radcliffe and Usher, the meals weren't arduous. I did most of the work – I wouldn't risk Elena burning her hands.

I resisted the urge to spike Madame's meals with the bottles in Dorien's apothecary kit. She made it clear in her barbed comments to me that she knows that *I* know what she's hiding, but if I put a foot out of place she'd hurt Elena. We were at a stalemate until I got Elena out of this house, but that meant marrying her off to Radcliffe. Why did that have to be our only option?

"I saw Clare." Ever since the night of the seance, Clare's face haunted my dreams. In my mind, her see-through skin and that yawning, blackened hole where her mouth should be had become superimposed over Elena's face. I glanced at the wall behind the fridge. *Where is the man she has spying on us? Is he here now, listening to every word to report back to her?* I leaned in close and lowered my voice to a whisper. "We should leave this place tonight. It's not safe here. The man in the walls *murdered* Heather."

Elena reached for the open bottle of red wine and took a swig, licking the claret from her lips. "You can leave, brother. But my fiancé is here. He protects me."

I glowered at her. The knife slammed into the chopping board with enough force to score the wood. We weren't the only ones who had a stalemate with Madame Usher. I remembered the stories I'd heard about Radcliffe – how he abruptly left a glittering international career a decade ago to teach at Manderley. There were rumors of a scandal hushed up, and a breakdown that left him trembling after every performance. When he arrived at the house and took up his residence in the stables, he seemed a funny, harmless little man who started every time the doorbell rang and often ran out of his private lessons to throw up. It was Madame Usher who forced him to keep up his contacts in the industry, to bring his composers and patrons and collaborators to the school to lend her the airs of respectability. He did everything she asked, and his endorsement alongside Victor's fame and the school's exclusivity made Madame Usher a name to be feared and revered in Classical circles.

No one sees what I see, because he seems harmless with his round glasses and kind voice.

Even Faye told me that I have to let Elena make her own decisions. But none of them were here in the beginning.

I remembered the day he took an interest in Elena. We were nine years old and we'd been at Manderley a little over a year. We were cleaning the Red Room between Victor's classes. Well, I was scrubbing student footprints off the pristine floor while she teased me by sitting at the piano pretending to be Victor scolding me. I was so angry at her because I was doing all the work, as usual, but she kept laughing her infectious *zâne* laugh until I was laughing with her. And then I caught the eye of Radcliffe. He hovered in the doorway, sheet music scattered at his feet where he had dropped them in his rapture. His eyes were fixed on Elena with a lecherous hunger that even then made ice drip down my spine.

Radcliffe couldn't protect my sister. He was in Madame Usher's debt. She had delivered to him the prize he'd so desperately pursued all these years. And when the wedding bells tolled, he would finally sate his vile hunger for my sister.

"If you're not going to help, you should practice." I snarled the words with more venom than I intended. "You are still competing for the Manderley Prize."

Not that it was a competition. Faye and Dorien were the only ones at school who had any real shot at beating Elena, and they were gone now.

Elena fidgeted at the table. She seemed to reach a decision, and pulled a paper from her pocket and set it down in front of me. "I found that in Maxim's study last night. You should give it to Faye. If she wants answers about the man in the walls, she will know what to do."

"What is it?" I snatched the paper.

"Ivan, please don't overreact. It might not even be about him. That's why you must show Faye."

I scanned the paper. It was an article from a newspaper in some small American town I never heard of, dated four years ago.

LOCAL MUSICIAN WITHDRAWS COMPLAINTS AGAINST ACADEMY

Donelle McCoy, a talented young local musician, was thrilled to be given a place at the prestigious Manderley Academy in upstate New York. But her joy turned sour and she left the school less than a year into her studies. Donelle alleged depraved goings-on at the school, including drug use among the students and deviant sexual proclivities among the staff. She said she'd been afraid for her life and her chastity, but today was withdrawing her claims, stating, "I was angry because I couldn't keep up with the workload. I made up everything I said. Manderley Academy is not a den of sin, and Victor Usher is an upstanding man of high moral character and a brilliant musician."

Neither Donelle nor her family could be reached for further comment.

I remembered Donelle. She was a pianist. She wasn't very good, and she spent more time praying her rosary and lecturing Madame Usher about the evils of drinking alcohol than she did practicing. She left abruptly in the middle of the second term, but that wasn't uncommon – the Ushers were strict about the school's standards and often kicked out students rather than continue to teach those who were doomed to mediocrity.

I tucked the article into my pocket. Donelle could have been imprinting her own morals onto the school. We have lived at Manderley long enough to know that students had their own ways of surviving this place. Aroha wasn't the first musician who needed drugs to survive, and I've seen plenty of sordid acts that would have put a Broken Muse tour to shame.

But the article talked about a teacher, and it was in Radcliffe's possession. I tried to remember him with Donelle, but I never paid attention unless he was with Elena. I never wanted the two of them to be alone.

And I knew one beastly woman who had the power to make a righteous girl retract her accusations. What did Radcliffe trade her for covering up his crimes?

I shoved the article into my pocket and glared at my sister. Her face crumpled. "Ivan, don't—"

I grabbed her arm, shaking her, wishing I could shake sense into her. "You cannot marry him. Radcliffe is tied up in whatever is going on in this house. He won't protect you. We have to leave this place."

"You cannot change my mind, brother." Elena's touched the

diamond on her finger. "Maxim has money. He has connections. He understands that I will not leave you behind. I marry him and I have the means to leave this place, and so do you. Can you not see? We will make a new life for ourselves with him as our patron."

I *could* see, and that was the problem. I could see that Elena was trading one type of servitude for another. The article burned a hole in my pocket.

Donelle called Manderley 'depraved.' The article didn't elaborate on the 'deviant sexual proclivities' she witnessed, but I could use my imagination.

What would Radcliffe do once he had Elena on his arm?

5

FAYE

"Relax, Faye. You're not in any trouble. We just want to ask you a few questions about Dorien Valencourt."

I shifted in the metal chair as Sheriff Laine Stanford set down a styrofoam coffee cup in front of me. She flashed me a smile that I *almost* believed could be friendly, but I knew her office was sharing information with Walpole and the NYPD. She couldn't be trusted. Beside her, a deputy rapped his pen on the table.

"Dorien didn't kill Heather," I said, ignoring the drink. "That's the only answer you need."

"You and Dorien were close, isn't that right?"

I gritted my teeth. I knew this interview was going to go to Valhalla in a wheelbarrow but I thought she'd at least butter me up first. "We were seeing each other, if that's what you mean."

She shuffled her papers. "According to other students and staff at the school, you were also dating Titus Thibodeaux and Ivan Nicolescu. Isn't that right?"

"If I was a guy, no one would bat an eyelid."

"Absolutely." She smiled at me then, trying to convince me that we were on the same side. Her deputy scoffed. "Can you tell me what happened the night of Heather's murder?"

I went over the story we all agreed on, that Dorien, Titus, and I had lied to Madame Usher about the recital so we could have a date, and we returned to find the Danvers, Valencourts, and Aaron Varney celebrating their engagement.

"You must've been upset when you saw Dorien proposed to Heather."

Mom and Natalie found me a lawyer, and I spoke to her and Rochester before I agreed to come to the station to answer Stanford's questions. We decided that I would go in alone, as having a lawyer present would give me a certain appearance. But she told me to say as little as possible, especially about all the tricks Madame Usher pulled.

So I shrugged. "Dorien is free to propose to whoever he wants."

"And then he went upstairs to talk to Heather?" she shuffled some papers in front of her.

"He did. We all watched him go. There wasn't enough time for him to go to the kitchen and grab a knife." I didn't mention the secret passages in the school. I didn't want it to get back to Madame Usher how much I knew.

"I don't think you're telling me the whole truth, Ms. de Winter." She threw a stack of photographs on the table. "You will do anything for Dorien Valencourt, isn't that true? Including violently attack an innocent man of God?"

I knew what the photographs were. I'd seen them before, in Aaron Varney's hands. And now, splashed all over the tabloids thanks to Madame Usher. "These are photoshopped."

"I need the bathroom." Stanford patted her stomach. "That coffee went right through me. Rivers, can you grab me the Varney file from my office? Faye, what do you say we take a break?"

"Whatever."

"Tape paused at 4:45PM." Stanford clicked off the recording device. As soon as Deputy Rivers left the room, she leaned across the table and grabbed my hand. I cried out, and she tightened her grip, her eyes widening as if she couldn't believe what she was about to do.

"Listen, we don't have much time. I know these photographs are faked. I looked up Varney's original complaint at the NYPD, and it has your name, but the file was altered recently." She glanced at the door. "That schoolteacher of yours, Usher, she's tight with Walpole, but I don't answer to him, and just because he's corrupt as fuck doesn't mean I have to be. Tell me the truth and I'll do what I can to get you and your man out of this shitstorm."

I wanted so badly to believe the earnestness in her eyes, but I'd been in Madame Usher's web for too long to trust that easy. I shook my head.

"Shit, de Winter. Don't be an idiot. If you stay silent, they get away with this…whatever it is. Throw me a bone here."

"I can't help you," I whispered. "But this is bigger than you think. Talk to Agent Rochester at the FBI about Aaron Varney and his god. And dig into the Usher family. Find out if it was convenient timing for Victor Usher to be pushing up daisies."

I wouldn't give her anything she could use to hang Dorien, but maybe, just maybe, if she was telling me the truth, she could help stop Varney or Usher before they hurt anyone else.

6

FAYE

I stepped outside into the parking lot behind the music store, blinking against the vibrant sunset that streaked across the sky. The shop was on the first floor of an office building, and the owner, Gregor, blocked out the windows with black paper because he labored under the mistaken impression it deterred thieves. Emerging after an eight-hour shift was like waking up your body with a cold shower of natural light.

My feet ached. My throat was dry from talking about pianos all day. I couldn't wait to stand under the rain shower at the hotel. I turned to lock the door behind me, and a brown hand cupped itself over my mouth.

I cried out as my assailant dragged me backward. *Shit, shit.* I dropped my bodyweight low, breaking their hold, and spun around and lunged out with my foot, hoping to trip them up so I could escape.

My foot connected with a shin, and my assailant went down. I sprung to my feet and grabbed for my bag and—

"Oof, what did you do that for?" a familiar voice snapped at me. My assailant rolled over, grasping at her leg, her dark eyes fixing me with an annoyed glare.

"Aroha?" I held out a hand and helped her up. "I thought you were a mugger."

"You see a dark skin in an alley and assume I'm a criminal? I expected better of a fellow brown girl, trash." Aroha fished around in her pocket and pulled out a packet of cigarettes. She tipped one into her hand and held the packet out to me. I accepted one gratefully and leaned up against the wall beside her. She lit our smokes and took a deep drag.

"I assume anyone's a mugger if they put their hand around my mouth in New York City," I shot back, but there was no bite.

"Fair enough."

I studied her face as I took a tentative puff. She looked terrible. Her black hair had spilled out of its tight bun, dancing wildly around her face. Her makeup was smudged, and her eyes glazed with the sheen of a chemical curtain. *She's high again.*

It didn't surprise me. Madame Usher had burned the anxiety medication she used to manage her moods. She needed something to help her through her performances. I just wished it didn't have to be this. Despite everything she'd done to me, I liked Aroha. She was prickly as fuck, but I respected the hell out of her and her vision for her career. In all the madness of the last few weeks, I hadn't given much thought to how she was a prisoner of Manderley, too.

I had a million questions to ask her, but I settled for an easy one. "How'd you escape Manderley?"

"I had a meeting with the philharmonic about doing a concerto in their Winter series, and I thought I'd see what you were up to now that you're no longer doing the old hag's bidding. Harrison's waiting down the block." She rolled her eyes. "He says we have to leave soon, or she'll get suspicious we came to see you."

I sucked in a deep drag. "I don't want you to get in trouble because of me."

"Too late, trash. Listen." She sounded serious. I turned toward her. "I told this to the police, but I'm telling you too because I don't trust that Walpole bastard. I saw Heather before she died. I was passing Dorien's room and I heard someone talking inside. Weird, because I knew he was out with you. So I pushed the door open a crack and saw Heather standing beside Dorien's bed, talking to the wall."

My tongue dried to the roof of my mouth. "Talking to a wall?"

She blinked, blowing out a row of perfect smoke rings. "Getting really pissy with it, stomping her foot and pouting and her whole act. She was still wearing that dress she used to take pictures down at the gazebo, too. I saw them all down there in the morning, and in the library editing it afterward. They really wanted to fuck Dorien over."

I winced at the memory of the photoshopped image of Dorien on his knees in the gazebo, proposing to Heather. It accompanied every lurid article about Heather's murder, and even though I knew it was fake, it made rage burn behind my eyes every time I saw it.

"What do you want me to do with this?" I asked her, curious about the answer.

Aroha rolled her eyes, sinking down to her knees. She giggled, and the giggle turned into a cackle that set my teeth on edge. "The bitch burned my medication. I was lucky Elena had some coke stashed behind the tank in the bathroom, or I'd have been a complete mess for this meeting today. Unlike you, I don't have my daddy's famous name to fall back on. I need that scholarship, or it's back to playing fucking church hymns for me. Raze Manderley to the ground if you have to, but at the end of it, let me walk away with a career, okay?"

Before I could say another word, Aroha stubbed out her cigarette on the ground and disappeared down the alley. I leaned my head back and drew the smoke deep into my lungs, letting the nicotine spin in my head, churning up this new dirt.

Heather had been talking to the wall.

Not just talking, by the sounds of it, but *scheming*.

An idea was forming in my mind.

I needed to get inside Manderley again. We needed the truth.

7

FAYE

*T*itus didn't say a word as he drove the winding roads to Manderley. What was there to say? Everything was completely fucked up.

He'd been called in by Sheriff Laine Stanford to give his statement as well. She'd even shown up at the hotel to talk to my mother. But whatever they said to Stanford had no impact, or maybe she was in Walpole's pocket after all, because the authorities were officially charging Dorien with first-degree murder. And now Ivan messaged me from his burner phone, with a picture of an old newspaper article about some previous drama at Manderley. Ivan thought it was about Radcliffe, but I wondered if it might match up with the reason our secret Manderley ghost had to disappear. I would look into it, but not today.

Today we found out who was hiding in the walls of Manderley.

Titus drummed his fingers on the steering wheel in time with an Iron Maiden track. It was weird to see him like this, filled with pent-up aggression. He'd been incredible these last few weeks as more salacious news stories came out about me and Dorien, as I schemed and investigated and worried about Ivan and Elena and Aroha stuck at Manderley with this murderer inside the walls.

The press might call Dorien the genius behind Broken Muse, but Titus was our rock. He anchored us to each other and kept our wild emotions from making us do irrational things.

Which was probably why he'd gone weird and silent – what we were doing today was pretty irrational.

As we rounded the bend and climbed along a narrow road hugging the side of the mountain, a chill crept into my veins. Through the trees, I could make out the gabled roof and gothic windows of Manderley. The twin eyes of my old attic bedroom windows glared back at me in silent accusation.

I don't want to be here.

I wanted to be back in my cozy hotel room with my mom, watching horror movies and throwing hilarious shade at the terrible room service tacos. But the only way to clear Dorien's name was to enter the belly of the beast.

The road turned abruptly, leaving a wide gravel shoulder that served as the starting point of one of the hiking trails, as well as a lookout across the valley. Titus slammed his foot down and we jerked to a stop. I peered out the window over the rickety safety rail to the deep valley far below, the treetops shrouded with mist and the river winding through them like a snake. Manderley's twin eyes burned into me.

"You don't have to go back there." Titus reached across to squeeze my arm. "We could ask Ivan and Elena to do this for us. Or better yet, wait until his FBI agent is ready to move against Usher."

I shook my head. "I need to see. I need to know."

I need to know if my father is inside those walls.

I need to know if he left us for her.

Titus made a choking sound, as if he sensed what I was thinking. He trailed his fingers along my arm, raising goosebumps on my skin that had nothing to do with my trepidation about returning to Manderley. I looked over to him, and he cocked an eyebrow at me, his dark eyes hard with determination. I knew I wasn't the only one who was afraid of Manderley.

"Manderley took from you, too." I slid my hand across his cheek. Beneath my fingers, his stubble scratched my skin, reminding me that in this world of spirits and shadows, he was with me. He was real.

I moved my hand along his jaw, his neck. I flicked a stray braid from his face. His eyes watched me. Not my hand. Me. The intensity of his gaze halted my breath. All my life, when people looked at me, they saw only my name – de Winter. My father, the great virtuoso. They didn't hear my music, only the ghost of his notes. But Titus saw me, all of me, even the dark and ugly sides I tried to keep hidden. And he loved them unconditionally.

Neither of us belonged at Manderley. But here, in this car, we had everything. We had each other. We shared the same song, the same sad notes and haunting melody.

I bent my head, resting my forehead against his. "Please," I whispered as the first flakes of snow fell outside the window. "Make me feel invincible."

Titus' fingers closed around my neck. Strong, domineering. He tilted my head back and took my mouth with his. He didn't rush, even though we very definitely had somewhere to be. He kissed me slowly, beautifully, his lips like a butterfly unfurling its wings for the first time. I tried to fall into him but the gearstick was in the way, and when I swung my leg over to straddle him, I jammed it against the steering wheel.

Titus laughed his low, sexy laugh as he leaned our seats back. Between his massive bulk and my curves, we couldn't maneuver easily, and it was too fucking cold outside to open a door. I tried to straddle him, but he plonked me down on the passenger seat. I peered up at him, disappointed that we couldn't make this work, but he pushed me back down.

"Let me take care of you," he smiled.

The words sent a flicker of heat through my body. Titus kissed a trail over my neck as he folded down the waistband of my leggings. I tried to reach down to help, but he slapped my hand away, chuckling against my lips.

I captured his rumbling laugh in my mouth, and it tasted like summer, like happiness.

"You don't need me to feel powerful," he murmured as he pushed my panties to one side. "You're Faye fucking de Winter. I want you to say it for me."

"I'm Faye de Winter."

"Say it properly." He teased my entrance with his finger. I could feel how wet I was already, how much my body needed him.

I bucked my hips toward him, trying to make him give me what I wanted. "I'm Faye fucking de Winter."

"Damn right. You're a queen riding into war. And I, your humble servant, will always be by your side. Or between your legs."

Titus lowered his head, his tongue lapping at my swollen clit as he thrust a finger inside me. My fingers tangled in his hair, pushing his head down as he danced his tongue over me until the ache inside me became a scream pressing against my lips.

Sound the fucktrumpets, musicians are the best in bed. Seriously. The rhythm, the tempo, the natural sense of pageantry. Titus played my body like a guitar, his fingers conjuring magic from my skin.

Liquid heat coursed through my body as he curled his finger inside me, rubbing that spot that drove me wild. I gripped his shoulders, bending into him, driving him deeper. "Titus, don't stop. You feel so good. You're perfect."

You're perfect.

We don't tell people that enough, that they're perfect just the way they are. I don't think Titus had ever heard those words before, even though his whole life had been about striving for perfection. He groaned against my clit, lost in the intensity of the moment. With a shuddering breath, I lost myself, too.

The orgasm crested, and I rode it into the snow-dusted valley below us. I rode it as my body came to pieces, as bursts of bright magic sizzled beneath my skin.

Titus laid a trail of kisses up my chest as he leaned forward, supporting his weight on the back of the chair as he tugged down his pants with one hand. His cock sprung free, and he laughed again at my expression when I saw it. I still wasn't quite sure how something that majestic could fit inside me. Magic.

Titus shuffled back between my legs. He pressed my thighs wide and plunged his cock inside me.

I saw stars. A universe opened up on the roof of the car as he thrust inside me, filling me, making me his. Being his perfect, wonderful self.

My breasts crushed against his chest, my knees smashing against the dashboard, a handbrake jabbing where no handbrake should ever jab. I loved every moment of it because it was raw and real and true. Because my Titus, my broken muse, was inside me, and for a brief moment, I believed I was invincible, and everything would be all right.

Getting Madame Usher out of the house was easier than I thought. All it took was asking Dorien to request a meeting with her in jail. I bet she thought he was going to agree to anything she wanted if she'd call in a favor from Walpole to get him to drop the charges.

After our distraction in the car, we had to race down the trail and through the wood to Manderley. We watched through the trees as Harrison drove Madame Usher away. A sprinkle of snow fell. Wet flakes dotted my face as I turned to watch them pass through the iron gates. As soon as the car disappeared around the bend of the road, Titus and I scrambled out of the trees and around the edge of the house to the backdoor, where I let us in with my copied key.

The sound of Aroha practicing one of her atonal pieces echoed through the halls. Otherwise, the house remained completely silent. We crept upstairs, careful to stand on the edges where the boards were less likely to creak. Using the keys Titus copied, I unlocked Ivan and Elena's door. Madame Usher was keeping them locked in their rooms when they didn't have classes or chores.

Elena breezed past me, air-kissing both my cheeks.

"I'll be over at Master Radcliffe's, providing a 'distraction.'" She waved as she bounced off. Ivan frowned as he came to the doorway. She hadn't elaborated on what she meant by distraction, but Ivan's jaw clenched as he watched her glide down the staircase, so I didn't want to ask.

"I missed you." I wrapped my arms around his neck and pressed my lips to his. I could still taste Titus' scent on my tongue – the taste of an ancient forest god; myrrh and musk, and roses dappled with dew. But I needed to taste Ivan, too. I needed to reassure myself that he was here, alive and safe – at least while he was in my arms.

Ivan grunted in surprise as I nipped at his lower lip, but he returned the kiss, his eyes no longer focused on the staircase but boring into me with cold and beautiful clarity.

I missed you.

I've been so afraid for you.

I deepened the kiss, pressing against him and devouring him as bit by bit the tension in his body unwound. He sank into me, giving into the connection we shared. We didn't need words to say the things we'd been thinking all these nights we've been apart.

I knew that loving Ivan meant loving Elena, too. They were a package deal, and I was lucky they were such a wonderful package. I didn't want Ivan to ever feel like he had to dull his devotion to her – it might've made some girls jealous, but I had no room for that shit in my life. It made me love him more. I would always be safe with him because I saw how he'd kept her safe for so many years.

I just wish...

I wish he was free to be himself. To learn about who he is and what he wants from his life if he's not protecting her. I wish he saw the wonderful person I see in him.

"Faye," Titus warned.

"Right, yes." I pulled away from Ivan reluctantly. His ice-blue eyes raked over me, like he was trying to commit me to memory. "We should do this."

We made our way down the hall to Dorien's room, where I used my keys to unlock it. The forensic teams finished with the room weeks ago, leaving it smelling faintly of bleach. Manderley's antique furniture and paintings were still in situ, but Dorien's things were gone – Ivan told me the Valencourts showed up with Father Aaron to take them away. I'd found some of Dorien's more well-known stage outfits – including the shirt he wore in the video for 'A Graveside Story' – on eBay. The Temple was getting desperate for money, which couldn't be a good sign.

Titus peered under the empty bed frame. "No ghosts here."

"Aroha said Heather was talking to that wall." I cast my eye around the room. Dorien never went in for band posters and Suicide Girls. Instead, he decorated the walls with artwork from Manderley's extensive collection, as well as his own acquisitions. The paintings remained in place, spectral reminders of the complicated boy who used to call this room home. His smell clung to the air, hidden beneath the antiseptic scent of the crime scene cleaners.

Above his desk was a painting that referenced the Hell panel of Hieronymus Bosch's *Garden of Earthly Delights* in a heavy-looking gilded frame. A Manderley piece, but not one that could be displayed in polite company. *How very Dorien.*

Heather was talking to the wall.

I moved to stand in the doorway. From Aroha's position, she couldn't have seen the desk wall. Anything – or anyone – there would be obscured for her.

I stepped up onto the desk and peered at the edge of the painting. It looked solid. As my fingers grazed the surface, I felt cold air brush against them. I'd felt drafts before in other rooms of Manderley – air rushing through gaps and cracks in the walls. I thought it was just part of living in an old house, but now…

"Help me lift this painting down," I said.

I stepped off the desk and Titus leaped up. Ivan started climbing up to help, but Titus shooed him away. Ivan pulled me into his arms, pressing his lips to mine for another breathless kiss.

"I have missed you," he murmured against my lips, his fingers trailing down my spine.

"Ditto." I ran my hands over his shoulders, trying to memorize the shape of him. I couldn't bear the thought of having to leave him here again.

"Faye, you should see this."

Reluctantly, I broke the kiss and turned toward Titus. He jabbed his finger at the gilded frame. "I can't move this," he said.

"Stand aside," Ivan commanded. "I'll do it—"

"Trust me, your puny Romanian arms won't make a dent. If I can't budge it, then it's stuck to the wall with some kind of super-human glue."

I climbed up beside Titus and stared at the frame again. In the corner – nestled amongst goat-demons feeding on human flash – was a man crucified on a harp, no doubt symbolizing the contrast between pleasure and pain.

Music.

I touched the harp, feeling the odd way the paint rose in ridges around it. Cold air nudged my fingers.

I pressed it.

The painting swung toward me. I flung myself off the desk, collapsing into Ivan's arms before the heavy bastard decapitated me. The painting hit the adjoining wall and stopped swinging, leaving a gaping hole in the wall behind it.

Sound the fucktrumpets.

Gotcha.

Titus held my hand as I clambered back on the desk and peered inside the hole. It was a crawl-space between the walls, wide enough only for a small person to walk through if they shuffled sideways. Titus wouldn't be able to fit. On the inside edge of the hole was a mechanism for operating the door. There was a bolt that could be slid in place, preventing the painting from being opened from the outside.

We got lucky. If that bolt had been shut today, we never would have found the secret door.

The crawl-space looked to stretch the entire length of the wall, but I could only see a few feet into the gloom – a yearning black hole threatening to swallow us. I patted my pocket for my phone, but then remembered I left it back in the car.

"I need a flashlight," I called over my shoulder.

Titus didn't have his phone on him, and Ivan's burner phone didn't have a flashlight app. We searched the drawers in Dorien's desk, but there was nothing. I ran downstairs to look in the kitchen. I found a packet of matches, which would do in a pinch, but I didn't want to risk burning the place down.

"I know where there will be a flashlight," I said. "Harrison's shed."

I didn't want to leave the house again, but we had at least two hours before Madame Usher could be back from her meeting with Dorien, and there was no way I was getting into that hole without a light. Ivan and I left Titus in Dorien's room, guarding the hole with the ax from the woodpile. We snuck back down-stairs and headed for the collection of outbuildings behind the stables.

Steam puffed from our lips as we made our way past the old shed where Titus secretly played his music. I tried the door of Harrison's maintenance shed. The door was locked, but my copied keys dealt with that.

Ivan made to step inside. I grabbed him by the collar and yanked him out again, holding him against me as he tried to avoid looking at me.

"You're not okay," I said. It wasn't a question.

Ivan looked toward the stables. Lights shone through the windows, and if I strained I could hear the faint notes of piano music. Elena was working on her 'distraction.'

"I keep thinking what that woman said in the article," Ivan said. "Deviant sexual proclivities."

I stroked his cheek. "They're just playing the piano."

"And what will he do to her once they're married?" he growled, his hands balling into fists.

"We don't know Donelle was talking about Radcliffe."

"Who else could it be?" he said bitterly. "Madame Usher barely touched Victor."

An image of the portrait in the attic burned inside my mind. *Maybe Donelle saw something between Madame and my father.*

If the man in the walls was Victor, he's been living there since his supposed death eighteen months ago. But my father has been missing for ten years. He couldn't really have been living in the walls all that time, could he? Not with *Victor* in the house, in *her* bed. It seemed insane.

We're going to find out.

I grabbed two flashlights from a shelf of tools and supplies and clicked them on to make sure they worked. We headed back down the path, keeping low to avoid been seen through the stable windows. From inside, I heard the keys stutter. Elena shrieked.

I looked back at Ivan. He stiffened, his entire body rigid. I reached for him, trying to urge him on, but I knew it was hopeless. He dived into the overgrown flowerbed, his fingers gripping the edge of the sill and pulling his body up so he could see inside.

Fuck it. In for a penny.

I shuffled in beside him, straining my head to see inside the dimly lit room. Snow dotted my hair, flakes melting into freezing drips that rolled under my collar and down my back. I had to cup my hands against the glass to see inside.

Elena didn't look like she was in trouble. In fact, she had a smile on her face as she sat at the piano, her back perfectly straight, her delicate neck long like a swan. Radcliffe leaned over her, his fingers cupping hers as he corrected her positioning. She gazed up at him with perfect adoration. He leaned in closer to murmur something to her, and his lips grazed her neck.

Beside me, Ivan ground his teeth together.

"There's nothing to see here." I tugged his arm. He didn't move. "Ivan. *Ivan?*"

He glared at the window. A low, pained sound escaped his throat.

"You're seeing what you expect to see. They're playing the piano. He kissed her neck. They *are* engaged to be married." I knitted my fingers in his and tugged him gently. "Can I remind you that we were doing much more depraved things on a piano months ago, and you haven't put a ring on it?"

Ivan cracked a smile, but it was a long time before he tore his gaze from the scene inside. When he looked at me again, his ice eyes burned with frigid ire. I gripped his fingers. "Whether Radcliffe is a deviant or not, if we want to free her from this marriage, we need to discover the secrets of Manderley. Come on."

He nodded and let me drag him out of the weeds. We rushed back inside, careful not to slam the kitchen door against the freezing air and alert Aroha to our presence. In the kitchen, I grabbed two knives from the rack. Whoever was in the walls was armed, so we should be, too.

Titus set down the ax when we entered the room. Ivan tossed him a flashlight and he pointed it into the hole. "This definitely goes all the way back toward my bedroom, but I'm not going to be any use." He handed back the flashlight. "I won't fit inside."

"Too many protein shakes," Ivan scoffed. It took me a moment to realize he'd cracked a joke, and I had to stifle a laugh with my hand.

Titus pointed to Ivan's violin, which was resting on the bed. "I took that from your room. I figure I'll play a few bars of, say, Saint-Saëns' *Danse Macabre*, if you need to get back here, and some Shostakovich if you need to stay silent and hide?"

"Mmmm, clever as well as gorgeous." I climbed up on the desk beside Titus and slid the largest carving knife into my belt. "Help me in."

Titus made a cup with his hands. I stepped into it and he boosted me up. I grabbed the edge of the hole and swung myself over. I gasped as I slid down into the darkness. It went deeper than I thought, and I shrieked as the walls closed around me and I disappeared into the gloom before my feet slammed into a hard wooden surface.

I clicked on my light. Wedged in sideways like this, I had to twist my neck at an awkward angle to aim the flashlight into the crawl space. The stale air burned my lungs. *Whoever's been wandering around in here, they can't have been comfortable.*

My hand flew to the knife handle. My breathing steadied, knowing it was there.

The space stretched all the way between the walls in both directions. I couldn't believe we never noticed from the outside how the house's walls were so deep.

"There's a ladder here." I felt around the strips of wood nailed into the wall. "Someone wanted to make it easier to climb in and out of the painting."

A moment later, Ivan's legs swung over the edge. I grabbed his ankle and guided it onto the first rung of the ladder. He swung himself over and dropped down beside me, holding his light up to peer at the walls. His flashlight made his pale skin luminescent, the cold of his blue eyes searing in the gloom.

"Stay behind me," he ordered, trying to push past me.

"No way." I crossed my arms over my boobs. "I'm not going to let you walk headfirst into danger." *If anyone is going to confront my father, it should be me.* "Besides, there's not enough room for you to get around me in here unless you have secret contortionist abilities."

I held up my flashlight and shone it into the gloom as we shuffled forward. We didn't have to go far before we reached a junction. We could continue straight ahead to Titus' room, or turn off down the walls that divided their rooms.

I noticed a pinprick of light stabbing through the wall.

"That's a peephole," I whispered, angling my body down the junction to get to it. I was too short to see out of the hole, but Ivan peered through. His features hardened.

"What is it?" I whispered.

"This peephole looks straight into Titus' room," Ivan said. "Whoever was in these walls would've been able to see and hear everything."

"That's how Madame Usher seemed to know what was going on in the house. She had someone spying on us."

My stomach churned as the full meaning of this peephole dawned on me.

Someone was watching us.

Someone watched me and Titus and Ivan on that bed.

That's fucking gross.

This branch was a dead end, so we backtracked and continued along the wall of Titus' room. It was tough to move in the narrow space. My ass scraped across the rough wood as I shuffled sideways. My tits were smushed against my chest. Behind me, Ivan grunted as he wrestled with his shoulders.

"We must be nearly at Titus' doorway. This looks like a dead end—"

I screamed as my foot slid away into nothing and I toppled forward into a dark abyss.

8

FAYE

*I*van grabbed me and yanked me backward, scraping my calf on rough wood as he hauled me to safety.

"Thanks." I nestled my head into his neck as I waited for my heart rate to return to normal. My leg stung, but I couldn't twist my body to look at it. I held it out for Ivan to inspect.

"You've scraped some skin off, and it's bleeding a little." He sounded concerned. "We should turn back."

"No way." I pointed my flashlight down into a dark hole that must lead to the ground floor. More wooden boards were nailed into the wall to create a ladder. I sucked in a few deep breaths of stale air. *I nearly fell down there. I could have broken my neck.*

Just like Clare.

"It goes up, as well." Ivan pointed with his flashlight. He didn't have to say what he was thinking. We both knew what that meant.

This tunnel leads into the storage room beside my bedroom.

Dorien and I had looked for a secret passage when we broke in there and couldn't find one. The button to operate the painting in his room was so well concealed I'm not surprised we didn't find a similar entrance in the attic. I leaned across the hole and grabbed a wooden board, testing my weight against it. It seemed sturdy. In fact, these boards looked as though they'd been hammered in recently, with modern nails. Ivan held my hips as I swung my legs across the hole and clambered up the ladder.

I moved through a small open hatch and stepped off the ladder into another narrow space. The ceiling of the tunnel was so low I had to stoop a little. Ivan looked ridiculous as he followed me, hunched over sideways in the tiny space. We crawled forward into the gloom. My heart hammered in my chest. Around every corner I expected to be pounced on by the tunnel's occupant.

Where is he?

Who is he?

If my father's face suddenly appeared like a ghoul in the darkness, what would I do?

The knife handle dug against my hip. As I dragged my legs forward, it felt like it weighed a million pounds. Or maybe that was my abandonment issues dragging behind me like dead weight.

Up ahead, two pinpricks of light pierced the gloom. I peered through one into my old bedroom – the peephole I found in the painting. This is where someone spied on me, and Clare before me.

The walls are talking.

But who was talking? Who?

The suspense of it weighed on my chest, so every step felt like moving through molasses. Ivan's presence behind me was the only thing stopping me from breaking down and yelling my accusations into the darkness.

A person could go insane hiding away in here. The walls tightened around me as I moved deeper. *How many horror films have I seen that start like this and end up with the heroine's guts splattered across the secret passage?*

I'm going to go insane if I don't get answers.

Where are you? Who are you?

From the corner of the storage room, we had to lie down and crawl through a low space, which I figured from the sloping wall and the map of the house I had in my head was the roof cavity beneath the attic windows. As I dragged myself forward on my elbows, I ran my fingers along the wall, crying out in triumph when my fingers brushed a mechanism – similar to the one we discovered behind the painting. I slid open the bolt, lifted the catch and a small hatch swung outward, into the storage room.

Dorien and I searched the whole room, but we never would have found this – it was too perfectly concealed in the paneling and it could only open from the inside.

I crawled out from the wall, shoving aside boxes and kicking up clouds of dust. I sucked in the hot air of the attic like it was the sweetest perfume. I clambered to my feet and swung my arms around. It felt so good to have *space*. I never thought I was claustrophobic or afraid of the dark, but my stomach cramped and my chest ached from being on edge.

Ivan climbed out after me. He winced as he rolled his shoulders and shone his light around the room, taking in the row of footsteps in the dust leading from the tunnel to the peephole and back again. His shoulders tensed. "This man will wish he's a ghost by the time I'm done with him."

"Get in line." My hands balled into fists.

All these months I lived up here, worried about my mom, hurting from the things the Muses did to me, someone was watching me, invading my privacy, finding fresh ways to torment me. And after I saw Clare I thought...I thought I was being visited by a ghostly friend. Someone who'd been just as much a victim of the house as I had.

But now I didn't know anymore.

The dead were still dead to me. But the living were determined to haunt my ass.

Ivan shone his light into the tunnel. "This passage keeps going."

"There's an entire network of tunnels," I breathed. I didn't want to go back into that narrow space, but we had to see where it led. *Who* it led to. I strained my ears to hear Titus – nothing, just a few stolen notes from Aroha's composition echoing and amplifying in the hollow walls. We were safe to keep going for now.

I kicked a box aside, no longer caring if they knew we discovered their secret. On my hands and knees, I turned my shoulders sideways and crawled back into the tunnel, aiming my flashlight into the unknown. My elbows scraped raw as I pulled myself along so Ivan could fit in after me. I heard a *CLICK* as he snapped the door shut behind us, snuffing out the thin beam of natural light.

My stifled breath came out in ragged gasps as I inched along the tunnel. My face felt hot, my lungs sticky, my temples pounding. I heard something squeak above me, and little feet *scritch-scritch-scritching* in the gloom. I shuffled faster, my elbows burning as the rough wood scraped off my skin.

At the end of the tunnel was another open trapdoor, another wooden ladder. As soon as we dropped down on the other side, the space around us widened out into a dark hallway, spacious enough for us to stand beside each other. The air still tasted stale and scratched the back of my throat, but at least I wasn't hemmed in on all sides.

Ivan clapped his hands over my shoulders, his breath coming out in ragged gasps. "That was horrible."

"No argument." I shone my flashlight down the corridor. "Look."

I noticed the tiny pinpricks of light dotting the hall. Little peepholes. I went up to one and looked out onto an ornate sitting room I'd never seen before. A Fazioli piano sat in the corner closest to us. I could only see the corner of it, beautifully polished despite the shabby condition of the other furniture. A violin rested on a stand beside it.

"I think…I think we're in Madame Usher's private wing."

"Look at this." Ivan tapped the opposite wall, showing me where a window had been boarded up from inside. I tried to map our location in my head. Many of the windows in Madame's private wing had the shades drawn constantly, so we couldn't see in from outside. *That's because she doesn't want anyone to know this corridor exists.*

Fear prickled in my chest, and the hairs on my arms and neck stood to attention. The air grew hotter, streaking my face with sweat. *He's here.* I *felt* him nearby, this creature of the gloom who had been haunting us. We were in his domain. He was watching us this very moment.

But where is he?

I tugged the knife from my belt and held it in front of me. Ivan did the same, holding his knife and taking my other hand in his.

Ivan squeezed my fingers as we made our way down the hallway, peeking through the peepholes into the different rooms of Madame's private wing – a master bedroom fit for a Russian Tsar, an opulent bathroom, all the furniture and fine objects coated in a thick layer of dust. Madame Usher certainly spared no expense on her own comfort, especially considering the rest of the house was in such a state of ruin.

The hallway stopped at a door. Ivan grabbed my wrist to stop me, but I shook him off.

I have to know.

The air sang with tension, pulled tight like a note ringing on an open string. I turned the handle, my breath catching. It was unlocked. I raised my knife and shoved the door open, and we stepped into the unknown.

9

———

FAYE

My breath caught in my throat as I aimed the flashlight beam into the dim room.

I don't know what I expected to find. A pile of skulls, perhaps. Or a nuclear weapon with a comically large countdown timer. But I definitely didn't expect the sight that greeted us.

The room was furnished with simple furniture. It must've been on the end of the wing, because it contained one of the tall gothic arched windows that made Manderley such an arresting sight. The window was boarded up, but the decorative rosette at the top had been left bare. The ancient glass was cracked slightly, letting in a blast of cold air. *That could be the source of the drafts in the houses.* Beneath the window, a narrow, single bed was made up with fresh sheets, and there were books stacked on a chair beside it. Crime thrillers mostly, and a biography of Mozart. Ratty men's clothing hung from a rack in the corner, with shoes and slippers lined up underneath. A bookshelf on the opposite wall held more volumes, as well as a small MP3 player and headphones, an electric kettle, and a supply of coffee and candy bars.

"Someone's been living here," I whispered. When we were sure there was no one in the room, I stepped inside, fingering the threadbare mattress, peering at the titles of the books. I longed to flick through the MP3 player, but I didn't want to put anything out of place.

We knew someone was hiding in the walls, but this room... this was someone's *life*. I couldn't imagine being hidden away in here day after day after day, away from light and love and music. *It's so sad.*

Angry tears pricked at the corners of my eyes. *Did my dad give up his life with Mom, with me, for this?*

"Look at this." Ivan moved behind the clothing rack. "There's another room back here."

He pushed the narrow door open and lurched forward, his knife glinting as he raised it high. I crowded in beside him as he swept his flashlight beam around the second room. It looked like some kind of laboratory. A narrow counter with a sink stood against one wall, with glass jars and beakers lined up on shelves above. A mortar and pestle sat in the sink alongside metal tongs and other strange implements. Boxes and old file cases littered the floor. The room smelt of sulfur and disinfectant.

Opposite the sink was a desk with a battered laptop, a printer, and stacks of books. Unable to hold back my curiosity, I picked up the top one and thumbed through it – it was a Victorian plant manual. Beneath it was a book on famous perfumers, and others on chemical compounds and medicinal herbs.

As Ivan turned pages in a notebook beside the computer, I picked up a bottle from the shelf. It had been labeled 'Brugmansia: Angel's Trumpet' and contained dried leaves and white flower petals. *I think I've seen these flowers before, in the poison garden...*

"Faye."

Ivan jabbed his finger at the notebook. It contained what looked like recipes. After scanning a couple, I realized they were notes on experiments with various flowers and herbs, with measurements and notations about temperatures and chemical reactions.

"I recognize this handwriting," Ivan said. "It belongs to Victor Usher."

Victor Usher.

My breath whooshed in relief. I didn't realize how much I'd been hoping my dad wasn't secretly living in the walls of Manderley until Ivan's words registered. A dead Donovan de Winter was better than one who chose this squalid hellhole over his family.

Ivan's fingers squeezed mine. "You are okay?"

I sucked in another deep breath. "Yes. I'm okay." I gestured to the shelves, the lab, the boxes. "So then what is this place? Some kind of Frankenstein lab?"

Ivan pulled a leather-bound volume off the shelf and opened it. "These are ledger books for that company the Usher's owned, Menabilly Holdings. They detail a lot of money moving around."

What the fuck is going on?

I moved deeper into the room. There was a second door, even smaller and narrower, facing into what I assumed to be Madame Usher's master suite. A hidden door that granted her and her husband access to this little bolthole. As I bent down to inspect the door, my foot brushed a cardboard box with a shipping label addressed to Menabilly Holdings.

I trained my beam on it and peeled back the flap. The box was filled with square paper bags. They looked familiar. My heart raced as I picked one up and held it under the light. "It's the herbal tea my mom used to drink."

In Cauda Venenum.

I lifted the box aside and looked at the stack behind it, my heart racing. There were boxes and boxes of the stuff, hidden in this secret laboratory behind Madame's bedroom wall. In horror, I whirled to face Ivan, who held up a page in the notebook. The word 'birthwort' jumped off the page.

"This is the poison," he whispered.

We've found it. We've found the evidence we need to get the bitch. We need to—

The faint sound of a solo violin pierced my ears. Not Aroha's atonal playing, but a familiar tune that opened with the *diabolus in musica*, dripping with darkness and urgency.

Saint-Saëns' *La Danse Macabre.*

Shit.

Get out. We have to get out now.

10

IVAN

Faye's eyes widened as the familiar tune sung in the air. She hugged the tea box to her chest, clinging to the truth like she needed it to remain upright. I grabbed her wrist and tugged her to her feet.

She whispered. "We have to put everything back how we found it."

My heart raced as I kicked the boxes back into the corner. Faye bent over the counter, her hair tumbling down her shoulders as she flipped the notebooks shut, hiding away evidence of Victor's complicity. I wished we'd thought to bring a phone to take photographs for evidence, but Faye left hers in the car and my burner couldn't even text in lower caps, let alone take photos.

Titus' playing sped up now, the bow tearing across the strings. I winced as he bungled the contrapuntal. He wasn't a skilled violinist, but I read the urgency in his notes.

I grabbed Faye's wrist again and yanked her toward the door. "We must go."

Faye slid the notebook back into its position beside the laptop. She cast a final, forlorn look at the room that contained all the answers we longed for, and a million new questions that would keep us awake at night.

And then we fled.

Back through Victor Usher's sad little bedroom. Back into the corridor connecting Madame Usher's private apartments to the secret tunnels throughout the house. Titus' music screeched in my ears. I had only one thought – get Faye out.

Keep her safe.

Faye dragged her feet behind me. She yanked down on her arm and freed it from my grasp. I grabbed for her but she twisted away. "What are you doing?"

She copped her hands over one of the peepholes. "I want to see Madame Usher."

"We have to get out of here," I whispered. "What if Victor comes back?"

"*Exactly.* He's not in his rooms. Why wasn't he in his bedroom or that lab or the tunnels? Because he's out *there*, in her quarters. I want to see them together. Then we'll know everything."

"We already know everything." Panic crawled through my stomach. I tugged on her hand. "Faye, *please.*"

She glared at me in defiance before turning back to the peephole. *Infuriating woman.* I paced across the corridor, wringing my hands in my hair before moving further down and choosing one of the other peepholes. Mine looked into the ornate reception room. I could clearly make out the door leading into the second-floor landing, where the student bedrooms and bathrooms led off.

Titus' music cut off abruptly. Faye and I exchanged a worried glance, but she refused to move. My stomach twisted in knots as I stared into that still room, waiting for something to happen. A few minutes later, the door banged open, shaking on its hinges. Madame Usher marched through the receiving room, her black skirts flying around her. Dust kicked up where she threw down her carpetbag. She unwound her shawl from her shoulders and tossed it angrily in the direction of a coat rack.

"That infernal boy," she yelled into the gloom. "I'll be glad when he's locked away for good."

She passed into the next room. I hardly dared to breathe as I moved with her, creeping along the wall to find another peephole. Madame Usher stood in the middle of her sitting room, her nails digging into the edge of the piano as she breathed through her nose.

"I'd like to see that swaggering boy locked in a jail cell," a male voice said, the sound muffled by the wall between us. His voice rose with obvious delight. "What did he want?"

I started. *He's right there. He's been right here all this time.*

Did he hear us? Our footsteps? Our whispers? Does he know we're inside the walls?

Why doesn't he tell her?

Even when we found the bedroom and lab, I didn't really believe it was possible until this very moment. But it's true.

It's him.

Victor Usher wasn't dead after all. He'd been living in the walls of Manderley, spying on us for his wife.

But why?

I couldn't see him from this angle, for he sat at the piano, his head to my left. I dared not move closer. I feared even my breathing could give us away.

Faye reached down the wall to me, hooking her pinkie finger in mine.

Madame Usher snorted. "He had the audacity to demand I intercede with the police, tell them he's innocent. He tried to threaten me with what he knows about the poison again, but this time he has no power over me. No one will believe a word from a trumped-up murdering shit. I don't need him any longer. Broken Muse will never play another show or make another record. That's for the best."

"What about our plan?" Victor's voice wheedled. "I needed Broken Muse."

"You destroyed the plan when you stabbed Heather," she snapped.

"I had to do it. If you heard the things she was saying… I had to protect—"

"I had it all planned. Every last detail was set in perfect motion. But as usual, you blundered in and made a mess of it." She flounced dramatically across the piano lid. "I never should have listened to you in the first place. If I hadn't done what you asked, none of this would have happened and you would have everything you deserve. Everything they took for granted could have been ours but you…you…"

"Shhhh." A hand reached out and tugged her onto the piano bench beside him. She was so close I could see the flyaway strands of dark hair that escaped her severe bun. He pulled her into him, so she rested her head on his shoulder. "My darling, please don't get worked up. We've worked too hard to give up now. You're right, of course. I messed up. But we can fix this. We will triumph. I know you have a brilliant new plan brewing in that beautiful head of yours."

She sniffed. "If Dorien goes away, Varney will get control over their estate. That will get him off our backs. Elena's wedding will secure Radcliffe's silence. All I have to do is keep the others from talking and we'll have the money we need to start over. It might not be what we imagined, but at least we'll no longer need to take in these wretched students."

"And Faye?" His voice was gentle, soothing. "What will you do with her?"

My stomach twisted as Madame Usher said, "You've become too soft. It's because of her our world is in disarray. I will take care of Faye, but you must trust me to do what's best for you."

"See? I knew you would think of everything." The floorboards creaked as the shadowed figure of Victor rose. I recognized the slope of his shoulders, the confident way he carried himself. "You have your lessons. I should get back to my lab. I will see you this evening."

Shit. *Shit.*

"Of course. Until tonight." She stood too, leaning over the piano. There was a wet, smacking sound as they kissed, and then she breezed from the room and Victor Usher started toward the bedroom and hidden door. I could see his back and his hair, long and tangled now, so different from Victor's usual tidy cut, and streaked with grey. He wore a perfectly-tailored suit streaked with dust. As he passed the violin, he tweaked the strings playfully.

As soon as he was out of sight in the bedroom, I let out the breath I'd been holding and grabbed Faye's hand. We'd taken two silent steps down the corridor when we heard a knocking on the wall.

"I know you're in there," Victor bellowed. "I heard you shuffling around, whispering to each other. Are you going to tell Faye? Because you should know the truth—"

At the sound of her name, Faye's face collapsed in fright. We bolted down the hallway, no longer caring how loud our footsteps were, how ragged our breathing. My elbow crashed against the wall as I slid my hands over her ass, helping her shimmy up the ladder. Behind us, the door to the bedroom crashed open.

"Go, go." I gave Faye one final push and she wiggled through the trapdoor, yelping as she hurt herself on something. Footsteps clattered behind me, but I didn't look back. I swung myself up and over just as the footsteps reached the ladder.

Victor cried, "Wait, please—"

Fuck no.

My elbows scraped raw as I scrambled after Faye. Her flashlight swung wildly as she tore along the narrow tunnel. Her skirt snagged on a nail, snapping her to a stop. She sobbed, but she couldn't turn around to free herself. I tore it away, straining to hear if he was coming behind us. At any moment I expected to feel Victor's long, bony fingers wrapped around my ankle.

But the fingers didn't come, and although I felt the itch of unseen eyes on me, when we turned the corner into the tunnel where we could stand upright and shuffled our way back to Dorien's bedroom, Victor didn't follow us.

"What happened?" Titus crawled out from under the bed as we pulled ourselves out of the painting. "I gave you the signal."

"It's my fault," Faye whimpered. "I wanted to see what Madame Usher did. And we found out...we found..."

Faye collapsed into his arms, her shoulders trembling with silent cries. Titus held her, rubbing circles on his back as he tore the answers from my eyes. I moved to hide behind the bureau, where I could watch both the painting and the doorway. I kept my knife poised to slice anyone who came for us.

We waited in tense silence until we heard Madame Usher enter the Red Room and berate Aroha for messing with the tempo. Titus reached inside the painting and ripped out the internal lock so we would always have a way into the secret passages. I pushed open the door and we crept down the hall, stepping over the places we knew had creaky floorboards. With every step my heart clattered so loudly against my ribs I felt certain I'd give us away. At any moment I expected Victor to burst from the walls and stab us, as he'd done to Heather.

We heard him confess. He did it, and they're deliberately framing Dorien for her murder. Does that mean they killed Clare, too?

So why isn't he coming after us now? Why didn't he keep chasing us or alert Madame Usher?

I didn't know, but I wasn't about to question it. At the top of the staircase, Faye paused, her hand lingering on mine. The look in her eyes said she didn't want to leave me.

I longed with every beat of my racing heart to follow her down that staircase, to escape into the bitter cold woods with them and be far, far away from this cursed place and the man in the walls who now knew we were onto him. I knew that sleep would never come to me at Manderley again.

But I couldn't leave Elena.

Especially not now.

Radcliffe wasn't the only danger to her.

And so we stood in silent parting. Faye's eyes pled with me, her fingers stroked my cheek, her lips quivered an unspoken promise. Titus tore her away, ripping my heart straight down the middle. I couldn't breathe. Something heavy squeezed my chest until stars blazed at the corners of my vision. The pain welled in my throat like tears until the warmth of her, the scent of her, was a ghost once more.

I stayed where I was at the top of the stairs for a long time, long after Faye and Titus disappeared into the hallway to the kitchen, long after Clare's face peered at me from around the corner of the balustrade. She was dressed in her maid's uniform, her wide mouth as black as the dress she wore as she waved a see-through duster over the carved banister.

Why is she shaking her head at me?

11

FAYE

Victor Usher is alive and living in the walls of Manderley.

I rested the Becker against my chin and drew my bow across the open strings, letting the sound ring in the empty hotel room as I decided what to play. I'd returned from another shift at the music shop to find Mom had gone to the hospital for another appointment. The quiet room assaulted me. The walls seemed to lean in, crushing my chest the way those narrow tunnels had done. I tasted the stale air on my tongue, and heard Madame Usher's chilling words pound against my skull. *I will take care of Faye.*

Despite myself, I found myself striking the strings to conjure a familiar, devilish tune. *Danse Macabre.* I closed my eyes as I lost myself in the furious fiddling – it was one of my favorite pieces to play, but today it felt ominous. I felt like Madame Usher was dangling us all from her fiddle, forcing us to dance in her fiendish revelry.

I left Ivan and Elena and Aroha in that house. I left them there knowing a murderer is hiding in the walls.

Ivan texted me every hour to let me know they were okay. He couldn't sleep and neither could I, so we stayed up theorizing over texts about why Victor was in the walls, what they meant by the things they said as they sat at the piano, and why they hadn't come after us yet.

Music had always been a friend to me. It comforted me after heartache, drove me to pursue my dreams, gave voice to my thoughts and fears and desires. And now – if I allowed myself to be consumed by it – it would give me answers.

I turned in agitated circles, focusing on my bowing as my mind conjured the scents of freshly dug grave dirt speckled with dew. This piece was written for orchestra, with an oboe representing a crow and a xylophone creating the sound of rattling bones. I closed my eyes and saw myself standing on the porch at Manderley as corpses rose from beneath the overgrown lawn to leap and gyrate.

Victor was alive. Madame Usher conjured him back from the dead and hid him from the world for eighteen months.

At least it's not Dad. At least the creep who's been spying on us through the walls isn't my own flesh and blood.

Everything that had happened at Manderley made a sick sense now. All the torments I blamed on my Muses, all the things Clare swore she hadn't done, it was Victor all along.

And he haunted Clare, too. *The walls are talking.* She left that message for the next maid. She knew he'd try the same tricks. And Donelle's accusations of deviancy…perhaps those peepholes had been in the walls long before Victor faked his death. But why us at all? Why risk exposing himself for the sake of frightening us?

Why bring me to Manderley at all? Why—

A knock sounded on the door, startling me from my thoughts. My bow screeched on the strings. *It must be Titus.* His parents had dragged him to another audition. He probably needed a good rant.

"You poor baby," I teased as I opened the door. "Tell me all about your evil parents wanting the best for you and making you audition for the London Academy of Music —"

I stopped dead.

Standing in the hall in a grease-stained shirt and an oversized grin was Creepy Cory.

How did he know I was here?

"Hey, Faye." Cory leaned against the frame, sliding his foot forward so I couldn't shut the door. I stepped back, my throat dry with fear. He still felt too close, like he sucked all the air from the room. I could see his greasy hair stuck to the skin behind his ears, and smell sugary alcohol on his breath.

"Cory, you…you…you didn't have to come here. I was going to call you." No one knew we were staying in this hotel except for Natalie and Broken Muse.

"I'd much rather see you in person, Faye. You're even more stunning than I remembered. I followed you from the hospital," he grinned, taking a step into the room as I shrunk from him. "Clever, right?"

No, not clever.

Seriously creepy.

"Um, sure. But it isn't safe for you to be here. These people I'm dealing with are dangerous." I leaned against the door, blocking his view of the room with my body. I didn't want him to see that I was alone. My hand slid into my pocket, and I wondered if I could unlock my phone one-handed and call one of the guys without Cory noticing. "It's not safe for you to be seen with me."

"If you're in danger, I can help you." Cory grabbed my wrist, his fingers squeezing so tight I cried out. I knew I made a mistake. He wasn't afraid of the Ushers. He liked the idea of being my white knight, my savior. It fed into the fantasy he'd created about himself.

It took everything I had not to yank my hand from his grasp. I didn't want to risk making him angry. Not yet. I swiped my thumb across my screen again, waiting to hear the click that said I'd made a call. "Did you have something to tell me about the Ushers?"

"I do. Can I come in?"

I shook my head. "Sorry, Mom's just got out of the shower."

"No, she's not. She's at the hospital." Cory grinned wider, giving him a maniacal clown vibe. "I know you're alone, Faye."

I swallowed, my muscles tensing. I swiped my thumb again but no click, no way to know if I had even unlocked the screen. *Can I shove my way past him and run for the elevators? Or back into the kitchen and grab a knife?*

The seconds counted down in silence. Cory's grin froze in a terrifying leer. His fingers tightened around my wrist, and I couldn't hold back the whimper that escaped my throat. "I'm not inviting you inside," I said, trying to keep my voice firm. "Please say what you came to tell me and leave."

"You don't have to be like that." His fingers rubbed circles on the inside of my wrist, and it was all I could do not to gag. "We have something special, something those rich fucks you go to school with could never compete with."

My muses are ten times the men you could ever hope to be, Creepy Cory. But I know I can't say anything to antagonize him. I was walking a knife edge. *If I keep him talking about the Ushers, I'll be able to figure out how to get out of this.*

I kept my wrist loose, not giving him any resistance, but not moving from the door, either. I lifted my chin and looked Cory straight in the eye, trying to keep my features neutral, interested but not inviting. Inside, my stomach churned. "You're clever to get this information for me. So tell me what you found out."

"The Usher family made their money in the perfume indus-try," Cory said. "That's what that company is for. Menabilly Holdings traded raw materials for perfumes and cosmetics. Your teacher Victor had a chemistry degree as well as his music quali-fications. He had been in Europe visiting artisanal brands the company was considering acquiring when he met his wife and gave up the family business for his music."

That explained some of the books we saw in the lab – Victor knew about perfumes and plants and mixing chemicals, which meant he had the skills to create poisons from the plants in the garden.

"And that's not all," Cory added. "The finances for the Usher School in New York City were more difficult to follow – a lot of money being funneled through accounts in the Cayman Islands – but it looks as if they were being paid huge sums of money."

"It was an expensive school." Mom worked three jobs to afford the tuition for me and my father to attend.

"Not this expensive. We're talking hundreds of thousands of dollars at a drop."

"Endowments from wealthy benefactors?" Dorien and I performed at various recitals and showcases in front of potential donors. Madame Usher would often wheel out my father as the final act to wow them into opening their wallets. It was one of the few times I was allowed to see him at the school, but even then I wasn't allowed to fawn over him in front of the guests.

"That's what I thought, and their accounts are set up to make it look like these were gifts from donors. But when I compared the Usher School to similar musical programs, it was given over thirty times as much money as Juilliard, and it's been gifted through shell companies that can be connected back to the Triumvirate – an alliance of three prominent West Coast crime families. This is illegal money."

Organized crime. My heart hammered in my chest, and not just because Cory was leaning closer, his tongue darting out to lick his lips. *My father was in debt to a crime family after purchasing the Becker. Is this related?*

"Does this money continue after the school shut down?" I asked.

"The opposite." Cory yanked on my wrist, pulling me against

his chest. His free hand grabbed for my other hand, but I jerked it away. "They are paying out huge sums of money to these same accounts. It looks as though their finances have been on tenuous ground ever since they opened Manderley Academy."

Sound the fucktrumpets, this is insane.

"Thank you so much for this, Cory. That's exactly what I was hoping you'd find." I backed into the room, my skin crawling where he touched me. "I appreciate the time it took you to do this. I'll drop some money into your account, and that's probably the last we'll see of each other—"

"I don't want your money, Faye." Cory twisted my wrist. I cried out as he forced me to turn around. He wrapped his free hand across my chest, grabbing my tits and fondling them roughly as he ground his hardness against my ass. He licked my ear. "The way I see it, we should finish what we started at the bar. All those nights you flirted with me, asked for my help with closing up. I know what you really wanted all along."

To demonstrate, he grunted, jamming his crotch against me.

"Let go of me." I kept my voice firm, calm, even though panic clawed at my lungs. I dug my nails into his arm, but that only made him grip me tighter, pinning my arms to my body. I tried to wriggle out of his grasp, but my thrashing about only excited him now.

Please, no. Not this.

"You're so feisty," he murmured as he shoved me toward the bed. My mind raced with full-blown panic. *If he gets on top of me, I won't be able to stop him.* "Those boys don't have to know what we get up to. You're sleeping with all three of them, like a filthy little slut. You're absolutely gagging for it. You wanted me the day you walked into the bar. We're going to—"

"What do you think you're doing?"

I cried out as Cory's fingers bent my wrist, but then Cory was flung away from me. I collapsed against the bed, tears rolling down my cheeks. I whirled around to see Titus holding Cory against the wall. Dark fingers wrapped around Cory's throat. He looked like he was about to shit himself in terror.

Good. He should be terrified.

"Titus." Tears of relief splashed onto my shirt. Titus growled as he leaned in close to Cory's face, close enough Cory could see the muscles bulging in his temples, the curl of Titus' lip as he contemplated exactly what to do with the rapist scum.

"Hello, bro." Cory tilted his head up to stare at Titus. And up. And up. He had to crane his neck at an awkward angle to take in all of my gentle giant. Titus didn't look so gentle now as he slammed Cory's back against the wall. Plaster rained from the ceiling.

"Hey, hey, there's no need to get all possessive alpha on me," Cory choked out. "You and your friends have all had a piece of her. I was just taking my turn—"

His words cut off as Titus' grip tightened around his neck. Titus' face twisted with a dark rage I'd never seen before. I grabbed his arm before he could swing.

"He's a cockroach," I whispered. "He'll go running to the police and say you assaulted him."

The implication hung in the air, the words unsaid. The police would take one look at Titus' skin color and my name splashed all over the media, and make things a thousand times worse for us. I wanted to see Cory bleed, but not at the expense of Titus' freedom.

Titus breathed hard. I knew he was trying to push through his rage, to get to a place where he could let Cory walk out of here alive. His shoulders tensed, his fist tightened, then released. He looked over at me, and his eyes were no longer hooded with hate. He was my Muse again.

"You're leaving now." Titus dropped Cory's collar and pointed to the elevators. "Don't come near Faye again, or I'll harvest your toes and make cello strings from your intestines."

"I know you share her around with your friends." Cory

reached for the pocket of his pants, apparently not knowing when to quit. "She's your chubby little whore. If it's a matter of money, I'll pay you to get in on the action—"

Titus' fist collided with Cory's face. I smiled at the satisfying smack as Cory's head hit the wall, spraying blood in the half-moon of an occult ritual and sending more plaster raining down. Cory slumped to the floor, his eyes flickering up to me, wide with pain and confusion, pleading for mercy.

Blood rushed in my ears.

Titus didn't hit him again.

When you step in front of a freight train, once is enough.

"You don't understand," he whimpered. "I'm in love with her. I can't live without her."

"Faye wouldn't be with a piece of shit like you. She only gave you the time of day because she's too nice and she felt sorry for you," Titus shot back. He shoved Cory's shoulder against the wall and withdrew his mobile phone from his pocket. Titus tossed the phone to me. "What am I going to find on here? Photographs? Maybe you've hacked her emails? Tell me the truth now, or I'll squeeze your brain out through your nostrils."

Cory nodded miserably.

"I thought so. This stops. *Now.* You will not see Faye. You will not follow her. You will not take photographs or video and you will leave her private things private. And if you even *think* about going to the police, I'll give them this phone and all the evidence on it. Stalking is so much worse than punching a dickweasel. Now get out of here, or I swear I will invert your ribcage and fill your eye sockets with urine."

Titus tore himself away from Cory, who didn't move, but slumped against the wall, his eyes reeling and blood streaming down his face. Titus leaned back and spat on Cory.

"I told you to leave." Titus cracked his knuckles.

Cory snapped out of his daze. He scrambled to his feet and lunged for the door, tripping over his own feet and face-planting in the hallway. His blood splattered the carpet as he got to his feet and ran for it.

"We won't be requiring your services again," I yelled after him.

When the elevator doors closed on Cory's stricken face, I collapsed into Titus' arms. "Thank you for being here, and for your oddly specific threats. I don't know what he would've done if you hadn't—"

"You'd have chopped his balls off, because you're amazing." Titus held me tight, crushing my body against his – my impenetrable fortress, behind which I was completely safe. "But I'm glad you didn't have to. That would have made an awful mess."

Wrapped in Titus' arms, the adrenaline faded and the sheer terror of what happened crept up on me. I started to shake, tears spilling down my cheeks. Titus pressed his lips to the top of my head. I sank into him, letting his strength hold me as I came to pieces.

"I'm sorry." Titus' huge hands cupped my cheeks, his forehead pressed against mine. "I'm sorry being a woman sucks so much. I'm sorry I didn't get here sooner."

"You have…nothing to be…sorry about." I struggled to get the words out between heaving sobs.

Titus stared over my shoulder at Cory's blood speckled across the wall. "I guess we can't use him to investigate the Usher's finances now."

I shook my head. "We won't get evidence from him, but he came here to tell me that Victor Usher had chemistry knowledge. The Ushers made their money in perfumes."

Titus rubbed his head. "That's true, although when Victor's parents went off to the retirement home, he stepped down from the business to focus on the music school. Sometimes he'd travel for board meetings, but he didn't seem to have much of a hand in the day-to-day running of the firm."

I nodded. "I think they only cared about the business as a front for other things." In a breathless stream, I told Titus everything Cory had found about the Menabilly Holdings and the Usher finances. "If we follow this trail, it will explain why they faked Victor's death. But it still doesn't explain what they planned to do to us. What did they mean when Victor said they needed Broken Muse? And how is my father connected? Finding out it's Victor in the walls instead of Donovan doesn't change the fact that Madame Usher has his portrait and his violin."

"You have the violin now." Titus' eyes fall on the instrument resting in its velvet-lined case.

"And I have no fucking idea what to do with it. Maybe it was a mistake taking it. Maybe it's stolen. Maybe it's cursed." I rested my head against his shoulder. "Maybe I'm cursed."

"Hey." Titus stroked a strand of my dark hair, curling it between his fingers. "We'll figure this out together."

"Everything we discover makes less and less sense. It's no secret Madame Usher maneuvered us all to that school. We know she wanted Elena and Ivan's money, but what about the others?" I stared at him. "What about you?"

Titus shrugged. "That's the thing. I had my choice of music programs across the country, especially with my parents' pedigree. I chose Manderley because that's where Dorien and Ivan were going. We wanted to stay together, see if we could keep that band alive."

Something niggled at me. "Your parents had no opinion about where you should study?" I found it hard to believe that Amos and Delphine didn't have their own ideas about Titus' schooling.

His face darkened. "Now that I think about it, yes. They did push me to choose Manderley. I...I...never realized it before."

I stroked his cheek, feeling his skin soften beneath me. "Are you okay?"

He kissed me, and there was such ferocity to the kiss that I knew the answer to my question was 'no.' And I knew the only thing I wanted to do was keep kissing him.

Manderley can wait. We're not under its spell anymore.

We flopped down on my bed. Titus kicked the door shut. He rested his elbows on either side of me, his cornrows flopping over to curtain our faces, creating this warm, soft, happy bubble for us. I lost myself in his smoky eyes – a cloudy grey so dark they were almost black, the edges ringed with deep, expressive midnight. Such beautiful, unique eyes – just like Titus himself.

He brushed his fingers over my cheek, and my heart did a little dance in my chest. He lifted an eyebrow in a cheeky way that was pure Dorien. He asked the question silently, not doing anything except stroking my skin until I gave him consent.

Tears threatened my eyes again. They weren't tears of fright, of anger. They were a deep welling of emotion at his thoughtfulness. Titus always saw what I needed before I did. He was just so impossibly *good* it broke my heart.

I leaned up and kissed him, letting my tongue linger on his for just a moment before pulling away. His mouth quirked up into a delighted smirk. He cupped my face in his huge hand and laid fluttery kisses on my nose, my eyelids, my forehead, before finally claiming my lips.

His lips started out all sweet and tender, light sweeps of his tongue on mine. But I could feel my hunger for him growing in my chest, swelling in my heart and between my legs as he deepened the kiss until we were biting, panting, crashing against each other.

"You're everything," Titus whispered as he splayed his fingers around my neck, pulling me closer for a demanding kiss. I could taste his hunger for me, and it made me drunk on him, my mind a fog of heat and need.

He slid off the end of the bed, kneeling on the carpet as he trailed his hands possessively over my body. He shoved the shirt dress I wore over my hips and tugged down my panties, spreading my knees wide and pushing them back into the bed with the heels of his hands. I breathed hard as his fingers trailed fire along my thighs. He followed the blaze with his tongue, nibbling at my skin before touching his lips to the ache between my legs. My fingers curled around the sheets.

Titus circled my entrance with his tongue, darting the tip inside to taste me. I was already a mess, tilting my pelvis up to demand more, to chase away the terrifying memory of Cory holding me down with Titus' warm, soft, lips. He laughed as he clamped his huge hands over my legs to hold me down. I was ready to pout, but then he tongued my clit with such gentle reverence I nearly floated off the bed.

The world spun around me, and all that existed was was his mouth and his hands and the delicious warmth that swelled inside me. This was so different from his birthday when he and Dorien sandwiched me between them, or from the car before we snuck back into Manderley. That had been pure, animal bliss. And this, this was worship. Reverence. This was Titus kneeling at the altar of Faye, and let me tell you, I was here for it.

The sheets were a knot in my hands. My legs shook against his relentless grip as he moved his tongue in those slow, beautiful circles. All rational thought leaked from my ears, and I couldn't have remembered Creepy Cory even if I wanted to. All that existed was Titus' lips on me and the way he made me feel.

Precious.

Adored.

Exalted.

Titus pressed the flat of his tongue against my clit, and I was gone. I thrashed against his grip as my body rode the wave of pleasure coursing through me. Titus crawled up beside me, touching my cheeks and grinning down at me, all happy alpha male because he made me lose my mind.

I tried to pull him back on top of me, but my arms didn't work anymore. *Damn orgasms, so inconvenient.* Titus chuckled, stroking the bare skin of my thighs as he bent his head to—

"Mi cielo, I'm home," Mom's voice called up the hallway. "And I brought tamales."

Holy bitchbadgers, Mom!

I tugged down my dress and kicked my panties under the bed, while Titus leaped into the armchair, crossing his legs to hide his raging hard-on. I slid off the bed onto shaking legs just as Mom threw open the door, her arms loaded down with takeout bags.

"You look like you've just rolled out of bed." She smirked as she dropped her keys on the vanity. "Hello, Titus."

"Hi, Marguerite." Titus leaned forward to kiss her offered cheek. "I'd get up to hug you, but…you know."

My cheeks burned with heat, but Mom only laughed. She dropped the bags on the table, and the delicious scent wafted through the room. "What have you been up to? I mean besides all the carnal shenanigans? Did you find out anything more about Dorien's case—"

Mom stopped in front of the wall, tapping the spray of droplets. "I don't remember this being here before. Is it me, or does that look like a bloodstain?"

Titus and I cracked up laughing.

As awful as Creepy Cory was, he did give us vital information. We knew without a doubt that the Ushers conspired to fake Victor's death, and that it likely had something to do with the huge payments made to their bank account from organized crime families before they closed the Usher School. I looked up the Triumvirate and found out there were three families – August, Dio, and Lucian – who ran their empire out of Emerald Beach, California. What interested me was that the August family were well known as purveyors of exquisite black market antiques, including musical instruments.

What I didn't know was what to do with that information.

Titus helped us devour the enormous stack of tamales. He said nothing about driving back to see his parents, and I didn't want him to go. We needed to put our heads together, Scooby-Doo style, and come up with a plan.

I decided it was time to fill Mom in on what we knew (leaving out some of the details that would get me in trouble, like the fact I snuck back to Manderley and went snooping into the walls). I dialed Ivan and put the phone on speaker so we could all tell our parts.

Mom lay in bed, her hair piled on top of her head. Her face grew ever more grim as Titus, Ivan and I filled her in on what we found out in the last few weeks. She jabbed her finger at my violin. "You're telling me that's the instrument your bastard father brought with dirty money?"

I nodded.

"You can't keep it," she hissed. "You have to get rid of it. Those are dangerous people, and if they know you have it they will—"

Her face twisted as she broke down into a coughing fit. I crawled up beside her, rubbing her back as she coughed into her hands. When she drew back, there was a thin splatter of blood on her fingers. "Please, Mom, don't upset yourself. I have no intention of keeping it. It's another piece of evidence that will take Madame Usher down."

"You shouldn't have kept this from me." She glared from me to Titus, even giving the phone on the bed an angry scowl. "I don't want you playing detective anymore. You need to tell the authorities everything you just told me. Now. Tonight."

"The police and the sheriff's office are under Madame Usher's spell. Walpole is helping to frame Dorien—"

"Sheriff Stanford is on the level," Mom shot back.

"We don't know that."

"*I* know. And when have I ever been wrong?" She thrust her hands on her hips, and she looked so much like the old Marguerite de Winter, the scourge of boardrooms and PR pitches across New York City, that I wanted to hug her. "I liked her the moment I met her. She's putting everything together. You have to trust her, mi cielo."

I shook my head. "If I knew how to get ahold of Dorien's FBI agent, I would. But Dorien's given him my details and he hasn't called, and I can't exactly dial information and ask for an agent's private number—"

"I think I can help with that," said a voice from the door.

DORIEN

"*D*orien?" Faye's eyes widened with shock as I stepped into the room.

That's right, I'm back.

I strode into the middle of their circle, my eyes never leaving her face. As Rochester drove me to the hotel, I wondered if maybe I'd made a mistake by not telling Faye I'd been sprung.

But as I swept her into my arms and planted my lips to hers, I knew my surprise was worth it. She sank into the kiss, melting into me like the sweetest, darkest chocolate s'mores. She tasted the way she smelled – like lavender and orange blossom, like childhood memories and dark wintery nights – and I fancied a little nip of Titus dancing on her tongue.

It was good to know he'd been looking after her while I'd been away. I couldn't believe I ever wanted to compete for Faye's love with my two best friends. They gave her so much that I couldn't, especially when I'd been going crazy in a jail cell without her.

Her tongue wrote magic on my soul. I kissed and kissed and I didn't want to ever breathe again without her. I vowed I would never, ever leave her side.

Faye broke the kiss to nuzzle her face into my neck. It felt so right to hold her again. My lips tingled with fire as I cast my eyes around the room, taking in the rest of the scene. The other people I cared about who I hadn't seen for weeks.

Titus lay across the bed, watching me with an expression that conveyed his relief at my liberty. Marguerite de Winter leaned forward, her tangled hair falling over her eyes as she watched with a mother's apprehension. Ivan's voice barked from the phone on the bed, demanding in his usual Romanian charm to know what was going on.

Almost everyone I cared about.

Jacob was still trapped with Father Aaron, and I couldn't rest until he was free.

Faye pulled back to look at me, as if reassuring herself I was really there. "How did you…how can you be…"

"They dropped the charges." I nodded to Rochester, who stood in the doorway. "Apparently, I have friends in high places."

"Thanks to you, Faye." Rochester strode forward, his hand extended to her. "Gavin Rochester. You told Sheriff Stanford to look for me. I've been able to get Dorien out of trouble, and she's acting as an informant in an undercover inquiry into Walpole and his officers while their departments continue to work together. Thanks to you, a bunch of corrupt as fuck cops will get what's coming to them."

Faye shook his hand firmly, then turned back to me. "I'm so happy you're here." She pulled me close again, clinging to me like I was all that held her upright.

"Who are you?" Marguerite stared at Rochester, her bright smile pinched. She patted her hair self-consciously, and I realized with a selfish pang that I should have called first, given Marguerite a chance to put some clothes on, do her hair, feel like a proper human being.

"As I said, I'm Agent Gavin Rochester, FBI." Gavin stepped around the bed and extended a hand to Marguerite. She peered at him with amusement as they shook. "I don't want to keep any of you awake, but I think we need to talk."

Marguerite patted a space at the end of her bed. "Sit down, Agent. Once Faye has finished necking her boyfriend, I'm sure she'll fix you some tea. And we have plenty of food to go around."

"Is Dorien there?" Ivan barked down the phone. "What is going on?"

Faye poked her tongue out at her mother, then resumed devouring my lips, which I had zero problem with whatsoever. Rochester clicked the door shut and perched on the end of the bed. Marguerite sighed dramatically and flounced out of bed, heading to the kitchenette to put the kettle on and unwrap the takeout. Out of the corner of my eye, I saw Rochester cast a look at Marguerite's back that was both fleeting and filled with longing. I wasn't surprised that he'd been taken by her in just a few moments of meeting – even in her robe she was startling, all tumbling dark hair and wide eyes that burned with fire.

Faye may have inherited her father's musical talent, but she got her soul from her mother.

When Marguerite had supplied everyone with food and drinks, and Faye had stealthy slipped her panties from under the bed into her pocket (naughty girl) and settled on my lap in the armchair, Rochester cleared his throat.

"I'm sorry that I left Dorien hanging as long as I did. I've been busy with the Temple investigation, and I wouldn't usually be able to interfere with a non-Federal case like this. I can't undo the damage done by the media, but Dorien's free now, and will remain so unless Walpole comes up with new evidence." His steely gaze settled on me. I nodded back, unable to speak as I'd stuffed my mouth so full of tamales. Jail food was ghastly and I swear I'd lost ten pounds on the inside.

Rochester continued. "I have a specific reason for wanting Dorien free."

"This is about the Temple." Faye shifted in my lap as she licked her fingers. I growled against her ear that her wriggling was doing evil things to me, especially since I now knew she wasn't wearing panties.

Rochester nodded. "We know Heather's death and Dorien's arrest must have repercussions, but we don't have any information about what's going on inside the organization. All we know is that the Danvers' have retreated to their estate and refuse to speak to the press. I don't know if they're even still involved with the Temple. Aaron Varney hasn't kept any of his appointments with the rich families he hoped to recruit. We don't even know for certain where he is. Our agents have seen some signs of life at Valencourt Manor, but when an officer tried to open the main gate, someone shot at him, which has never happened in all the times we've sent teams out to monitor the cult. This change in behavior concerns my team, especially given what we knew about the arranged marriage and the day of ascension. We need to move against the Temple soon, and it would be better if we had someone on the inside."

He didn't have to elaborate. Faye buried her face in my shoulder. "You?" she whispered. I nodded.

Just thinking about Jacob made my stomach twist in knots and bile rise in my throat. All the time I'd been in jail, dread had been mounting in my gut. Heather's death ruined all the Temple's plans. What would Aaron do to him to punish me? Did they send him to the Penalty Room and subject him to unimaginable horrors?

"Not just Dorien. We want you to help him try to make contact with his parents," Rochester said.

I shook my head. "Not Faye. I'm not putting her in danger."

She squeezed my hand. "If it's for Jacob, I'll do it."

"I won't send you anywhere near that place." I glared at Rochester. How did he forget to mention this to me? From the way he avoided my eyes, I knew he intended to ask Faye all along.

"I never thought I'd say this, but I agree with Dorien."

Marguerite kicked Rochester's thigh under the covers. "You're not sending my daughter into a cult stronghold to make nice with a madman."

"I wouldn't ask if there was any other way." Rochester touched his thigh where my mother kicked him. "We need intel of Varney before we can make a move. We need to cut off the head before we can hope to save the body. At this stage, we don't even know if they're still at Valencourt Manor. When a cult goes underground like this…" he shook his head, and my gut churned with hopelessness.

Faye shuddered. I squeezed her hand. "Why us?" she asked. "Surely you have agents who could—"

"It doesn't matter," Marguerite's eyes flashed with determination. "Because you're not doing it."

"Agreed," Titus added.

"Varney will sniff out our people at this late stage. It has to be someone they're willing to trust. We know they approved of your relationship with Dorien at one point. We think it's the best chance we have of getting inside."

"But they were prepared to frame Faye for assaulting Varney." I curled my hand into a fist, ready to slam it into Rochester's face. How could he even suggest this? I won't take Faye into that hellhole. "They hate her."

"Now that Heather Danvers is no longer in the picture, they may have changed their minds again."

"What if they try to hurt us?" Faye's lip trembled.

"We'll have a team covering you the entire time," Rochester assured. "We don't need you to get inside or record a conversation or anything like that. All we need is confirmation that the cult is still at Valencourt Manor with Aaron, and that Jacob is still alive."

I blanched at his words. *He has to still be alive.*

"I'll do it," Faye said.

"No," Marguerite and I shouted at the same time.

"Yes." Faye's eyes blazed. "I'm not going to stand on the sidelines when I can help an innocent kid. Mom, you'd do the exact same thing. You know you would."

Marguerite's eyes fluttered shut, and for a moment I saw her not as I remembered her – strong and wild and terrifying – but as she was now, her eyes sunken and lined with crows' feet, her skin sickly, her de Winter curves wasted away and her lips dry from the medication. She swallowed, and her eyes opened. She nodded at her daughter.

Faye glared down at me, daring me to try to speak for her again. "We'll get him back," she whispered, pressing her lips to my forehead. "I promise."

I pulled her face to mine, taking her mouth for a deep kiss. After everything I put her through this past year, after all those years of happiness the Temple robbed from us, she was willing to do this for me? "You're incredible, did you know that?"

"I've heard a rumor," Faye laughed as her tongue played against mine.

"Thank you, Faye." Rochester pulled a slim file from his briefcase. "If you don't mind me hanging around, I can go over some details of the operation with you and Dorien. We want to move quickly."

"That's fine, and I should probably tell you what we've uncovered," Faye said. "Madame Usher's husband is still alive."

"What?" I stared at her. "Victor? That's impossible. I saw his body."

"You sure about that?" Faye grinned.

Fuck. This is insane.

"If you're going to be staying, Gavin, you need to be properly attired." Marguerite tossed the other hotel bathrobe at Gavin's head. She lifted the receiver and dialed room service. "We'll need more food. And margaritas. *All* the margaritas. Every margarita in the universe."

"Mo-om, you're not supposed to drink alcohol."

"And you're not supposed to run headfirst into a cult stronghold with Dorien fucking Valencourt," she shot back, daring any of us to argue.

Faye went to the bathroom as Rochester pulled on his robe and Marguerite busied herself with the room service menu. I knew she was putting her panties back on – and I couldn't help feeling disappointed. I liked knowing she was bare with everyone in the room. When she returned, she told us how she and Ivan had snuck into the tunnels at Manderley and found Victor Usher's laboratory, as well as what Creepy Cory had told them about the Usher's finances.

By the time we finished off the food and my head swam from the sugar margaritas, Rochester was rubbing his eyes. He extricated himself from the duvet and shrugged off the bathrobe. "Thank you for a surprisingly lovely evening. They're too far between in my line of work. I'll leave you to your own devices for now but..." he looked over to Marguerite, who was frowning at her virgin margarita and, I thought, deliberately not meeting his eyes, "...I want you to know I've booked a room just down the hall. I'll have another agent staying with me. Her name is Amelia Velasquez. We'll take it in shifts to keep an eye out for you all. You're safe here."

"You'd better have a hundred agents when you send my daughter into that hellhole," Marguerite yelled at his departing figure. "And flame-throwers. And grenade launchers. And a fucking dinosaur cannon."

"What's a dinosaur cannon?" Faye snickered as Rochester pulled the door shut behind him.

"Armored vehicle pulled by a T-Rex, that launches baby T-Rexes over the wall to gobble up the enemy before you get there. I don't know. I made it up." She wagged her finger at Faye. "But if he doesn't have one, you tell me and I'll make him pay."

Faye and I exchanged a glance, the air heavy between us. I'd been nursing a hard-on for several hours, and if I didn't peel her clothes off and fuck her right now I was going to experience serious testicular damage. But I couldn't exactly throw Faye down on the bed with her mother here, but I also didn't want to drag her away to my own room when I knew that beneath her facade Marguerite was afraid for her.

Marguerite threw off the covers. "I'll be heading out."

"Mom, it's late." Faye slid off me and tried to lead her back to bed. I crossed my leg, wincing as my sore balls rubbed against the leg of my jeans. Marguerite shook her daughter off.

"Yes, but it's the crack of dawn in New Zealand, and I'm ready to shake off these margaritas. Titus is going to take me dancing." I glanced at Titus, who looked apprehensive. I remembered he spent New Year's Eve being dragged around New York City clubs by Marguerite, and I wasn't sure he was ready to relive the trauma of the experience.

Too bad. Right now, if it would get me alone with Faye, I'd fire my best friend from the dinosaur cannon.

I waited in agony while Marguerite chose a dress – an off-the-shoulder indigo number with a flared skirt that looked killer with her tousled dark hair and red lips – and fussed over Titus' hair before ushering him out the door with winks and promises that she'd keep him out all night.

"Help me," Titus whispered as the door shut behind him.

Sorry, friend.

As soon as the door slammed behind them, we crashed together, our bodies drawn by the pull of our need. Our teeth clashed, our lips burned against each other, raw and hungry and desperate.

"It's only been a few weeks," Faye teased, but her fingers tugged at the hem of my shirt with urgency.

"Every minute on the inside without you is agony." I swept her into my arms. I wanted to crawl inside this woman, build my life in her flesh.

She giggled. "On the inside, huh? So, my hardened criminal, did you learn any tricks in the prison showers?"

Her giggles turned to moans as I ground my cock against her thigh. "*Hardened* criminal is right. This is what you do to me, Sprite."

"Dorien…"

I shoved her down, so she was sitting on the edge of the bed, gazing up at me with those wide green eyes. I drowned in those eyes. "Take off your dress."

Faye's eyes glimmered at the authority in my voice, but she moved to obey. She slipped her shirt-dress over her head, revealing her breasts swelling from a pink bra and matching pink panties with lace around the edges. They clung to her pussy where she was already wet. For me.

My mouth went dry. *She's everything.*

"Have you been a good girl while I've been gone?" I loved seeing her squirm when I took on this tone with her.

She shook her head, leaning back on her palms, her tits thrusting out to give me an amazing view of cleavage that could crush a man. I undid my belt, fussed with my buttons, making her wait. My hands brushed over my throbbing cock and the pain tore a moan from my throat. Faye's lip parted. She liked seeing how much I wanted her.

"That's what I like to hear. Do you like a criminal telling you what to do?"

"Maybe." She said it cheekily, with demands of her own. "As long as he tells me to do things that make me feel good."

"Have you been thinking about me? Have you been touching yourself while you imagined what I'd do to you once I was free? What I'd do to you with Titus and Ivan in the same room?" I tugged down her panties. I pressed her knees wider, taking in the sight I'd been deprived of for too long.

She's swollen and wet and hot for me.

I breathed hard. I wanted this to be amazing for her, but I wouldn't last long faced with so much perfection.

"Yes." Faye's green eyes dared me to push her.

I cupped her breast in my hand, rubbing my fingers over her nipple through the fabric. Faye's lips fell wider, and she arched her back to give me more access. She demanded more, but I wasn't ready to give it to her just yet.

I knelt in front of her and pressed my lips to her inner thigh. She groaned with frustration. "I tasted Titus on your lips. Has he tasted you here, too? Has my friend licked your pussy already today?"

"Yes."

I used my fingers to spread her wide. She was so wet. I slid a finger inside her, feeling how swollen she was, how much she wanted me. I kissed her clit, my tongue fluttering over the bud. Just thinking that earlier today my best friend knelt in the same place, worshipping her, made her taste all the sweeter.

My cock throbbed painfully. *How the fuck am I going to last?* I could come right now just from the friction against my jeans and the way her thighs trembled and her mouth moaned little obscenities.

I pushed my tongue in beside my finger, then licked my way back to her clit, continuing with the fluttery circles.

"Dorien, fuck, please…" Faye's thighs rose off the bed. I had to hold her down with a firm hand. "Fuck, you cockpoodle. Harder. Don't play around. Fuck—"

But I wasn't ready for her to come yet. I was a man who'd been lost in the desert for so long. I'd finally reached water but I couldn't gulp it down or I'd drown myself. I wanted to savor her. I wanted this moment written across my memory forever. So I kept up the light kisses, the soft strokes that almost *but not quite* tipped her over the edge.

Faye grabbed my hair, grinding my face against her clit. I breathed in her sweet scent and gave her what she demanded. I thrust a second finger inside her, curling them to rub at her G-spot. My lips were slick with her need.

She breathed hard, her fingers digging into my skull. I slid a third finger inside, and with a cry, her hips clenched and her walls closed around me. Her whole body vibrated as the orgasm shot through her, and I almost lost it right then with her clamped around me.

My lungs felt full of water, full of her. It was hard to breathe. I crawled up her body, dropping my jeans to the floor. My cock brushed her thigh and I was so close…

I buried myself inside her. *So hot. So soft. So warm.* Faye brought her legs up to clamp around my back, angling her hips to drive me deeper. My thumb ground against her clit, dragging another climax from her as I thrust inside her like a man possessed.

I am possessed. Faye is everything, she's everywhere to me. She can haunt me any time she fucking likes.

She ground her pelvis against me as she came. It was glorious, feeling her walls contract around my cock, hearing her sweet cries as I fell over the edge and let my ghost capture me.

Faye de Winter was mine again. Madame Usher didn't control me anymore. And Aaron Varney wasn't going to know what hit him.

13

IVAN

$\mathcal{N}$ow that I knew about the way Victor was getting around the house, I felt his presence everywhere. Eyes pricked my back as I scrubbed the floors and dusted the pianos. They scratched at my back as I sat in the corner of Elena's private lessons, and watched over my shoulder as she crawled into my bed and burrowed into my shoulder at night.

I wondered if Victor had a passage to get out to the stables. If he was spying on Elena when she was with Radcliffe.

I wondered what he'd think if he found my sister bending over a piano for that vile man. The thought made me see stars. Elena said it hadn't happened yet, but it was only a matter of time. I could practically see Radcliffe licking his lips as he led her away from me for yet another date in his private rooms.

Unlike Victor, who skulked in the shadows, Clare grew bolder. She hung out with me in the kitchen, swinging her legs through the table as she watched me chop vegetables. She sat on our bed at night, helping Elena decide how to pin her hair. I couldn't find her frightening anymore – she was a friend, a victim of Manderley, just like us.

Life at Manderley without Faye and the others had reverted

back to the days of our childhood, except that now we had a friendly ghost and a creepy man watching our every move. Madame Usher had me and Elena doing the chores, and with Elena preoccupied with her upcoming wedding and a steady stream of recitals and parties to attend with Radcliffe, I was doing it all. My classes were mostly a farce now. I couldn't hide my disdain for Radcliffe, and the idea of completing my degree seemed foreign – a pointless dream from another life. I was here to protect Elena. Nothing else mattered.

But being trapped at Manderley had its benefits, and I would not waste this opportunity. Instead of attending classes and practicing my repertoire, I pored through the library, searching for anything that would help us.

The Manderley library included one of the world's most impressive collections of texts on Baroque music, acquired by the Ushers on their various tours of Europe – or so the official story went. I had to wonder if the August crime family had their fingerprints on the more valuable texts. But buried on a dusty shelf in the corner where Madame Usher had obviously forgotten their existence was a collection of Victor's father's history books, including volumes written in Victor Senior's own hand about the history of his family and the house.

I set aside a history of the Usher perfume company and dug out the leather-bound volume on the house I started reading the other day. I couldn't spend too long in the library or Madame Usher would start to get suspicious. I turned the pages, scanning Victor's sloping handwriting for something we could use.

I learned that the house was built in the eighteenth century by the Usher family patriarch, confusingly *also* named Victor. At the time, the Ushers had acquired a great wealth importing perfumes from Europe for the burgeoning colonial upper class, but when the Seven Years War threatened their newfound prosperity, Victor the First became fearful of losing his wealth or his life, so when he built his family home, he added the tunnels to hide his family and gold from invading forces.

As I turned the page, a folded paper slid out of the book, yellowed with age. I unfolded it, resisting the urge to yell with triumph as it revealed a set of building floor plans. They were from the original house before it was expanded and renovated. The wing that now served as Madame Usher's private quarters was only half the size, the kitchens hadn't yet been enlarged, and some of the internal room configurations were slightly different. Drawn between the rooms were the narrow passages we discovered. Markings in Dorien's room, the attic, and what was now the Red Room showed where doorways opened into the tunnels.

It also showed a tunnel heading from the Red Room under the house, with an exit down beside the stream. An escape route, so the family could make their way down to the river and presumably get ahead of their enemies.

I glanced over my shoulder, peering at the library walls as my skin prickled with unease. Clare was off watching Elena's private tutorial. Was Victor watching? Would he see what I was about to do? The prickling on my neck intensified as I drew my secret phone from my pocket and quickly snapped a few pictures, which I forwarded to Faye. It would be helpful to know where the tunnels led, and where exactly in the house Victor could – or could not – go.

As soon as the photographs were sent, I shut off the phone, put away the books, and secreted my phone back into its hiding spot – taped to the tank in the bathroom, where Elena used to sometimes hide drugs for Aroha. The plans didn't show any hidden passages along our bathroom walls. I couldn't be certain they hadn't been added later, but I'd already inspected every inch of the bathroom before I started hiding my phone there, and I was certain there were no peepholes or secret doors.

I heard Madame Usher yelling for me, and headed back to finish my chores, feeling Victor's eyes on me the whole time.

Why doesn't he tell his wife he found us in the tunnels?

Madame's overheard words chilled me to the bone. "All I have to do is keep the others from talking and we'll have the money we need to start over."

Our money. The money from Broken Muse record sales and Elena's performances that Madame Usher held in trust for us. That had to be what she was referring to. We weren't able to access it until we reached our twenty-fifth birthday, unless we married first. If Elena married Radcliffe, Madame Usher wouldn't have access to our money any longer. *So what does she mean by this? Is she talking about some other funds, or...*

...or...she has a deal with Radcliffe – she keeps the money. He gets my sister. After all, she was the one who delivered Elena into his depraved arms.

Over my dead fucking body.

That night, I lifted Elena's arm from where she slung it across my chest and slipped from bed. Our bedroom door had been locked from the outside, but I didn't need to get out. I padded to the bathroom, untaped my mobile phone, and turned it on. Faye had sent me a string of text updates about the maps and helping Agent Rochester break out Jacob, and her mom dragging Titus to an underground swing club and forcing him to dance so hard he nearly broke his hip.

Faye. I missed her so much my chest burned with it. Every minute of the day I thought about what she was doing out there, the danger she was in. The danger she escaped. I didn't understand why Victor hadn't told Madame that he saw us in the tunnels.

I squeezed the phone in my hand and gritted my teeth against the frustrated scream building inside me.

Dorien was out. Which meant that Madame Usher's hold on the police wasn't as strong as she thought. And that made her position precarious. She was a tiger backed into a corner, made all the more dangerous because of her desperation.

And Elena was still here, in the heart of the tiger's den.

Faye's texts blurred together as I fought my frustration. I hated feeling helpless, stuck here while they were outside, trying to make a difference. Through the haze of rage, I noticed her final text message. My heart caught in my throat. I had to read it five times to make sure it said what I thought it said.

I tracked down Donelle from the articles. I'm going to call her in the morning and see if I can get her to talk about the things she experienced at Manderley. Sleep well, my Ice Prince. I love you.

She'd added Donelle's phone number and email address.

I clutched the phone in my fingers as my heart hammered against my chest. *Faye is going to call her. Faye should be the one to call her – she's good at making people do what she wants. I only have to wait until tomorrow to find out...*

I touched my chest, where Elena's arm had draped only a few minutes before. My sister's days were counting down.

I couldn't wait. This was too important.

I rolled up the towels and pressed them into the gap at the bottom of the door, hoping that would muffle the sound of my voice. I sat on the toilet lid and pulled up Donelle's number on the screen.

I hit 'CALL.'

The phone rang once, twice, three times. It was nearly midnight, too late to be polite. She had to pick up the phone. She just *had* to.

RING RING.

This is a mistake. Faye is right. I should have waited for her to make the call. I'm too cold. I'll frighten her. I'll—

"Hello?"

A woman's voice on the other end. She sounded groggy, her voice thick with sleep. I opened my mouth but all that came out was a dry croak.

"Who is this? Why are you calling so late?"

Just say it. Just tell her you're calling from Manderley and you're afraid. She's been here. She'll understand.

"Hello? If this is one of those overseas phone scams, then I'm hanging up now—"

"Help me," I managed to choke out. "You have to help me. Please?"

"Is that you, Robbie?" Her tone turned soft, kind. "I showed you where the church spare key is kept. If you need to get off the street, just go down to the youth group room and there are some pillows and blankets. I don't want you outside on a night like this—"

"No, I'm not Robbie. My name is Ivan Nicolescu. You might remember me. I'm calling from Manderley and—"

"Manderley?" Her voice turned sharp. "Is this some kind of sick joke?"

"No. I need your help. It's about an article in your local newspaper four years ago. I need to know if—"

"*She* sent you to harass me again, didn't she?" Donelle spat. "Well, you tell her I don't want another cent of her filthy blood money. I wrote her stupid retraction and gave all the money to my church, so we can fight against the forces of Satan here on Earth, including her and that husband of hers and that disgusting school of degenerates. I haven't opened my mouth about that horrid place and the ungodly things that went on there. God sees all, and he will strike her down for her sins."

"Yes, but what sins?" I wanted to reach through the phone and throttle her. "Could you elaborate—"

"I won't let another word about her sully my tongue or poison my soul. She can't come after me again. I haven't broken our agreement. I'm not an innocent girl anymore. I'll fight her. My church will fight her. If she comes after me, we will tell the world that Satan lives inside her!"

This woman sounds unhinged. "Please understand, I don't work for Madame Usher. I'm one of her students. My sister is in danger. I want—"

"Your sister?" Donelle laughed cruelly. "If she's at Manderley, buckle her chastity belt and pray. Pray for her immortal soul. Pray she makes it out alive. Call me again, and I go to the police."

She hung up, taking my only chance to find out the truth about Radcliffe's depravity with her.

14

DORIEN

"**R**emember, whatever you do, don't provoke Varney. If he doesn't let you see Jacob, don't ask to. Just get in, talk to whoever you can talk to, and get out again."

I nodded to Agent Velasquez, who was taping the wire to my chest over my IN CAUDA VENENUM ink with perhaps more enthusiasm than a female FBI agent should be showing. Faye watched me from across the back of the cramped van, where we were being prepped for our encounter with the Temple. Faye licked her lips, and I knew she didn't care that Velasquez was giving my pecs a good squeeze.

I guess she doesn't mind sharing, either.

I would have said something filthy to her if I wasn't so distracted with freaking the fuck out about going into my family home. I knew I wasn't supposed to try anything heroic, but if I saw Jacob I didn't know what I would do. *How can they expect me to just leave him there with Aaron Varney?*

I have to be strong. I have to do this their way. It's the best chance Jacob has.

Velasquez taped the last of the wire and patted my arm.

"You're all set, Dorien." I pulled on my shirt and jacket, hoping like hell the Temple wouldn't think to search me. If they demanded it, we were under orders to turn around and leave. Loyalty was everything in my family. My parents would never in a million years believe I'd go to the Feds, but I couldn't predict Aaron.

All I knew was that I had to get Jacob away from him, no matter what.

Rochester threw open the rear doors of the van, and we climbed out and into my Porsche. Faye clasped my hand across the seat. Rochester patted my back. "Do you want to go over the plan one last time?"

I offered him a weak smile. Every muscle in my body was being squeezed in a vise. "I'm used to memorizing entire symphonies. The plan isn't the problem."

"I know." Darkness hooded Rochester's blue eyes. "Good luck, Dorien. We've got your back in there."

I watched him walk back the van, his shoulders hunched with tension. This was a big day for him, too. He lost his parents to the Temple. He had to help his sister walk off a mountain in a snow-storm to save her life. I felt the weight of his pain on my shoulders. He felt responsible for what happened to his parents. This was his day for redemption.

Satan knows I'd had so many of those – for all the evil it wrought, Manderley gave me the chance to start over with Faye, to undo the hurt I caused her. Despite fucking Ivan's and Titus' and Elena's life over completely, they still stood by me.

I wanted to give Rochester his redemption.

And more than anything, I wanted to feel Jacob's arms around me again. I wanted my brother to have the life I had, to have the chance to scrape his knees and travel the world and fall in love and make mistakes.

Faye squeezed my leg. "I'll be right by your side."

When Rochester first suggested she come with me into the mouth of hell, I wanted to throttle the bastard. But now, I couldn't imagine doing this without her. I placed my hand over hers and gunned the engine.

I'm coming to get you, Jacob. Just like I promised.

The van followed us at a safe distance. I kept an eye on them in the rearview mirror as we drove the winding country roads toward Valencourt Manor. My fingers tightened on the wheel until cramps seized my arms. I saw the stone wall topped with barbed wire, the rolling hills covered with trees that hid the mansion from view. Every fiber of my body told me to turn around and get away from this place. I spent my whole life fleeing my parents, and going back made me feel like a kid again – alone, terrified. But this wasn't about me any longer – it was about Jacob.

I should have pulled him out years ago.

Faye squeezed my knee. "Dorien, what's that?"

"Shit." I slammed my foot to the floor as I saw what Faye was pointing at. A pillar of smoke rose from the trees surrounding the house to pierce the frigid sky. My phone rang, the sound shrill and urgent. Faye picked it up. "It's Rochester," she said. "Hi. Yes, we see it. What is it—"

Her words cut off as I accelerated. The tires bit the road as I tore around the corner, passing a gap in the trees through which I could always catch a glimpse of the northeast turret of Valencourt Manor.

"Dorien, slow down."

I couldn't slow down. I had to see. I had to know.

The car hurtled past, and I glimpsed a flash of the turret and the black smoke billowing from its windows.

Smoke.

Fire.

The day of ascension.

"No." I pounded the wheel in frustration as the car kicked and bounced along the uneven road. The NO TRESPASSING signs flew by in a blur. Rochester yelled down the phone to Faye, but I didn't register his words. I saw the gates up ahead. They were closed and chained shut with a comically large padlock. Faye yelled as I planted my foot and drove straight at them. She braced her arms at her sides as we slammed into the gates.

Adrenaline surged through my body as we hit. It was like plunging over a rollercoaster – the moments before the impact hung in the air for a long time, long enough for me to realize what a fucking idiot I was for ramming a gate with my Porsche.

Then we hit.

It was like getting whacked in the head with a baseball bat after leaving one of Titus' heavy metal concerts with your ears buzzing and your brain filled with fog. Sound buzzed in my ears, a crunch, a scream, and then deafness that was louder than anything I'd ever heard before. I gasped for air as the airbags exploded. My neck ached. My whole body ached. I tried to swim through the airbag to get to Faye, but it felt like trying to push water aside – it kept filling in the gaps of air, choking me, drowning me. I tried to cry out but my mouth was full of blood.

Faye, are you okay? I'm an idiot. Why did I do that?

Faye, fuck, please be okay...

A warm hand clasped mine. Faye's face appeared in the corner of my vision. She yelled something at me, but I couldn't hear it. She broke down into a coughing fit as she shoved open her car door and tumbled out.

My door opened. Rough hands grabbed me, dragging me free of the airbags. Rochester dropped me on the ground, yelling something in my face that I couldn't hear. I was dimly aware of others circling me, of Faye stumbling toward me, but as I turned my neck painfully toward the sky, the black smoke curled across grey clouds, and I knew what I had to do.

I staggered to my feet, shoving Rochester aside. I had to get to the house. The van skidded on the cracked driveway in front of me, and Velasquez threw open the rear door, gesturing wildly for us to jump in.

Rochester helped me and Faye stagger inside. He didn't even have the doors shut before the van tore up the hill. Velasquez and Rochester yelled back and forth, their words dull thuds against my battered skull. Faye held me and I held the surveillance rig as the van's shitty suspension struggled up the broken driveway. The adrenaline from the crash was starting to cool, giving me full body shivers. Or maybe that was from watching the black smoke billow from the trees to surround the van. We rounded the final corner, the smoke now so thick I couldn't see a foot from the van.

The van was still moving when I slipped under Faye's arm and threw the doors open. Faye yelled something at me but I couldn't hear. "Don't follow me," I tried to yell back, but as soon as I opened my mouth, smoke poured in and my lungs collapsed. My feet hit the ground. My ankle crunched and I was dimly away that it hurt, but the adrenaline was back and I couldn't feel anything over the burning in my lungs. I broke into a run, coughing into my hand as my eyes streamed with tears. I couldn't see the house. I couldn't see anything. I crashed into a tree, picked myself up, kept running.

I stumbled on the broken concrete drive and toppled into a pile of scrap metal. Something sliced through my hand, which was going to hurt like a bitch later, but I didn't stop.

Jacob, I'm coming!

I fumbled my way across the parking area, around the dried-up fountain, and up the stone steps two at a time. A flash of memory assailed me – me standing with my father on those same steps as my mother returned from the hospital carrying the bundle of blankets that held my kid brother. She stooping down to show me Jacob's tiny screwed-up face, and I poked him until he woke up because I was a little shit and I promised the howling baby right then and there that I'd be the best big brother in the world.

In the distance, I could hear sirens.

"Dorien, wait." The words sounded muted, like they were being yelled underwater.

I didn't wait. My eyes stung so fucking bad. I kept them screwed shut as I slammed into the door, staggering inside.

A wall of heat and smoke burst from the depths of the house. It slammed into me, bowling me over. I slammed my tailbone into the stone as I skidded across the stone porch. Pain rocketed up my spine. I rolled over and dragged myself to my feet, my chest heaving as a fresh coughing fit bent me double.

"Jacob?" I cried, but my voice was lost, burned away. He couldn't hear me over the roar of the fire, the crash of ceiling beams falling and windows blowing out. I couldn't even hear myself.

I staggered through the entrance hall, bracing myself against the heat. I crashed into the kitchen, holding my sleeve against my mouth and nose to try to keep out the worst of the smoke. I couldn't see, so I stumbled in the direction of the courtyard door.

It's no use. I'm never going to find him.

My hip scraped along the kitchen island. Pots and pans toppled at my feet, the metal burning where it touched my skin. I kicked them aside and pushed onward. My shoulder hit the glass of the door, and it burst from the heat and the impact, spraying shards across the floor. They thudded against my skin, but I couldn't feel a thing in this heat, this demonic heat. I fumbled for the door handle. Too hot. Too hot. My fingers closed around it and they melted against the metal. I screamed and screamed as pain ate my fingers, swallowing them into a hellish black hole of terror.

Somehow, through a feat of inhuman strength I didn't know I possessed, I tore my hand from the door handle. The pain still rocketed through my body, and I didn't feel invincible anymore. Despite the heat, my body shuddered with the chill of certain death. With the fear that I wouldn't see my brother again. Red welts danced in front of my vision, and the roar and crackle of the fire tearing through the house penetrated through my deafness. I yanked my sleeve over my fingers and managed to turn the handle and shove the door open without blacking out from the pain. The rush of heat shoved me through the gap, sending me sprawling across the courtyard.

I lay on the cobbles, gasping for fresh air. I dragged myself forward, rubbing my eyes with my burned hand. "Jacob?" I coughed. "Are you out here?"

I bet he's hiding in his secret place.

I crawled across the cobbles. My knees scraped raw on the hard stone. My fingers touched something sticky. Water? In this inferno? I raised my fingers to my face. No, not water. It smelled awful. Poisoned. Like copper and dead animals and—

Whatever it was, it was dripping on my head. I felt the wet splotches sticking to my hair.

I looked up.

I wished I hadn't.

I wished for blindness, for madness – something that could wipe the horror of what I saw from my memory forever.

They were tied side by side to a makeshift scaffold, arms spread wide and legs tied together in a cruel mockery of their god's son. Metal nails had been driven through their hands and feet into the wood. From the dried blood caked to their skin and the wooden cross, I knew these wounds had bled profusely. The horror etched onto their broken faces told the story of their suffering.

Their chests were torn open with long slashes, so their guts spilled out, entrails decorating the ground around their feet. Bile choked my throat as I realized what dripped on me had come from their stomach cavities. The smoke and heat had dried their skin, so the edges pulled back and flaked off, scattered in the air like sadistic confetti.

They spent their final hours together in agony, with an over-grown garden their only witness.

My parents.

Crucified.

15

FAYE

"Dorien?" I clambered up the stone steps after him. But I'd twisted my ankle when they pulled me out of the car, so I could only hobble. Dorien seemed possessed of super-human power. He crashed into the smoke like it didn't touch him, like his lungs weren't burning and his eyes weren't glued shut by the blinding pain.

My ankle screamed with pain as I dragged it up the steps. Something crashed above me, and I leaped back as a piece of the roof collapsed, caving in the entrance above the front door. Glass shattered as the French windows blew out. My heart leaped into my throat. *Dorien's inside.*

"Dorien?"

Hands wrapped around me, dragging me back from the house. "Don't you die in there, too," Rochester yelled. I tried to wriggle out of his grasp, but he held me firm.

Sirens wailed as fire engines and police vehicles swerved into the driveway. I watched with a detached horror as the firefighters unrolled hoses and Rochester thrust me at Velasquez. He moved amongst the officers on the scene, issuing orders like he rescued headstrong musicians from burning mansions every second

Sunday. Velasquez had her arm around my shoulders – outwardly, it looked like an expression of empathy, but I could tell by her vise-like grip that she was preventing my escape.

"Dorien's in there," I struggled against her. "I have to find him."

"The firefighters will get to him faster if they're not looking for two of you," she yelled back.

Another crash shattered the forest. The section of the roof over the kitchen collapsed. Someone screamed.

It took me a moment to realize the person screaming was me.

Smoke stung my eyes, but I couldn't tear my gaze away from the horror in front of me as bit by bit the flames consumed the house. Firefighters trained their hoses on the worst of the blaze, running into the burning ruin and yelling instructions to each other over the roar of the conflagration.

From the haze of smoke, figures emerged. Rochester, wearing a firefighter's jacket. He had his arms around someone else, dragging him to safety.

Dorien.

Dorien. He's alive.

I didn't know it was possible to smile so much with smoke burning my lungs.

They hobbled toward the waiting ambulance. Paramedics swarmed, wrapping Dorien in blankets, thrusting oxygen into his face, checking his body for injuries. Velasquez lost her grip on me, and I elbowed my way through the crowd to get to him.

"Dorien, are you okay?" I bent down to smooth back his hair. A patch of it crumbled to dust in my hands. His eyebrows had burned away, and he smelled *delightful*.

He stared out at me, his eyes haunted. I'd never seen him like that before, like he'd stared into the face of evil itself. I wanted to slap him around the head and call him a cockpoodle for running into that fire, but he'd seen something inside. Something that had shaken him to his core.

"You idiot." Rochester ran up beside us, his own shoulders covered in a security blanket. A paramedic snapped at him to come back so he could finish his checkup, but he grabbed Dorien's shoulder and shook him. "What did you think you were doing, running into a burning building like that?"

Dorien tore off the oxygen mask, his face grave. "Jacob's not here."

Rochester patted his arm. "We're looking for him. But we had to spend precious minutes saving your ass. Don't ever do that again—"

"He's not here," Dorien said forcefully.

"I know. We'll do a thorough search of the property, of course. But this fire was deliberately set. I don't expect him to be here. I think Aaron has taken him—"

"He'll be at the Danvers'." Dorien leaped to his feet, shrugging off the rescue blanket. "We have to get there tonight."

"You're not going anywhere." Rochester shoved him back down. "You need to be treated by these good people or you'll do yourself permanent damage."

"My parents are in the courtyard. Aaron *crucified* them. If Jacob's with him then he's in real danger. We have to—" Dorien broke down into a coughing fit.

Crucified?

Holy cumpuddle, that's insane.

Dorien's eyes swam with pain. He looked like he was going to lose his shit any moment. I leaned in close and took him into my arms. "You'll be no good to him if you're all banged up. Please, let the paramedics do their jobs. I'll be right here."

His shoulders shuddered. I know he had a complicated relationship with his parents. He hated them, but like any kid who was made to feel unwelcome, he desperately wanted their approval, their love. But they'd chosen this nightmare over him, and now he'd never get the chance to prove himself.

"I couldn't save them," he whispered into my shoulder as the pain of it undid him. "Aaron got to them, and now he has Jacob."

*D*orien was in the hospital for a couple of weeks. When he was given the all-clear, we took him back to the hotel and laid him out in the king-sized bed. Mom told Natalie what happened and she kindly upgraded us to a suite with three beds and an incredible view across the New York skyline.

My muse really was broken – half his beautiful hair had been burned away, not to mention his eyebrows. Without them, his face looked naked and permanently surprised. He had a twisted ankle and second-degree burns on his hand and lower legs. Looking at him tucked up in bed made my chest constrict, and when I opened my mouth to talk to him, I couldn't find words.

Because of the way he grabbed the door handle, only his pinkie finger was badly damaged. The doctors rebuilt it and put him on a rehabilitation schedule to regain movement, but he would never have the mobility to play piano at a professional level in the Classical world again.

Nothing I could say would be able to comfort him. Not after what he saw inside that house. Not knowing that Jacob was still in Aaron's hands, or that he had lost the music.

Mom brought Dorien a cup of tea and held a cold washcloth over his head. She dragged me over to the kitchenette and started opening cupboards. "I need you to go out for ingredients while I start making the tortillas."

This was what we did in my family. If someone was sick, you cooked for them, even if it meant making a mess of a tiny hotel kitchen.

By the time Dorien woke up, we laid out a feast of homemade food. I helped him to sit up in bed, and presented him with a plate of his favorites. His mouth twisted into an awful smile, a smile that felt like a betrayal of everything he witnessed.

"Someone's here to see you." I stepped aside, giving him a clear view of the armchair in the corner and the white-haired Romanian slumped in it, long legs dangling and icicle eyes watching us with a mixture of concern and loathing.

He'd been texting me less than usual, punishing himself for calling Donelle and losing the lead. So when he hadn't replied to my message about Dorien's discharge, I assumed he was ignoring me. Then he'd turned up in the hotel lobby as we wheeled a sedated Dorien upstairs. He must have broken several laws to get here from Manderley so fast.

"Well, I'll be damned." Dorien's voice croaked over the words. The doctors said it might be more than a month before he would sound normal again. Luckily, his hearing returned after a couple of days. I don't know what he would have done if he couldn't hear music again.

"Hello, Dorien," Ivan said. His gaze dipped to Dorien's bandaged finger before returning to his eyes. An unspoken message passed between them. I knew Dorien was asking about Elena and Ivan was telling him to mind his own fucking business.

But there was more to it. A palpable heat clung to the air. This *thing* that festered between them for so long engorged and fed and filled the room. My mother cleared her throat. Even she could sense it.

Ivan loved Dorien. It was obvious from the way his icicle eyes swept his body, cataloging every scar, every injury, every injustice. The thought that Dorien couldn't play again made his heart hurt, as it did mine. Ivan had spent his whole life living in the shadow of his sister's light. In Dorien, he'd found the one place where he could be his own man, and that man was adored.

And Dorien... I didn't know if he could ever love Ivan the way he wanted to be loved, because he blamed himself for Ivan's incarceration at Manderley. And now that his finger had been injured…he might not be able to love music the same way again, and Ivan and music were intrinsically linked. But as Dorien's eyes crinkled at the edges and his face broke out into that wicked smile, I could see he was trying.

I handed around plates just as Titus arrived, his arms loaded down with boxes of pizza and french fries. No one said much – it was enough to eat together, knowing how close we came to losing Dorien.

As we all dug in, someone rapped on the door. Mom started to get to her feet, but I held her back. Cory's assault flashed in my mind, and my body jerked with the memory of him pressing himself against me.

Titus went to the door and peeked into the hallway. "It's Rochester." He opened the door and the agent stepped in.

Dorien folded his arms. "Well? Do you have Aaron in custody yet?"

Rochester accepted a seat on the end of the bed and a heaping plate of food from my mother. He didn't have much choice in the matter. He looked haggard, the bags under his eyes ruining his All-American good looks.

"We've surrounded the Danvers' property in California. You were right, Dorien. The Temple has made it their new home. We've sighted five members patrolling the grounds with assault rifles. We don't know how many people are inside, but the information on your brother's map of Valencourt gives us a very good idea of how they set things up. He and Pearl also gave us a list of the cult members whose names they knew, and we've been able to track down some of their families for more information."

"When are you going in?"

Rochester spread his arms, his palms facing up in a pleading gesture. "Even if I knew, I couldn't tell you. We're waiting on orders from higher up. I *know* it's terrible waiting like this, but it's the way things work. Varney won't walk away from this."

Dorien's hand fisted the sheets. I could tell he wanted to bite back, but the truth was, the only person who knew the agony he was living through was Rochester.

"In the meantime, they can't leave the property without us knowing about it, and our people will move in at the slightest sign of something amiss. The best thing you can do right now is stay in that bed and heal, because Jacob is going to need you once he's free."

We finished up the meal in awkward silence. Rochester rose with a reluctant glance at my mother, and excused himself to sleep. Ivan rose, too. "I should return to Manderley. Madame Usher doesn't know I'm gone."

I grabbed his arm. "Stay. Please."

He stared down at me, his eyes twin storms that betrayed the demons inside him. He almost lost Dorien. He wanted to stay. He wanted to hold us both close and never let go. But Elena was at Manderley, and he couldn't bear the idea of something happening to her without him there to protect her.

Ivan's eyes flicked to the door.

I dropped his wrist. "Ivan, I'm sorry."

I shouldn't have asked him. I shouldn't have made him feel as though he had to choose. I had Titus and Dorien. Elena needed him.

Ivan's hand went around my neck, pulling my face to his. "I will stay," he promised, as his lips brushed mine. It felt like months since I tasted him last – the chilled apple and salt-tang of him, all that ice and lust wrapped into one delicious package. He struggled so much with moments like these, with letting his true feelings shine through. But he was making progress. His lips burst with love and wanting.

"I'm happy you're staying." I touched his cheek, drawing away because I knew my mother was watching. She was pretty awesome, but it was one thing to know your daughter was dating three guys and quite another to watch them at it.

I called the front desk and asked for a foldout bed, which they brought up for us. Titus and I made up the foldout while Ivan helped Mom with the dishes and Dorien directed proceedings from bed like an overzealous conductor.

"Your mom looks good," Titus said as he tucked the corners into perfect angles.

"She does." I smiled as she twirled in front of the windows, wearing one of her favorite cocktail dresses. "Dr. Nelson is a miracle worker. Once we knew the poison, they could give her the right drugs. She'll never heal perfectly, but she's able to be up and about now, and she's been enjoying life so much more."

"Don't I know it." Titus winced, rubbing the spot on his hip where he had a bruise from being kicked by an over-exuberant salsa dancer at Mom's favorite club.

There was a knock at the suite door.

"That's Natalie." Mom picked up her purse. "I'm off."

I leaped across the room and blocked the door with my body. "What are you doing?"

Mom glanced over her shoulder, nodding at my three Muses. "Mi cielo, this room isn't big enough for me and you and your harem of beautiful men. Natalie is taking me to a gallery opening downtown. They're supposed to have amazing cocktails. *Non-alcoholic* cocktails." She rolled her eyes at my expression. "I'll stay the night at her place. Please don't worry about me. I have to get my life back, too."

She blew kisses to us all as she left, leaving me alone with Broken Muse.

Dorien cracked a smile that was pure evil. He patted his lap. "Come here, Sprite."

It wasn't a command so much as a prayer. I crawled across the bed toward him, desperate to drive that hopelessness from his voice. *He might never play piano again.* Nothing I could do would repair his finger. But I could gift him tonight.

I straddled him, taking care not to rub against his bad ankle and his worst burns. Dorien's eyes fluttered shut, and he let out a sigh as he trailed his fingers along my arms before tangling them through my hair and bringing my face to meet his.

His kiss began soft, tender. His lips were soft and questioning. He was unsure now, of what was going to happen in this room, of what the future held for all of us. Seeing Ivan outside of Manderley's walls had thrown him off, made him consider what our lives could be like on the other side of this horror, if we could fight our way to that place.

I knew, because I had the same thoughts.

I returned his kiss with demanding certainty. I needed him to know that whatever happened in the future, I would be here for him, for all of them. Tonight belonged to us, and I wanted to taste every inch of Dorien Valencourt – the boy who was burned but not broken. My brave, stupid Muse.

The bed sagged as Titus lay down beside us, his fingers replacing Dorien's on my arm, trailing slow circles over my skin. Behind me, I heard Ivan draw a sharp breath. A moment later, he joined us on the other side, his hand resting with uncertain possession on the small of my back while I deepened the kiss with Dorien. Titus touched my cheek. "Faye." He whispered my name like an incantation.

I leaned over to kiss him, long and hard and deep. He kissed so differently than Dorien. He tasted different, too – dark and chaotic, but dappled with light, like early morning dew on an ancient forest. His fingers wrapped around my neck, and I felt so safe in his arms, so protected. I gasped a little as I ground myself down on Dorien's crotch and made him groan.

As I drew back, Titus' eyes devoured my body before flicking to Dorien and Ivan. I knew what they were discussing in those silent glances. They had shared other women together on tour, but those were groupies – throwaway faces and bodies to keep them warm, to make them forget their troubles for a few hours. I was so much more to them. And I'd been with two of them several times, but never all three.

I turned to Ivan, running my finger across his cheek. "If you want to go back to her, I won't stop you," I whispered. "It won't change anything between us. I'll still love you with my whole heart."

"There's nowhere else I'd rather be." Ivan's fingers closed over mine, and his cold eyes burned with determination as he kissed me. He gave me the kiss he was supposed to give me at the *Engine Ward* club, the kiss that burned all our doubts to ash.

As Ivan's lips blazed heat into my core, Dorien's fingers trailed over my skin. I didn't know how he and Titus got my clothes off. Everything became such a mess of kisses and caresses and the next thing I knew, my dress got tangled in the ceiling fan and Dorien's boxers were hanging over the lampshade, and the three of us were naked on top of the duvet, me sandwiched between them with my back against Dorien and my fingers tracing the line of Ivan's sharp jaw.

Titus lifted my knee, his breath coming out in ragged gasps as he touched his lips to my clit. I shuddered against Dorien, who held me tight as Titus ate me, savored me, fluttered his tongue against my clit like a goddamn butterfly. Ivan flashed Dorien a look of such longing that I would have bashed their heads together if my body wasn't currently building toward the best orgasm of my life. He tore his gaze away and bent to take my nipple in his mouth.

Their scents blended together in the air, and I didn't need music to conjure memories. As Dorien opened my legs wider and slid inside me, as each of my Muses touched me and stroked me and brought me to the edge, I saw in my mind everything we'd been through together, every moment of doubt and fear that we conquered, and every moment that might be ours in the future.

Music sung in my veins. This was how it was always supposed to be – the four of us, entwined together, for one night, for one moment, for eternity.

16

FAYE

I woke to warmth tingling down my legs.

I opened one sleepy eye and took in the scene. Sunlight streamed in through the windows. We hadn't bothered to close the curtains. Clothing was strewn everywhere, and I couldn't tell where my limbs stopped and the boys began, so tangled together were we, the sheets warm from the heat of our bodies, the air thick with our mingled scent.

Between my legs, someone gripped my thighs with calloused, musicians' fingers, their head firmly wedged in as they flicked their tongue over my clit and dipped it into my pussy, tasting the juices that already made me wet and wanting.

Mmmmm, this is the best way to wake up.

I reached down. My fingers tangled in short, fine hair. Ivan. As he realized I was awake, he curved his hands under my ass, lifting my hips to give better access to his punishing tongue. He swapped from flicks to small swirls, writing promises against my clit that had me writhing and cursing his name.

Heat pulsed inside me, building steadily to an ache that clawed along my spine. Ivan had my hips off the bed, twisting the bedspread into wild knots. Titus, who could sleep through a hurricane, remained a snoring rock, but Dorien stirred beside me. He threw a hand casually over my chest. His eyes widened as he saw what Ivan was doing.

Dorien quirked his lip into a cruel smile. He lifted the edge of the duvet and peered down at his friend. "What do we have here?"

Ivan lifted his eyes to look at Dorien as he pressed the flat of his tongue against me. The need in that look sent me over the edge. Dorien captured my mouth with his, swallowing my cry as the orgasm pulsed through me. Ivan stuck his tongue inside me again, tasting me as I soaked the sheets.

When my body quieted, Dorien pulled back and lifted the sheet again. The two of us peered down at Ivan, who planted a long, lingering kiss on my swollen clit before oh-so-casually reaching across to tug at Dorien's boxers.

Dorien was rock hard.

Dorien's cock jerked as Ivan's fingers brushed it through the silky fabric. His breath stuttered. The air fell still, expectant. Ivan lifted the hem and dragged the boxers down, down, down, over Dorien's thighs, freeing his cock.

Ivan looked to Dorien again, his eyes full of questions.

"I want you to suck it." Dorien's voice was husky but thick with power. Ivan closed his eyes, and a tremble rocked through his body. He bent down and brushed his lips reverently over the tip.

As I watched, Ivan's head bobbed down on Dorien's cock. Dorien couldn't take his eyes off his friend. He stroked Ivan's hair lovingly, like he was patting a beloved cat. All I could do was watch, grinding my pelvis into the bed as the ache between my legs burst anew.

It was so fucking hot.

To see Ivan getting exactly what he wanted, to hear Dorien's little grunts of pleasure as Ivan's mouth stroked him just the way he liked, to feel Dorien's fingers tugging at my hair, reminding me that none of this would be possible without the love and trust we shared.

Ivan's eyes never left Dorien's face as he sucked his cock in deep. I knew this was a thing that had been stirring between them for some time, and maybe this was the end of Ivan's worship of Dorien, or maybe it was the beginning of something more.

Huge hands wrapped around me. They threw off the covers and dragged me back, plonking me straight down on Titus' cock. "Oh," I cried out as he filled my pussy, his enormous shaft touching me in places only he could touch. I dragged my feet beneath me, so I knelt on him in reverse cowgirl, rocking against his cock as I watched Ivan suck Dorien off.

I ground down on Titus, driving him deeper, chasing the orgasm that teased at the tips of my toes. He was so big that it hurt a little, especially because I was still sore from last night, but it was the best kind of hurt.

Ivan's Adam's apple bobbed as he took Dorien in deep, his hand splayed under his thigh the way he did for me, thrusting Dorien's hips up to give him better access. I loved the expression on Dorien's face because I knew exactly what he was feeling. Ivan was very good at giving head.

Dorien threw his head back. His hands clamped on Ivan's shoulders as he came with a shudder that rocked the whole bed. Titus gripped my hips and ground me against him, filling me, stretching me.

"Come here," Dorien commanded. He grabbed Ivan under the arms and dragged him up the bed to lie beside him. "I want to taste myself on your tongue."

He took Ivan's lips with his own. Ivan's eyes widened like he couldn't quite believe this was happening. His body stiffened, but as Dorien deepened this kiss he relaxed, his body fitting against Dorien's like they were made for each other. Dorien tugged at Ivan's hair, nipped at his lip, scraped his teeth along his neck as he fisted Ivan's cock. His rough treatment made Ivan's eyes roll back in his head with pleasure.

This wasn't about giving me something to watch, even though seeing them made me grind down harder on Titus as my pleasure rose like a storm inside me. This was them taking the first steps into a dark, enchanted forest, slicing and cutting their way through the tangled vines of their emotions.

Ivan had spent his entire life living for his sister, trying to save her from the evil of the world. Dorien was the only person who'd ever put Ivan first, who thought *he* was worthy of saving. Dorien's fist worked Ivan's cock, and Ivan's back muscles tightened and his eyes grew wide with wonder and need, and he came in pale ribbons across Dorien's stomach.

Dorien looked down at him with such arrogant pleasure, like a spoiled king humoring a loyal subject. I half expected him to command Ivan to clean him with his mouth, but instead, he rolled over and pinched my nipple.

That little bite of pain was all I needed to send me tumbling over the edge. I ground myself down on Titus, feeling my walls clench around him as I rode the wave of pleasure unfurling inside me. His nails dug into my thighs as he thrust up to meet me, and he grunted as he too came, his cock twitching and jerking inside me.

Good thing this hotel had extra well-soundproofed walls, because we had no intention of leaving the bed for the rest of the day.

"What was that?" I grinned as I wrapped my arms around Ivan, pulling him back under the covers.

"I do not know." Ivan rested his head on my shoulder and smiled. His smile was so sweet and sad. "It was a dream, Faye."

We both glanced toward the bathroom. Steam curled from

under the door as Dorien's booming voice sang 'Avant de quitter' from the opera *Faust*, which is the most Dorien shower-opera song ever.

We were both thinking the same thing – what happened today meant the world to Ivan, but what was it for Dorien? Was it another one of his games? Another way for him to wrestle back control when he was teetering so dangerously close to losing everything?

"I have to go back to Manderley," Ivan said.

I nodded. I knew nothing I could say would talk him out of returning. "You need to get her out of that house. She has to know she doesn't have to go through with this marriage now."

"She's determined to marry him," he said, his voice hopeful. "Maybe she truly loves him?"

Ivan had such a broken puppy dog face I wanted to rub him behind the ears until he wagged his tail again.

I shook my head, remembering walking with Elena by the gazebo, the determination in her voice as she spoke about her brother and what she would do to escape Manderley. *I am a woman now,* she'd said. *I am not innocent, and I refuse to die locked away in this crumbling shithole because he won't do what needs to be done.*

"I need you to talk to her," Ivan said. "She may listen to you."

I nodded. "I need to look after Dorien right now, but if you arrange it, I'll do everything I can."

Ivan rose reluctantly, picking his clothes from the mess on the floor. "Tell Dorien goodbye for me." He cast a forlorn glance to the bathroom as he picked up his backpack. "Tell him I—I'm sorry about his finger."

"Tell him yourself."

Ivan laughed hollowly. "If he steps out of that shower all haughty and glistening, I won't be able to leave."

I flashed him a grin. "I believe it."

We kissed goodbye. I wanted to drag him back into bed and

use every trick in the book to make him stay, but that wasn't fair. Ivan needed to be with his sister, and I needed to stay with Dorien while Rochester and his team stormed the Danvers' mansion.

Last night and this morning we managed to make Dorien forget about his brother, Jacob. But now a knife of unease twisted in my gut. What would happen when the Feds broke inside the Temple? Would Dorien get his orphaned brother back? What would that mean for his future? For our future?

17

DORIEN

*J*acob.

I gazed up at the Danvers' California estate through the trees, all garish Greco-Roman columns and gaudy carvings – a modern Barbie dreamhouse that seemed so at odds with the supposed values of the Temple of Earthly Truths. The skin on my injured finger pulled painfully, but I could barely feel it. Somewhere inside was my kid brother, and Aaron Varney had control of him.

I balled my hands into fists at my sides.

Faye and I had flown out to California two days ago to be on site when Rochester's team went in. They were in negotiations with Aaron Varney – they were hoping he would allow two of their team to enter the compound for a talk. This would enable the Feds to gather information about what was going on inside, maybe even allow Jacob and some of the other children to leave. Rochester wanted me nearby in case I would make a good bargaining chip – they wouldn't send me in blind now that they'd seen what Aaron did to my parents, but I was happy to be a chess piece they could move around the board if it meant I got Jacob back.

Rochester and Velasquez had been inside the house for four hours. They weren't on comms because that was one of Aaron's stipulations, and they hadn't checked in since they entered the double gilded doors, which wasn't good. Faye and I sat together in the back of the van, listening to the members of Rochester's team panic and bark orders at each other. Sometimes, the bushes would rustle a little – a sign of life from the officers closing in on the perimeter.

"I never knew FBI raids could be this boring." Faye rolled her eyes. I knew she was trying to distract me. "We should have brought snacks."

Baldwin, who was working the comms station, reached into an empty rifle case and drew out a bag of corn chips. "Rookie mistake. I've got food stashed all over this van. There are at least three packages of Oreos hidden under the front seat."

"You, sir, are a genius. I don't suppose you happen to have any salsa hidden in that server stack—"

Faye's words were cut off by a series of loud POPs from the house and a window shattering. I bolted to my feet. "What the fuck was that?"

But no one answered. Baldwin was barking into his comms, and I saw a flash of movement in the bushes as the officers closed in. My stomach flew to my throat. *Were those gunshots? Please let Jacob be okay—*

After the flurry of activity, the house fell silent – an oppressive silence that chilled my heart. Faye slipped her fingers into mine, squeezing my hand so tight she'd break bones if I had any left, but I was a quivering mess.

Hours seemed to pass as we watched that silent house. The gilded door squeaked and grated and swung open. Two figures stepped outside. They held hands, and their long brown robes swept around their feet. They each carried an assault rifle, not pointed at anyone but resting on their shoulder, indicating they could start shooting at any moment. As they moved toward the gate, the officers surged forward, guns trained, yelling at them to stop.

"Don't shoot," I yelled. "That's my brother."

It's him. It's Jacob.

My brother held up his hand and waved at me, his face breaking into a cheerful smile. My heart swelled in my chest and broke open, and I was laughing and crying and babbling. *Jacob is out. He's alive, and he's outside.*

Beside Jacob, Pearl folded her arms and glared at the officers advancing on them.

"You took your time getting here," she rebuked the nearest officer.

I surged forward, but Baldwin grabbed the scruff of my neck and yanked me back. "You can't go to him yet, son. It might be a trap. We've seen it before."

A trap...my mind reeled as I understood what he meant. Aaron might've put a bomb on Jacob.

Fuck, no, please.

Beside me, Faye whimpered. "Why haven't Rochester and Velasquez come out?"

She's right. The gilded doors yawned open, revealing a foyer dripping with crystal chandeliers. But no one appeared behind them, no triumphant Rochester or beaming Velasquez. Everything was too still, too quiet.

Something isn't right. It is a trap.

The officers circled Jacob and Pearl, ordering them to stop. Jacob set his gun on the ground, and he nodded at Pearl to do the same. "It's okay," he said to the officers. "You can go inside. Everyone is asleep. Even your friends are asleep, but they'll be okay."

"Jacob!" I yelled, shrugging out of Baldwin's grasp. Before I could reach him, he and Pearl were swarmed by officers. They closed around the children, barking orders as they took the guns and swept them for explosives and other weapons.

'All clear." They pushed the children toward the gate and the waiting medical unit. Toward me and Faye and freedom.

Jacob ran to me with a wide smile and fell into my arms. "You came for me. I was so scared that you were dead, too. But you came to get me, just like you said you would."

I rubbed Jacob's back, feeling his ribs poking through his skin like dinosaur spines. For a fifteen-year-old, he was so small and light – a twig that could snap at any moment. Tears streamed down my cheeks.

Don't thank me for this, brother. I should have pulled you out a long time ago. But I promise I will never, ever let anyone take your power from you again.

We held each other for a long time, until he wriggled with impatience, until I cried my body's volume in tears. I took his hand in mine and led him over to the van, where Faye was watching us with a broad grin on her face. "Jacob, I'd like you to meet my girlfriend, Faye. You're going to live with us now, if you want to."

"Hi, Jacob." Faye bent down, so she was at his height. "I'm so excited to meet you. Dorien has been telling me so much about you. I can't wait to hang out."

Jacob slunk behind me. A shadow passed over his eyes as he glared back at Faye. *It's nothing to worry about, he's nervous of strangers. He hasn't been outside the Temple in years.*

But as Faye stepped back and Jacob's frown deepened, I couldn't help but wonder if it was as simple as that. *What lies has Aaron been filling his head with? Jacob can't believe everything Aaron told him, otherwise he wouldn't be out here. But he doesn't know what's real and what's lies.*

Behind us, officers marched into the property. Minutes later, they were dragging bodies out on stretchers, covered in sheets with oxygen masks over their faces. I saw them lift Rochester into the medical unit, and my stomach tightened.

I looked down at my brother. A chill struck my veins. "What happened, Jacob? Did you do something to these people?"

"We didn't hurt them," he said, a little petulantly. "Pearl and I made the tea, and we put some stuff in it so they would fall asleep. Then we used the guns to shoot the padlock on the front door and came outside."

The gunshots we heard.

"It was all Pearl's idea." Jacob waved to his friend, who was standing in the medical van, refusing to sit down as she explained their daring escape in a dramatic voice.

Something about what Jacob said niggled at me. "What stuff did you put in the tea? Is it dangerous? You have to tell the medics so they can treat these people. That man over there helped me to save your life."

Jacob shrugged. "I don't know what it was called. Pearl's sister Heather gave her an old bottle. She said she took it from you at Manderley, and it made people sleepy."

It took me a few minutes to figure out what Jacob was referring to. The apothecary set Clare and I found in the attic. I showed it to Heather. The first day Faye showed up at Manderley, we used the syrup of ipecac to make her sick, and we got chloroform to knock Faye out before the party. Faye and I used a Victorian drug called chloral to knock out Madame Usher so we could copy her keys and explore the attic room. I hadn't looked at the apothecary set since then, but I was betting the bottle of chloral was missing.

I saw Heather's actions in a new light. She'd tried to fuck us all over and hurt Faye, and I'd never forgive her for that, and her brutal death didn't change the fact she was a 'class A bitchbadger,' as Faye would say. But her two younger sisters were trapped inside the cult. She must have seen what happened to my family and been determined not to let it happened to hers.

Thank you, Heather.

I pressed Jacob to me again, and I met Faye's eyes over his

shoulder. She'd figured out the same thing I had, that Heather had been trying to save her sister. She'd been just as much a prisoner of Manderley as the rest of us.

Together, we turned to the gilded doors just as they brought out Aaron on a stretcher. He looked blissful in sleep, the edges of his mouth turned up into a contented smile. I *burned* to make him pay for destroying my family. He would wake up in a cell, and be put on trial for murder, and likely be locked up for life, but it wasn't enough. It would never be enough for the torment he caused for his god complex.

But he was only one part of this puzzle. Madame Usher was still the spider at the center of this web. And if I couldn't wrap my hands around Aaron's throat and squeeze until the life drained from his eyes, I could sure as hell bring her to her knees.

18

DORIEN

"He's doing great." Dr. Nelson peered at me over the chart. She wasn't even Jacob's doctor, but when she heard we were back in the hospital getting him assessed, she offered to help. "Apart from a few abrasions and the damage on his feet, he's healthier than I expected. He's severely malnourished, but he's receiving fluids, and he's making great progress. He'll need continued monitoring and care, and I'm making a recommendation for a child psychologist, who will determine his mental age and help with deprogramming. He became agitated when the doctors checked him over. I strongly advise you to take him to a dentist at your first opportunity, but he's a strong boy and with lots of love I think he'll thrive. You'll be able to take him home with you by the end of the week."

Home. What a joke. I didn't have a home. Valencourt Manor burned to the ground, and I couldn't live in a hotel room on Natalie's dime forever. I didn't even have a car anymore – crashing the Porsche into the gate completely wrote it off.

With my pinkie finger damaged, I'd likely never play the piano like I could before. The only thing in my life I was actually good at had been taken from me.

Jacob desperately needed stability and safety in his life, and I was anything but. I was a mess.

I'm already failing him.

Dr. Nelson must have sensed my apprehension because she patted my shoulder. "There's no easy fix here, Dorien. This is a long, hard road you're walking with Jacob. Children who come out of cults carry trauma they will struggle to understand. He'll be confused, angry, anxious, maybe even depressed. He may suffer PTSD from the terrible things he experienced in Aaron's care, but he's also been ripped from the only family he's known. He's been programmed to believe that everything outside the Temple is unsafe, evil, and corrupt, and that includes you. It's going to be tough, but if you're gentle and patient, he'll come out the other side a strong, resilient young man, just like his older brother."

I blinked back tears. It wasn't fair. Jacob didn't deserve any of this. I took Dr. Nelson's papers in shaking hands. Psychologists. Group therapy. Dental work. Jacob needed all of this to get better, and Medicaid would pay for some of it, but where the fuck would I get the money to look after my brother?

"Can we see him?" Faye asked Dr. Nelson, her hand never leaving mine. She'd been by my side ever since Jacob walked out of the Danvers' estate – I would have collapsed with grief by now if it weren't for her steadiness.

Dr. Nelson stepped aside, and Faye held open the door for me. I swallowed down my tears. Jacob needed my strength now. Looking at him reminded me of my own guilt, my failure, but I couldn't put that on him. He'd already endured so much.

My feet dragged as I walked through the door. He sat up in bed when he saw me. He was so impossibly tiny, like a little kid. "Hey, buddy."

Jacob smiled at me, and that smile broke my heart. "Dorien. They gave me jelly beans. Look."

He pushed his fingers through a rainbow of colorful candies on his tray, his eyes wide with wonder.

"That's great." I swallowed back the lump welling in my throat. "You seem better today. It was so brave what you did, putting everyone to sleep and walking outside like that."

"It was Pearl's idea. She's been telling me about jelly beans! And school and go-karts and wrestling and baseball and Pop-Tarts!" He smiled again, but the smile was a little manic.

"Well, the good news is soon I'm going to take you out of here and we'll go and try all those things. Anything you want to do, you can do it."

But Jacob was frowning. "Where's Pearl?"

"She's in a hospital just like this, but in California," Faye said.

"I didn't ask you," Jacob snapped at her. I started at his tone – I'd never heard my gentle brother speak to someone like that before, his voice dripping with disdain. Faye looked unperturbed, but I felt my heart sinking. I remembered those fleeting visits I've had with him over the years, how meek and kind and anxious he was. But this Jacob…I didn't know how to deal with him.

I wonder if that's how Father Aaron talks to the women in the Temple.

"Faye's telling the truth." I try to keep my voice gentle. "Pearl's cousins are looking after her while her parents get better—"

"You're lying." Jacob's face fell, and when he peered up at me, his slate-grey eyes were dark with rage. "God punished her, didn't he? God punished her and now she's dead because I didn't save her."

"No, that's not true. She's in California. I can set up a video call with her if you want—"

"No no no." Jacob's face screwed up, his tiny fists beating at my chest. Every blow felt like the sword of Damocles slicing off my head. "Father Aaron said she was wicked and sinful. He said it was my job to make her godly and good, but instead, I helped her and now she's burning to hell." Jacob shoved the tray so hard it rolled across the room. The jelly beans rolled over the edge and scattered on the floor. "You're going to hell too."

I know.

"I'm not going to hell. I'm going to be right here with you, buddy." I reached out to touch his hair. "Father Aaron has told you lots of things that aren't true, but I'm going to help you—"

"No!" he yelled, pummeling my chest again. "I don't want you. I don't want your whore. I want Mommy. Where are Mommy and Daddy?"

"Dorien, I think you should come outside now," Dr. Nelson called out from the doorway.

I can't. I can't leave him like this.

Jacob's fists pummeled my back, my chest, my arms. Faye had to pull him off me. When she touched his arm, he hissed at her, like a cat cornered by an overexcited puppy.

Even when I drew away I could still feel his blows raining down on me. "I hate you, I hate you," he screamed as Dr. Nelson hurried in, the door swinging shut behind her.

*T*he news of the federal raid on the Temple of Earthly Truths and Father Aaron's arrest made headlines. The hospital did a great job keeping the press away from Jacob, but once they figured out the connection between me and the cult (with a little help from Madame Usher, according to Ivan), they hounded us relentlessly. They banged on the car windows as we pulled into the hospital parking lot, chased us into the lobby of the hotel, and stalked us as we met with Rochester to give our statements about Aaron's treatment of my family. Marguerite and Natalie were working as our unpaid PR team, fielding media calls and releasing statements, and Broken Muse topped the Classical Music charts for the first time since our last album released three years ago. It was a river of lies flowing beneath a mountain of shit, and we could do nothing but ride the current and hope we didn't get pulled under.

The press weren't even the worst thing hounding me. Nightmares kept me awake – the twisted faces of my parents leering down at me from their cross, reminding me that I was a failure. I assumed Jacob had seen them too, for he was haunted by his own nightmares – visions that sent him screaming and flinging himself from his hospital bed. But that could have been from any one of the horrors Aaron visited on him over the years.

At least Aaron was behind bars now, and from the looks of the case Rochester and his team put together, he'd be staying there for a long time. The thirty-five adults and seven children who drank the poisoned tea were being released from the hospital back to their families, and some were starting to speak about what went on within the cult. I tried to read their stories, but my eyes blurred with rage and regret and I couldn't see the words anymore.

My ruined finger mocked me, a fitting punishment for my crime. *I'll never be able to forgive myself for going to Europe with Broken Muse instead of doing everything I could to get Jacob out.*

I couldn't change my mistakes, but I had my chance for redemption. Jacob would be coming home with me in a matter of days. I went to visit him in the hospital every day. He was brighter and happier when Faye wasn't in the room, but his emotions wavered all over the place, from relief to anxiety to excitement to anger.

I can't help him. I don't have the emotional maturity to deal with my own shit, let alone his trauma.

But it didn't matter how useless I was as a brother. I was all Jacob had left now. What a great prize I was.

Back in the hotel suite after a tiring day with Jacob, Faye and I made plans. As much as I didn't want to deal with the fallout of my parents' murder, I had a meeting with their lawyer to prepare for. Social services needed to talk to me about Jacob's guardianship, and we couldn't keep staying in the hotel with the media circus, but every apartment in the city cost seven million dollars in rent.

"You're going to love this." Faye made a face as she tossed the newspaper down in front of me. "As if we didn't have enough problems to deal with."

I picked it up and scanned the headlines. It was an exclusive interview with Madame Usher, who styled herself as my artistic mentor and a close family friend. She spoke with astonishing conviction about how much she cared about me, and how the cult might have influenced my actions in the house. She implied Clare and Heather had been afraid of me, and that the cult had given me the skills to manipulate them.

"This doesn't seem like her." I slid the paper back across the table and reached for one of the little bottles of minibar Scotch Faye lined up down the center of the table. "It reeks of desperation."

"I know." Faye sipped her coffee. "She's lashing out because she knows we know her secrets. She's discrediting us before we speak up about Victor."

"Why haven't we spoken up about Victor?" If she wanted to fight this battle in the court of public opinion, she could be my guest. I'd been making headlines since Broken Muse first released our debut single, 'A Graveside Story.' She shouldn't pick her battles in her enemy's front garden.

"Because Ivan and Elena are still inside that house, and I don't want to give her any reason to hurt them." Faye popped the cork on her own bottle and took a long slug. "We need more than just this wild story of a fake death and a creepy old man hiding in the walls. We need the story, the reasons. We need to follow that money."

"This is where we're going to live for a while."

Jacob's eyes widened as he took in the apartment. Even though she hadn't lived there long, Marguerite had done an amazing job making it ready for us all. There were two bedrooms, one for her and one for Jacob, and a large kitchen and living room (at least, large by NYC standards) where Faye and I could sleep on a foldout sofa. She painted his room with a soft green that reminded me of the rolling lawns of Manderley, and filled it with everything a boy needed – toys and video games and new clothing and toiletries.

When Marguerite saw Madame Usher's article, she declared war. Madame Usher might've been a venomous spider, but she couldn't play the media like Marguerite de Winter. Faye's mom sold her own story of poison and stolen husbands to a rival paper, and used the check to lease a three months' apartment for all of us.

Now, she leaned against the doorframe, watching Jacob with a shy smile as he circled the room, touching all the new things she placed there for him.

"This is Marguerite. She's going to be living with us, and she'll look after you when I'm not here." *Because I have to get a job.*

I'd never had a job before that wasn't 'rockstar' – but with my finger unlikely to regain its previous mobility, Madame Usher determined to sully my name, Ivan trapped at Manderley and Titus on track for Juilliard, the band was over.

Faye's mother bent down, so she was at his level, even though I could see it caused her pain. "Hello, Jacob. It's so nice to meet you. I heard you know my daughter, Faye. I got you these things so you feel at home here. I hope you like them."

Jacob sat on the edge of the bed, his eyes wide as he took in all the stuff. He wouldn't even remember owning toys or clothes he didn't have to sew himself from old towels. From Rochester's damning reports of the Danvers' residence, Jacob might not even have had a bed. There was evidence the children slept on piles of old blankets on the floor.

Both Jacob and I still woke several times a night, screaming from the nightmarish visions of our parents hanging from a cross.

Jacob didn't say anything. He picked up a stack of perfectly folded t-shirts and tossed them on the floor.

"These things are evil. They make me unclean. We shouldn't have them here."

"Hey, buddy, hey." I sat down beside him and clasped his hand in mine. "I know that's what Aaron told you, but look. I wear all sorts of clothes. So does everyone else who you've met, remember? It's okay to wear these clothes and feel comfortable. You can even choose your own, in whatever colors you want."

The therapist we started seeing (yet another reason I needed an income source other than paltry Spotify royalty checks, stat) said that I should challenge the logic of Aaron's teachings. If Jacob sees Aaron's rules being broken without consequence, he'll start to understand the rules themselves were false. *Hopefully.* The therapist was always quick to warn that every child was different and some couldn't break the patterns of manipulation from a cult. But that wasn't going to be my brother. Not while I was here to help him.

"I want to go home." He stomped his foot. "You said I could go home."

I clasped my hand over his before he could wreck more of Marguerite's hard work. "This is what I meant, buddy. This is our home for now. And Pearl is going to visit soon. You wanted to see Pearl again."

I was nervous about Jacob seeing Pearl. I thought seeing someone from the Temple might trigger Jacob. The therapist who charged more per hour than we used to make in t-shirt sales from an entire *tour* believed that because Jacob trusts Pearl, and she didn't grow up in the Temple and knew about the outside world, she could be a good influence on him, help him to adjust. So I arranged with her cousins to have her visit in a month, just before she started at school.

"I don't like this place. I want to go back to our house. I want Mommy." Angry tears clouded his face.

"Jacob, you remember what happened to Mommy." I had to tread carefully here. The therapist said we couldn't indulge delusions, but we had to do it in a way that wouldn't trigger the trauma of Jacob's memories. I don't know how much he saw of what Aaron did to our parents. Forensics said they died several hours before the fire took hold. Knowing Aaron's ways, he would have made an example of them in front of his followers. "Father Aaron did that, and so that means I have to keep you here so you're safe from him—"

"You said you'd keep me safe, but you let them die. They just wanted you to come home so we could be a real family. Aaron's right. You're evil." He kicked the bedside table.

I wrapped my arms around him, holding him still as a tsunami of emotion welled inside him. He kicked and screamed and railed against the world. His tiny fists pummeled my chest and every blow twisted inside me like a knife slicing me to pieces.

He wasn't wrong. I am evil. I left him in Aaron's clutches and now he's broken. Just like me.

Jacob raged until his anger spent. He collapsed in a pile of his ruined things, his eyes closed. Marguerite helped me to my feet and led me outside, closing the door behind us. "Give him time, Dorien. He's been through hell." She touched my arm. "You both have."

"I don't—" I fought for words between the sob rising from my chest. "I don't know what to do to help him."

"You're doing everything you need to by being there." She gave me a warm hug, the first she'd given me since I walked back into Faye's life. "Follow me, I'll make you some cocoa. Everything is better after a pot of my cocoa, mostly because of the large amount of whisky I put in it. But don't tell my daughter."

As I followed Marguerite to the kitchen, I wondered. What if Jacob never got better? What if he could never learn to trust me, or Marguerite, or Ivan and Titus, or Faye? If Jacob didn't improve, I couldn't keep him here where every day he was greeted by the life I built without him. That wasn't fair to him.

Would saving my brother mean giving up everything I won, including Faye's heart?

19

FAYE

I traipsed up the stairs to the apartment, cursing the cockpoodle who decided elevators in NYC apartment buildings were a bourgeois luxury. My back hurt. My feet hurt. I smelled like furniture wax and old cabbage (piano shops always smelled like old cabbage, don't ask me why. I don't make the rules). All I wanted was a glass of wine and maybe for Dorien to fuck a smile onto my face. As I inserted the key into the lock, I could hear Jacob screaming.

Poor kid. No matter how much my life sucked at the moment, Jacob had it worse. Some days he was all smiles and kindness with Dorien, but his mood would turn on a violin string. He didn't like me. He spoke to me in this haughty, condescending tone that reminded me far too much of his older brother during my early days at Manderley.

Jacob had the same slate-grey eyes as Dorien, and the same crooked smile that melted your heart. But while Dorien's grin flirted with devils, Jacob's smile – when he allowed us to see it – was pure kindness and innocence.

I wanted to help him so much, but what he was going through was more than any of us could ever comprehend. We had to be there for him through every awful mood and every cutting remark. And that meant when I turned the key in the door I plastered a smile on my face.

Mom greeted me, throwing her coat over her shoulders and tossing her keys into her purse. She had to yell to be heard over the screaming. "There you are. I'm running late for my appointment with Dr. Nelson. Jacob's hasn't eaten a bite all day, but he'd been happily watching cartoons for hours until one of the characters set another on fire." She blew a kiss. "I'll be home in a couple of hours. Maybe longer."

"You can't leave me here." I stared over her shoulder at the boy on the sofa, lying on his back kicking his feet while he tore his lungs out. Panic crawled through my chest.

"I'm sorry, mi cielo. I'm getting test results back and Dr. Nelson wants to introduce me to another specialist. But you'll be fine with Jacob for a little bit."

Doubtful. "Where's Dorien? Why can't he watch Jacob?"

"Dorien has the meeting with his lawyer." Mom glanced at her watch. "He was supposed to be done an hour ago, but they must have had a lot to talk about. I have to go. You'll be fine. Just… um…you'll be fine. Byeeeeee." She air-kissed my cheeks as she dashed into the corridor. Was it my imagination, or did she breathe a sigh of relief as she darted toward the stairwell?

Great.

I set down my bag, noticing my violin case hidden behind the potted plant. I hadn't practiced in a while – thinking about music depressed me. The only reason I was able to attend Manderley was because of Madame Usher. I couldn't afford another music program and no school would offer me a scholarship with my name splashed across lurid headlines. But right then, there was nothing I wanted to do more than draw my bow across the strings and transport myself somewhere far away.

I unclipped the case, pulling out the Becker and setting it against my chin. Jacob watched me from the sofa as I drew the bow across the strings, twisting the pegs to get the proper tuning. He kept screaming, but without enthusiasm.

"Don't come any closer." Jacob's face clouded with rage. He looked so like the Dorien I remembered from Madame Usher's school it made my chest ache. I wanted to wrap Jacob in my arms and make him laugh and teach him about horror films and Mexican food and buy him so much ice cream he got sick, but that wasn't my role. I had to give him the space to learn to trust me. Maybe he never would. Maybe Aaron had already corrupted his relationships with women beyond repair.

"I promise I'll stay over here. I won't touch you or talk to you." I struck the strings to emphasize my promise. "I'm just going to play for a little bit. You don't even have to listen. You can go right on screaming."

Jacob frowned at me as I raised the violin and started to play. I chose Sarasate's *Zigeunerweisen Op. 20* – a piece composed for piano and orchestra that Dorien arranged for violin and piano for one of our duets at the Usher School. I tried hard not to look at Jacob as I played, but it was impossible – those dark eyes that were so much like Dorien's bore into me as I dove deeper into my memories.

Dorien's enchanting scent wove around me, that dark heart of cinnamon and frankincense dappled with sweet violets dragging me under its spell. This wasn't simply the lingering residue of Dorien's recent presence in the room – it was a memory from long ago conjured by the music. It was me and Dorien practicing this piece in an echoey room, accompanied by the slightly boiled pork odor that wafted from the school's old furnace vents.

It was a time when all I thought about was classes and violin and making my dad see me and Dorien's perfect grey eyes.

During the melancholic third section, which is played muted, Jacob stopped screaming. He curled his feet beneath him and sat watching me as the piece swelled and dipped. The Spanish composer Sarasate drew inspiration from Hungarian folk music, although he thought they were Romani gypsy tunes. The fourth and final section called for frenzied playing of long spiccato runs, double stops, and left-hand pizzicato. His eyes widened as he watched my fingers, his body moving in a jerky dance as if the music controlled his limbs. When I finished with a breathless flourish, I lowered my bow and met his eyes. Tears glistened in the corners.

"I think…" he screwed up his face. "I remember that song."

I tried to hide my surprise. "I used to play with your brother at a music school in New York City. I'm surprised you remember it at all; you must've been barely five years old."

He shook his head. "I don't know if I do remember. I don't remember the school. I don't remember you. But I remember the music. It makes me want to dance."

I dared a smile. "Me too. But it's hard to dance and play at the same time. Dorien can do it, and he plays the piano. He makes every song into a performance, and not many people can do that."

"My mother said Dorien has a gift."

"She's right. Your brother is exceptionally gifted. Has he played you any of his music?"

Jacob shook his head. I didn't blame Dorien for not showing him Broken Muse. The songs were quite dark, and the band's existence was tied to Dorien's guilt for leaving his brother inside the Temple.

"I could play one for you." I picked up the remote and navigated through my favorite playlist, selecting one of their lighter songs and pumping the volume up until the music swelled from the speakers. Jacob's eyes widened again as Ivan's violin added a melancholic air, while Titus' deep cello dueled for supremacy with Dorien's florid playing. When it was over, he begged for another.

I paused. I didn't want to overstep, and Dorien was so nervous about Jacob feeling betrayed by his absence. But Jacob didn't look betrayed. He looked like a little kid in awe of his big brother. So I put on another song and navigated to a folder I kept of images from their tours and fan pages (If Dorien finds out I kept tabs on him all these years, I'd never hear the end of it), and brought them up on the screen.

"Here's Dorien performing at the Wiener Musikverein in Vienna, and this is from their show at the Royal Albert Hall in London." I flipped past a photograph of Dorien crowd surfing in the famous venue. "Here is Dorien with Titus and Ivan on a photoshoot in Prague. They've been all over the world playing for their fans."

"Wow." Jacob pointed to a photograph. "Who's that with him?"

I peered at the photograph. It was of Dorien and Titus at a music award event in London, dressed in their stage costumes and surrounded by men and women in black tie. They smiled at the camera with their arms around an older couple, but the smile didn't reach their eyes.

"Her name is Madame Usher, and that was her husband, Victor Usher. He died nearly two years ago. She runs the music school Dorien and I have been attending. She's not a nice person."

"She came to the Temple once. I remember her. She met with my parents and Father Aaron in the kitchen. We baked a special loaf of bread for her visit."

What? A cold fist clenched around my heart. "When was this?"

Jacob counted on his fingers. "I think...five summers ago. I remember because we had an amazing orange crop that year, so we made an orange seed cake to go with the bread."

"Was she alone, or did she have anyone else with her?"

Jacob shook his head. "She was all by herself. Father Aaron must not have wanted her to feel lonely, because he invited her to sleep over in his bedroom."

Did he now...

I leaned toward him, heart pounding. I didn't want to push

Jacob, but this was important. "Did you happen to overhear what she and Aaron talked about?"

Jacob frowned. "Eavesdropping is a sin."

"You're right. I'm sorry. I just meant…what did you all talk about when you were together?"

"She talked about Dorien lots, and how he was in Europe with his band, and he had this great power to spread the Temple's message all over the world but he was wasting it with sinful music. She and Aaron and Mother agreed on that a lot. She had one of those glittery keys pinned to her neck, like my mom used to wear. When she left, she gave Father Aaron a big brown envelope." His eyes flicked to the ground. "I asked him if it was a present and he said it was none of my business. He wouldn't even let me have any orange seed cake."

I wanted to keep pressing him, but I had an idea. A way to connect to Jacob. A way to help him draw a line between the things that made him happy about Temple and the big, wide, scary world he lived in now.

"I bet that orange cake was amazing, too. I heard you're an excellent baker." I felt my lips curling into a smile. "Hey, do you want to learn how to make tortillas? That's flat bread from Mexico, where my mother comes from. You roll them up and fill them with meat and vegetables and spices, and they're delicious."

Jacob scrambled off the couch. "Flat bread? That's totally crazy."

As I tied an apron around Jake's narrow waist, my mind whirred a mile a minute. Madame Usher was visiting Father Aaron. That was before Dorien tried to help Ivan and Elena escape, before she trapped all three Broken Muses at Manderley. So what was she doing with Father Aaron? Why did I have a terrible feeling we'd only scratched the surface of what was going on?

20

DORIEN

When I came home from the appointment with my lawyers, Jacob and Faye were in the kitchen. He was rolling out the dough for tortillas while Faye chopped and mixed fillings. She'd put a playlist of Broken Muse songs on quiet in the background, and was sashaying her gorgeous hips as she moved around the kitchen. When Jacob looked up at me, he actually *smiled*.

After what I just learned, the scene made my throat tighten. I slid into a chair and breathed in the delicious scent of fresh tortillas. "I'm sorry I'm later than I planned. It looks like you two are having fun."

"Faye taught me to make tortillas," Jacob held up a lopsided circle of dough proudly. "Look."

"That's amazing."

"We've got to fry it first, silly." Faye had a frilly apron tied backward around her middle, so it covered her butt, with the strings dangling down between her legs. The front of her shirt was dusted with flour, which might have given me ghost Clare flashbacks if I wasn't so distracted by Jacob's broad smile. He wore a newspaper chef's hat and was just as coated in flour.

The pair of them bustled around, preparing food for me. Jacob presented a plate of fish tacos with a flourish. I exchanged a glance with Faye as I dug in. *You're a genius,* I mouthed. She found a way to connect with him through baking – an activity that felt familiar to him. It was perfect.

After we'd all eaten our fill of tacos, Jacob went to his room to play with his toys. I grabbed Faye around the waist and twirled her, planting kisses along her jaw until she pushed me away.

"I have to tell you something," she said. "You're not going to like it."

"No. Me first." Faye sounded grave, but I had a feeling once she heard my news, hers wouldn't seem as bad. "I've been dying to tell you how the meeting with the lawyer went."

"Okay, fine. You first."

"As I suspected, both Jacob's and my trust fund had been cleared out by Father Aaron, as have most of their investments."

"I'm sorry, Dorien." Faye laid her head on my shoulder.

"It's actually a blessing, in a way. They changed their will several years ago to give everything to The Temple, which means that we'd spend the rest of our lives fighting the cult in court for that money, and now we don't have to, because it's all gone… except the house."

"What?"

"Mom and Dad left Valencourt Manor – the house, the grounds, the whole property – to me and Jacob, to be shared equally between us. I don't know if they simply overlooked it or if somewhere in the back of their warped brains they knew Aaron was taking them for a ride. But the house is ours. Even with the fire and the piles of trash and the decades of neglect, the estate is prime land. It's worth a few million, at least."

Faye pressed her hand to her mouth. "I can't believe it."

"I can't, either." I spun her around until she squealed. "The lawyers are working through the tangled web that is my parents' finances now, and then we could put the place up for sale. And then we'll have money – real money we can spend on giving Jacob the best possible future, the life they stole from him."

"Dorien, that's amazing." Faye held my cheeks. "You can't call it our money, though. This is your money, not mine. Yours and Jacob's. Please, don't spend a cent of it on me."

"I can give Jacob a great life and still buy my girl a new frying pan." I lift the thrift-store pan to show her the cracks running across the handle. Faye grabbed it and tried to swat me with it, but I ducked out of her grasp.

"Seriously, I have to tell you about my thing now." She set down the frying pan. "I want you to promise you won't grill Jacob about it. We made real progress today and I don't want to frighten him."

That cold lump in my throat returned. "You're scaring me. Spit it out, Sprite."

She took a deep breath. "Jacob said Madame Usher visited your parents and Father Aaron at their house, about five years ago. They made a special cake for her and she spoke about you, and she *stayed the night.* In Aaron's room. Apparently, when she left, Father Aaron was in a good mood."

She didn't have to elaborate on what this meant.

Father Aaron was another one of Madame Usher's pawns.

Over the next couple of weeks, I spent every waking moment with Jacob. We went for slow, meandering walks around the nearby park, stopping to purchase chestnuts from a peddler and to feed the ducks in the pond. We returned only when Jacob's ruined feet made it impossible for him to walk, and I'd carry him back on my shoulders like he was a kid.

I bought him picture books to help with his reading, and sports equipment and action figures and enough junk food to put the meat back on his bones. He smiled more and more.

His smiles made me angry. Mostly at myself. He was fifteen years old. He wasn't supposed to be struggling his way through picture books and feeding ducks at the pond. At the park, we passed a group of boys his age having a snowball fight, and Jacob hid behind me.

He'd had his whole life taken from him. I should have got him out years ago, Madame Usher be damned. I'd been selfish, so happy to escape the sinking ship that was my family that I went on tour with Broken Muse. I'd like to say I at least thought about Jacob all the time, that I was planning and plotting to free him. But that would be a lie. And I paid for that lie with my finger and any chance at continuing my career as a musician. I was too angry at myself to be sad about it.

I was determined that from now on I'd make sure he had everything to make up for the shitty brother he'd been given.

And that started with selling off Valencourt Manor as soon as possible so I could get my hands on that money. I was scrolling through my laptop, looking for the name of a local company that could clean up the property, when Faye waved at me over the screen. She had her phone in her hand.

"That was Titus. His parents are dragging him back to New Orleans. They invited me down as well. I think his mother believes I'll talk some sense into him about choosing a new school." She frowned. "I'd love to go, but that would leave you here on your own with Jacob and Mom, and with everything going on and Ivan still at Manderley—"

"Go." I waved my hand at her. "There's nothing much more we can do about Manderley and Madame Usher. It's in Rochester's hands now. I want you to enjoy yourself."

"Are you sure?"

I thought of my time in New Orleans during the early days of Broken Muse – trawling the jazz clubs with Titus, puking into the Mardi Gras Fountain after a night on the absinthe, hooking my veins directly into the lifeblood of music and culture and magic. Faye would have an amazing time. "I'm sure. It'll give me a chance to spend some time alone with Jacob. We've got a lot to talk about, and soon, hopefully a lot of money to spend."

She kissed my forehead. "You're doing great with him, you know that?"

"It doesn't feel like it," I growled, the anger bubbling to the surface again.

She smiled at me. "You have to be patient, which I know you suck at."

"I can be patient."

"Says the boy who would throw his sheet music across the room if he couldn't master a piece first time through."

"I'm not—" A laugh caught in my throat. "Okay, yeah. That's me. I just…I waited too long to get Jacob out of there, and he's lost so much. I want him to start his life now."

"He's already started," Faye said. "Every time you see him smile, remember that's a smile you gave him. He may not ever be like other kids, and that's okay. We weren't like other kids, either. And we turned out all right. If you'll excuse me, I need to start packing. We leave in a few days."

Faye sashayed her hips as she left the room. I stared at the spot she occupied long after she'd gone. It was true what I said – we'd reached a stalemate with Madame Usher. Despite what Faye and Ivan overheard, she hadn't made any move against us beyond that article trying to paint her as a concerned teacher. According to Ivan, she hadn't stepped up her torture at Manderley. In fact, she seemed to have lost interest in him and Broken Muse.

I knew better than to assume Madame Usher had forgotten us completely. She and Victor were planning something diabolical. But she had already taken so much from us, and while we knew what she hid at Manderley, we had more over her than she had on us. We had the power. So it was safe for Faye to leave for a bit.

Wasn't it?

21

FAYE

I was packing my bags for New Orleans when Ivan stormed through the door. Jacob dropped the wooden blocks he was playing with and dived behind the sofa. Dorien gathered his brother in his arms and glared at Ivan, but our Romanian didn't notice.

He stood in front of me, his shoulders shaking, a square of white card clutched in his hands. He looked like he was going to explode.

"What's wrong?" I shot to my feet and wrapped my arms around him. He remained stiff and irresponsible – an Ivan made of stone instead of flesh.

It took Ivan a couple of tries to form words.

"I am to give you this." He thrust the card into my hands.

I held it up. It was an invitation printed on cream card stock with a gold border, asking me to attend the wedding ceremony for Elena Nicolescu and Maxim Radcliffe, at Manderley, a week from today.

"I don't understand…" I frowned at the card. "Their wedding wasn't supposed to happen until June. I addressed the envelopes myself. What about all those important musicians and directors and patrons Madame Usher invited?"

"Elena decided she didn't want to wait." Ivan's face twisted with rage. He gripped my wrist. "You have to come with me. You have to talk to her."

He dragged me downstairs. Harrison waited outside in the limo. He smiled as Ivan bundled me into the back while horns sounded around us. The moment gave me a flashback to my very first day at Manderley, where Harrison showed up at my Bushwick apartment in the limo. Only this time, I was stepping back into the spider's lair to save Elena instead of my mother.

"Miss Faye, it's lovely to see you again."

"Hi, Harrison." I buckled my seatbelt. Ivan climbed up beside me and reached for the vodka in the bar. "How are things at Manderley?"

"Quiet without all you students around." Harrison frowned. "So much trouble, I don't like it. It's not good for my nerves."

I wanted to tell Harrison about Victor living in the walls, but he looked so much older and more frail than I remembered him. I didn't want to give him a fright, especially since it seemed Madame Usher left him alone. Instead, I tried a different tack. "I was wondering, could you tell me more about Madame Usher and Victor? What were they like as a couple?"

Harrison's lip curled back, showing me without a single word what he thought. "In the early days, Victor was besotted. It was as if she bewitched him. He thought the sun shone out her asshole, pardon my language. But over the years, there was a distance between them, especially after they closed up the city school and started teaching at Manderley. Victor loved having his house filled with music and bright students and international musicians, but she…well, you know what she's like."

"A spider," I said before I could stop myself.

"That's right. A spider. Victor told me once that she wanted —" Harrison swallowed. I expected him to continue the thought, but he stopped himself. "Do not misunderstand me, they had many loving moments between them. I got the feeling there were financial troubles, which can be a strain on any relationship, but it's no business of mine. I just cut the roses."

As we made the long drive out to Manderley and Harrison distracted himself singing along with his music, Ivan filled me in on everything that had been going on at the house. How Elena had been frantic with wedding preparations. How Madame Usher seemed to have given up all pretenses of running a school or of holding them prisoner. How Aroha had become increasingly erratic – Ivan often found her walking the halls at night, or banging her head repeatedly against a window.

He didn't talk about Victor, but I read his concern in his icy gaze.

The high iron gates of Manderley loomed over us as the limo bumped along the overgrown drive. We pulled into a parking space beneath the trees, next to the twins' truck, which hadn't been used in a long time, judging by the thick layer of dead leaves obscuring it. Ivan told me Madame Usher confiscated the keys.

I pushed the door open, my face tilted up just as the first icy drops of a snowstorm hit my skin. Harrison wrapped a long, dark coat around me, and the pair of them bundled me around the back of the house to the stables. Elena opened the door and ushered us inside.

I'd never been inside Master Radcliffe's living quarters before. It looked exactly as I imagined the home of an older bachelor to look – a dark oak desk and floor-to-ceiling bookshelves lined the living area, with a couple of threadbare armchairs and a Turkish ottoman. There was no TV. In the center of the room, a beautiful polished Fazioli grand piano dominated the space, the carpet around it strewn with sheet music and scribbled notes.

Elena flopped down on the piano stool and patted the cushion beside her.

"Play with me," she said.

"Elena, I wanted to—"

"I know Ivan brought you here to talk me out of marrying Maxim. I want to play with my best friend."

"I didn't bring my bow."

She snapped her fingers at an instrument in the corner. I noticed a beautiful violin nestled on a stand, as if it had been reluctantly set down while its owner did some unfortunate chore. Master Radcliffe's instrument. I rarely saw him play the violin – he taught mainly composition, which he said came more naturally to him on the piano. Even so, I didn't want to touch it – there was something sacred about a musician's instrument, and I shouldn't play without permission – but I couldn't refuse Elena.

I picked up the violin.

Elena opened with Beethoven's *Violin Sonata No. 9*. I played the raw, emotionally-charged piece with her, my fingers flying over the familiar notes. I watched as she played, her eyelashes fluttering closed and a look of complete and utter contentment on her lips. She truly was magic. Being able to conjure music with her was one of my life's greatest joys.

And I knew in that moment that I would never change her mind. Because Elena didn't comprehend love the way I did. She didn't seek wild yearning the way I did with Ivan and Titus and Dorien, because she'd already found that love in her music. She loved the music in a way none of us fully understood. She was doing this because Radcliffe could give her something Ivan couldn't, something no other man could – access to the world's stage, where she could weave her magic for an adoring audience until the day she died.

As the final notes died away, Elena lifted her shapely fingers from the keys and peered up at me. "I know my brother has brought you here to convince me not to go through with this marriage," she said.

"He did. But I'm not going to do that." I placed my hand over hers. "I only ask one thing – make sure you get access to your trust fund. It should be in your name, not Radcliffe's."

Elena played a few bars. "Maxim has taken care of all that boring stuff."

"I know you're not that naive."

"Faye, I'm fine. Everything is wonderful between me and Maxim. We're to be husband and wife, and we will go off to Europe and leave this damp, disgusting house behind us. Maxim has already booked me on a ten-city tour over the summer. I am happy, and if Ivan cannot see that, I have nothing to say to either of you." She rose. "Harrison will drive you home."

"Elena, I—"

She turned away, waving her hand at me. "I will not discuss it anymore. I will see you at the wedding."

Too soon, I was in the back of the limo on the way to Manderley once more. Titus gripped my leg as we turned the narrow corners of the mountain road, the wheels skating over deep puddles as rain pelted down in sheets. Beside me, Dorien braced himself against the side of the car and poured his second Scotch of the day.

"I don't know what I'll do when I see Usher again," he murmured, curling his lips around the glass.

"You won't do anything," I said. "You will smile and you will shake hands and you won't do a single thing to ruin Elena's day. Because there is life for all of us after Madame Usher, and you need to remember that."

As I said the words, I curled my fingers around Titus' body. He looked at me nervously. We would leave for New Orleans tomorrow, and neither of us knew what to expect from his parents when we got there. He'd been accepted into both the Royal Academy of Music in London and the Sibelius Academy in Finland, and I had a feeling they were going to put the pressure on him to choose soon. Honestly, I thought both programs sounded amazing. I'd kill for that opportunity. Even if Dorien could get enough movement back in his finger to play at the same level, his notoriety had probably killed any chance he had at being taken seriously by the classical scene. But Titus could still build a traditional career. Plus, being in a country far from his parents would give him a chance to shine in his own light.

But I knew that wasn't what Titus wanted. And I wasn't going to push him toward a future that made him miserable.

We turned into Manderley and my stomach sank to my knees. Despite the fucking abysmal weather and the fact the wedding had been moved up several months, the parking lot was jammed with cars. I shouldn't have been surprised. The musical world loved to gossip, and anyone who was anyone wanted an excuse to set foot inside the walls of Manderley, crawl over Heather's corpse, and see the magical Elena Nicolescu in the flesh.

Ivan met us in the foyer. I didn't even have my coat off when he grabbed my hand and dragged me toward the stairs. "Elena wants you in her room."

We wove our way through guests standing on the staircase as they sipped Champagne and admired the remaining gilded portraits. I noticed Madame had ordered some modern artworks and large floral arrangements to cover the bare spaces after Clare (or Victor) destroyed the antiques to manipulate Madame Usher to let me stay.

Why did he do that? Why did he do any of it – kill Heather, and probably Clare, too?

I debated knocking on the hollow wall and asking him, but we didn't have time.

I pushed open the twins' door. No locks – there's no point. Elena sat in front of her mirror, applying makeup. A snow-white dress swirled around her ankles, the sweetheart neckline perfectly accentuating her narrow shoulders and nipped-in waist, while giving her the barest hint of cleavage. (A pox on all flat-chested women. I have to strap my girls in like they're competing in Daytona). She shooed Ivan out and closed the door behind us.

"Help me with my hair."

She settled back into her chair, and I swept her white-blonde hair into my hands and began to twist and pin it. It felt like spun silk in my fingers, so impossibly soft and smooth. She had clips with little glittering diamonds on them, and I used these to secure it in place. It looked like her hair was held together with glittering snowflakes. She was a winter princess, a *zâne* blessing us with her magic.

She preened in the mirror, turning her shoulders to admire herself from every angle. "If you wish to tell me that I still have time to pull out of this marriage—"

"I'm here for one reason only," I swiveled her chair around so I could tuck in a loose strand at the front. "To make you the most beautiful bride Manderley has ever seen."

"And tonight, we will party." She grinned salaciously. *There's that wicked Elena I know and love.*

"I wish we had more time to be students together," I said, feeling a wistful sadness wash over me. Instead of attending wild parties and kissing boys, I spent my last year of high school working multiple jobs and worrying my mother wouldn't wake up from a coma. Music school was supposed to be my chance to let loose a little – I could work hard, but have fun, too. But Madame Usher took that away from me. Both Elena and I have had to grow up too fast. I wished we could have been young and reckless together.

"You are so silly sometimes! Married women still get to party, especially when they can finally lay hands on their own money. We will stay here at Manderley until the end of the semester," she said. "It is between me and Aroha for the Manderley Prize, so I don't think I shall have any problems, even if I take a few days to come and see you in the city."

"I'd like that," I smiled. "My mom knows all the good clubs."

"You'll look after my brother." Elena clasped my hands to her breast. She tilted her face to mine and her eyes…something flashed in them that filled me with dread. "We don't all of us get to choose for love, and if I can give him that, he might one day forgive me."

I closed my eyes, willing away the lump of emotion that swelled inside me. "You deserve more than this, Elena."

"I won't hear another word about it. Now," she dropped my hand. The dreadful thing in her eyes evaporated, leaving behind my calm, beautiful friend. She held the jeweled comb up to her hair. "I think you should fasten this just so."

A knock sounded at the door. I rose to see who it was, but the door flung open, hitting the wall behind with such force the picture frames twitched on their strings. Madame Usher stood in the hallway, her black gown gathered at the waist with a jeweled clasp. At her throat dripped a necklace of blood-red rubies. A very familiar necklace.

My necklace.

She must have rescued it before she burned all my belongings. And now she dared wear it like it was hers?

Madame Usher stared daggers at me as she tapped her finger on her wrist. "Elena, it is time to go."

Elena stood and wafted to the door, turning her nose high as she breezed past Madame. The pair exchanged a look that was as perplexing as it was loaded with meaning. Madame looked every bit the triumphant spider, but Elena…she looked at Madame as if she were a bug she was about to squash.

A shiver ran down my spine.

Whatever Madame Usher had traded for Elena's hand in marriage, Elena didn't intend to be anyone's prize. I just wish she'd confide in me what she was thinking.

I rose to follow Elena. I tried to slide past Madame Usher without touching her, without acknowledging her. She caught my wrist, twisting it back so I had no choice but to turn and gaze into those cold eyes. Her cloying perfume invaded my nostrils – the sickly sweet flowers that clung to her like a funeral wreath. Behind her head, a sad face appeared, floating against the flocked wallpaper.

Clare.

"This is not the end," Madame Usher hissed. "You may have got Dorien out of prison, but I can reach you wherever you hide, Faye de Winter. I know their secrets. I will destroy them all just to watch you suffer."

My neck prickled with the weight of her threat. It took everything I had not to turn toward the wall, where I knew her husband was sitting, peering at us through one of his peepholes.

Instead, I flung up my hand, clasped the necklace, and tore it from her neck. She winced as the chain bit into her pale skin before the clasp snapped, and it came away in my hand.

Mine, bitch.

Behind her head, Clare's ghost smiled.

"You want to be careful about threatening me. Don't think that just because you're still walking around being a hateful witch that I've forgotten you poisoned my mother. *In Cauda Venenum,* Gizella. I'm not the only one with secrets that can destroy." I yanked my wrist down, snapping her hold on me but not the spell of her harrowing gaze. I shoved my way past her and stomped down the stairs, the prickling feeling following me like Clare's ghost.

22

FAYE

As dusk fell, Radcliffe and Elena spoke their vows in front of the crumbling gazebo. Aroha and I had wrapped fairy lights and sprigs of dried herbs around the gazebo, giving the scene a fae-like quality. Elena's white dress billowed around her, and she wrapped her fur-lined cloak close to her throat to ward off the chill. She looked like an elven queen.

The ceremony was beautiful. Enchanting. And yet, as she spoke her vows in that breathy, wooden voice, I couldn't help but wish she said them to someone of her choosing, someone other than a man at least forty years her senior.

She made this choice with eyes wide open.

I thought of that superior tilt of her chin and the cold, calculating look in her eyes as she breezed past Madame Usher earlier, and a chill ran down my spine that had nothing to do with the wintery mountain air.

Afterward, we gathered in the ballroom for drinks and canapés. The crowd spilled out into the hallway, the Red Room, and the Yellow Room, talking and laughing in tight circles as they sipped on Victor's finest port. Madame had brought in caterers. The food was not as good as mine.

Elena lit up the room as she moved between the groups, bending her graceful neck to speak to every person. At her side, Master Radcliffe beamed as he showed her off to his friends and colleagues. His jewel. His prize.

We gathered in the corner, beneath the heavy drapes. Titus had twisted a safety pin through the broken clasp of my necklace so I could wear the rubies, which glittered at my throat like a warning of blood to be spilled. Hardly anyone spoke to us, but they all whispered about us. Aroha came over, her plate loaded down with mediocre food, and chatted to us.

I noticed she swayed as she stood. Her eyes were glazed over. I thought she might be on drugs again, but before I could ask her anything more, Elena and Radcliffe joined our group.

The conversation died. I watched Ivan as he worked his jaw, trying to find the words to say something to his sister. The silence stretched between them. Elena's shoulders' sagged as she realized she wouldn't get what she wanted most from him. She turned to me, and I hugged her.

"I'm happy for you," I said. I meant it.

I think I meant it.

Aroha fell against her. "You're going to be amazing," she said in a stage whisper. "Did you leave anything in the bathroom for me?"

So Elena had given Aroha cocaine. I wasn't surprised, but it made me sad. Aroha had so much talent. If she could just get over her stage fright, she'd be a star. She'd been doing so well before Madame Usher threw away her medication. I didn't blame her for falling back into her coke habit. In our world, you had to do what you could to survive. But I wished Elena hadn't indulged her.

Titus and Dorien embraced Elena next, then shook Radcliffe's hand. Judging by the way Radcliffe's chin wobbled, I suspected Titus crushed his fingers.

Ivan leaned forward and kissed Elena's cheeks, pausing long

enough to whisper something in her ear in Romanian. He gripped her waist with trembling hands, and I didn't think he'd let go, but he finally tore himself away.

Radcliffe extended a hand. Ivan stared at it for a long time before he shoved his own hand forward to shake it.

The moment their hands touched, it was as though a spark ignited. Darkness closed over Ivan's blue eyes.

He drew back his free hand and slammed it into Radcliffe's face.

23

IVAN

"I can't believe you did that." Dorien slapped me on the shoulder as we piled into the car.

I flexed my knuckles, enjoyed the sting across them from where they connected with Radcliffe's smug fucking face. Over and over I replayed the moment when my fist connected. Bone crunched. Blood spurted from his nose. His rheumy eyes froze with shock before the pain hit and his face crumpled into his hands. He staggered backward, knocking over a table piled high with food, sending petit fours and salmon puffs cascading to the floor. The guests scattered in chaos, and Elena screamed at me as she ran to his side.

"Get out of here," Madame Usher barked in my face. "You are released from my care. I do not want to see you ever again."

And just like that, I was banished from Manderley. I was free. Homeless and penniless and now, sisterless. But free.

It was probably for the best that I now watched through the back window as the dark towers of Manderley were swallowed by the mountains. If I had to hear the sounds of Elena's wedding night through the walls, I couldn't be held responsible for what I might do.

Their wedding night.

I couldn't reply to Dorien. If I opened my mouth, all that would come out was a scream.

After all these years of fighting, all these years of sacrifice, Elena had chained herself to that man and his deviant sexual proclivities. I knew on the surface it looked like she was getting everything she wanted, but no one knew her like I did.

"You know that she had to do this." Faye ran her fingers over my bruised knuckles.

"No," I rasped.

"You saw her tonight. She loves the music. And Master Radcliffe loves her. He will give her everything she's ever wanted. And I think, for her, that's perfect." Her fingers laced in mine, and she squeezed hard enough to crack the bones. Hard enough to draw me from my dark thoughts.

Harrison wound down the window between the two cars. "I promise you that I will look after Elena for as long as she's at Manderley."

The rest of the journey passed in wrathful silence. Harrison swore at the drivers as we hit New York City's impossible traffic. We finally reached Faye and Dorien's apartment, and each of us hugged Harrison for the last time. Faye held him close, and he patted her back and whispered to her, and I wondered if he saw her in some ways as the daughter he never had. He'd been the same with Clare, I remembered.

"Don't go upstairs," Dorien's eyes twinkled as he clasped Faye's wrist. "I have a surprise for you all."

"We're going to New Orleans tomorrow," Faye pointed out. "Titus and I should get an early night."

"Sleep is for the old," Dorien said. "Besides, I can see Ivan needs something more from tonight."

Dorien was right. I wouldn't sleep, not with this rage burning inside me, not with the sting of Radcliffe's blood on my knuckles.

"Should we change?" Faye touched the necklace of rubies. "I would hate for the safety pin to snap while we were at a club."

I exchanged glances with the others. The necklace was one of the many mysteries we still hadn't solved. The night of the recital, when Dorien and Heather trapped Faye in a bag far from Manderley, someone set her free and left her clothes downstairs for her, along with that necklace.

It had to be Victor, but why? He didn't tell Madame Usher he saw us in the walls. For some reason, Victor wanted to help Faye. But we didn't yet understand why.

"Don't change," Dorien kissed her neck, his teeth tugging lightly at the chain. "I want you just the way you are tonight."

"Okay, but this can't be an all-night thing. Seriously, Dorien. We leave…" Faye glanced at the screen on her phone, "in twenty-six hours."

"That's right," Dorien grinned that wild grin of his as he hailed a taxi. "We have all the time in the world."

The taxi driver let Dorien put on his playlist, and Beethoven's *5th* boomed through his speakers. I didn't think he'd want to listen to music again with his injured finger, but it was almost like he didn't care.

Instead of drawing me out of the darkness, the music pulled me deeper. If I wanted to wallow down here in blood and hate, Faye and Dorien and Titus would be right here with me.

Faye rested against my shoulder, and I wrapped my arm around her waist, holding her close. Her eyes hooded with sleep and in a few moments, she was nodding off.

I was nearly asleep myself, lost in the music and my memories, when the taxi pulled over. I looked up, expecting to see the glittering lights of a club. Instead, we were parked in front of a decrepit building with high ionic columns. It looked like a bank or government building. It also looked completely abandoned, with graffiti strewn across the stone and dead leaves gathered in the portico.

"Where are we?" Titus asked.

"I can't believe it." Faye punched Dorien in the arm. "What have you brought us here?"

I thought I understood, but Dorien didn't confirm. Instead, he threw a brick at the window. I cringed as the glass shattered, piercing the night. But no one came running, no wailing siren alerted us to an alarm. This was New York City. No one wanted to get involved with the ghosts.

Titus boosted Dorien up and he clambered in the window. A few moments later, the large carved doors swung outward, and Dorien welcomed us inside.

The building had once been grand. Plush carpet, now damp and musty, squelched under my feet. Trash stacked along the walls, and one of the crystal chandeliers in the grand entranceway had come down, breaking the marble tiles and scattering shards of glass everywhere. The other chandelier was thick with spiderwebs. The air stank of piss and rotting food, and I saw a sleeping bag and trash bags covered with rat droppings. Someone had been squatting in here.

We followed Dorien along another grand corridor, kicking up clouds of dust. He stopped in front of a door, breathing hard. Faye's fingers dug into my arm. Dorien shoved the door open and ushered us into the darkness.

"Let there be light." Dorien clicked on his phone's flashlight and shone it into the gloom.

We stood in a studio. It was all clean lines, polished floors, and acoustic battling – the kind of modern space I loved, so far removed from the stuffy antiques of Manderley. Our feet made a rich resonant sound as we walked through the space, even though the floor was coated in a thick layer of dust and the soundproof foam had been torn to shreds. A white sheet at one end of the room covered the unmistakable shape of a piano. At the other end were piles of beanbags.

I turned to Dorien. Bathed in the light of his phone, he

appeared otherworldly – a demon summoned by the *diabolus in musica*. He walked over to the piano and threw aside the ghostly sheet.

"This is the Usher School." Dorien's fingers trailed along the piano. Dust swirled around him as he left claw marks against the wood. A tug at the corner of his mouth was the only clue that he couldn't move his pinkie finger the way he wanted. "This is where I first saw Faye de Winter play."

I couldn't speak. My lungs felt full of blood.

Dorien blew the dust from the keys. His face screwed up as he perched on the edge of the filthy stool. He bent down beside the piano and swept something into his hands. A violin case, battered from years of being carried around by music students. He cradled the case like it was a child. "I decided to look it up the other day. I assumed they sold the building – it must be worth a fortune – but they've left it here to rot."

I exchanged a glance with Faye. Titus moved to the end of the room and tossed some of the beanbags aside. "The ones underneath aren't dusty and gross."

Dorien beckoned me and Faye forward with a curled finger. When I was beside him, he held out the case to me.

"Play," he commanded.

If Dorien ordered it, I would obey. I lifted the violin from its velvet lining, gripped the bow in my fingers, and played. I played snatches of songs, pieces from the old Romanian folk songs Elena and I performed on street corners for coins, movements from my favorite classical pieces, bits of Paganini I heard Faye play in her intense theatrical style that I would never be able to master. I played the Broken Muse songs that I wrote with Dorien when I realized I was fucking in love with him – songs of hope and longing.

I played the shattered pieces of my soul.

I played my story.

At some point, I became aware that I no longer played alone.

The instruments inside my head had become living, breathing music. Titus and Faye had found another violin and a cello somewhere. The cello was missing a string, but Titus made it work. Dorien sat at the piano, conjuring dark magic with his fingers, expertly improvising to avoid stretching his pinkie beyond its limited range of motion.

He hadn't sat at a piano since the fire. We'd been walking on eggshells around the question – could he play again? Would he? But tonight, he dashed those fears to dust. Dorien Valencourt might have a more limited range now, but that only made his music more powerful.

Into the night we played, bodies and instruments swirling around each other. No one spoke about needing to sleep, about Titus and Faye leaving tomorrow, or about Elena tucked into Radcliffe's bed. The room felt charged with electricity. We didn't dare stop for fear of breaking the spell.

As the sun peeked over the city, Dorien's fingers slid off the keys, and he grabbed me by the collar and dragged me over to the beanbags. Titus had piled the clean ones up together to create a kind of nest.

Dorien removed his black wool coat and laid it over the beanbags. He tugged my collar to him, forcing me against his body. His fingers wiped a trail beneath my eyes. I didn't even realize I'd been crying until I felt the wet tears touch his skin.

"You have a family," he whispered. "The best kind of family, one who doesn't mind doing depraved things to you."

Before I could reply, Dorien claimed my mouth with his just as delicate fingers yanked down my fly. Faye's hand reached inside and tugged out my dick. Her hot mouth circled the tip as Dorien's tongue dipped into my mouth. I breathed him in until he was my blood, my body, bonded to me.

Dorien took the kiss with arrogance. He knew how much I wanted it, craved it. I'd lived in cramped hotel rooms on tour with this guy. I'd seen him at his absolute worst and it never was enough. I'd never have my fill of rich asshole Dorien Valencourt. I'd never get tired of him biting my lip, staking his claim.

My fingers curled in Faye's hair as she sucked me in deep. It was because of her that Dorien was kissing me right now. She saw this thing that haunted me, and she made it real. She made all my dreams come true. I would never stop loving her and this gift she has given me, the gift she gave me every day she looked at me with eyes warm with love instead of cold with jealousy.

Titus lay back on Dorien's coat, stroking himself as he watched the three of us. His eyes met mine, and I felt our connection, too. Nothing that needing fucking out of us, but something deeper, better, that branded itself into my skin.

My brother.

My family.

Everyone I ever needed to be whole.

"I want to try something." Dorien bent toward Faye and whispered in her ear. Even in the dim light of the rising sun, I could see the heat flare in her cheeks. *It must be filthy.* But she nodded.

"Lie back, Titus," Dorien declared. This was always his role, to command, to take control. On those nights in hotel rooms with groupies he barked orders and they scrambled to obey. But we'd never done anything like this before – not with someone we loved. Not when our hearts were raw and open and bleeding.

Titus did as he was told, tossing off his clothes and leaning back on the coat with his hands folded behind his head. His skin was almost invisible against the fabric, his cock standing proud. Cornrows swept across the planes of his chest. Dorien whispered to Faye, who slid up between Titus' legs so that her back was pressed against his chest. Dorien tapped me on the shoulder.

"You're next."

Faye spread her legs wide, and I could see her cunt glistening in the low light. *She wants this. She loves us. She trusts us.* Titus crept a hand around her middle, pressing a finger to her clit and circling, slowly, slowly, as we three watched her wriggle and squirm. Titus clenched his teeth as she ground her ass against him.

"Ivan, get down here now before she makes me come early," Titus gritted out.

Dorien's fingers circled my wrist, his grip tight, holding me in place. A whimper of excitement escaped my throat.

"Will you let this be mine tonight?" Dorien palmed my ass. His words bit against my earlobe. My stomach soared as the force of his words hit me.

"I was always yours," I answered.

It was the truth.

I belonged to Dorien Valencourt the day he tried to save me and Elena. And I'd belonged to Faye since the day she saved me from Dorien. I needed them both like I needed the air I breathed.

Dorien removed my clothes, his fingers unbuttoning my shirt. He chuckled as my stomach jerked against his touch. He slid my feet free from my shoes, leaving my socks on as he rolled my pants over my hips, trailing fire with his evil fingers until I was so hard from being denied him I wanted to burst.

I knelt down in front of Faye. She stared up at me with heavy-lidded eyes, her raven hair spilling over her shoulders. "You're so beautiful," she whispered, touching my cheek, so soft, too soft for what Dorien wanted us to do.

I touched her skin, danced my fingers over her, committing her curves and dips and perfect rounded breasts to memory. I placed my hands on either side of her, touching Titus' warm skin.

"Fuck her," Dorien whispered roughly. "I want to watch your beautiful cock move inside her."

I must obey.

I slid up inside Faye, gasping at the wet heat of her. *So warm and soft and slick.* Faye tilted her chin up at me, her wide eyes filling me with love. I drew back, giving myself a moment to catch my breath, to collect myself. I couldn't come now. That would ruin Dorien's plan, and I very much did not want to do that.

Dorien's fingers grabbed the skin of my ass. He shoved against me, using his momentum to manage my speed, my strokes. It was as if we were only fucking because he commanded it, he controlled it, and I never thought I'd get off on that, but I was struggling to breathe and my balls were tightening up into my body.

"Now, Titus…" Dorien's voice was right beside my ear, hot and rasping as he leaned over me. The silk of his shirt brushed my skin. "You fit yourself inside her too."

He handed Titus a bottle of lube. While I thrust slowly into Faye, lifting her hips high for him, he got himself into position. I felt the pressure of his finger inside her ass through the thin wall of her, and I had to stop thrusting for a moment because it felt too good. When Titus pushed his cock inside Faye, inch by inch, her eyes rolled back in her head.

"It's…" Her eyelids fluttered closed. "It's intense."

Titus met my eyes over Faye's shoulder, and I could tell he was struggling with the intensity of it, too. I know I was with the two of us inside her like this. I drew out, long and slow, as he thrust in deeper. It took us a few strokes, but we fell into an easy rhythm. We were musicians, after all.

Faye leaned back against Titus as we continued to thrust together. Her nails dug into my arms and her pretty, perfect lips fell open as she reveled in the sensation of it. I kissed her neck, nibbled at her lower lip until I smudged red lipstick across her skin.

Dorien's lips found my neck, biting down until I sucked in a breath through my teeth. Warm fingers trailed along the bare skin of my back, and a moment later Dorien's hot breath kissed my ear. "Are you ready for me?"

I swallowed, my body rigid.

"I want you to say it, Ivan." Dorien curled his fingers around my neck, not squeezing, not hurting, just promising that he *could*, if he wanted to. He could make me hurt so fucking good.

"Yes."

"Good." Dorien chuckled. I heard the squirt of the lube, and then Dorien had me in his grip, one hand bracing my shoulder as I thrust into Faye, the other stroking over my skin, pressing at my hole. His slippery fingers opening me for him.

I can't this is too much I need to catch my breath I need to fucking stop I need...

"Just a second—" I started to say, but he pushed a finger inside me and there were no more seconds left. I was here and Dorien had his finger in me and Faye scraped her teeth along my jaw and I thought I might break apart from the joy of it.

Dorien kissed Faye over my shoulder, his tongue darting between her waiting lips. "Hey, Sprite." He grinned. "How does it feel to have all three Broken Muses at your mercy?"

In my wrecked mind, it seemed like an odd thing to say, because she was sandwiched between us. But it was also the truest thing Dorien had ever said. Everything we had in this moment that was good and perfect came to us because of Faye. Dorien might be making commands, but she was in total control.

"Like coming home," she whispered, and it was true. It was so true. This, tonight, is what it felt like to have a home.

I'm exactly where I belong.

Dorien pushed a second finger in beside the first, pumping them inside me until I no longer gritted my teeth, until I arched my back against him and begged for more.

He removed his fingers and I cried out to be bereft of him. But for only a moment. Then the head of his cock was against my entrance and my toes curled and he angled my hips back and thrust inside.

At first, it was like a kiss, but then the kiss grew into painful pressure as he glided deeper, pushing his crown past the tight rim. And then the pressure became a wild piercing – an invasion so deep and intense and satisfying that I forgot to breathe. I couldn't think.

Dorien drew back his hips, giving me a moment of respite as my cock jerked inside Faye, a moment to breathe, to sense, to be. He bit down on my neck.

"Don't you worry," he whispered against my ear. "I will never forget you."

He thrust inside me, hard and fast and needy, and I saw stars. The sunrise collapsed in on itself, and the darkness crept in from the edges, punctured by bright pinpricks of violent light.

I'm lost.

Dorien wasn't gentle. He didn't give me another moment to catch my breath. Inside me, he was a man possessed. He shoved me forward so my chest pressed against Faye, so his body bore down on all three of us, controlling every stroke, just the way he liked it.

He grunted, moving against me with animal cruelty, lost completely to his possession. With each thrust, he pushed me into Faye, who sank deeper onto Titus, and so it was as if we were no longer four bodies but one writhing mess of humanity sating our need with each other.

It felt like a line of fire stretching directly from her through to him – a chain of bloody hearts and broken promises that bound us together.

"I love you," Dorien whispered. "You're mine now, all of you. And I love you."

It was like a hot poke slicing through my chest. Dorien's teeth dug into my neck. My balls squeezed up inside my body. And then…I let go. I released with short, violent strokes into Faye as her walls clenched around me. And it was like a rolling wave that kept crashing, an ocean of pleasure that would never end.

And I didn't want it to, because who wouldn't want to have a family like this?

24

DORIEN

I extracted my arm from beneath Faye and stood up. For a while I sat at the piano, tinkering with the keys, feeling the tug in my burned finger where the muscles wouldn't quite do what they used to. The ghost of a melody plagued me, something beautiful to capture the emotion of tonight. But I didn't want to play it imperfectly into the world and wake them all up. I needed to let the sound linger, to allow the new song to take shape.

The way Ivan looked at me sometimes, I knew he thinks I plan these things. That I have some devious scheme always in my head he longed to be let in on. But I didn't know this would happen tonight. I didn't know I'd wake up the happiest spoiled rich prince that ever lived.

Me and Ivan; that'd been on the cards for years. I would've jumped that tight ass of his sooner if only he'd given the slightest indication that was what he wanted. But he was too good at hiding and I was too skilled at only seeing what I wanted to see.

Before, the two of us together would have complicated every-thing. It might've been the end of Broken Muse. But here, in the rubble of our lowest point, when our future looked so dark and uncertain, it felt like the beginning of something beautiful.

I left the three of them curled in a pile on the beanbags. I clicked on my flashlight app and set about exploring the derelict building.

It occurred to me that it was odd the Ushers never sold the school. I think of the illegal money entering their accounts while the school was open, and how it reversed then they closed the school. If all this was about money, then surely Madame Usher could have sold the school and got on with her life. She wouldn't have needed Broken Muse or Faye for whatever insane thing she had planned.

I knew there had to be something inside this building she couldn't let anyone find out.

Which was why I took everyone here. Well, that and I wanted to fuck in this place where Faye and I began our story. But mostly it was for the mystery.

I moved down the hallway, peering into the old studios and practice rooms with their ghostly furniture covered in sheets, the costume wing and the administration office with its shelves of dusty files. I kicked an old scorebook, watching as the pages scattered across the floor.

My feet dragged me to the staircase. Upstairs were more practice rooms and a larger hall we used for recitals. Downstairs was a basement. I hesitated on the first step before my feet dragged me downward, my shoulders pushed forward as though some invisible hand shoved me from behind.

In the basement was a giant old furnace that heated the building. When it was on in winter it made the whole school smell like boiled pork. All us kids were too afraid to go down there because this beast of a thing looked like it ate children. Madame Usher encouraged our stories, barking at students who flubbed their notes that they were so useless at music that she could throw them in the furnace, and then at least they'd be good at keeping the rest of us warm.

The old fear clawed at my stomach as I made my way down the narrow steps into the furnace room. But after everything I saw at my parents' house, a creepy basement in an abandoned music school couldn't keep me away.

I shone my flashlight around the basement. It was filled with weird-ass stuff – broken chairs and instruments, file boxes, weird shapeless lumps I couldn't identify. I felt that prickling in my neck I felt at Manderley – the sense of being watched.

Something's down here. I'm close. I know it.

I knew behind the furnace was a second room with a dirt floor, where coal bags were stored. I went to move around the furnace, but my hand was compelled to grab the rusted handle. I felt like I was being directed by some external force to open the door and shine my flashlight inside.

What's that?

I picked up the object nestled in the ashes, bringing it into the beam of my flashlight. From its blackened color, I knew someone had tried to burn it. It was round and convex, uneven, with a jagged edge where it had been broken—

No.

I cried out as I realized what I was holding.

It was the top of a human skull.

25

DORIEN

"Fuck."

I dropped the skull back in the furnace. My instinct was to run as far away as fucking possible, but I was here because we needed answers. And a skull in the fucking furnace was a good start.

I swallowed back the bile and shone my flashlight into the furnace, using an old wrench to push around the thick layer of ash and coal dust crusted to the bottom. There were other shapes that looked like bone fragments and…yup, those were teeth.

As Sprite would say, sound the fucktrumpets.

I steadied myself against the belly of the beast as I hauled myself to my feet. My legs trembled as I walked around the other side of it, locating the wooden door to the second room. The door was padlocked, but the wood was so rotten that a couple of swift kicks knocked the lock from the frame. The door swung inward, and I swung my phone in front of me to peer inside.

What I saw made blood rush to my head.

The dirt floor had been disturbed – it was no longer flat and compacted but rucked up into random piles and littered with debris. As I scraped my boot through the dirt, I kicked up an object. A leather shoe with elaborate broguing around the toes. A men's shoe.

With the bone of a foot sticking out.

I had to hold my hand over my mouth to hold back my gagging as I swept the room with my flashlight. I recognized more shapes poking from the dirt – bones, skulls, a neat row of teeth. A few metal scraps of cufflinks and belt buckles. The bits of bodies that wouldn't completely burn away.

Bodies.

The entire room had been filled with bodies.

Yup. That's not good.

It looked like some attempt had initially been made to bury them in the dirt, but then they were just shoved into the room. There were dark patches in the dirt around a pile in the corner, but I would not go any further because I could hear the scritching of rats and I wasn't fucking stupid.

My foot caught on something. I jerked it away, kicking an object out of the loose dirt. It glinted in the light. That same eerie presence that shoved me down the stairs buzzed around me, urging me to pick it up.

I bent down. It turned out what I kicked was a skeletal hand, still held together in places with the frayed fabric of a shirt and… other stuff I didn't want to consider. I had the wrench in my hand and I used it to knock the shiny object free. It toppled into my hand, and I rubbed off the dirt to reveal its shape.

It was a silver cufflink. It depicted a treble clef wrapped around a violin, with the bow crossed over to make it look like a coat of arms.

I remembered Faye working with a fancy jewelry designer in Soho on this design. I remembered her showing me the sketches while we practiced sonatas together for our recital. She and Marguerite had the cufflinks made as a surprise gift for Donovan after he won the prestigious Vienna Award. Faye wanted to give him something unique, something he couldn't find in any store so he would remember her when he was overseas. According to the papers, Donovan wore them to every performance.

He'd been wearing them the day he disappeared.

Holy shit. This belonged to Donovan de Winter.

26

DORIEN

*F*aye's *father is buried here.*

I staggered out of the corpse room, slamming the door behind me as I fought to keep my stomach contents inside my body.

Donovan de Winter has been here all along.

This is why the Ushers never sold this building. They couldn't risk another owner discovering what they'd been up to down in the basement. But who are these other bodies they burned down there? How long has this been going on?

Were these people dying down here while we learned scales in the school above?

I remembered Madame's lips curling back as she threatened a student with being burned in the furnace. Was the music school heated with burning flesh?

I couldn't stomach any more of it. My skin burned where it touched the cufflink. I didn't want to deliver this news to Faye, but I had to. I pounded up the stairs. *I need to get the others. We have to leave. If Madame Usher figures out we found this, she'll—*

I slammed into something warm and hard.

Ivan cried out as he lost his balance and crashed to the floor.

He bit his lip as he looked up at me. It was so delicious I almost fell on him there and then. But I couldn't be distracted by hot little Romanians. Instead, I reached down and hauled him to his feet.

"What were you running from?" Ivan tried to peer around me into the gloomy corridor.

"You won't believe it. There are a bunch of bodies in the basement. Burned bodies and bits of bodies. Someone was using the building's furnace to dispose of people."

Ivan frowned. "Be serious."

"I *said* you wouldn't believe it. And it gets worse." I opened my hand to show him the cufflink. "This belonged to Faye's father. It's a one-of-a-kind piece. Donovan de Winter's body is down there."

Ivan studied my face, his teeth biting into his lip again. This time I couldn't bear it. I leaned forward and kissed him. He yelped in surprise, but responded by opening his lips to grant me access. I

"You really did see bodies?"

I nodded. "We found the reason the Ushers never sold this building. It probably explains why Victor had to disappear, too. We know the Ushers were taking money from organized crime. Perhaps this is why. They were using the furnace to dispose of anyone the gangs needed to get rid of. My guess is Donovan found out, and…" I couldn't finish the sentence.

"What will we tell Faye?" He glanced back toward the studio, where I could hear Faye and Titus talking together.

"The truth. She deserves to know after all this time. I just hope she doesn't cancel her trip with Titus. Donovan and Madame Usher have already taken enough from her. Speaking of which." I clamped a hand on his shoulder, dragging him close so his nose touched mine. "Elena leaves with Radcliffe for Europe in a couple of weeks. She now has access to your money. All of us are free of Manderley now. Whatever Madame Usher and her creepy stalker husband tried to pull off, she failed." I stepped closer, kicking my boots against his to push his feet wide so I could slide right up against his body. So I could feel how hard he was for me again. I tugged his lip between my teeth. "You're free, Ivan."

"I have nowhere to go," he choked out.

I shrugged. "Come and stay with me and Jacob."

"You just got your brother back. I can't intrude—"

"You're my brother, too." There was no mistaking the command in my voice. Ivan's eyes fluttered shut, his chest heaving as he let the words sink in. "Stay with me. I'll look after you while Faye and Titus are in the Big Easy. We'll make this work. We'll figure out your future together, okay?"

He flinched as I thrust out my hand toward him. *I've gone too far. It's too much. I've frightened him away.* But then he surprised me by surging forward and clasping my fingers in his. "I would love to."

"Good. Now," I tugged him away from the basement. "Let's call Rochester and get these skeletons dug up. I want to know what secrets the Ushers have been hiding down there."

27

FAYE

It was hard to say goodbye to Dorien and Ivan with everything going on. But they needed some space from us too, to figure out what the thing between them meant. So as a sleepy-eyed Dorien led Rochester and a forensics team into the Usher School basement, I climbed into a taxi with Titus and sped to the airport.

All through our flight, I clasped that tiny silver cufflink. I kept my earbuds in my ears and hoped Titus didn't notice I played my father's music over and over, as if I might find some answers in his intricate compositions.

My dad is dead.

All these years...I always knew it was a possibility. Mom certainly believed he'd fallen foul of the crime family he'd been in debt to. It was strange how calm I felt, how much I realized that knowing the truth about him didn't make any difference. He still left us. His death was his final betrayal.

I begged Mom to get these cufflinks made for his Vienna Award ceremony. She spent money we couldn't spare so I could work with a jeweler to create the unique design. I knew Dad liked everything in his life to be unique, special, glittery. He beamed when I presented them to him, counting the diamonds inlaid in the tiny violin. He wore those cufflinks at every performance and proudly told reporters that his daughter had them made for him, and they gave him good luck.

He loved those cufflinks more than he loved me.

I refused to cry for him. I'd already cried so much.

Delphine traveled with us. Amos had already gone south a couple of weeks ago to prepare for their winter tour. As we wheeled her heavy suitcases through the airport, she kept up a steady stream of friendly conversation about musicians and touring and some of the cities they would visit. Not once did a word about Manderley Academy or the electric guitar leave her lips.

Titus' parents lived in a modest house in the Garden District, but they gave us the keys to a little place they owned in the French Quarter. Titus referred to it as the 'shotgun' house. It was long and narrow – the front door opened directly into the living room. Behind that was a bedroom and ensuite, and a kitchen right down the back. Titus said they called this style shotgun houses because every room left off another, so if you shot a bullet through the front door it would pass through every doorway and out the back without damaging anything.

It was past 11PM when we got in, so Delphine went back to her place, and Titus and I went straight to bed. It felt weird to be so far from New York and everything going on there. So far from my dad's body and the case mounting against Madame Usher. The sounds of the city were so different here.

Titus fell into a deep sleep, but I tossed and turned and struggled to quiet my whirring brain. Dorien had texted to say Rochester had confirmed DNA matches for some of the remains recovered from the Usher School – three notorious crime lords who disappeared after falling foul of the Triumvirate. It was looking more and more like the Ushers were paid by the gangs to dispose of their dead. Nothing on my father yet, but Donovan de

Winter didn't have a criminal record so he wasn't in their database, and I wasn't in a hurry to get back and give them a sample. I had the cufflink. I knew what I needed to know.

My father was dead.

They had a team of forensic accountants working on the Menabilly Holdings accounts, trying to get the dirt they needed to build a case. I was positive if they followed the money they'd be able to connect Madame Usher not just to the Triumvirate, but also to the Temple of Earthly Truths. I hoped we'd get justice for everyone who'd been wronged by the Ushers.

All those people buried under the music school. Who were they? What had they done to die in such a brutal way? I shuddered to think how close we came to joining them.

Eventually, I fell into a restless sleep. When I woke, sunlight streamed through the windows, and even though my clock said it was barely 7AM, the city already teamed with life. Down the street, someone was playing the saxophone. I rubbed my eyes. *It's no good. Sleep won't happen. New Orleans is already working her spell on me.*

I extricated myself from Titus' slumbering embrace and took my violin out onto the front porch, which was done up with bright, gingerbread trim. The saxophonist was across the street and a few doors down. I raised my bow to my chin and answered him with a jaunty reel. We dueled back and forth for a bit, pulling funny faces at each other, until—

"Hello, Faye."

I jumped out of my skin, nearly dropping my bow. "Delphine?" I whirled around to see Faye's mother sitting on the steps watching me. "I didn't know you were there."

"You were lost in the music." She smiled. "I understand. Would you like some breakfast?"

I nodded and followed her inside. Too late I realized we had to walk through our bedroom to get to the kitchen. My face burned as I took in my clothing strewn everywhere and our rumpled bed with Titus snoring away, but Delphine didn't say a word about it. She headed straight to the stove and started the coffee machine.

"I brought beignets." She pointed to the bakery bag she'd placed on the table, which emitted a delicious scent. "A New Orleans special."

I pulled out one of the delicious squares of dough. Sugar dusted my chin as I took a big bite. Delphine set a steaming cup of coffee in front of me and grabbed her own beignet from the stack, and we chewed happily.

"These were Titus' favorites growing up." She finished the beignet without leaving a single granule of sugar on her skin.

How does she do that? I look like I'd been dipped in sugar.

"I can see why. These are amazing."

She gazed out the window. "Tell me about your life, Faye. Titus says you grew up with your mother."

Luckily for Delphine, one of my favorite topics was Marguerite de Winter. I told her about my mother growing up as an immigrant in New York City, meeting Donovan, and building her PR firm from the ground up. I told her about how my mother made our life fun, our house full of great food and loud music, and how she hadn't let her current medical setbacks stop her from living her life on her own terms. Delphine nodded and seemed genuinely interested. I thought they would get along like old friends if they ever met.

As Delphine made us second cups of coffee, I found myself talking about Dad. The corner of the cufflink jabbed my thigh through my pocket. I told her how I did everything I could to make him *see* me. I wanted to please him so badly. On the surface he made all the right noises – he told every reporter who interviewed him about his brilliant daughter. When we saw his performances, he'd invite me on stage at the end to present him with flowers. He encouraged me in my lessons and insisted I had only the best tutors, even though we couldn't afford them.

But he only saw me as an extension of himself. When he was on tour, he would forget to call us. He never played a game with me or asked me how I was. He used me to charm influential people and score points in a game with rules I never understood. He rarely came to my recitals, and if he did, he'd bring along a horde of reporters to write about what a great father he was. "He was so different than you and Amos," I said. "My father was a narcissist. He charmed people into loving him, then killed that love with neglect. Titus is lucky to have parents who care so much about him."

"I met your father many times," she said, skillfully avoiding any talk about Titus. "We moved in the same circles. I remember how charming he could be. I understand if you don't want to talk about him. I know how grief can make us all mute. But if you ever have questions, if you want to know him as his peers knew him, I will answer them for you."

And suddenly, I did want to know very much. I reached into my pocket and fingered the cufflink. "Tell me about him. Please."

"He was a magnet. The moment he walked into a room, heads swirled." She sighed. "But there was always something that didn't add up. He lived a flashy life, the life of a rockstar – not a classical violinist. He never revealed where he got the money to fund his lifestyle, but people speculated, of course. There were wild stories about a mystery inheritance, an affair with a wealthy patron, a link to organized crime. Donovan encouraged the gossip to fuel his image in the press, a little like your friend Dorien does now. He drove up to events in fancy cars, he wore designer suits, and his instruments... the last time I saw him play, he had a Becker. That instrument alone cost more than Amos and I make in a year."

My fingers closed around the handle of my violin case. She must not have seen the instrument I played. I knew the Becker was valuable, but Delphine reminded me that it was probably paid for with dirty money. The violin in my hands probably sent my dad's body into that basement.

"I wondered if I could ask you something," I said. "It's about Manderley Academy. Titus said you encouraged him to choose that school. I guess I wondered why? Surely it's not as prestigious as some of his other options."

"If I'd known that place was so…haunted, I never would have let him go," she sighed. "It was very strange. We were so excited when he got into the Royal Academy of Music. But then Madame Usher and Master Radcliffe showed up at our door. Radcliffe's friends in Vienna wanted us to headline their next season, but as Manderley was sponsoring, it could only happen if we were connected to the school. I didn't want to influence Titus' decision. It felt too much like accepting a bribe. But Amos said we had to take every diamond offered to us, because the world would give us only scraps. And Titus wanted to be where his friends were, so we thought it was a win for everyone. Titus thinks his father doesn't see him, and he might be right. But not because Amos sees Micah. I think he sees his own failing—oh, son, you're awake?"

I turned to see Titus in the doorway. I wondered how much he'd overheard. He frowned at the empty bag on the table. "Did you eat all the beignets?"

I pretended to hide the last two beignets behind my coffee cup. "Sorry, big boy. You snooze, you lose."

He poked his tongue out at me as he swiped the donut on his way across the room to kiss his mother on the forehead and make his own coffee.

Delphine rose, leaning in to kiss Titus on the cheek. "I'll leave the two of you to explore the city. Don't forget the party tonight, darling."

Titus pulled back, so she kissed the air instead. His body went rigid. "How could I forget?"

The screen door banged as Delphine left.

"Party?" I asked.

Titus frowned as he stuffed the beignet into his mouth. "Ifff-duffmmmmmmeretssssssshooooooffff."

"Pardon?"

He swallowed. "It's just my parents trying to show us off. All their friends are going to be there. Everyone will take turns around the piano."

"It sounds like fun."

He slammed his coffee cup down with such force he broke the handle off. "They want me to play. Well, they want *us* to play."

"Nice of you to tell me," I said lightly. I knew this wasn't about me.

"This is Amos putting his foot down. He's worried about the media attention around you and Dorien and Manderley. He doesn't want our family associated with any of that *unpleasantness*. So he wants us to show up and be polite and civil and charming, and play polite, civil, charming music so everyone will congratulate him on having one almost perfect son left."

"Do you think that's fair?"

"It's the truth," he growled.

I took his hand and wrapped it around my waist. With my free hand, I reached for the last beignet and held it against his lips. "Your parents made their names by defying what the world expected of them. I know they're afraid because of what they've lost, but I think if they experienced your music for themselves, and the effect it has on people, they won't stand in your way."

Titus swallowed. "That's your mother, Faye. Not mine. They just want me to do what they say and not rock the boat for them."

"I think we should give them a chance." I twirled one of his cornrows between my fingers. "What do you say? Let's bring them a real party."

28

FAYE

We spent the day exploring the city. I loved New Orleans. I especially loved being there with Titus. It reminded me of touring Prague and Romania with Ivan – it was one thing to travel and be new to a place, but to see it through the eyes of someone who had lived there, loved there, grown and changed there made it completely magical. It gave every encounter hidden meaning and depth. On every corner, Titus battled against memories – some happy, some upsetting. All of them part of who he was.

We went shopping in the French Quarter, and I purchased a fuchsia evening dress with layers of tulle and a plunging neckline. It turns out, the woman at the boutique had a matching fuchsia shirt that fit Titus perfectly. Never in a million years would I have expected to love Titus in a pink shirt, but he looked so fucking hot with his narrow waist and braids spilling over his broad shoulders that it made my knees weak. I think it made him feel bold, and he needed every ounce of boldness tonight.

By the time we arrived at the Thibodeaux' house, the party was already in full swing. Lively jazz music bled out into the street as couples gathered on the narrow balcony, laughing and toasting. Someone howled at the rising moon. It was that kind of night.

Delphine greeted us the moment we stepped inside and thrust glasses into our hands. I lifted mine to my lips and sniffed the strong cocktail. "Sazerac," Delphine explained. "Rye whiskey, bitters, sugar, and a dash of absinthe. The official drink of New Orleans. Drink up. Son, I've made you a non-alcoholic punch."

"Careful," Titus whispered as I took a generous mouthful. "I need you with a clear head and perfect form for our performance."

"One thing you should know about me by now is that I can play perfectly anywhere, with any kind of alcohol in my stomach." I grinned, but he wasn't wrong. The Sazerac had a mighty kick.

Titus gripped my hand so hard I had to grit my teeth against the pain. Our instrument cases banged against our legs as we entered a beautiful open-plan living space decorated with Delphine's lush modern style. There was hardly space to move. The place was wall-to-wall people dressed in glittering evening wear and tables laden with amazing-smelling food, but we squeezed through the crowd.

Amos sat at the piano, his fingers flying over the keys as a gorgeous woman with dark ringlets and the voice of an angel sung Nina Simone's 'Sinnerman' with such throaty sexiness that I swear Nina herself was in the room with us. Amos pounded the keys with aplomb, enjoying the attention of his fans.

When he finished, his gaze fell on us. He regarded his son as if he was wary, as if Titus was a wild animal sent to Amos for taming, and the maestro didn't quite know what to do with him.

"Titus, Faye, come meet our friends." He took my hand and sat me on the bench beside him, introducing me to a sea of people whose names I had no hope of remembering. Not-Nina leaned forward as Amos repeated my name.

"Donovan de Winter's daughter?" asked Not-Nina.

"She is a maestra in her own right," Amos declared. And even though I was angry at him for the way he treated Titus, I warmed to him a hell of a lot in that moment for not letting them lump me in with my father. "Perhaps we can twist her arm to play something for us? I've heard she's a particular fan of Paganini."

"Consider my arm twisted." I set down my case and drew out the instrument. Delphine's eyes widened as she noticed the Becker, and I knew she recognized it as the instrument my father played at the end of his life. But she didn't say anything, and I was grateful for that. Amos' eyes trained on me as I tuned. I launched into one of Paganini's tricky caprices.

Performing Paganini was a chance for a violinist to show off their skills, provided you could nail the sometimes-impossible fingering. Paganini was famous for his demonic performances, and I played into that, letting my body move a little as I performed, screwing up my features and pointing my bow to tell a story.

When I finished, there was a beat of silence in the room. Then Amos erupted with applause and his friends followed suit. Their clapping rumbled like thunder in my chest. There's a tradition in Classical spaces of not clapping until the very end of the evening's performances so as not to interrupt the enjoyment of the music for others, and I had to admit sometimes I thought it was dumb. Feedback from the audience was addictive. No wonder Titus loved heavy metal – how cool would it be to have fans screaming your name?

Speaking of Titus…I fixed my eyes on Amos. "Titus and I would like to play something for you."

"Of course." He waved his arms, pushing his friends back to make enough space for Titus to bring in his cello case. I nodded to Titus. He looked over at his parents, and for a moment he wavered. His shoulders slumped, and I felt sure he was going to back out.

I stepped forward and touched his arm. That seemed to be enough. He squared his shoulders and unclipped the case.

Nestled inside was his St. Moritz SG.

Tony Iommi's guitar, with its evil black finish and body curling into spikes like devil horns.

Amos' cheeks puffed out. Delphine let out an audible gasp. Now the room fell truly silent. Titus lifted out the instrument and plugged it into the portable amp the jazz musicians were using. Amos' breath rasped, his chest heaving. I expected him to yell, to rage, but he remained frozen in place.

Titus wouldn't look at his parents as he tuned and tested the effects pedals. But I watched them. I watched Amos' jaw working with anger and Delphine hiding her face in her husband's shoulder. The rest of the room buzzed with nervous energy. The guests leaned forward, drinks clutching in whitened knuckles, waiting to see what we came out with.

I raised my bow and nodded to Titus. He bent over his guitar, letting his braids fall over his face. A curtain to protect himself from his parents' ire. And he struck the first sinister riff.

After four bars I came in with the melody. It was a cover of Black Sabbath's 'War Pigs' we arranged for guitar and violin. We chose this song deliberately because there was no mistaking what it was. I knew many in the room would recognize it. I knew Amos and Delphine recognized it, because it had been one of Micah's favorites.

Titus' fingers tore at the strings, his whole body swinging with the riff as he found his groove in the music. We traded riffs, dueling each other for supremacy within the music. His braids flew wild around his head, and that guitar *purred* in his hands.

By the time we finished the song with a pulsing, pounding riff, we were sweaty and smiling. Whatever happened now, we had a blast, and Titus had never played better.

Titus raised his chin, his gaze to heaven as sweat dripped from his brow. Tears pooled in the corners of his eyes, and I knew he felt his brother in every riff. As the final note rang through the amp, the silence in the room was more deafening than ever.

Titus slowly lowered his face. He stepped toward me. His hand shook as he cupped my cheek, but the lips that brushed mine burned with fire. *We did it. We—*

SLAM.

We both jumped as Amos dropped the lid on the piano. Titus bit my lip, and I sucked the blood that spurted from the cut. He turned to his parents.

Tears rolled down Delphine's cheeks, speckling the front of her silk gown. She didn't hide her face but wept silently and openly, her grief terrifying in its rawness. I longed to pull her into my arms, but I didn't know what she'd do if I touched her right now.

Amos' grief had turned him hard as granite, though the blood the burned in his veins was so hot with rage that it cracked the stone of his skin, seeping out of every pore. He leered at his son, his face monstrous. Women whimpered and shied away.

Amos took a step toward his son, his hands raised. I stepped in front of Titus, certain Amos was about to slide his hands around his throat. Instead, he let out an inhuman howl, spun on his heel, and shoved his way through the crowd. A moment later, a door slammed deep within the house.

Not-Nina began to shoo the guests from the room. "Go. This party is over. Get out of here."

Titus' chest heaved. Delphine leaned over the piano, seeking its strength to hold her upright. Her tears splashed on the keys.

Only when the room was empty, when the only sound was the chime of a clock and the slam of car doors and scandalized voices on the street outside, did Delphine rise up to her full height. She smoothed down her dress and glided toward her son. Titus shrunk from her as she raised a trembling hand, fearing the physical and emotional blow that would surely follow.

Delphine lowered her hand, placing it on his shoulder. Her fingers curled around him, and she pulled him close. Their arms went around each other in the same moment, and they collapsed like they'd come home at last. Titus buried his face in her shoulder.

"His spirit lives in you, son," she sobbed.

Titus' shoulders shook as he held her, as together they did what they should have done years ago and honored Micah with their tears, their togetherness, their music.

Delphine leaned back, her lips tugging into a wobbly smile as she stroked his cheeks. "I'm sorry, my beautiful boy. I'm so so sorry I didn't see you through my grief."

I reached up to touch my own cheek, and found it wet with tears. Titus needed this moment. As much as he tried to do his own thing and not care what anyone thought of him, I knew that he would never be happy unless they were happy, too. That was part of what I loved about him – that he wanted to honor the legacy they built for him.

"What about Dad?" Titus sniffed.

Delphine's shoulders tightened. "I won't do him the disservice of speaking for him. Your father loves you, Titus. You know he does. But this isn't the life he sees for you."

"But shouldn't he be happy Titus has chosen his own path?" I asked. "That's what you both did."

My voice cut through the poison air, breaking her gaze with her son. Delphine's eyes fluttered shut. She'd fallen into a memory that gouged out her heart. "We wanted Titus to have what we didn't have. That was the gift we wished to give both our sons – the gift of a world where they didn't have to work twice as hard just to get a seat at the table."

He kissed her forehead. "I know, Mom."

"I don't think you do, son. We know we've failed you in so many ways. You cannot imagine the grief of a parent who outlives their child. I've learned to harden my skin and resist my tears, but when something joyful happens, no matter how small – the roses in the garden bloom after a long winter, I hear a song that makes my heart – it's as if the levees open and it all comes crashing down again. And you, my beautiful, bright son, you are my greatest joy." She caressed his cheek, and I thought my heart might burst from my chest for how much Titus needed to hear her words. "We never meant to force you into Micah's shadow. So much that was good in him lives in you, and I'd be heartsick to think I snuffed that out because I was afraid and ashamed. We're never guaranteed a happy ending in this life, but a happy beginning and a happy middle – those are in my power to give you. Please, son, play your music if it makes your heart light and free. Micah would be so, so proud of you."

"Thanks, Mom. I—" Titus' words caught in his throat. He stared at the door through which Amos had disappeared. "Tell Dad…tell him I'm sorry we ruined his party. Tell him that if he wants to talk to me, he knows where to find me. I won't be going back to school to study the cello. I hope one day he'll understand."

With that, Titus released his mother's embrace. He slipped my hand into his arm, and with his ax slung over his shoulder, we stepped over the empty cello case and strode from the house, out into the night.

29

TITUS

"Here." Faye slapped an amber drink in front of me, along with a basket of po boys. "I'll drink it if you change your mind."

I wrapped my fingers around the glass. It was 10AM the day after my parents' party. I'd barely slept thinking about my father's face as he stormed out and my mother's heartfelt apology. Faye finally got sick of me moping and thinking, and dragged me to this diner, where I'd surprised myself by ordering a Sazerac.

I didn't drink because I knew alcohol played a part in Micah's accident. I wanted my mind and wits about me so I could save the people I loved from their own drunken stupidity. And my sobriety had definitely come in handy on the road, especially with Dorien being...well, *Dorien*. But I realized that, like so many things I did, I chose not to drink because I thought it would please my parents. But after last night, I felt as though that weight had come off my shoulders. My mother loved me for who I was, and my father...well, I would never please him, no matter what I did. It was time to stop living for them and start figuring out who I was.

I raised the Sazerac to my lips with a trembling hand. My lips still burned from my mother's kiss. Her tears left pricks of fire against my skin. I felt strange all over as I sipped – fuzzy and heavy with grief, but light at the same time.

Micah.

I *felt* him with me when I played last night – his breath on my shoulders, his infectious energy making my fingers dance along the fretboard. His smile bright in every riff. I could never have my brother back, but I could keep his memory alive through music. And now my mother could see that.

I just wish Dad could understand...

"I smelled something," Faye leaned back in her chair, dangling her own glass from her fingers. "When we played that song, I could smell coffee and sweet cherries, very rich and dark. I thought it might be someone's perfume, but it seemed to be everywhere, all around us."

My back stiffened. Faye had told me about this strange ability of hers, about the scents she smelt when she played sometimes – scents that were intrinsically linked to her own memories, but this… "That's Micah's aftershave."

His old girlfriend gave Micah that scent – she loved him drenched in the stuff, so she brought him a lifetime supply. Everything he owned smelled like it. I had some old concert t-shirts of his I stole from his drawer before my parents got rid of his things, and I wore them for months without washing them because they were soaked in coffee and cherries.

Faye picked up one of the po boys and took a huge bite. Juices dribbled down her chin. "I hope you're not regretting what we did. This is progress, Titus."

I slid across the booth and wrapped my arms around her, pulling her close. This was why I loved her, because she was a perfect mirror of me. She made me brave and bold, like her.

"Did you know this was the very bar where Dorien first came up with the idea for Broken Muse?"

Faye sat forward, her lip curling with excitement. "It was?"

I told her the story about Dorien leaping on stage and attracting all those girls. "Broken Muse played one of our first ever gigs right there." I pointed to the stage in the corner. "There were only twenty people in the place. Some of my brother's old friends mostly, and a couple of dudes we knew from summer music camp. It was wild. Dorien poured whiskey all over the piano and some girl licked it off."

"Typical Dorien." Faye laughed. "I wish I could have been there."

"I miss them." It felt good to say it. "Ever since we had to cancel the tour and go to Manderley, nothing's been the same. I feel anxious and on edge all the time. I miss playing music with my friends. We've been so caught up in our shit that we forgot why we started the band in the first place, and now it's done."

"Is it done?" Faye asked. "You're free of Madame Usher now. Broken Muse can play again if you want to."

I shook my head. "The songs were a moment in time, and the moment is over. It doesn't matter what really happened at Manderley; the image the world has when they think of us is Dorien pulling a knife out of Heather's back. We can't change that."

"Do you have to change it?" Faye asked. "Ozzy Osbourne bit the head off a bat. Paganini sold his soul to the devil so he could sell out concert halls. Varg Vikernes stabbed his bandmate, and he's got a successful YouTube channel. Okay, Varg's a terrible example, but what I'm saying is that Madame Usher was counting on all this bad press to destroy the band, but we know that controversy sells records. Broken Muse has never had more press, and if you were to go out on tour or release a new song now…"

"I just can't see it," I sighed. "Maybe we'll play together again one day. But I think we all have to do our own things for a while, try not to fuck everything up this time, especially with Dorien's finger—"

"Well, sound the fucktrumpets, that makes things a bit awkward."

"What does?"

Faye held up her phone. "I maaaaay have already invited Dorien and Ivan down here to have a little fun with us, just like you used to on tour. Dorien said they're heading to the airport now – they'll be here in a couple of hours."

What?

She did what?

I stared at the tiny stage where my story with Dorien Valencourt had began, where we set in motion a series of events that would bring Faye into my life and intrinsically link me to my bandmates forever.

"Perfect." I grinned. "Let's get wild."

*A*s day turned into evening and evening became a deep, rich night, Faye and I danced from bar to bar, stuffing our faces with po boys and gumbo and sampling the finest Sazeracs until my head spun and I felt a tap on my shoulder. I turned around to see Dorien's evil grin. Behind him, Ivan stood like an ice king surveying his kingdom.

"You made it!" Faye threw her arms around Ivan. He melted in her arms, wrapping her in his embrace and swinging her off the ground so her legs knocked over several barstools and the waitress shot us a filthy look.

Dorien leaned across the bar, his hair falling in his face. Something was different about him, and it took me a few moments to put my finger on what it was. *Ivan.*

Decent cock will give a man a glow.

I watched Ivan burn with jealousy every night Dorien walked up to his hotel room with some random guy or girl. The three of us had shared enough girls that I'd seen the longing behind Ivan's icy glare.

Faye brought them together. She gave them the gift of each other. She didn't believe she had to be enough for either of them, just as each of us on our own weren't enough for her. That made me love her even more.

"Where's Jacob?" I asked Dorien.

"Marguerite has him for the weekend." Dorien's eyes danced at the mention of his brother. "She's taking him to the zoo. He's excited."

"I want to hear all about it."

And I did. I truly did. We went back to the bar where Dorien and I sat all those years ago and dreamed up the concept of Broken Muse. The stage still stood in the corner, although it was smaller now with crimson curtains as a backdrop and no grand piano in sight. We ordered another round of Sazeracs and fried shrimp po boys, and Dorien regaled us with stories of Jacob's recovery. Ivan and Dorien took him to an ice skating rink, and he had an absolute blast until they had to clear the ice because a hockey league had their practice. They'd stayed to watch, and when Jacob realized the enormous guys bashing each other around out there were his age, he went quiet. He didn't talk for days. Sadness tinged Dorien's words as he grappled with the reality that his younger brother might always experience the world differently and live on the outside of his peers.

"I've been taking him to church," Dorien told me. "I don't like it. I *hate* it, actually. I don't want religious shit messing up his head. But it's familiar to Jacob and the pastor seems like a good guy. Jacob joined the youth group and…it's too early to hope, but he might even be making friends."

It felt so strange, so wild, to be sitting together in a bar in New Orleans, *the* bar where Broken Muse started, with Madame Usher a distant memory. She wasn't gone from our lives completely, but right now we were free of her. And it felt amazing. Judging by Faye's giddy laugh and Dorien's aristocratic smile, I wasn't the only one who thought so.

Only Ivan couldn't give himself over one hundred percent to the moment, and I understood why. He would never be free of Manderley until Elena was, and we all knew that wouldn't happen while she was chained to Radcliffe.

We didn't have all our answers, but it was out of our hands now. We needed to trust Rochester and his team to do their jobs. Answers would come.

As the band on stage wound down their set and packed out their gear, the waitress came over with more baskets of po boys and curly fries. As she set them on the table, her eyes narrowed at each of us before settling on Dorien. "You're from Broken Muse? I remember you – the arrogant little shit who took over my stage without so much as a 'please and thank you, ma'am.'"

"Broken Muse doesn't exist anymore." Ivan tipped back his drink.

"I remember you, Laverne." Dorien turned his thousand-megawatt smile to her. "Did we finally turn you into a fan?"

"Can't be a fan of a band that doesn't exist," Laverne smirked, but I could see Dorien's charm wearing away her sharp edges. "I heard y'all broke up. I heard there was some big scandal. Your fiancee dead with a knife in her back, and her blood on your hands."

"I was never charged with anything," Dorien held up his hands, turning them over so she could see they were clean. "I'm innocent."

"Too bad." The waitress rolled her eyes. "Innocent is so much less rock'n'roll."

"I told you," Faye mouthed as she nudged my hand.

"See that guy?" The waitress pointed to the saxophonist as he hobbled off the stage. "He spent twenty-two years in prison for a crime he didn't commit. He still comes in here every week and plays the roof off."

Ivan started to say something, but Laverne whirled around and jabbed her finger at a woman nursing a lavish cocktail. "She was a rising jazz singer until she had a love-child with her manager. He promised her the world. When she got pregnant, he tossed her out to chase after the next floozy. She's on stage in an hour and she'll pack this place out."

"What's your point?" Dorien growled.

"My point is that no one gives a fuck what's on your rap sheet if you can play a groove we can lose ourselves in. The music comes first, and the music isn't about you, it's about your audience." She narrowed her eyes at each of us in turn. "At least, it's supposed to. I'll give you an hour."

"What?"

"Your set. I'll bump my final act. You have an hour on stage. Now get your asses up there." She tapped her wrist. "Times' a ticking."

I shook my head, but Dorien leaned across the table. "You serious, Laverne?"

"I don't joke about music." She dropped a po boy in Dorien's lap and flounced away.

I stared down at my food. The last thing I wanted to do was get up there and play. It had been so long since we played those songs. Did we even remember what to do?

But of course, Dorien couldn't resist. "We have to do this. Ivan's got his violin in our rental car, and we can send a cab to grab Titus' ax."

"You mean my cello," I said, thinking of the instrument resting on its stand at the shotgun house, where Faye left it after she fitted my guitar into the cello case for the party.

"I meant what I fucking said," Dorien's blue-blooded smirk stoked a fire in my veins. "You should play our songs the way you want to play them. I know you can do it."

"What about you?" Faye asked him. Dorien's instrument wasn't exactly portable.

"I'm not worried." Dorien waved Laverne back. "You still have a piano somewhere? I'll even take a keyboard in a pinch."

"Son, this is New Orleans." Laverne gestured for us to follow her onto the stage. She yanked back the curtains, revealing a deeper stage area. She threw off a dusty sheet, revealing an polished Fazioli baby grand. Dorien sucked in his breath. He wasn't in control of his hands as they reached out and stroked the keys. His whole body swayed. It was a beautiful instrument, but I knew that wasn't what had arrested him.

I felt it too – the tingle in my fingers, the pulse in my veins. The desire to *play*, to be Broken Muse once more. I was still supping on the thrill of playing in front of my parents, of finally standing up to Dad and admitting who I was. I *could* play our songs the way they deserved to be played, the way I always imagined them.

I looked straight up into Faye's eyes. She burned bright in the dim bar, her halo of dark hair sparkling under the red-soaked lights.

I wrapped my arms around Dorien and Ivan. "Fuck it, let's do it."

No less than ten minutes later, I was backstage with my guitar in my hands. Dorien sat at the piano, practicing finger exercises and scales to warm up his muscles. Ivan paced the length of the stage, his violin rested on his chin. He looked like he was going to be sick.

Memories rushed at me – of other nights, other clubs, other nervous pre-concert rituals and post-concert debauchery. Of the fire and flames I walked through to make music with these two, my brothers. It was the same fire burning inside us now and it… it was completely different.

The weight of my ax around my neck steadied me. *I am Titus Thibodeaux, and I know who I am.*

Laverne, who turned out to be the bar's owner, stepped on stage and addressed the room. "Ladies and gentlemen, we have a surprise for you tonight. You might've heard of a band named Broken Muse. The press dubbed them The Bad Boys of Baroque for their fiery reinterpretations of classical music and their hedonistic antics. They've been in hiding for a long time now but tonight, Broken Muse is back in town and they want you to party like it's 1799. Are you ready?"

We stormed on stage as the lights went up. And even though we'd only decided to play twenty minutes ago when the bar was practically empty, it was now packed with people. Laverne worked fast. She'd sent runners to some of the nearby clubs to tell them what was going down, and word of our impromptu set had spread like wildfire over social media, attracting our local fans like the call of the sirens.

The roar of the crowd washed over me, cleansing me of my sins and making me anew. At the piano, Dorien grinned like a blue-blooded Cheshire Cat. Even Ivan cracked a smile.

We started to play.

The moment my fingers touched the strings, I *remembered*. Every song, every note, came to me with perfect clarity. I remembered what I loved about this music, *our* music, how it told our stories in a way that opened veins and bled our lives across the stage. Our pain and our hopes and our fears on display so that our audience could find themselves in the music.

And now I got to tell my story in my own words.

I missed this. Fuck how I missed this.

I missed playing the music I loved for people like me. I missed looking out into a sea of faces, rapt as I brought them to their knees.

I was used to giving the stage over to Dorien. Even an instrumental band like ours needed a frontman, and Dorien filled that role with aplomb. But tonight, he let Ivan and I share the spotlight – this wasn't just his moment, it was for all of us. Tonight, I leaped across the stage, swinging that guitar on my hips, kicking out my legs and letting my hair fly wild around my face. I could have been in Iron Maiden or Metallica instead of a weird gothy classical trio. It was perfect.

It was *me*.

I gazed out into the sea of rapt faces. I saw only one. Faye was in the front row, throwing her hair around, jumping and screaming and yelling. Our Faye. Our muse. She brought us together again. She brought us all home.

Back to where we belonged. With each other.

With our music.

And as the crowd screamed my name, as they roared for their hometown boy, their Jesus risen from the dead, as they stamped their feet and cried for more, I felt a peace sweep over my body. It didn't matter what Madame Usher tried to do. It didn't even matter if my father never spoke to me again.

Somewhere above, Micah's light shone down on me.

30

FAYE

"That was incredible," I breathed as Broken Muse climbed off stage, each of them falling into my arms for a sweaty, stinky hug. Titus' ax brushed against my hips and my dress snapped on Ivan's bow, but I didn't care.

They were *perfection*. I'd never seen a live show like it. I've seen plenty of live bands – not just in concert halls, but in bars and stadiums, too. No one had a presence like Broken Muse. Maybe I was biased because I loved them with a fierceness that clawed at my chest, but they were the best. The fucking *best*.

We pulled apart to see Laverne standing there, holding out four Sazeracs with a wicked smile on her face. "Next time you're back in town, you play here." She thrust the drinks into our hands and stormed off to serve the crowd at the bar.

"To the best night of my life." Dorien raised his glass.

"I thought the night you and Ivan had me over the piano stool was the best night?" I teased him, but I clinked glasses. I knew what he meant. I leaned in and kissed Dorien, long and hard, giving him a promise of what he could expect later. He was snatched away from me by a trio of adoring fans.

He wasn't the only one. Ivan had been cornered by an

intense-looking goth girl who was grilling him about Count Dracula, while Titus laughed as he tried to stop a tiny girl with cute black pigtails from climbing on his shoulders.

Maybe other girls would feel jealous and protective of the attention they were getting, but I reveled in it. These were my Muses and they were beautiful and perfect and fucking hot and they deserved to have every person in this room fall at their feet. I threw my arms around fans and snapped pictures for them with their favorite Muse boys and listened to a girl gush for twenty-two minutes about Ivan's eyebrows and I loved every sordid moment of it.

"What are you going to do now?" I asked when I was able to catch a breath again.

It was 2AM. We made our way across town with a horde of Broken Muse groupies in tow, ending up at a smoky jazz club off Bourbon Street nursing potent Sazeracs because we were in New Orleans and that's what you did. Dorien had lipstick smeared across his face, but I knew from his heavy-lidded eyes when he looked at me that he had only eyes for me.

"More absinthe." Titus slammed down a tray of green shots.

"I think we've drunk all the absinthe in the city." Ivan collapsed on the table, one finger rubbing his temple. "It certainly feels like it."

"I meant, what are you doing about Broken Muse?" I said. "Is this the last ever show?"

The three of them exchanged a glance.

"I fucking miss the band," Dorien said. "I miss being on stage with you both."

Ivan nodded, then winced as he realized how much he didn't want to move his head. Titus tossed his braids over his shoulder, and the smile that stretched from ear to ear was all the answer he needed to give.

"I say we keep going," Dorien said. "I know my finger is an issue, but I think if we adjust the compositions for Titus' guitar, we can re-allocate some of my trickier parts. Madame Usher can rail against us in the press all she wants. Anything she says is only going to help us sell out a tour. The Bad Boys of Baroque are back, and we're more dangerous than ever. But we do things differently this time. We don't let anyone dictate what we do, where we play, or what we can do with the money we make. It's the three of us, no management, no label, no Usher in the background pulling the strings. What do you say?"

Titus wrapped his arms around me and Dorien and Ivan, crushing us in a hug. Ivan managed to choke out a quiet. "I agree."

And just like that, Broken Muse was back.

As the sun rose, they regaled me with more wild stories from the road. I reveled in their past, for the first time feeling as though I was part of their story.

Titus dragged us down the street to a twenty-four-hour burger place. Ivan glanced down at his phone. The carefree twist fell from his face, replaced by a frown.

"What is it?" I asked.

"It's from Elena," he said. "She says we have to come back to Manderley."

"What? Why?"

"She doesn't say." Ivan held the phone to his ear, his eyes swimming as his fear slammed against his encroaching hangover. I heard Elena's chirpy voice on the other end. "It's going straight to voicemail."

Titus whipped out his phone and was frantically tapping the screen. "Shit, all the planes to New York are grounded."

"What?" Ivan looked murderous.

"There's a wicked Nor'easter rolling down the coast, heading straight for Manderley. They're predicting five feet of snow by tomorrow evening."

Ivan drew back his hand, preparing to shatter his glass against the wall. Dorien caught his wrist, pulling Ivan against him so

Ivan could rail against his body instead of the innocent establishment. "We will get to her, I promise."

Titus slid his phone back into his pocket and tossed some bills on the table to pay for our burgers. "I've got us a flight to Baltimore – that's as close as we can get. We'll rent a car at the airport. If we want to make it at all, we have to go *now*."

31

FAYE

Ivan was a mess the whole flight. He spilled water all over his lap, barked at the flight attendants, and crushed my fingers in his iron grip. But we touched down in Baltimore just as they announced all flights were grounded. At least we were closer.

Elena, please be all right.

Titus and Dorien took turns driving. I sat in the back with Ivan, white-knuckling it the whole way as the pair broke every road rule and speed limit. Ivan called Elena every ten minutes until his phone ran out of battery, and then he bugged Dorien for his spare battery cord until Dorien tossed it out the window.

We crossed into New York just as the snow started to fall harder. Fifty miles later it was so thick we could barely see the next car in front of us. I gripped the edge of the seat as Titus flung the car around the bends. We made it to the foot of the mountains and started climbing. Ivan gritted his teeth in frustration as we crawled along, watching out for patches of ice. We didn't pass a single car on the road.

"What could have happened to her?" Ivan snapped. "Why won't she answer her phone?"

Dorien tapped the screen of his own phone. "I think the lines are down. There's no signal."

Ivan leaned forward, his eyes glued on the window, his fingers laced in mine. Wind battered the car from all sides, and the snow fell so thick and hard I had no idea how Titus kept us on the road.

It seemed to take days to crawl through the storm to the gates of Manderley. Lights were on in Harrison's cottage, but we didn't stop to say hello. As Titus jerked the car to a stop in front of the busted fountain, Dorien reached into the glove compartment and pulled out a pistol.

"What the fuck?"

"I bought it at the airport, can you believe it?" Dorien grinned. "God bless America."

"Put that away." I snapped. "We're not going into that house shooting, and that's final."

Dorien looked like he wanted to argue, but Titus wrestled the weapon from his fingers and shoved it back into the glove box, and that was the end of it. The moment I opened the door, the wind blasted me with an icy chill. We staggered up the front steps and inched our way around the edge of the porch, where the wood was sturdiest. I had to grip the railing as my feet slipped and slid on the icy porch. A foot of snow had blown against the door, with more piled up around the pillars. I turned back to the car, seeing it was already nearly obscured by the rapid snowfall.

We were trapped at Manderley until the storm passed.

Ivan hammered his fists on the door. "Elena, open up." He jiggled the handle, but the door was locked. I didn't have my Manderley keys with me – it seemed pointless to bring them to New Orleans, so I'd left them with Dorien, and he left them at the apartment when he'd rushed down to meet us.

No one answered. Snow blasted us sideways. I was cold right through, cold in my bones and my heart.

"We should try the stables," I yelled. The wind whipped away my words, but Ivan was already running back down the steps and around the side of the school. Dorien powered after him, his crimson scarf whipping in the wind. Titus helped me down the steps, steadying me so I didn't slip on the ice.

By the time we trudged through the snow to the stables, Ivan and Dorien had broken down the front door. It hung open, banging against the wall as the wind howled inside. Titus dragged me in and slammed the door shut behind us.

"Elena?" Ivan yelled from deeper in the house. Dorien stood in the middle of the room, staring at the mess strewn on the floor. The whole house was a disaster zone – Elena's clothing and makeup scattered everywhere, plates smashed on the kitchen floor, torn sheet music blowing about like confetti. It looked as though a tornado had ripped through the place. I rubbed my freezing hands together as I picked my way through the house, toward the bathroom. I wished instead of a gun, Dorien had bought some gloves at the airport.

The bathroom light was on. I turned in the dim circle, taking in the bloody handprints on the edge of the basin, the smashed mirror, and the bottles and lotions strewn across the tiles with a sinking feeling in my stomach. My feet scuffed more clothing and torn pages, dusted with snow blown in from outside.

What happened here? Who made all this mess, and where is Elena? Did someone break in and attack her? Is that why she called Ivan so frantically, and then her phone went dead—

I screamed as a dark shape lunged from the shadows of the linen cupboard and grabbed me around the neck.

IVAN

Faye's scream curled through my body. I raced from the bedroom to find her in the door of the bathroom, struggling with an intruder hidden in shadow.

Victor Usher.

Anger surged through me as I took in the man's fingers wrapped around her neck. *We never should have left Elena here, knowing Victor lived in the walls. Now he's got Faye.*

I lunged at them, all the rage and fear coalescing inside me. *I will kill this bastard.*

I grabbed Victor's wrist and twisted it behind him before he could hurt her. Victor whimpered, and I noticed how thin his wrist was, how soft his skin, and that I could break it one quick motion if I so desired—

"Ivan? Please stop. You're *hurting* me."

My blood froze in my veins. *Not Victor.*

"Elena?"

My beautiful sister staggered from the shadows. She didn't look so beautiful now. Her eyes were wide with terror, her skirt was torn, and her pale skin was marred with bruises and dried blood.

"Ivan, help me."

Her voice trembled with terror. I dropped her wrist and she fell into my arms, her cheeks wet with tears, her shoulders heaving. I held her as she sobbed, and the story told by the broken furniture, the torn music sheets and the bruises clawed at my insides, turning my anger into a rage that boiled in my veins.

Deviant sexual proclivities.

Radcliffe did this to her.

I'll kill the bastard. When I find him I'll string his balls from the ceiling with piano wire and—

My heart stopped as I looked over my sister's shoulder at the piano and realized someone already had.

Radcliffe lay on the floor beside the piano stool, his pants pulled down around his ankles and his hairy, knobbly legs twisted underneath him. His face turned toward me, a pair of glassy eyes staring right through me, the mouth open in slack-jawed surprise. A dark halo of dried blood circled his head – a stain on the Persian rug no amount of scrubbing would ever be able to lift.

Dorien loomed over Radcliffe, the tip of his Barker Blacks scuffing the bloodstain. "There's a wound on the side of his head, and blood on the corner of the piano. I think someone hit him, and he fell and hit his head, and that's what killed him."

I looked down at my sister trembling in my arms. At the broken jug handle she clutched in her hands, the corners stained with blood. At the shattered pieces of the jug lying around Radcliffe's body. I held her at arm's length and watched her face crumple as I asked, "Elena, what did you do?"

33

FAYE

*E*lena's lip trembled under the intensity of Ivan's gaze. She dropped the object she'd been holding, which I could see now was the handle and part of the side of a broken jug. It rolled across the rug, coming to rest against Radcliffe's thigh. Dark blood stained the rim. It looked exactly like the broken shards that were scattered around the body.

Radcliffe's body.

He's dead. He's not a person any longer, just a corpse.

"I...I needed you," Elena whispered, so that only Ivan and I could hear. The words punched Ivan in the gut. His face crumpled and he jammed his sister's face into his shoulder, as if he could squash the demons out of her. I knew he was hating himself for leaving her, even though she told him to go.

I stepped around the twins and bent down beside Master Radcliffe, careful not to touch his clothes or the dried blood. We couldn't risk getting our fingerprints on anything. I pulled a tissue from my pocket and used that to cover my fingers as I touched his wrist. No pulse. I didn't expect there to be.

"He's dead," I said.

"Thank you, Sprite the Obvious," Dorien said, a hint of dark sarcasm in his voice. He looked rattled, and I knew he was remembering the last dead bodies he saw – his parents. Elena buried her head in Ivan's shoulder.

I leaned over and peered at Radcliffe's face, at the sheen on his skin and the glassy, surprised look in his eyes. He felt cold and stiff – I knew from the number of horror films and true crime I watched that rigor mortis was normally over after thirty-six hours, but the freezing temperature had probably helped to prolong it. He'd been dead a couple of days, definitely before Elena called Ivan.

What the fuck?

"Elena, you have to tell us what happened." I tried to take her hand in mine, but she clung to Ivan and shook her head.

"*Elena,*" Dorien said with more force than kindness. "We nearly killed ourselves getting here to help you. Whatever went down, we are on your side. You know this. But we need to *know* what we're dealing with here so we can figure out what to do. And I'm assuming Madame Usher doesn't know about this—" he indicated Radcliffe's body "—but if she sees our car in the snow, she could be over here any moment. So talk quickly, please."

Ivan glared at Dorien, but Elena bit her lip and nodded.

Titus found the only remaining chair that wasn't broken and dragged it over. Elena collapsed into it, her long limbs flapping out the sides like a frightened bird. Ivan stood behind her, his hands on her shoulders, playing with her bedraggled hair. I knelt on the carpet and took her hands in mine.

She sniffed. "He…he was a different person after we said our vows. If he had been the Radcliffe of before – the kindly, chivalrous old man – I could have lived with it. He looked after me. He wanted me to be famous, to have a career that overshadowed his. But as soon as the ring was on my fingers, he turned beastly. If he'd shown his true nature earlier, I would have run a mile, but he acted the perfect gentleman. Waiting until our wedding night to reveal himself was part of the game to him. He had what he wanted, and so did *she*." Elena turned her gaze to the window, where Manderley's east wing loomed. I could almost *sense* Madame Usher's eyes fixed on us – like the eye of Sauron, lidless and ever-watching.

"Was this about your money?" Dorien asked, gently this time.

Elena shook her head. "I don't think Madame Usher has even given him access to our trust. I don't think she ever intended to. They had an agreement – I heard them speak of it late at night when they thought I was asleep. She enticed him to come to Manderley by dangling me in front of him. She played him recordings of me, and he came here to seduce me. It was a game to him, and we played right into her trap. She always intended for me to marry him, a sacrificial lamb to his peculiar tastes in exchange for something she wanted."

"What?" Dorien's eyes blazed. He looked like he was ready to shake it out of her.

"I do not know," Elena sobbed. "It was something to do with his nervous breakdown, why he retreated from performances. And there is something else about him you do not know. I must show you. But it doesn't explain why she gave me to him – his little toy."

"Did he hurt you?" I gripped her hands. My mind went to a dark place, where Creepy Cory held me beneath him and I couldn't move and all I could taste was his deep-fried stickiness as his hands—

Elena nodded slowly. "He has visited more injustice upon my body than a human being can endure. I tried to fight him off, but you see what happened." She gestured at the destruction around us. "When he touched me, it was like a snake slithering under my skin. And even then I thought I must endure it for what he could give me, for in a few days we would go to Europe for our tour and I would play in all those beautiful concert halls and at least I would know some happiness. But when he came at me that night he told me he would put a child in my belly. He chose me because of my talents – so I would breed with him to create his true legacy, his next maestro. The glittering career he promised me was not to be mine – that belonged to our child. But I will not be caged again. I will not bring a child into this world to be raised by him, not knowing what he's capable of. We fought. He lunged at me and I..." she glared at the jug and shuddered. Ivan pulled her to his chest. "I hit him and he fell. I didn't mean for it to happen. I knew Ivan could help me."

She sobbed into Ivan's shoulder. I looked down at Radcliffe's body, at his white legs and speckled ass. My stomach turned. I resisted the urge to kick him. He hurt Elena. I couldn't feel sorry for him. I wanted to bring him back to life so that I could kill him again myself.

I noticed bruises on his arms. *That must've been where she fought back. That's my girl.*

"What was the other thing you found out about him?" Dorien asked. He peered around the room with a puzzled expression on his face.

"Look at those papers." Elena pointed to a stack on top of the piano.

I peered over Dorien's shoulder as he read them. My stomach churned as I saw the splatters of blood across the page. Dorien frowned as he looked at the names on the documents.

"This is..." he said. "I don't understand."

"Aaron Varney is Master Radcliffe's son," Elena said. "That is the legacy of the man I married."

34

FAYE

Wait...what the fuck?

How is that possible? How did everyone miss that? Rochester has been chasing Varney for years. Surely he would have figured out his connection to Radcliffe, to Manderley?

Dorien's hands trembled as he flipped the papers over, scanning each line.

"Aaron uses his mother's name," Elena explained. "I confronted Maxim about it and he said she was a flautist he met on tour with the National Youth Orchestra. She was a member of a radical religious sect that believed God and demons could speak through music. Maxim didn't even know he had a son until Aaron found him a decade ago."

Around the time Radcliffe stepped away from performing because of a scandal.

My mind whirred. I could imagine it – Aaron Varney, would-be religious leader and desperate for quick and easy cash, discovered his father is a world-famous classical musician. Elena hadn't said it out loud, but I was certain Aaron's mother was underage when Radcliffe slept with her. So Aaron found Radcliffe and... what? Tried to convince him to join his burgeoning Temple? But if Radcliffe refused…we knew that Aaron would use every tool at his disposal to further his cause. He probably threatened Radcliffe to go to the papers, maybe even have his mother press charges. Radcliffe would be ruined, his career in tatters.

And that was where Madame Usher came in, with her connections in law enforcement. She offered Radcliffe a job at Manderley, and in exchange, perhaps she would keep Aaron's cult and the truth about his paternity out of the public eye. Radcliffe owed her his freedom, his reputation, as long as she kept Aaron off his back by any means necessary.

But he could also give her what she needed – his contacts in the music world, a means to place Manderley on the global stage as a fine institution. He lent her the legitimacy of a real music school while in the background she schemed and maneuvered to…what? We still didn't have the final piece of the puzzle – Madame Usher's real motivations.

I didn't know if that was the full story, but I felt certain I'd hit on the crux of it. It explained Madame Usher's link to the Temple, and Radcliffe's need to hide behind her. Judging by the murderous look on Dorien's face, he came to the same conclusion.

This is completely fucked up.

"What do we do now?" Titus said.

An excellent question. We still had a dead body on our hands.

"We call the police," Dorien said. "We tell them exactly what happened. Radcliffe was a brute with a fetish for young women and Elena defended herself. This is self-defense – anyone can see that."

"And you think they will believe me?" Elena shot back. "I am a foreigner, and he's a respected musician and my husband. With everything going on in the house and Walpole in Madame Usher's pocket, they will send me to prison for his murder. They will say I did it to take his money. Now everything that is his belongs to me."

I glanced at Dorien, and I could see him thinking the same as me. Elena was right. Madame Usher had the police commissioner in her pocket. She was the one who sold Elena to Radcliffe for his awful scheme. She'd already nearly successfully framed Dorien once before, so she had no qualms about planting evidence and lying to get the result she wanted. If Elena's case had a fair trial, I didn't think a jury would convict her, but I couldn't be sure.

"We could go to Rochester," Dorien said. "He knows Walpole is crooked, and he's closing his net around Madame Usher. Knowing Aaron is Radcliffe's son is the final piece of the puzzle."

"I don't trust him." Elena folded her arms. But Ivan nodded to Dorien. He looked so small. This was too big for us.

Dorien tapped his phone, then frowned. "Fuck, I forgot we didn't have signal."

"The storm knocked it out," Elena sniffed, tucking a lank strand of hair behind her ear. "That's why I couldn't call you again. I've been waiting in here with him for *days*, hoping you'd come to rescue me. But instead, you want to turn me in to the police!"

Her voice rose with distress, and she threw herself into Ivan's arms. He shot Dorien a reproachful look.

"We could try to make it back down the road," Dorien said hopefully. "If we go slow in the car, I'm sure we'll be fine."

I glanced out the window at the snow pelting down. At this rate, we'd have to dig the car out. Even as Dorien said the words, his face betrayed him. He knew it was pointless.

We're not going anywhere.

"What do you propose, Elena?" Ivan's tone was harsher than I'd ever heard him use with her before.

Her chin trembled as she glanced down at her husband. "I don't want to go to jail."

"You won't." Ivan's fingers laced around her neck. He held her fiercely, his eyes boring into mine over her shoulder. "We won't let that happen."

I read his intention in that icy glare.

"We can't do that." I shook my head.

"It is our only choice," Ivan said sadly, stroking Elena's hair.

It wasn't. Of course it wasn't. We were panicked, stressed, driven to the end of our rope by the terror of Radcliffe's body and Madame Usher's final betrayal. It was obvious we weren't thinking clearly.

But we had to do *something*. We couldn't just leave him there. And we were all alone out here, with no one but Harrison, Aroha, and Mad Madame Usher and her crazy husband living in the walls. Who knew what they'd do to us if they found out what happened?

I leaned against the bathroom door, trying to think.

"We wait out the storm," I said. "The phone tower will be repaired and we'll be able to get through to Rochester."

"And Elena goes to jail," Ivan snapped.

"We don't know that for a fact." I looked down at Radcliffe, and I knew that as much as I had liked the man while he was alive, I wouldn't let Elena be blamed for his death. He was Aaron's father. His DNA was part of the man who broke Dorien's family and tormented Jacob and deprived him of a normal life. And look what he did to Elena. All this time we thought Madame Usher was the enemy, but Radcliffe was a *beast*. The monster hiding in plain sight.

People go missing in storms all the time. Perhaps Radcliffe was walking in the woods and got caught in the snow. If we take him far away and bury him deep, no one will ever find his body. He'll be just another of Manderley's secrets.

It became impossible to breathe. I rushed into the bathroom and cracked the window, gasping at the frigid blast of air.

Dorien appeared in the doorway. "Sprite?"

"We can't bury him in this storm," I said, thinking fast. "It's too dangerous. But we can't leave him here, either. Madame Usher or Harrison or Aroha could walk in at any moment and we lose our chance. We have to hide the body until the weather clears, and we need to clean this place up and agree on a story."

"Okay," said Dorien. "Okay." He looked haunted. His jaw worked, like he wanted to say something but thought better of it. Instead, he opened his arms and I fell into them. I didn't realize how much I needed a soft place to fall until my head rested on his shoulder and hot tears burned down my cheeks.

We pulled down the shower curtain and rolled Radcliffe into it, careful not to touch anything in his exposed crotch area. *Too fucking gross.* His limbs were still a little stiff, making him ungainly to lift, but at least he wasn't a large man. Elena and I cleaned up the broken objects and stuffed the pieces into trash bags. Ivan got to work cleaning down the piano, removing every last trace of blood from the wood.

"What do we do about the bloodstain?" I pointed to the rug.

Titus grunted as he lifted the piano, while Dorien rolled up the rug and set it on top of our trash pile. There was now a large bright square under the piano where the wood around the rug had faded.

"Ivan, wipe the floor carefully with bleach. We can't take any chances. We'll take the rug with us when we leave," Dorien said. "We can dump the trash in the pit at the old timber mill. No one will look there. I think there's an old rug in that storage room in the attic at the house. We can bring that in here and lay it under the piano and no one will ever notice a change."

We worked in panicked silence, filling five garbage bags with broken objects. Titus screwed the legs back on chairs and used glue to repair some of the more expensive pieces. Elena and I wiped down the kitchen counters and cupboards. If we were going with the story that Radcliffe went out for firewood and never came back, then we needed this place to be spotless.

Through our cleaning, the body of Radcliffe lay in the doorway. Even through the shower curtain, his glassy eyes seemed to follow me as I moved around the room.

"Where are we going to hide him?"

"Not in here," Dorien said. "We don't want any more DNA or other material to end up in the stables, because if we report him as a missing person, the police *will* look here first."

"It's snowing worse than ever." Elena shuddered against Ivan as the wind rattled the shingles. "We cannot hope to dig a grave in this."

I couldn't help but notice how quickly she'd resigned herself to covering up the crime. Something about her story niggled at me, but I couldn't put my finger on it.

"We won't be able to get him to the mausoleum." I thought about hiding him in Victor's empty grave, but we'd kill ourselves trying to drag him all the way there and back in this weather.

"It's simple," Dorien said. "We hide him behind the painting in my old room."

I glared at him. "Be serious."

"I am. It's perfect. Even if the police search the house, they'll never think of looking *inside* the walls."

"What about Madam Usher?" I hissed. "She's going to notice when he doesn't show up for classes, and she'll see all of us sneaking around. Or Victor will find the body in the tunnels and tell her, and it's over for us."

"Sure. Victor could go to the police and say, what? I've been living in the walls creeping on young girls at my wife's school, and I saw them dump a body in here? Madame Usher won't report it because it'll expose the tunnels," Dorien shot back. "They have too much to lose. And speaking of Madame Usher, we should lock her in her rooms."

"Well, at least you have a solid plan," I said sarcastically.

"She might know we're at the house, but she can't know what we're up to. Ivan has the map showing the other exits for Victor's tunnels. We block them all, and when we leave, there's no evidence we were ever here."

"This is insane. We could be stuck here for days while this storm clears. He's going to start to smell."

"The cold air blowing through the walls will help keep him cool," Ivan said. "I am with Dorien. I think it is our best option."

Dorien nodded. He glanced at Elena again, and that strange, haunted look passed over his eyes again. I wanted to ask what he was thinking, but I was too grossed out by our plan to dig into it. "We don't have our keys with us. Elena, you've got that spare key I cut for you? I need you to go back to the house and lock Usher and Aroha in their rooms."

She nodded, and leaned forward to kiss Dorien's cheek. He held her arm and whispered something in her ear that made her body go stiff. I knew he was telling her what he suspected, asking for her to confirm or deny. Instead, she pulled away, her eyes downcast. "I will return."

I don't know how long she was gone, but it felt like forever. Ivan paced the room, wringing his hands and occasionally stopping to give Radcliffe's corpse a violent kick. Dorien sat at the piano, his hands in his lap and his head hanging. Titus held me tight, and I squeezed him as waves of nausea and fear rocked my body. *What the fuck are we doing? Not even ten hours ago we were in New Orleans, celebrating the return of Broken Muse. And now we're trying to dispose of a dead body.*

The door slammed open, startling us out of our skins. Elena rushed in and sank against it to hold back the storm. Her pale cheeks were flushed with color.

"I did it," she whispered, hugging herself. "They are locked inside their rooms."

"Okay." Dorien stood, dusting off his hands on his pants. "Let's do this, then."

The four of us each picked up one corner of the curtain. Elena held the door open for us as we struggled out into the snow.

Bitter wind pelted us, nearly ripping Radcliffe from my hands. Somehow, with lots of staggering and swearing and falling over, we managed to make it across the back garden.

Elena held the kitchen door for us, and we shuffled inside. As quietly as we could, we huffed and struggled upstairs and into Dorien's old room. I dropped my leg on the rug and rubbed my screaming arms while Dorien jumped on the desk to open the painting. Luckily, we'd thought to dismantle the internal lock last time, so we could get inside.

Dorien peered into the wall cavity. "Victor? Are you in there?"

"Stop fucking around and give me space," Titus grunted as he lifted the body onto his shoulders. "This bastard is heavy."

Ivan and I moved in beside Titus to help lift the body while Dorien maneuvered it into the hole. Elena leaned against the wall, watching us. As I turned to help push, I caught a glimpse of her. She was smiling – a sweet, eerily-calm Elena smile.

The smile of someone who got exactly what she wanted.

As we strained under Radcliffe's deadweight, Dorien met my eyes. He saw her smile, too.

In his gaze, I read the same duplicitous thought that had entered my head. Elena had been close to Radcliffe for months and never shown any fear of him. We'd all taken classes with him and he seemed to be a perfect gentleman. It was her word against his about what happened in that room, and now he was dead. We believed it because we read Donelle's article about the 'deviant sexual proclivities,' but she never mentioned Radcliffe by name. She could have been talking about Victor or Madame Usher or even one of the visiting teachers.

And the scene in the stables…that's what was bothering me. All that broken furniture and smashed crockery – it seemed too erratic, too spread out. It was odd, wasn't it, to have such chaos in every room of the house, not concentrated in the living room where Radcliffe fell? If I didn't know better, I'd say it wasn't caused by a vicious fight, but someone deliberately and maliciously turning the place over.

It seemed perfectly designed for maximum impact – to agitate Ivan to the point where he'd do anything to secure Elena's safety.

As if…as if it had been staged.

Wait, what am I thinking?

Elena was my friend, and too many women had been silenced by the threat of not being believed. I had a feminist duty to stand by her.

She looked so upset when we found her in the stables, so lost and broken. And Ivan said he noticed Radcliffe lusting after her from a young age.

And yet…Radcliffe's pants around his ankles…the shards of pottery on top of his body, as if they'd been smashed after he died…the surprised look on his face…

It was *too* perfect.

I remembered something else, too. I remembered Elena's words back in Sighisoara, when she first told us she was engaged. "This is real life, and there's no good and evil. I'm not the pure virgin who needs saving."

I remembered looking into her cold icicle eyes – so much like Ivan's, and yet infinitely more impassable – and feeling *certain* she had no intention of going through with her marriage to Radcliffe.

Is Elena really the victim of a violent, depraved man?

Or did she lure him into the marriage and then hit him over the head? Did she plan this? Was this always her endgame – to get rid of Radcliffe and have Ivan cover it up for her so she could take Radcliffe's money and fame and run?

35

FAYE

"There." Dorien fell against the painting, his forehead coated with sweat. "It's done."

I got the bucket and mop and cleaned the floor in his bedroom. Then, we went to Aroha's room. If we were going to wait out the storm at Manderley, we were doing it together. There was no noise from inside. "Aroha?" I knocked gently. "It's Faye. Can we come in?"

No answer. I took the key from Elena and shoved it into the lock. Dorien pushed open the door. Aroha lay on her bed, her face pointed at the ceiling, her arms crossed over her stomach. She didn't move.

"Aroha?" My heart raced as I knelt beside her. Dorien shook her, but she didn't wake up. Her limbs flopped about uselessly, and her lips fell open.

"She's alive," Dorien pressed his fingers into her wrist. "But her pulse is erratic. Her breathing is slow. And look at her eyes. She's overdosed on something."

Ivan held up a bottle. "This? It looks like it's from your apothecary set."

Dorien snatched the bottle from Ivan's hand. "This is chloral.

But I don't understand. Heather gave the bottle from the set to Pearl, so why…"

His eyes met mine as the answer occurred to us at the same time. *Victor.* He had a ton of these old apothecary bottles in his little laboratory. He must have given the bottle to Aroha. He clearly couldn't stop himself from talking with students – we know he'd chatted with Heather before he killed her, but he'd also tried to scare me, and he'd obviously been talking to Clare as well. *Did he intend for Aroha to be his next victim…*

I tried to remember what I'd read about chloral when we were planning to use it on Madame Usher. The Victorians had used it as a cure for insomnia, but also to treat melancholy. It was highly addictive and poisonous in large doses, and could also cause hallucinations, nausea, and a range of other non-fun symptoms, including death.

Shit. Aroha, no.

"What do we do?" Elena leaned over her, concern written over her features. I felt awful for suspecting her of murdering Radcliffe. I *knew* Elena – she was kind and good and truthful. She couldn't possibly have planned such a fiendish thing.

"I don't think there's much we can do except wait with her and hope she pulls through." I rearranged Aroha's pillows and rolled her onto her side into the recovery position, so she wouldn't choke if she threw up. We couldn't call an ambulance – not even the rescue helicopter would make it up the mountain in this weather. We couldn't even use the internet to see if it had any clever (or not so clever) suggestions.

So we waited. Elena and I parked ourselves on Aroha's bed. I stroked her hair and Elena sang Romanian folk songs in her sweet, breathy voice. The Muses went from room to room in the house, checking doors and windows and blocking off all the exits of Victor's tunnels.

I don't know how many hours passed. Aroha's breathing grew

stronger. She started to murmur and thrash, clutching at her stomach. I had to hope that meant she was improving.

At some point, Madame Usher realized she was locked in and started banging and cursing at the door. Weirdly, the sound of her anger soothed me. She was in there and we were out here. Manderley belonged to us now.

Thankfully, despite the storm raging outside, the lights remained on. We were able to keep Aroha's room warm and bright during our long night-time vigil at her side.

Sometime later, as the sun once again threatened the horizon, Aroha opened her eyes. "What are you doing here, trash?" She gripped my arm so hard she pinched my skin.

"Elena called us. Radcliffe disappeared in the storm, and Madame Usher…" I racked my brain for some lie to explain why we locked her in, then decided not to bother. Aroha winced, doubling over with pain. "Are you okay?"

"I think I need to shit…or puke…" Aroha gasped. "Or both… yup, definitely both."

Ivan brought food and fresh water. Aroha spent the day moving back and forth between the bathroom and her bed. We changed her sheets three times, tossing the sweaty, soiled ones into Heather's old room. Madame Usher had abandoned her assault on the door and was now playing Mozart at top volume from her record player. The walls of Manderley shook from the assault of the music.

When Aroha declared she was well enough to brave the stairs, we all gathered in the Red Room. I tried the house phone, but the line was still dead, so I couldn't let Harrison know we were here. Titus helped me bring in a load of wood and we lit a roaring fire. We passed around port glasses and I heated up some chili I stored in the freezer.

"What happened?" I asked Aroha.

She winced, pushing her chili bowl aside as she clutched her stomach. "What does it look like? I have been going fucking mad, is what happened. The competition is coming up, but it's like no one gives a shit. It's as if the school is just a facade for something else, and the cloak is slipping and all the spiders are crawling out. There's no one here except Dopey and Mopey over there," she gestured her elbow at Elena and Ivan, "and Radcliffe who is so lovesick he doesn't come to my lessons half the time, and *her*. And she's fucking mad. Good thing you've got her locked away upstairs, because I think she'd kill us all. But maybe that's just me going mental. I'm all alone with my thoughts all the time and this house… this fucking *house*…" she rolled her eyes at the ceiling. "I snorted all Elena's coke. Usher refused to let me get the drugs I *actually* need, so fuck her. But he said this would help and I was fucking desperate. I wasn't trying to off myself, just to get the voices to stop."

"Who said the chloral would help you?" I already knew the answer, but I needed to hear it from her.

"The man in the walls. The one Clare and Heather talked to, obviously." Aroha rolled her eyes. "I thought you knew all about him. He never stops going on about you. Faye this, Faye that, isn't she amazing? He's such a wanker."

"Where is the man in the walls now?" Dorien stared at the spot behind my head, and I know what he's thinking – is Victor about to burst through the walls with an ax and murder us all? It had definitely crossed my mind.

Dorien touched his hand to his pocket. I knew he'd gone back to the car and retrieved the gun. I didn't like it, but I didn't say anything.

"Probably back in his hole. He says he has a room where Madame keeps him. She locks the door so he can't see us without her permission. He's afraid of her, it's fucking pathetic—"

Aroha's words broke off into a coughing fit that racked her whole body.

When she withdrew her hands from her mouth, they were covered with blood.

Shit. This isn't good. We need to get her to a hospital.

But the snow and wind and hail battered the house all day and into the night, determined to keep us trapped in Manderley's belly.

The power went out in the night, plunging the house into a darkness so complete I knew it was what death must feel like. Luckily, we had planned in advance and had boxes of candles placed next to the fireplace in the Red Room. We all slept in there together, huddled on the opulent sofas with blankets drawn up to our chins.

I warmed soup over the fire for breakfast, and we spent the day reading ghost stories to each other and playing music together. Aroha was still sick – just a mouthful of soup made her double over with pain. But she managed to drink some water and warm tea, so that was something. She hadn't coughed up any more blood, but I noticed her hobbling off to the bathroom every few minutes.

"We have a problem." Dorien grabbed my hand and yanked me out of the room. He glanced over his shoulder as he slammed the door, and I knew he didn't want the others to hear us.

"Elena?" I wondered if he was going to address the fears we hadn't voiced.

But Dorien shook his head. He turned his head to the staircase and inhaled deeply. "Sniff."

I followed his example, surprised to get a lungful of sickly sweet air, with the faintest undercurrent of putrid rot.

Dorien pinched his nose. "I think our friend upstairs is succumbing."

"The heat from the fires must be traveling through the wall cavities," I said. "It's going to speed up the decay. We have to live with it. We'll freeze in here if we don't keep the fires going—"

A noise from the second floor startled us. Madame Usher was banging on her door again. She screamed and howled, more wild and desperate than angry. *She must smell him, too.*

Maybe Victor has discovered him.

Maybe they're both up there wondering if they'll be next.

Good.

"I want to talk to her," I told Dorien. "We should probably bring her some food."

"You think that's a good idea?" He raised an eyebrow.

"No. But we're doing it. This stalemate of ours ends now."

Dorien poked his head into the room and beckoned Titus to join us – we needed his muscle. We went to the kitchen, and Titus held a candle for me while I made up a tray of simple food – an apple that was only a little mushy, a couple of candy bars, a handful of almonds. A small glass of slightly rancid-smelling milk. I was being a petty bitch but I didn't care.

We took the tray upstairs. With every step into the darkened hallway, I expected Clare's ghost to waft out of the walls and warn us away. But she didn't, which probably meant she was watching somewhere and smiling.

Titus and Dorien flanked the door. I held the tray with both hands, trying to calm my racing heart. Dorien slipped the key into the lock and flung the door open. It hit Madame Usher in the face. She staggered backward, howling and clutching her forehead. Blood seeped through her fingers where the door had torn her skin.

Her eyes widened when she saw me holding the tray. For the first time, she appeared genuinely surprised. Victor was either trapped in the wing with her, or he decided not to tell her we were in the house. I thought about what Aroha said, about him being obsessed with me, and wondered again why he seemed to be on my side even as he tormented me.

"We know what you did," I snapped at her before she could talk. "We know about the bodies under the Usher School and the

Triumvirate's money and Radcliffe's connection to the Temple. We know you've been hiding Victor in the walls of Manderley. We got all the evidence we need to put you away for a long time, and your friend Walpole won't be able to stop us. Maybe we'll go to the police, or maybe we'll keep you here and torture you, the way you tortured us. I haven't decided yet. Either way, we're trapped in this house together until the storm passes, so I suggest you do what we say, because I might feel calm now but I can't say how I'll feel in a few hours. You're not leaving this room. Someone will guard this door at all times. We've blocked Victor's exits, and if we find him in the walls, we'll kill him. Do you understand?"

Madame Usher tossed back her head and laughed. Although using the word 'laugh' couldn't convey the sheer terror of her banshee howl. Titus and I exchanged a glance. I didn't know what to say to that.

She didn't give me a chance to respond. She grabbed the tray from my hands and kicked the door with her foot. It slammed shut in my face.

"Get in there," I nudged Dorien. "We're not letting her out of our sight. Show her your gun if you need her to cooperate. If Victor wants to save her, he can show his face."

Dorien made a face at me, but followed her inside. I heard him bark at her to sit down and shut up, but as Titus and I descended the staircase, her unhinged laughter boomed off the walls around us, filling the silent house with dread.

By the third night, the smell became unbearable. At dinner, everyone pushed their food around their plates. No one would eat a bite because my improvised fireplace stew tasted like decay, like death.

The smell clung to our clothes, our hair. It burned into our skin and burrowed into our eye sockets. We couldn't distract ourselves with parlor games or ghost stories any longer. A man was decomposing in the walls and we were forced to bear witness.

But still the storm refused to relent. I stuffed my feet into rain boots to stand outside on the porch every few hours just for a respite from the stench, but I could only handle a minute before I had to rush back into the warmth. We had no window with which to steal away into the forest to dig him a grave. Dorien and Ivan decided to head out on their own to try and make a start, but returned twenty minutes later after they'd nearly lost each other in the tree line.

At least Aroha was feeling stronger. We filled her in on the whole sordid story – everything we knew so far. She was still groggy and drugged, saying strange things that didn't make sense. But then she sang to us in the language of her people, and she was clear and bright, her words barbed and powerful. Her song gave me the strength to endure what I had to do next.

"It's my turn." I set down the book I'd been staring at for the last hour without reading a word, and went upstairs. I knocked on the door to Madame Usher's wing. "Titus?"

He'd been sitting with Usher for the last four hours. Ivan, Dorien, Elena, they'd all had their turn. They all said the same thing – that as much as they tried to ignore her, they couldn't block out the cruel words she spat at them, the secrets she dangled like carrots if only they would grant her freedom. Aroha was too weak to be of use now. That left one person who hadn't sat with her – me.

I didn't want to be alone in a room with Madame Usher and a gun. I didn't trust myself not to use it.

Titus still hadn't come to the door. I called him again. Nothing. I listened for footsteps on the other side, but all I heard was the wind howling against the house and the ticking of that infernal grandfather clock. My chest tightened. I fumbled in my dress for the other set of keys we found and shoved it into the slot.

I stepped into the room. My breath hitched as I crossed the receiving room, noticing Titus' huge footprints in the dust. He had crossed this room, but he never returned.

With a racing heart, I entered the sitting room. I'd only ever seen this room from the peepholes in Victor's tunnels. From this angle, I could see the holes had been cunningly hidden in gilded portraits of Usher family ancestors. A portrait of Victor hung over the piano, a crystal perfume bottle in his hands.

"Titus?"

He wasn't in this room, and neither was Madame Usher. Panic surged inside me. I grabbed a fire poker from the stand – noticing as I did the small ax for chopping kindling was also gone – and rushed into the bedroom.

"Titus?"

He was slumped in a chair beside the bed, his chin to his chest, his huge feet jutting out at odd angles. I dropped the poker and grabbed his face, tipping his head up. Glassy eyes stared back at me. A sheen of sweat made his skin cold and clammy. He was breathing, slow and shallow, but when I slapped his cheeks, he didn't stir.

Titus, no, no.

"What's she done to you?" I picked up a broken teacup from the floor and sniffed. It smelled faintly of pears. "You gullible bastard. You should've known not to accept anything from her. Fuck."

I searched his lap, but of course Dorien's gun was gone. I picked up the poker and made a search of the bedroom, but Madame Usher wasn't anywhere in her apartments. I rushed to the door and yelled downstairs.

"Dorien, Ivan, help me."

They were by my side a moment later. Dorien set down the

silver candelabra he brought up and picked up Titus' wrist, watching it flop limply across his lap. "What happened?"

"Exactly what it looks like – Usher drugged him and took his gun." I glanced at the spot on the wall where the secret door was concealed in the paneling. "She's gone into the tunnels with Victor. She knew we closed the entrances, so they either have an escape route we don't know about, or they're hoping to hide and wait out the storm. We can't let them leave this house."

"We need weapons," Dorien said. Ivan nodded and darted away. He returned a few moments later carrying two curved rapier swords he'd torn from one of the antique displays. Ivan tossed one to Dorien. My hands tightened around my poker.

Dorien located a spring in the panel. The door didn't open – I assumed they locked it behind them – but Dorien sawed through the paneling with his sword, making a hole large enough to reach through with his hand and release the lock. His eyes met mine, their edges laced with danger. "Take Titus downstairs. Give him the same treatment as Aroha. Luckily, it looks like he hasn't had enough to hurt him, just to put him to sleep. I'll call you if I find anything—"

"I'm coming with you." I shoved past Ivan and lunged for the door. Dorien threw out his body to block me.

"Sprite, you can't—"

I shoved him into the hidden room. "You don't have time to argue with me."

"Fine." Dorien looked miserable, but he knew I was right. "Ivan, take Titus back to the Red Room and keep everyone there. Bar the door as best you can."

Ivan nodded, his sword swinging at his side like some kind of elfin prince as he lifted Titus' arm across his back and managed to drag him away. Dorien turned to me and shoved the candelabra into my hands. "It's just you and me now, Sprite."

He went first, sweeping the weapon around the room while I held out the candelabra to give us some light. I noticed some of the bottles on the shelves had been disturbed. *How much goddamn chloral does he have in here? I guess with his chemistry degree he can make as much as they need.*

We passed into the next room. The bed was unmade. Seeing a different book on the nightstand made my stomach turn. To think that the Ushers were somewhere in the walls of this house, trying to make their escape, while Titus was out cold and they'd nearly killed Aroha... After everything they'd done, they deserved to *burn.*

I won't let you get away with this.

"Careful, Sprite."

I surged ahead of Dorien in the long corridor. We had to find them. If they got away they'd take the truth with them. Dorien elbowed me out of the way to hoist himself up the ladder first. My veins itched with fire as I held up the candelabra to give him enough light. I needed to find them. I needed answers.

"We could really use Clare's help finding them," Dorien mused. "She chose a fine time to ghost us."

"Ha ha. Keep going up," I whispered. "To the attic." I didn't know why, but something told me they would go to the storage room and try to come down the attic stairs. We nailed a board across the door, but if they had the ax, they could just chop their way to freedom.

Dorien disappeared into the shaft. I handed him the candelabra and he held it from me as I pulled myself up after him. We crawled our way into the roof space, pulling ourselves along on our elbows. The candles flickered wildly as warm air rushed through the space, bringing with it the sickly, cloying scent of decay. I coughed, desperate to clear it from my lungs, and blew out one of the candles.

Dorien's boots twitched. "They broke through the door. They're in the house." He shuffled forward and kicked off the rest of the door, thrusting his weapon into the room while I tried to give him enough light.

"I can't see them. And the door is open." Dorien slid out, feet first, then reached back to help me. As I dragged myself to my feet and lifted the candelabra, my eyes caught the light glittering from two orbs in the corner of the room.

A pair of eyes glaring at us from the gloom.

My heart stopped beating.

She's here.

"This ends here, Usher." Dorien kept the tip of his sword trained on the figure as he inched forward. He displayed more confidence than I felt. The Ushers had the gun, which meant at least one of us was taking a bullet tonight. And I wasn't going to let it be Dorien.

I don't want to die.

"You want to fight in the shadows like a coward?" Dorien took another step. "I'm fine with that."

The shadow stepped into the square of light.

Dorien cursed.

I gasped as his features stood out against the pale moon. Those high, proud cheekbones. That strong jaw. And the eyes of clear crystal green.

My eyes.

"My love." Donovan de Winter staggered toward me, hand outstretched, fingers brushing my cheek. "My beautiful daughter. You're mine at last."

FAYE

It can't be him.
It's impossible.
It's a trick. He's a ghost.

But his hand on my cheek was warm. It had form, substance. His green eyes bore into mine as his features twisted in ecstasy – a distorted mirror of my own horror. His breath made a circle of mist in the chilly attic. His dark curls fell wild around his face.

If Donovan de Winter was a ghost, he was doing a fucking great job of pretending to be living.

"Stay back," Dorien rasped, jabbing the sword at my father's head. "I'm warning you."

"You don't know how long I've waited for this day." Tears rolled down Dad's cheeks. "Look at you, Faye. I've seen you from afar, but up close, you're even more beautiful than I expected."

I tried to speak, but words wouldn't come. There was no word in any language to describe what I felt as I let my father run his fingers across my cheek.

"I said, get away from her." Dorien grabbed Dad by his collar and slammed him against the wall. The wood creaked in protest as Dorien slammed the blade against his throat. "You don't deserve her. You don't deserve to breathe the same air as her."

"Daddy." The word escaped my throat before I could stop it. It rose up from a deep memory I'd locked away inside me, a desperate longing for him to wrap me in his arms and tell me I was good enough, talented enough, clever enough, beautiful enough, to deserve his love.

Dorien winced as though I physically slapped him with the word. Tears welled in my eyes and broke through my defenses. *It's him. It's my daddy.*

I wanted to hate him. I wanted to curl my hands around his throat and choke the life from him for what he did to us. But the little girl inside me who desperately wanted to be worthy of him, she cried and wept and keened because her daddy had come back to her at long last.

It was too much.

"Faye, my love, don't cry. Please don't cry. I'm here now. Daddy's here."

"You don't get to say that to her. You weren't there when she needed you. You weren't there when she cried herself to sleep in my arms because her daddy never loved her." Dorien's eyes flicked to me. "Remember, Faye? Remember what he did to you. What he's doing to you right now."

I swallowed hard, swallowed back the little girl who wanted to fall into his arms and have him kiss away her pain. Dorien was right. I had him, and Titus, and Ivan. I didn't need my scumbag of a father.

"Start talking," Dorien shoved the blade against his skin. Dad swallowed, and a thin line of blood bloomed on his skin. "Where are the Ushers?"

His eyes closed. "We heard you coming and Gizella ran downstairs, but I wanted to see you."

"And Victor?"

Dad looked confused. "Victor Usher is dead."

Victor Usher is dead.

And just like that, the pieces slotted into place.

We thought Victor was the one hiding in the walls, spying on us for his wife. Ivan said he recognized his voice through the wall, and the books in the lab were in his handwriting. But it was my dad. He was the one who left the fairy tale book for me to find. He smashed my violin so that I'd find his Becker, and he played the haunting music in the storage room night after night, keeping me awake so he could duet with me.

Even now, I was still just an extension of Donovan de Winter's own narcissism. He made me dance for his amusement while he hid in the walls with his lover. *But for what?*

"You're lying," Dorien snarled. "We opened Victor's grave. We know it's empty."

"He's not lying, Dorien." I stepped in close, so close I could smell the rot and dust that clung to my father's worn clothing. Beneath it, the sage and bergamot scent that belonged to my memories assaulted my nostrils. I closed my eyes, letting the box of memories inside me fall open and the pieces of my childhood tumble free.

Or rather, all the pieces that didn't include him. All the times he missed my birthday parties or recitals because he was off doing his own music. All the times he looked right through me like I was the ghost. All those nights my mom came home from her third job with bags under her eyes and horrors heaped on her shoulders, while he came home smelling of Madame Usher's sickly floral perfume.

I remembered my mother waking up at 6AM after a grueling night shift to hide Easter eggs around our apartment. I remembered her beaming at me from the front row of every recital, and taking me and Dorien out for ice cream when his parents forgot to pick him up. I remembered building blanket forts and shrieking at horror films and stuffing my face with tamales and churros until I threw up. I remembered love that burst from my veins like spring flowers. And none of that love belonged to him.

Mom gave me everything so I would never need him. And now, I needed every ounce of strength she'd given me to face this monster.

"My baby girl," he whimpered.

"How could you do this to me?" The memories churned inside me, becoming a storm of rage and power. "You *chose* to live in these walls as a ghost, didn't you? You chose her over me. I'm *not* your baby girl."

"No, no, no. You don't understand!" he cried. "I had to leave. I had to leave to save you. I lost *everything*. You don't know what it's like, the big tours, the stardom, the glitter and glamor. I got swept away by it. I didn't see the finances. I thought my good fortune would just go on and on forever, I'd live for the moment and pay them back with the next record, the next check, the next big award. Gizella encouraged me – she wanted me to have everything I deserved, everything I earned. She introduced me to her friends who had money they were willing to lend to artists like me. But every dollar I spent was soaked in blood, and I didn't understand that until it was too late. I borrowed from the wrong people, and they were coming after you. You and Marguerite. They would hurt you if I didn't pay. Gizella agreed to help me pay back my loans, but only if I walked away from you forever. I thought it was for the best. I was such a fuck-up that I'd put your lives at risk. You were better off without me."

Tears spilled down his cheeks. Beside me, Dorien breathed deep and jagged. I touched my hands to his shoulders. I needed his strength, his fire. I needed his strong body to hold me upright because I was in danger of floating away.

"And look at you. I was right all along. You were better off without me. You've become so beautiful, so accomplished. Marguerite must be so proud." He reached up to touch my face again. "I never should have brought you here. But I missed you so much."

What?

I jerked away, as if he slapped me with his words.

"What do you mean, you brought Faye here?" Dorien's eyes blazed. His sword arm twitched. He was on the edge of losing control, and I didn't think I could stop him even if I wanted to, and I wasn't sure I wanted to.

"Of course I did. I was tormented being away from you, my darling, missing out on seeing you growing up. This was just supposed to be a temporary arrangement. Gizella had a plan for my comeback. We had to pay my debt in full, she had to divorce Victor, and we had to fix things with the Triumvirate so no one could come after me in the future. But then everything took so much longer than we thought. Months turned into years and I was still a ghost in the walls and then finally, *finally*, Victor got sick and I could at least live most of my time in her private wing."

"You…you lived in the walls of Manderley for *ten years?*" I couldn't believe it. I'd been in those claustrophobic spaces. No wonder his eyes looked wild, and his speech was so erratic and poorly constructed – not the immaculately tailored charmer I remembered.

"It took Gizella that long to pay off my debts. Don't blame her, blame the greedy thugs who kept asking for more, more, more, even after all she and Victor had done for them in the past. And then Victor died and I was ready to make my return to the world, but she had a plan. She had the perfect project for me, but we needed to wait until all the pieces were in place." His Adam's apple bobbed. "Everything she's done has been for me, for the music. She's so different from Marguerite, who never understood us, Faye. A good woman, but she never understood us. We need more than good people. We need fire. We need blood. Your man here understands that."

"Don't talk about my mother like that," I growled. "She has fire enough to burn the world."

"But her fire was for earthly things. Not for the heavens. Not for music. She didn't understand me like Gizella did." His eyes flicked away from mine, staring into the shadows, and I wondered if he was deliberately speaking in the past tense. He sucked in a quick breath, and continued.

"But the years without sunlight, without people, without stimulation…I was going mad. I could only play music when Victor was away on tour or outside in the woods with Harrison. I had to sit in the walls and listen to clumsy students flub their notes and have awkward sex. Gizella kept saying things would change, but they never did. And then Clare moved into the attic. I was lonely, and so was she." His eyes flicked toward the bedroom Clare had before me, and the hole he made in the wall so he could watch her. "The peephole wasn't for perverted reasons. I just wanted to see when she was up there so I could talk to her. That's all we did, just talk. Oh, we wrote a song together. You've been playing it with me."

Bile stung my throat. All these years I'd mourned him, cried for him, raged against his mysterious disappearance, and he was here comforting another girl, being the friend he'd never been to me.

"You told Clare you were a ghost," I whispered.

"It was easier than explaining. I couldn't very well have her run off and tell someone and spoil Gizella's plan. But Clare was clever – she figured out who I was. She compared the composition we made to some of my recordings. She saw my portrait in the hall and asked about me and found out about Gizella's affair. She was going to tell you, Dorien. She was going to tell everyone. And all these years I lived in the walls would have been for nothing."

"So you pushed her down the stairs." Dorien's jaw locked. His sword arm trembled with rage.

"I didn't mean for her to die! I wanted to talk to her in person, show her who I really was. I wanted to tell the truth. I lost the chance with my real daughter, but maybe with Clare, I could love someone the way they deserved to be loved." His shoulders trembled. "I'm so so sorry. I wanted to show her that she wasn't alone, but when I stepped out of the wall I frightened her, and she fell backward and I—I—I—didn't mean for her to die!"

His body shuddered with silent sobs. Dorien worked his jaw. A bead of my father's blood rolled off the tip of the sword.

"Keep talking," I said. "We need to hear everything. We need to understand."

Dad sniffed. "After Clare's death, I didn't want this life anymore. But Gizella told me she worked too hard for me to back out now. I knew I wouldn't survive another year without someone else to love. I told Gizella I could not live another day in these walls, listening to inferior musicians get the opportunities my daughter and Clare should have had. I packed my things. I told her I was leaving, and then she said that if I stayed, she'd make sure you came to Manderley, that I'd see you again. She said she would bring you to me, but it would be your choice if you stayed. She really did try to bring us together, my darling. I think if things had worked out the way they were supposed to, in time you could have loved Gizella like a mother."

He's mad. He's mad if he thinks for a second I could have loved a woman who took my father from me, forced him to live in the walls, and then dangled me in front of him only to torment me into leaving. Does he not realize what she was trying to do? She didn't want me here, but she couldn't kick me out because she would lose him. It had to be my choice to leave. That's why she enlisted Broken Muse to torture me – she was trying to drive me away.

Dorien watched my face, his eyes darkening as he realized what he'd been part of. Every move of Madame Usher's was a carefully designed gambit to keep my father in line.

"She poisoned Mom to bring me here," I gasped out. "Did you know that? Did you help her? I saw that lab back there…"

"The lab belonged to Victor, and his father before him, for designing their perfumes – although he hardly used it. I would never hurt Marguerite. You needed her." Tears rolled down his cheeks. "I did everything I could to make your stay at Manderley happy, even when I figured out what Gizella was doing. I played music for you and with you. I gave you gifts. I watched every performance, all those performances I missed. I was a better father as a ghost than I ever was in real life."

I gulped back a sob. He was right. And it hurt so so much that he was right. It felt like Dorien's blade slicing through my chest over and over again.

I told Dorien once that I loved him and hated him in equal measure, and it was true then, because of how much he hurt me. But hate is part of love – you can only hate someone if you first loved them with your whole heart. And I *hated* my father. I hated him with a white-hot rage that burned my eyes to embers.

And I loathed myself for my hatred, because it was my weakness. Because beneath it, my love still festered like rot that couldn't be cut out. My weakness made me stand here and listen to a man utterly incapable of love try to justify a lifetime of hurt and neglect. It made me lock eyes with Dorien Valencourt, a boy who only *ever* loved me, who done stupid and reckless and dangerous things because he loved me, and wish and wish and wish for my daddy, as if my father's love could somehow make whole the wounds his neglect inflicted.

Everything made sense now.

It was my father all this time.

Nothing would ever make sense again.

"Daddy?"

The word choked on my tongue – a desperate little girl wishing to be more than an afterthought.

Dorien sighed. He tore his blade from Dad's throat and

stepped back, his hand searching for mine in the dark. Blood dribbled down Dad's stained blazer as he staggered toward me, arms outstretched. He wanted to hold me.

I *ached* to be held. I hated that I ached.

I *wished*.

Daddy.

"My Faye." Tears mingled with the blood streaming from his wound. "All those years I thought I loved Gizella, but I was wrong. So wrong. Clare taught me that I never loved you the way you deserved. I want to be a good dad to you once again—"

His voice cut off abruptly.

"Daddy?"

His face contorted in silent agony. He tried to speak, but all that came out was a ruptured gurgle.

He crumpled to the floor.

I screamed as my flickering candles illuminated a dark pool of blood spreading around his still body, and the small kindling ax buried in his back.

A shadowed figure loomed in the doorway. Madame Usher leaned into the light, a sadistic smile on her face.

37

DORIEN

"You killed him," I said. I tried to sound matter-of-fact about it, as if we were chatting about the weather. I needed to keep this shit calm so I could get Faye away from Madame Usher.

It was just as well I was doing the talking, because Faye looked as though if she opened her mouth, she would scream. I tried not to think about the body of her father at my feet, or about my own parents hanging from the cross with nails through their hands and their stomachs sliced open. *We* were alive, and I needed to keep it that way.

"He was weak." Madame Usher fixed her eyes on the tip of my sword, which I kept pointed at her throat. A lifetime of exclusive boarding schools had turned me into a mediocre fencer, but it didn't take much skill to drive a sharp blade through flesh. And I'd do it – I saw in her eyes she knew I'd do it to save Faye.

Sprite, I'm so sorry.

Faye leaned against me, her whole body trembling, her eyes burning with tears she didn't want to cry for the man who fucked her up and fucked her over. I wished I could take away the pain tearing her apart and make it my own. I wish I could feel everything she felt right now so she didn't have to. I already knew that pain so well. Sprite and I were too much alike. We both spent our whole lives looking for the approval of people who didn't love us, didn't deserve us, and now they were dead and we didn't even get the comfort of anger. They were dead and we still wanted them to love us.

Faye screamed as Madame Usher kicked her father. Madame Usher whipped her hand to the pocket of her dress to retrieve my pistol, which she aimed at Faye's head. "After all I did for him, he comes crawling back to you, begging for love as if he had been bereft of it? What about *my* love? What about everything I sacrificed?"

"You took him from his family, locked him up to wither away as a ghost in the walls, and tried to destroy his daughter in front of his eyes," I shot back. My hand twitched. I was holding the sword with my injured hand, and my pinkie finger wasn't up to the task. I had to hope Madame Usher didn't notice. I used my other hand to shove Faye behind me, placing my body between her and the barrel of the gun, between her and the rapidly-spreading pool of her father's blood. "You're evil. How can anyone love a monster like you?"

Behind me, Faye whimpered.

Madame Usher's face reddened with rage. She kept her body turned toward me, but her poisoned words – and her aim – were for Faye.

"You think you're so amazing, just because you carry his blood," she hissed, stomping her boot in the crimson pool at her feet. "You see now how easily blood can be spilled, spoiled, destroyed. You may wear his name like a fashion accessory, but you'll never have his talent. You and that ungrateful mother of yours tried to drain the life from him, always so clingy, so demanding of his attention. I had to get him away from you both, don't you see? He was becoming distracted by your petty concerns. He had greater things to do, to be."

"It's you who doesn't understand," I cried back. "By depriving him of his family, you prevented him from becoming the great musician he could have been. It wasn't Marguerite and Faye who made him crave the finer things, the fame, the trappings of success. You blinded him with baubles and made him into a shallow, uninspired shell of greatness. The best art is about truth – it's the mundane made beautiful, the human experiences that are uniquely ours and yet also shared by everyone. Frida Kahlo painted flowers so they wouldn't die. But what truth could Donovan de Winter breathe to life in his art if he lived a shallow, heartless lie? You killed his talent, not them."

"Is that what you think?" she spat back. "Then you are even more arrogant and oblivious than I imagined. You with your pampered life and your songs of teenage angst. You're nothing but a foolish child. Everything you ever wanted has been handed to you on a silver platter. You've never known pain or hardship. I gave those gifts to you, and you squandered them, as you squandered every opportunity you've had in life. You've never had to make a tough choice or make a sacrifice for your art, and that's why you will never surpass him. Great art comes from hardship, from loss, from *longing*. Donovan de Winter needed to lose everything before he could be *magnificent*."

"But he never became magnificent, did he?" I didn't dare break her gaze to look down at Donovan, but I could feel his blood oozing beneath the soles of my shoes. "He withered away inside Manderley's wall. You never gave him the chance to be reborn."

"He was going to make his return," she said. "I had it all planned out, a way for him to make his mark on the musical world. You'd done so much of my work for me, you beautiful, simple boy. But first, you needed to prove you were worthy of him. I needed you to be absolutely loyal to me, to the house of Usher. I took care of Marguerite, and I gave you one simple assignment – drive Faye away from him, get rid of his last distraction."

"That's what this is about?" I snorted as her words sank in. "You did all this because you wanted Donovan to join Broken Muse?"

Did she think we would just let Faye's once-dead father into the band, a band made famous from songs I wrote about longing for Faye? But then, Madame Usher didn't have to convince us. She had manipulated everything behind the scenes so expertly that we would have had no choice but to agree. Donovan would be in Broken Muse, or we would be utterly ruined.

She's insane. She's an absolute fucking psychopath.

"He would have made you legendary." Madame frowned at me. "You would have gone on to fame and fortune the likes of which even you could only dream of. And I would have been behind you, managing it all. It was perfect. But you had to mess everything up by falling in love with *her*."

She spat at Faye, who shuddered against me.

Madame Usher smiled, and it was almost a sad smile, but I was certain she had no capacity for true emotion. Her eyes were black pinpricks, without light or warmth. She pulled back the safety and pointed the gun square at my head. "But never mind that now. It is time to put everything right."

She squeezed the trigger.

38

DORIEN

My eyes slammed shut. I couldn't look down the barrel to the triumphant grin of Madame Usher as she took my life.

I love you Faye. I love you, Jacob. I'm so sorry—

But the shot didn't come. There was no loud bang, no searing pain, no final moment of clarity before I rushed toward the light. There was a faint clicking nose, and a frustrated grunt.

I opened my eyes.

Madame Usher squeezed the trigger again. *Click, click, click.* Nothing happened.

"Dorien," Faye's voice cracked. "Did you by change purchase a gun, but no ammunition?"

"I thought they came pre-loaded?" I cocked an eyebrow at Madame Usher. "I guess you've been foiled by my stupidity."

Madame Usher *snarled.* She bent down and jerked the ax from Donovan's back. Faye screamed as blood spurted from the wound, splattering us. An arc of crimson decorated the front of Usher's dress, a few speckles dotting the pale skin of her neck.

I lunged at her, but she dodged around my sword and swung

down with her ax. I shoved Faye back. The ax hooked on my shirt, ripping the fabric and whispering against my skin.

Faye screamed again as her back pressed into the wall. Madame Usher's grin was wild, triumphant. I thrust at her face, but the angle was wrong, weak. She whacked the sword with her ax and knocked it out of my hands.

Fuck. Fuck.

I cast around for something else to use as a weapon. She roared as she came at us, ax raised. I picked up the first thing I laid hands on – the portrait of Donovan – and swung it at her just as the ax came down, right toward my skull—

The ax splintered the wooden frame and tore through the canvas. Madame Usher's body toppled forward, thrown off-balance by the momentum. I lunged for my sword. Usher roared and slammed down on top of me, her bony elbow crushing my neck.

"Sprite—" I gasped, my fingers reaching, reaching, brushing the sword's hilt but not close enough to grab it. Madame ground her elbow into me, pushing the air from my lungs. Red welts danced in front of my eyes. Blood rushed in my ears. *Any second now I'll pass out and—*

"When I think how many times I longed to slip a little poison into your food," Madame purred in my ear, wrapping her other arm around my neck and bending my head back. The gun was still in her fingers, so close but completely out of reach. My chest burned like I'd swallowed hot coals. Pain rushed my temples as I fought for air, but I could already feel the tips of my fingers, my legs, going numb. Her voice sounded far away, and I wasn't sure if I heard her words or just imagined them as the dark at the edge of my vision closed in. "My husband kept impeccable diaries – the one helpful thing he did in his whole useless life. It was too easy to follow his instructions and use plants from the garden to poison Marguerite. But if you hadn't used the chloral on me, I never would have thought to make a supply for my own purposes. Do you think that oaf Titus will ever wake up? It's a pity he's not here to save you..."

Her voice trailed off as red blossomed over my eyes. I thought I must have finally run out of air. My chest no longer burned and an ethereal white light burst in the center of the red and rushed toward me. *All I have to do is head toward the light...*

But I could hear someone screaming. And no one should be screaming in heaven, unless...

Madame Usher was no longer on top of me. My chest heaved, my lips burned as I gasped and sucked and gorged myself on air. Every breath burned, but I was breathing, I was alive and the light…

The light was Clare.

She glowed with a pale light that had no source. She floated across the room, moving toward us with deliberate, menacing slowness, her green eyes filled with malicious delight, her mouth open in a ghastly cry of defiance.

Madame Usher was screaming.

I coughed, my lungs on fire. My fingers closed around the hilt of the sword.

Madame didn't try to stop me. She was frozen, glaring at the ghost as though she could stop Clare with the force of her hatred. "You ungrateful wretch. I took you in when no one else would. I gave you a home, a job. I even let that dolt Radcliffe give you lessons. And you had to go and turn him against me. You were lucky you fell down the stairs, because you didn't succumb to the arsenic I'd been rubbing on your violin strings."

Clare stretched out her fingers toward Madame Usher's neck, her blackened mouth opening, yawning. The temperature dropped to freezing, and even though we knew Clare couldn't move objects, that all the ghostly things were really Donovan's doing, I believed this time may be an exception.

Madame Usher staggered backward, just out of reach. "That's right, every time you and Donovan betrayed me, you killed yourself. So I know you can't hurt me."

Clare's fingers brushed her neck, and Madame's eyes bugged out. She flinched away. She *felt* Clare's icy grasp.

You killed me, the air whispered. *You killed me and now you will pay.*

"Get away from me!" Madame Usher grabbed the candelabra from Faye's frozen fingers and threw it at Clare. It sailed right through her, hitting the rolled-up rug in the corner of the room, which burst into flames.

"Shit." I leaped to my feet and tried to tip the carpet on its side to smother the flames, but all I succeeded in doing was spreading the fire to the boxes stacked behind it. Behind me, Madame Usher screamed. Faye stood behind her, still staring blankly at her father's broken body. She didn't seem to have even registered Clare's presence at all.

"Faye." I held out my hand to her. "I need you to come here."

"Daddy." She pulled on his boot. "We can't leave him here. We have to save him."

Fuck. Shit. Fuck.

My strong, beautiful, fearsome Sprite. In the last ten minutes, she'd learned enough truths to undo her utterly, and now I needed to pull her away from the body of the one man she'd spent the last ten years hoping to see alive.

"Faye." I choked on her name as the room started to fill with smoke. I stumbled over Donovan's body and grabbed her shoulders, giving her a gentle shake. "I wish I had the time to give you the mental breakdown you so desperately deserve. But we have to leave. *Now.*"

I wrapped my arm around her shoulders and dragged her toward the door, turning her away from Clare just as Madame Usher let out a bloodcurdling scream. I wanted so badly to turn around and witness Clare's revenge, because it would be beautiful and so, so deserved. I wished I could jerk the pistol from her fingers, because I didn't like turning my back on a woman with a gun. But I had to get Faye out.

As I staggered out of the storage room, a dark shape appeared in the narrow stairwell. Faye screamed as Titus grabbed her around the waist and threw her over his shoulder. He shot me a look fraught with pain before stumbling back toward the stairs. He gripped the banister with both hands and half slid, half shuffled, down. *He must've woken up, then.*

At the bottom, Ivan tried to take Faye from him, but he growled incoherently and continued his shuffle toward the main staircase. By now, I could smell the smoke curling through the air, and the orange flames leaped so high they provided up a square of flickering light. Madame Usher's screams became one long, agonized wail – a sound I knew I'd hear in my nightmares for the rest of my days.

"What's going on?" Elena cried out, taking the stairs two at a time to meet us as we shuffled down. "I smell smoke."

"No time to explain. The house is on fire." I shoved her toward the front door. "We have to go. Ivan, get Aroha."

"What about Madame Usher?" Elena's eyes bore into mine, and I knew what she was really asking.

"We leave her."

Ivan returned with Aroha under his arm. She bent double, her body racked with a coughing fit. I pressed the sleeve of my shirt to my mouth and nose as the acrid smoke began to sting. Titus held a squabbling Faye over his shoulder as he threw open the door. "It's no use," he said groggily, surveying the solid wall of snow piled the full height of the door. He punched it a couple of times. "There's too much snow. We'll be dead before I can dig through this."

Not to mention the fact that you barely have use of your arms and legs, I thought but didn't say.

"The kitchen." I raced ahead, ducking into the kitchen and

turning the handle on the back door. It pushed open with ease. I yelled in triumph for the others to follow, but as I did, a giant clump of snow fell loose from the eaves above and dropped in the doorway. I staggered back as an avalanche of snow slid into the kitchen, splattering my legs with wet ice and completely blocking our exit.

"What now?" Elena cried. "The smoke is getting thicker."

Upstairs, something crashed. I could no longer hear Madame screaming. I whirled around, staring at the faces of my stricken friends. Faye was usually the one who had clever ideas, but her father's death had destroyed her, and I needed to step the fuck up. *Think, Dorien. We could try smashing a window, maybe even going back upstairs and sliding off the porch roof onto the snow—*

"The tunnels," Faye whispered.

Okay, so maybe she was still our beautiful, clever Faye.

"Yeah, nah. I'm not getting into some rank-ass tunnel while the house is burning," Aroha shot back. "We don't know if there's an outdoor exit. We'll get stuck and burn."

"No, we can get outside," Faye argued. "The night of the parents' recital, Daddy came from the house and followed Dorien through the woods. Then he had to get back into the house to leave those items for me in the kitchen without Harrison or any of the other party guests seeing. There's an outside exit, I'm sure of it—"

"It was on the map," Ivan said. "I remember it clearly. It goes from the Red Room to down beside the stream."

I raced into the Red Room and tore the boards we nailed over the hidden entrance. I drew back my leg and kicked the paneled wall with everything I had. It didn't even make a dent. Titus shoved me out of the way and threw his body at the wall. With a crack, the wood splintered. Titus tossed the pieces away, revealing a dark hole leading along the wall.

"Quickly." Titus grabbed Faye's arm, pulling her close to him and caging her in his arms. She seemed to be free of her father's spell, and with him behind her she wouldn't be able to run back for her father's body. Faye accepted another silver candlestick from Aroha and stepped into the gloom. As she disappeared, Titus turned sideways to squeeze his broard shoulders inside. He gasped as he had to wriggle to fit in the narrow gap. Ivan helped Elena inside next. That left me to help Aroha.

The room was dense with smoke now. I could barely see Aroha's body as I grabbed her arm. She shook her head. "I'm staying."

"No, you're not."

"This is the only place I ever did something worthwhile," she muttered. "My insides are on fire. I'd rather die here than in a bloody mess in a hospital bed."

"Don't be stupid." I yanked her close. "This house has taken too many victims."

She struggled against me, but I picked her up and plonked her in the hole, climbing in after her so she could only move forward. I knew Aroha could kick my ass if she needed to. She didn't want to stay behind. She wanted someone to save her. Didn't we all?

I shoved her into the tunnel, kicking at her heels to make her run faster. Inside the walls, the rotting smell was unbearable. It mingled with the smoke to create a poison that made my whole body burn. Every step was agony as my lungs and stomach cramped and disgorged, and my eyes had clamped shut with protest so I couldn't see a thing. I kept moving into the darkness, not knowing if we were even going in the right direction, but trusting Faye.

"I see a doorway," Faye called from somewhere above. I picked up the pace, urging Aroha onward as more crashes sounded behind us. Light punched the air around Aroha's shoulders, and I found my breath came a little easier, the burn a little duller.

Frigid cold air enveloped me, but it was blissfully fresh and free of burning. The world opened up around me and my Barker Blacks scuffed in fluffy snow.

We collapsed into a heap in the snow, holding each other as we emptied our lungs and stomachs of the foulness of Manderley. I gasped in mouthfuls of frigid mountain air. Behind us, the fire blazed, an unholy conflagration that consumed the house from the inside out.

39

FAYE

*M*anderley was burning.

In all my nightmares, I'd never imagined such a sight. We huddled in a tight circle to warm ourselves as we watched. The fire spread through the rooms on the first floor, tearing at the ancient drapes and blowing out the windows with a sound like gunshots. Flames licked like orange tongues as they eviscerated the ancient house of Usher. Stone walls broke apart as the heavy wooden ceiling beams collapsed upon them, and the beautiful carved wooden gables dashed themselves against the ground.

Madame Usher is inside.

So is my father.

I've always thought of fire as a destructive force, wild in its hunger and undiscerning in its tastes. But as Manderley burned beneath a raging sky, I saw something else. I saw that fire *cleansed* – it burned away the rot, the evil, the bad seeds, leaving behind a clean slate.

What we saw tonight was the exorcism of Manderley.

As we stared up at the burning building, I thought I caught the faint snatch of music on the wind. The same song I'd played in my room at night, the song my father wrote with Clare, the notes twining in the breeze – their funeral dirge.

We made our way to the broken fountain just as the porch collapsed, sending up a cloud of black smoke that burned my lungs. The flames tore through the building, gutting the second floor, moving like dancers – a living fire to brighten this dark night, transforming the house into an altar where all the ghosts of Madame's deeds sacrificed for absolution.

The sound of it was incredible – the roar rumbling through the valley, the howl of the wind tearing through the skeleton, the crackle like drums beating, and the crash and shatter of beautiful objects consigned to ashes. And above it all, the sickening melody of a horrible, inhuman scream.

"I see her." Ivan pointed to a window in the east wing. It took me a moment to recognize her face staring out of the orange flames.

Madame Usher.

The moment froze in time, like a movie paused in my memory to provide one final horror – Madame Usher's body wreathed in flames, her black skirts ablaze, her hands black and her mouth open in a scream of bitter terror. She met my eyes and for a moment, she recognized me. She saw that she had lost.

Then she fell.

The crunch as she hit the ground would haunt my dreams for the rest of my life.

She didn't move.

We rushed to her. Ivan rolled her over, beating out the flames with his foot. There was no saving her. Her neck bent at an impossible angle, and her eyes peered up at me, glassy and unseeing.

She was gone.

Numbness settled in my veins. I should have been happy. She was evil, and now she could never hurt another human soul. But I felt nothing for her, only an ache in my heart.

She did all of it for love. For the love of my father. But that love corrupted her, turning her heart into coal. And I felt certain my heart would become coal, too.

I turned my gaze to the window where she'd fallen, startled to see another face peering down. The figure held out both hands, as if she had just shoved something heavy out the window. Piercing green eyes, a cute turned-up nose, and a blackened mouth outlined in orange flames.

Clare.

The flames crackled and moved, and a second figure joined her. My father put his arm around Clare's shoulders, pulling her head into him, the way he never did with me.

She smiled. And it was the most beautiful smile I'd ever seen.

Fire blazed around them, and they disappeared.

"We should get to Harrison," I said, balling my fists into my eye sockets in a vain attempt to hold the tears inside. "He has a satellite phone."

Because while cleansing fire is a good thing when it comes to creepy houses and their malevolent mistresses, I do not want to see this thing burn through the pristine, beautiful forest.

Dorien held me as we trudged through the snow, stepping into the ruts Titus made with his body as he shoved his way ahead of us. Wind blasted the skin from our faces, and for every step forward we seemed to be blown three steps back. We had to circle around to the front of the house, taking a wide berth as the wall of heat shoved us away from Manderley, and then make our way down the drive. Our candles had blown out long ago, and we followed each other blindly until Titus called out with triumph and I could just make out the glow of light from Harrison's windows, so very faint and far away.

The wall of heat rose up behind us, and fear clawed at my chest. If the forest caught fire, we'd be in big trouble. We had to get word to the authorities. Aroha still needed medical attention.

Maybe there's a chance they could put out the fire before it spreads.

I couldn't think about it. I had to focus on putting one foot in front of the other.

Finally, *finally,* we reached Harrison's gatehouse. Snow piled into my boots as I swung myself up the steps.

"Harrison." I slammed into the door, pounding with my fists. Nothing moved inside, but the fire flickered brightly from the hearth. "It's Faye. Open up. Manderley is on fire!"

Nothing moved or stirred inside. Manderley's destruction reflected in the window, but when I cupped my hands against the glass I thought I could see the fire crackling in his hearth. "Harrison?" I stepped down and banged on the high window of his living room. "It's Faye. Please, help us."

"He might've fallen asleep. Watch out." Titus wrapped his scarf around his fist and punched out the glass pane in the kitchen window. He reached through and unlocked the door. We piled inside, drawn toward the roaring fire. Two chairs were pulled close to the blaze, facing the flames. Harrison leaped up from one, his face a storm.

"How dare you break in here?" he boomed, his face beet red. "Get out!"

I never knew our kindly groundskeeper had such demons in him. Dorien rounded Harrison's chair, his eyes wide. Harrison stormed toward him, arms outstretched, roaring with defiance, and I honestly thought he was going to flatten us all.

"We're sorry for barging in, but you have to help us. Madame Usher is dead, Manderley is on fire, and my father...his body...We need to use your satellite phone to call—" I stopped short as Harrison shoved Dorien from the room. Dorien was fighting him, trying to force his shoulder into Harrison's gut to get around him.

"You ungrateful, wretched boy. You've ruined *everything.*"

"Faye, look in the chair," Dorien cried out as Harrison pushed him out the door and down into the snow. "Look in the other chair."

"Don't!" Harrison barked. I jerked my head around, but all I could see was the wingback with the top of someone's head reclined there, and a thin, skeletal hand on the rest, the fingers curled around an empty whiskey glass. Harrison had a guest, but why hadn't he moved—

Wait a second...

I took a step closer. Bile rose in my chest as I moved into the light of the fire, as I saw the terrifying sight that Dorien warned me about.

A human skeleton had been arranged perfectly in the chair, its feet in fluffy slippers, the fingers of its other hand clutching a fat cigar. The bones had been lovingly cleaned and dressed in pressed trousers and a plaid shirt. In some places, bits of leathery skin and gristle still clung to them, and I could see wires and wooden pegs propping the body in position.

The skull of Victor Usher grinned up at me, his eye sockets black as night.

40

FAYE

"Harrison," I choked out. "What's going on?"

He stood in the doorway and plucked his rifle from its rack. He hung his head with sadness as he loaded two bullets into the chamber. "You shouldn't have barged in here like this, Miss Faye. A man's business is his own."

"That's Victor Usher, isn't it?" Dorien cried from outside. "You dug up Victor Usher's corpse. But why?"

"Why? Because he never should have died!" Harrison roared. "That witch never loved him, but she strung him along in a loveless marriage because if she lost him, she'd lose this house. After Victor's parents died, we thought we would finally have a chance to be together. All those years waiting, pretending, wishing for a world that would accept us. And when Victor's parents finally bit the dust, we thought we would be able to live out our days together in the solitude of Manderley. But she wouldn't dream of it. She refused to divorce him, to accept the generous settlement he offered to be rid of her tyranny. She used his secret against him, binding him to her in a marriage of misery while she finally took him from me."

He's in love with Victor Usher.

Of course he was. I couldn't believe I hadn't realized it earlier. The way he talked about Victor and the Usher family, about growing up in this house and walking the grounds and hunting together. I remembered the photograph hanging in Madame Usher's office – the wedding portrait with Harrison on a ladder behind them, glaring at the newlyweds with untamed hatred. *He was glaring at Madame Usher because she took his love from him.*

"Manderley died with Victor," Harrison sobbed. "The flowers haven't bloomed since he drew his last breath. I tried everything to make this place blossom again, but she prefers it to be rot and weeds."

Tears rolled down Harrison's cheeks as he snapped the barrel closed and stepped toward the door. "I just wanted the time that had been stolen from us. I was going to put him back in the mausoleum, but I couldn't bear to part with him."

He sighed, his shoulders shaking, as he raised the gun and pointed it at Dorien.

"Faye, I'm so so sorry," Harrison said. "I've tried to protect you all from her evil, but if you tell them about me, they'll take me away from Manderley. I'll lose him, and I can't bear to be apart from him. So you see what I have to do."

He lifted the gun and aimed it at Dorien's chest.

41

FAYE

"Wait. You don't have to do this," I cried. "We all understand what it's like to have to love in secret. We all know what it's like to lose someone. We won't tell a soul what we saw tonight, will we?"

Dorien, Titus, Ivan, Elena, and Aroha all shook their heads.

"Please, Harrison, don't do this. It's not you. You're not a murderer. You—"

Harrison sighed. "I'm sorry, Miss Faye. it's too late. I promise I'll make it quick. Not like Madame Usher. She would have you suffer out of spite." He glanced out the window. "The fire will hide the evidence."

He raised the rifle again. Dorien blew me a kiss, his eyes wide and dark and impossibly sad.

I screamed as a shot rang out.

TITUS

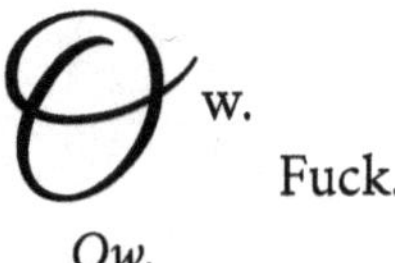

Ow. Fuck.

FAYE

*E*verything happened so fast.

I surged forward as Titus leaped in front of Dorien, his hands wrapped around the barrel of the rifle. My gentle giant collapsed, clutching his abdomen. The snow around him turned pink with blood. Harrison froze, stunned by the scene, and Ivan took the chance to tackle him, knocking him into the snow.

"Titus, no."

I fell at his side, pulling his braids away from his face. He peered up at me, his eyes swimming with pain. *No. This can't be how it ends.*

He's not dying tonight. He's not. I forbid it.

"Faye…" the word gurgled in Titus' throat. Blood dribbled from the wound. He pawed at the snow, trying to grab the rifle that had fallen beside him. But his body was slipping into shock and he couldn't make his hand work properly. The pink snow grew around him.

I grabbed his hand and held it to my chest, pressing it against my heart. "Titus, stop. Please, listen to me. You have to—"

My words died as blood spurted from the corner of his mouth, splattering the front of his shirt.

That's not good. That can't be good.

Titus closed his eyes as he battled with his demons. He jerked his hand from mine and fell on the gun, trying to pick it up, but someone knocked him out of the way. Before I could scream, Ivan tore the rifle from Titus, flung his body around, and fired.

BANG.

The shot rang out across the valley, echoing through the mountains. Harrison's body slumped into the snow. He didn't move.

"No," Titus murmured. "I was supposed to carry that guilt. I was…"

His eyes fluttered closed, and his body slumped in the snow.

"No, Titus." I held his head up and slapped his cheek, pulled on his eyelids, kissed his freezing lips. "Wake up. You have to wake up, you beautiful, impossible man."

Tears froze on my cheeks. I knew what he'd tried to do. In his dying moments Titus had decided to kill Harrison to save us all, because he didn't want any of us to have to live with the guilt of pulling the trigger. He never once in his whole life put himself before others. And he wouldn't do that even at the edge of death.

You can't die. Not now. You're not allowed. We were supposed to have our whole lives ahead of us. We were supposed to make music together and have a beautiful family and travel the world and you can't die you can't you can't—

"Fuck." Dorien crawled forward, lifting Titus' drooping head. "Man, you have to stay awake, okay? Please, stay awake for Faye. Stay awake for me. Can you do that?"

Dorien knew Titus wouldn't fight for himself. But he'd fight for *us*. Titus' lips parted, and a quiet moan escaped, or maybe it was my big stupid heart imagining it.

"Please, Titus. Keep fighting. I need you. We all need you."

Ivan staggered over, dropping the gun as he knelt beside me. His shirt was splattered with blood and his cold eyes haunted with what he'd done.

"Ivan," Elena rushed to her brother's side, planting kisses on his cheeks. "You saved us all. You are my hero."

"There is no time for that," he barked, pushing her off. "Titus is shot."

"And we can't drive anywhere because of the bloody snow." Dorien rose shakily to his feet. "We need a rescue helicopter. Wait with Titus, I'll find Harrison's satellite phone."

"Elena, I need your help." I shrugged off my jacket and balled it up, pressing it against Titus' gunshot wound. "Hold this here. Try to staunch the bleeding. You can pack a bit of snow behind it, too."

I cradled Titus' head into my lap, and looked up at the burning house in the background. I sucked in a breath as I caught sight of two figures walking through the snow, their bodies translucent and circled in light. A smell shifted in the air – it was like nothing I'd ever smelled before, a cacophony of scents that stirred a surge of memories inside me. Some of them belonged to me – my father kissing my mom after a concert, and smiling shyly as he handed me my first ever violin. But others were not mine – Dorien snuggled in the attic bedroom with Clare, Ivan bringing Dorien's hand to his lips and kissing his ruined finger, Titus headbanging with Micah as they jumped on his bed.

The beautiful dead – the memories that Manderley couldn't take from us.

I turned up my hand and waved at my father and Clare.

"Faye." Elena squinted at the house. "What are you waving at?"

I blinked, and they were gone.

"Nothing." I drew my gaze back to Titus' face. The music swelled in my ears, driving out the roar of the fire. "Nothing at all."

Elena rested her cheek against mine as she pressed against the wound. Ivan held us both close, his body sheltering us from the icy snow. I did not look back at Manderley as the final snatches of my father's song faded into the cold night.

EPILOGUE: FAYE

"Are you ready for this?" Dorien knitted his fingers in mine. He leaned in close, the dark smudges of eyeliner making his face appear demonic, but in the best possible way. Demons were all about possession, and this man was welcome to my eternal soul if he kept looking at me like *that*.

"I was born ready." I squeezed his fingers, wishing I could squeeze away the butterflies in my stomach.

I was lying.

I am not ready.

This is insane.

Sound the fucktrumpets. Why did I think I could do this?

Dorien planted his lips on mine, the rush of heat coursing through my body, tugging at my nerves and making the edges fray even worse than before. He pulled away and flashed me that wicked grin of pure aristocratic confidence. "You're going to slay tonight."

I glanced over his shoulder, picking out Titus and Ivan standing behind me in the dim light. Ivan nodded, and Titus flashed me the devil horns.

That's right. That's why I'm doing this.

For them. For us. For our future.

The light dimmed on stage. *That's our cue. Too late to back out now.*

Fog swirled around my ankles as I dragged my leaden feet to my designated spot. Dorien flashed me his megawatt grin as he settled himself behind the piano, then gave a signal to the crew.

The lights went up, and Titus strummed his guitar. A haunting, somber note rang through the club, and six hundred Broken Muse fans erupted into raucous applause.

Their reaction nearly knocked me off my feet. I'd never heard a sound like it – a physical force that grabbed my heart, tugged it right out of my chest, and tossed it into an electrical socket. My body buzzed with sizzling energy – the same wild abandon that came over me whenever I kissed my Muses, only amplified and returned to me a hundredfold.

Dorien punched the keys, and a few bars later Ivan came in with a scorching melody. Spotlights flickered between them, highlighting Ivan's sharp cheekbones and Dorien's devious grin and Titus' wild and beautiful smile.

A smile that I almost lost eight months ago.

Miraculously, Harrison's shot missed Titus' vital organs. He'd spent weeks in the hospital and months hobbling around with a cane, and he couldn't quite leap around stage yet like he wanted to, but he was gloriously alive and that was what mattered. He was living proof Manderley could grant life as well as take it away.

His father hadn't left his side during his recovery. Amos and Delphine Thibodeaux were in the audience tonight. They were still filled with pain over Micah's death, but they were working hard to rebuild their relationship with their living son.

They weren't the only special guests here tonight. My mom, Agent Rochester and Natalie were in a private box with Jacob. Mom and Natalie had joined forces again to build a PR consultancy. Mom was also looking after Jacob while Dorien was on tour, and the pair of them had bonded. I loved seeing her share her energy with another kid, and Jacob thrived under her care. He'd stopped asking about Father Aaron (who had died in a prison brawl – and I can't say anyone would mourn him). He moved up a year in school, and was taking dance classes with her and Rochester.

That's right – Mom and Rochester were an item now. It was weird at first, but she looked so happy and he looked so completely smitten with her that I sensed the flutter of true love in the air.

I raised my violin to my chin, and I struck the strings. The spotlight bathed me in brilliant light as we launched into *The Fall of the House of Usher* – the composition Dorien and I wrote together.

A new song for a new era of Broken Muse.

I twirled around my Muses, dancing with Titus as his fingers assaulted the strings, dueling with Ivan as we played the complex *spiccato*. I lay across the piano and kissed Dorien's head as his fingers fluttered over scales. He beamed up at me like I was a goddess, never once betraying the pain in his hand from his old injury. There were still some pieces he'd never be able to play again, but he was happy to be behind the piano with his family, and he was getting more into composition now, where it didn't matter how many working fingers he had.

We finished the song to rapturous applause. Dorien leaned forward to speak into his microphone. "Thank you so much for being here tonight. You're the first to meet the new and very much improved Broken Muse. Faye de Winter joins us on violin, and you'll be seeing a lot of her since she's now a permanent member of the band. We think you'll love her just as much as we do."

Judging by the wild whistles and applause that greet my name, he's right. My cheeks flushed with color as I took a deep bow, then returned my violin to my chin to begin the next song.

We tore through the rest of our set, a mix of classic Broken Muse songs, some fun covers, and another new piece Dorien had written especially for us, called *Manderley Burns*.

As I ground up against Ivan during our violin duel in 'Manderley Burns,' I realized that Madame Usher was right about one thing – Broken Muse was better as a foursome. But it wasn't Donovan de Winter who would accompany them to stardom, it was me.

Something wonderful sparked on stage that night – a bit of Elena's *zâne* magic scented the air. I felt as though I'd stepped into my future, and it looked bright and full of adventures and music and love.

We emerged from stage after the show, sweaty and beaming. Elena bounced in the wings, rushing forward to shower us with kisses. She had been lucky to catch this show – her solo tour just happened to be in New York City this same weekend. "You are all amazing." I was grinning so hard I could barely feel her kisses touch my cheeks.

"You didn't make me violently ill, trash." Aroha wrapped her arms around me. She was back in America after a stint in a rehab center back in New Zealand. She and Titus were recording this weird album of atonal music inspired by addiction and mental health, with all the proceeds going to support mental health services for her Iwi (tribe) back home. She signed with a label and the press were calling her the Maori Chelsea Wolfe, a comparison she wore with pride.

In the green room, Dorien flopped onto the sofa, kicking off his boots and massaging his sore finger. Titus sat down opposite him, resting the guitar on his knee and playing a Black Sabbath riff, his braids falling over his face. Ivan hovered at the table, where the venue had laid out a rider of all our favorites. He poured a glass of port for each of us – a tradition we kept from our time at Manderley.

I waved the glass away. "Not for me tonight."

He lifted an eyebrow. It was the third night in a row I hadn't imbibed. I'd been waiting until after we got through this first show to tell them, but from the excited glint in Ivan's icicle eyes, I think he figured it out.

"You're…" He couldn't even get the words out, he was so excited. I nodded.

Ivan broke into a wild grin. It was this crack in this armor that alerted the other two.

Titus' head snapped up. "You're not drinking again?"

I shrugged, barely able to keep the grin off my own face. "Maybe I just don't feel like it."

"Or could there be another reason, Sprite?" The corner of Dorien's mouth quirked up.

"Sound the fucktrumpets, you're *pregnant?*" Titus' eyes bugged out of his head. He picked me up, crushing me to his chest and spinning me around so my legs flew out at crazy angles.

"Careful, you'll spin the little peanut right out of me," I laughed.

Titus sat me down and the three of them crowded around me, kissing me and peppering me with questions about the baby. *Our baby.* I still couldn't believe it myself.

The timing wasn't great – we planned to tour for a year – but as I touched my stomach and felt a surge of intense love for the peanut growing there, I knew it would be okay. Better than okay. It would be amazing. We would be amazing.

Our child wouldn't have a normal life. Not with a mom and three dads and an uncle who survived a cult and a grandmother who loved to go dancing and a godmother who was a famous classical violinist and another godmother who was a ghost. But who cared about normal? We had our family, and we had the music flowing in our veins, and that was all we needed.

Not one of them asked whose baby it was. They didn't need to. It was all of ours. A new Broken Muse. A new life we would love and cherish and who would fill our lives with a different type of music – the kind of music that sings in the heart.

"We don't have to do this," Titus reached across and squeezed my knee. "We can turn around and go home if you want to."

"Don't drive so wildly," Ivan snapped, reaching across to steady Dorien's hand. "This isn't the Monaco GP. In fact, don't drive at all. Pull over, I'm taking the wheel."

"I love it when you order me around like that," Dorien shot back. "It's *adorable*."

While the two of them bickered in the front seat and Titus rubbed reassuring circles on my leg, I trained my eyes out the window, looking for the turrets of Manderley poking through the trees. Even though objectively I knew they weren't there any longer, that nothing at the house could ever hurt me again, I couldn't help the fear twisting in my gut as we neared the tall iron gates.

Beside me, our daughter, Claire, made a gurgling noise in her sleep. Her long eyelashes fluttered as she stirred, but didn't wake. I touched my finger to her tiny hand, the love in my chest swelling as I reveled in how soft and small and perfect she was. She had light brown skin like mine and a mop of glorious dark hair.

When she'd first been born, I thought she had Titus' dark eyes – they were so impossibly deep and she wore such a serious expression that she always appeared to be considering the problems of the universe, rather than contemplating her next poop. But at three months old, it was clear to me that Dorien was the father – her cheeky grin was all him.

It didn't matter who contributed her DNA. She was ours, and we were hers. Completely and utterly. My muses were the most amazing fathers. Dorien spent hours playing peekaboo with her and zooming her around the room like an airplane while she giggled with delight. Ivan took her for long walks every day, and Titus loved to fuss over her – sourcing the best baby food and changing her diapers and carefully folding her tiny baby clothes.

The Broken Muse tour was so successful we were able to take six months off to spend time together as a family while Dorien wrote new music. We were going to make our base in Prague for the summer, but before we left America there was one thing we had to do.

I held my breath as we drove through the gates, half expecting some bolt of lightning to shoot from the sky and fry us. Harrison's old gatehouse loomed beside us, empty now and being consumed by the forest. Vines twisted across the walls and crawled through the broken window and open door. We had Harrison buried in the Usher crypt, in the tomb beside Victor that had been reserved for Madame Usher. It felt right, even after what he tried to do to us.

We pulled into the parking spot underneath the trees. Elena was already there, leaning against the hood of her shiny new Bentley, a cigarette dangling from her jaws. Behind her, Manderley sprawled across my vision – no longer the grand and imposing house that dwarfed the ancient trees surrounding it, but a blackened scar on the landscape.

Just a pile of ashes and bones.

"I want to meet my goddaughter." Elena rapped on the window before Dorien had even turned off the engine. Grinning, I unclipped Claire's carseat, flipped the handle, and brought her out to show her off.

"She's sleeping," Ivan said, throwing her arm around his sister's shoulders and kissing her forehead. They hadn't seen each other since the first show of our tour. Elena had a six-month residency in Vienna, and we'd been doing shows every second night across Europe and Asia. We even went down to Australia and New Zealand. Aroha and her family showed us around the country, and it was so beautiful, I wanted to live there. Maybe one day.

We had so many wonderful days ahead of us.

"Well, wake her up." Elena stubbed out her cigarette with her. "We need to be properly introduced."

I laughed at Elena, who didn't understand a thing about babies. She declared that she would never have one – a trauma she carried from her short marriage to Radcliffe. She said she wanted to focus on her career, but I think it was more than that. Between her father, who effectively sold her, and the Ushers, she didn't exactly have great role models. I understood – I'd been so worried that I would turn out to be like my father, but that curse died with him because I loved my daughter more than life itself. And Ivan had proven he was an amazing dad, which I never doubted.

Claire opened her eyes then, and we let Elena have cuddles and spent some time catching up before we decided to make our move toward the ruins. My boots crunched on the gravel, kicking aside dead leaves and bits of charred debris. The winter weather and the encroaching forest hadn't been kind to Manderley – the eastern end wall had been standing when we were helicoptered to safety, but now it lay in pieces atop the rest of the structure. Vines and weeds tangled amongst the charred remains of the house that had become a tomb. An eerie silence pervaded, as if trees didn't dare rustle and birds were forbidden to sing. Madame Usher had silenced the music of Manderley forever.

The police were able to analyze Victor's remains and determined he'd been poisoned. It was exactly as Harrison said – Madame Usher got rid of Victor so she could control the house, the finances, and my father. *In Cauda Venenum* – that's the secret she thought Dorien had figured out.

As for Madame Usher, her body was never recovered. The fire department said that there was no way she could have survived the fall, but even though they scoured the whole area where we said we saw her, they hadn't been able to locate her body. They believed she might have been dragged off by wolves.

Thinking about it gave me an uneasy feeling. My gaze flicked to the trees at the edge of the overgrown gardens. Had her burned, broken body been sacrificed to the mountains, scattered across the landscape by animals, forever separated from the house she cursed with her malice and never allowed to rest in peace? Or did we just imagine seeing her body with its broken neck? Was that the final horror Manderley visited upon us? Was she still out there, alive after dragging herself free of the fire? Was she licking her wounds and lying in wait to spring another trap for us?

Neither option felt right, or just. But you don't always get closure in life. So much about Madame Usher would be forever a mystery to me.

The firefighters did manage to pull my father's remains from the house. Mom refused to give him a funeral, and we buried him in a small, cheap grave in the Bushwick cemetery, close to the crappy apartment I rented after Mom became ill. I hadn't visited him, and I never would.

As for the third body consumed by Manderley, the body of Maxim Radcliffe hidden in the walls, that had also been recovered. He was too badly damaged for the police to conclude anything from forensics. His death was ruled a sad accident.

"Here it is." Titus set down the object he'd taken from the trunk of the car, unwrapping the blanket to reveal a round, smooth lump of granite. We'd had it engraved with a simple message.

For Clare and Donovan. Who brought about the fall of the House of Usher.

Titus dragged over a bag of quick-dry cement and a spade, and the boys dug a shallow hole where the front door had stood and set the stone inside. There was a gap at the side of our marker, where Titus had dug the hole extra-wide. I removed an object from my pocket and dropped it into the earth.

My father's cufflink.

Rochester had the furnace room and all its remains carefully studied. They found the remains of at least twenty-six people. He concluded that the Ushers were being paid by the Triumvirate to get rid of bodies. "Crime families always leave a trail of collateral damage in their wake," he told us. He believed when Madame Usher decided to make my father disappear, she had his clothes burned in the furnace with the last of the bodies.

I'd thought about returning my father's violin to Manderley. It seemed right, symbolically, but I couldn't quite stomach burying a Becker in the dirt, especially knowing where it came from. Instead, we wrapped it carefully and had it delivered anonymously to Nero Lucian, a casino owner in Emerald Beach who Rochester was able to connect to the Triumvirate. Hopefully now, all debts were repaid.

I stepped back, admiring the marker as the guys cemented the stone inside. Now anyone who set foot at Manderley would know its legacy. Hopefully, the ghosts would finally be able to rest in peace.

I half expected to see Clare's ghost staring back at us, but I knew she was gone. We'd given her the justice she needed to be free of Manderley. I liked to think that Dad and Clare were together in the afterlife. Dad brought me to Manderley in search of his own redemption, but I didn't need a parent. Clare did. I hoped that wherever they were now, they were together, and happy. Even if I did want to punch his stupid ghost in its stupid face.

"I wonder what's going to happen to this place now," I said, kicking one of the charred beams that once held up the ceiling of the Red Room. Beneath it, sunlight twinkled off shards of crystal that had once been Madame's antique port decanter.

"You do not need to wonder," Elena piped up. "I own it."

"What?"

"Madame Usher willed it to me in the event of her death," Elena said, reaching into her pocket to tip out another cigarette. "Apparently, she wrote that I was the one woman capable of following in her footsteps. But I do not think it should be a school any longer. We should let sleeping ghosts lie. Instead, I think a wildlife sanctuary. We will give the land back to the wolves and the trees. I've already set up a trust, and I found an expert named Eli Hart down in Emerald Beach who's putting a team together to manage it."

She flashed that beautiful, enigmatic smile as she gazed out across her husband's funeral pyre. And I wondered again, as I had wondered so many times since that awful night, if Elena was a victim or a cold, calculating murderess. Did she accidentally kill Radcliffe trying to defend herself from his vicious advances, or did she catch him by surprise with a blow to the head and then staged the scene by pulling down his pants and smashing up the house? Was Donelle talking about Radcliffe when she wrote about the 'deviant sexual proclivities' she witnessed, or was she an ordinary old homophobe who couldn't stomach seeing Victor and Harrison together?

Just another mystery that would be buried with Manderley.

I threw my arms around my friend and kissed her cheek. Dorien came up beside us and wrapped his arms around us both. Ivan and Titus joined us, Titus jiggling our daughter on his hip. I rested my face on Ivan's shoulder and thanked the ghosts of Manderley. This place had taken so much for all of us, but it hadn't taken our love. The music that beat in our hearts for each other still thrummed in our veins.

Hand in hand, we turned our backs on the charred remains of Manderley Academy, and stepped forward into our future.

THE END

Want to meet the dark and dangerous men of the Triumvirate and the girl who holds their heart? Check out this new dark reverse harem series by Steffanie Holmes:

Psst. I have a secret.

Are you ready?

I'm Mackenzie Malloy, and everyone thinks they know who I am.

Five years ago, I disappeared.

No one has seen me or my family outside the walls of Malloy Manor since.
But now I'm coming to reclaim my throne:
The Ice Queen of Stonehurst Prep is back.

Standing between me and my everything?
Three things can bring me down:
The sweet guy who wants answers from his former friend.
The rock god who wants to f*ck me.
The king who'll crush me before giving up his crown.

They think they can ruin me, wreck it all, but I won't let them.
I'm not the Mackenzie Eli used to know.
Hot boys and rock gods like Gabriel won't win me over.
And just like Noah, I'll kill to keep my crown.

I'm just a poor little rich girl with the stolen life.
I'm here to tear down three princes,
before they destroy me.

Read now:
http://books2read.com/mystolenlife

Get your free copy of *Cabinet of Curiosities*, a Steffanie Holmes compendium of short stories and bonus scenes. To get this collection, all you need to do is sign up for updates with the Steffanie Holmes newsletter.

http://www.steffanieholmes.com/newsletter

You've been waiting a long time for the final book in Faye's series, and for that I'm so grateful. Thank you for your patience with this artsy-fartsy author, especially as she navigates life and writing during a global pandemic.

In writing Manderley Academy, I drew on numerous novels, poison manuals, and true hauntings for inspiration. If you're a fan of gothic literature, you may notice some of the illusions and names in homage to my literary heroes and heroines. At the centre of it all is Manderley – named in honour of the grand house at the centre of Daphne du Maurier's *Rebecca*, one of my favourite books of all time. If you haven't read it, I encourage you to do so, although you may not be able to turn the lights out until you reach the last page.

I've waited to the very end to tell you about the true story that inspired these books. I didn't want to give you any spoilers. I'd like to tell you now.

Walburga Oesterreich was a housewife in the early 20th century, married to Fred – the owner of a Milwaukee apron factory. Fred's business was successful and he gave Dolly (everyone called her Dolly because you would, with a name like

Walburga, wouldn't you?) everything she wanted – a nice house, lovely clothes, lots of antiques and objects and things, a good life. He was also away from home a lot, and when he was home he drank. And got mean. Fred and Dolly had huge screaming rows that caught the attention of neighbours in their upper-class street. Those neighbours often gossiped about Dolly's 'wandering eye' and flirtations with men who weren't her husband.

One day in 1913, Dolly's sewing machine stopped working. She called up Fred in a tizzy and he sent over 'a boy' from the factory to fix it. That boy was 17-year-old Otto Sanhuber.

Dolly and Otto began their affair that day. At first, they met at a hotel, but soon Dolly was inviting Otto over to her home when Fred was away. But those nosy neighbours started to notice Otto's comings and goings. Dolly tried to cover up the affair by telling people Otto was her 'vagabond half-brother' but no one was buying it.

Word got back to Fred, and he told his wife to choose – her lover or her lavish lifestyle. She chose the house and the money and the fancy clothes and Fred. And Otto disappeared from their lives.

But all was not well. Fred was drinking more than ever, and he'd become convinced their house was haunted. He'd find items moved from where he left them, noises in the house when he and Dolly were in a room together, food missing from the kitchen, and the sensation of being watched. It was starting to freak him out.

The couple moved to Los Angeles for a new start and to expand Fred's business, but the ghost followed them to their new home. Dolly was preoccupied setting up their lavish new pad with all her beloved things, so she might not have noticed that Fred's drinking was worse. Or that he would never be alone in the house – if she was out, he would invite a friend around. She never saw his paranoia – Fred was convinced this nameless phantom intended to do him harm.

Dolly and Fred went out to a friend's house. They came home around midnight and got into a screaming fight. Neighbours heard the argument, and then they heard gunshots. They kicked in the front door and found Fred's dead body on the floor, shot three times, and thumping and knocking coming from upstairs. They followed the sound and found Dolly crying, locked in a closet. They found no trace of the intruder, but Fred's cash, gold watch, and other valuables had been taken. However, no one had seen an intruder entering or leaving the neighbourhood. For a long time, the crime went unsolved.

A year later, Dolly was in a relationship with Roy Clum, a film producer. One day, she handed him a pistol and asked him to dispose of it in the Le Brea Tar Pits. Roy agreed to do it, but a few months afterward their relationship went sour, and Roy realised the gun was the exact one used to kill Fred. He went to the police with his story, and Dolly was arrested.

Dolly's attorney, Herman Shapiro, was quick to point out at her trial that she couldn't be the murderer, since she was locked in the closet. Herman – who was Dolly's new lover – wore a watch that looked suspiciously identical to the one taken from Fred's body.

One day during the trial, Dolly came to Herman and gave him some strange instructions. Herman was intrigued, but he did what Dolly said. He went home and prepared a meal, placed it on a tray, and took it upstairs to Dolly's room. He set the food down in the closet and whistled. A moment later, a panel slid open in the closet wall and a man's face appeared.

The man in the wall told Herman everything. He *was* Otto Sanhuber. He had been living in the walls and attic of Dolly's homes for over a decade, ever since Fred forced her to break off their affair. He had been the one making the noises that had so terrified Fred. And he had heard their screaming fight on the night of the party.

Otto was concerned Fred would hurt Dolly, so he took Fred's

gun and went downstairs. Fred attacked Otto, and the gun went off twice into his chest. Fred fell to the ground, and Otto shot him again to make sure he was gone.

Herman told Otto to run away. He knew that Dolly wouldn't be convicted of murder because she'd been locked in the closet. If he took Otto to the police, Herman's reputation would be ruined. So Otto went to Canada and in 1925, Dolly got off scot free.

(There's even more to this story, as Otto returns to LA in 1930 and gets arrested, but I've already rambled enough).

I heard this story on a podcast called *Lore*, which explores true stories of our dark past. I think you'd probably enjoy it.

I've created a playlist for the Broken Muses of Manderley Academy series. You'll find it on Spotify here. I've tried to include every song I mention in the text, as well as some I love that I feel Faye and the Broken Muse boys would adore. I've included some more modern music, too – a bit of goth, a smidge of metal (for many metal musicians, like Titus, are classically-trained and heavily inspired by classical roots). Maybe it will spark your own 'Come to Dorien' moment, or you'll find some cool new tunes to jam along.

As always, it takes a village to bring a book to life. I'd like to thank my cantankerous drummer husband for reading this manuscript and giving me so many ideas to make it better. And for being my lighthouse. And for putting up with me blasting Bach at full volume.

To Kit, Bri, Elaina, Katya, the SpecFicNZ community, and the Noods for all the writerly encouragement and advice. To Meg and Eveis for the epically helpful editing job, and to Lori for the stunning covers. To Sam and Iris, for the daily Facebook shenanigans that help keep me sane while I spend my days stuck at home covered in cats.

To you, the reader, for going on this journey with me, even though it's led to some dark places. If you're enjoying *Manderley Academy* and want to read more from me, check out my dark reverse harem bully romance series, *Kings of Miskatonic Prep.* HP Lovecraft meets *Cruel Intentions* in this dark paranormal reverse harem bully romance that's definitely not for the faint of heart. Hazel is the most badass FMC I've ever written, and I think you'll love meeting her. Read here: http://books2read.com/shunned.

You might enjoy another of my reverse harem series – The Nevermore Bookshop Mysteries is what you'd get if you crossed Agatha Christie with Black Books and added a harem of famous literary men. It's my most popular series to date, and it's a lot more light-hearted and fun (despite all the murder). Start book 1, *A Dead and Stormy Night* – http://books2read.com/adeadandstormynight.

Every week I send out a newsletter to fans – it features a spooky story about a real-life haunting or strange criminal case that has inspired one of my books, as well as news about upcoming releases and a free book of bonus scenes called *Cabinet of Curiosities.* To get on the mailing list all you gotta do is head to my website: http://www.steffanieholmes.com/newsletter

If you want to hang out and talk about all things Broken Muse, my readers are sharing their theories and discussing the book over in my Facebook group, Books That Bite. Come join the fun.

I'm so happy you enjoyed this story! I'd love it if you wanted to leave a review on Amazon or Goodreads. It will help other readers to find their next read.

Thank you, thank you! I love you heaps! Until next time.

Steff

EXCERPT: STONEHURST PREP, BOOK 1
READ THE FIRST CHAPTER OF MY STOLEN LIFE

Enjoy this short teaser from book 1 of Stonehurst Prep, My Stolen Life.
http://books2read.com/mystolenlife

I roll over in bed and slam against a wall.

Huh? Odd.

My bed isn't pushed against a wall. I must've twisted around in my sleep and hit the headboard. I do thrash around a lot, especially when I have bad dreams, and tonights was particularly gruesome. My mind stretches into the silence, searching for the tendrils of my nightmare. *I'm lying in bed and some dark shadow comes and lifts me up, pinning my arms so they hurt. He drags me downstairs to my mother, slumped in her favorite chair. At first, I think she passed out drunk after a night at the club, but then I see the dark pool expanding around her feet, staining the designer rug.*

I see the knife handle sticking out of her neck.

I see her glassy eyes rolled toward the ceiling.

I see the window behind her head, and my own reflection in the glass, my face streaked with blood, my eyes dark voids of pain and hatred.

But it's okay now. It was just a dream. It's—

OW.

I hit the headboard again. I reach down to rub my elbow, and my hand grazes a solid wall of satin. On my other side.

What the hell?

I open my eyes into a darkness that is oppressive and complete, the kind of darkness I'd never see inside my princess bedroom with its flimsy purple curtains letting in the glittering skyline of the city. The kind of darkness that folds in on me, pressing me against the hard, un-bedlike surface I lie on.

Now the panic hits.

I throw out my arms, kick with my legs. I hit walls. Walls all around me, lined with satin, dense with an immense weight pressing from all sides. Walls so close I can't sit up or bend my knees. I scream, and my scream bounces back at me, hollow and weak.

I'm in a coffin. I'm in a motherfucking coffin, and I'm *still alive.*

I scream and scream and scream. The sound fills my head and stabs at my brain. I know all I'm doing is using up my precious oxygen, but I can't make myself stop. In that scream I lose myself, and every memory of who I am dissolves into a puddle of terror.

When I do stop, finally, I gasp and pant, and I taste blood and stale air on my tongue. A cold fear seeps into my bones. Am I dying? My throat crawls with invisible bugs. Is this what it feels like to die?

I hunt around in my pockets, but I'm wearing purple pajamas, and the only thing inside is a bookmark Daddy gave me. I can't see it of course, but I know it has a quote from Julius Caesar on it. *Alea iacta est. The die is cast.*

Like fuck it is.

I think of Daddy, of everything he taught me – memories too dark to be obliterated by fear. Bile rises in my throat. I swallow, choke it back. Daddy always told me our world is forged in blood. I might be only thirteen, but I know who he is, what he's capable of. I've heard the whispers. I've seen the way people hurry to appease him whenever he enters a room. I've had the lessons from Antony in what to do if I find myself alone with one of Daddy's enemies.

Of course, they never taught me what to do if one of those enemies *buries me alive.*

I can't give up.

I claw at the satin on the lid. It tears under my fingers, and I pull out puffs of stuffing to reach the wood beneath. I claw at the surface, digging splinters under my nails. Cramps arc along my arm from the awkward angle. I know it's hopeless; I know I'll never be able to scratch my way through the wood. Even if I can, I *feel* the weight of several feet of dirt above me. I'd be crushed in moments. But I have to try.

I'm my father's daughter, and this is not how I die.

I claw and scratch and tear. I lose track of how much time passes in the tiny space. My ears buzz. My skin weeps with cold sweat.

A noise reaches my ears. A faint shifting. A scuffle. A scrape and thud above my head. Muffled and far away.

Someone piling the dirt in my grave.

Or maybe...

...maybe someone digging it out again.

Fuck, fuck, please.

"Help." My throat is hoarse from screaming. I bang the lid with my fists, not even feeling the splinters piercing my skin. "Help me!"

THUD. Something hits the lid. The coffin groans. My veins burn with fear and hope and terror.

The wood cracks. The lid is flung away. Dirt rains down on me, but I don't care. I suck in lungfuls of fresh, crisp air. A circle of light blinds me. I fling my body up, up into the unknown. Warm arms catch me, hold me close.

"I found you, Claws." Only Antony calls me by that nickname.

Of course, it would be my cousin who saves me. Antony drags me over the lip of the grave, *my* grave, and we fall into crackling leaves and damp grass.

I sob into his shoulder. Antony rolls me over, his fingers pressing all over my body, checking if I'm hurt. He rests my back against cold stone. "I have to take care of this," he says. I watch through tear-filled eyes as he pushes the dirt back into the hole – into what was supposed to be my grave – and brushes dead leaves on top. When he's done, it's impossible to tell the ground's been disturbed at all.

I tremble all over. I can't make myself stop shaking. Antony comes back to me and wraps me in his arms. He staggers to his feet, holding me like I'm weightless. He's only just turned eighteen, but already he's built like a tank.

I let out a terrified sob. Antony glances over his shoulder, and there's panic in his eyes. "You've got to be quiet, Claws," he whispers. "They might be nearby. I'm going to get you out of here."

I can't speak. My voice is gone, left in the coffin with my screams. Antony hoists me up and darts into the shadows. He runs with ease, ducking between rows of crumbling gravestones and beneath bent and gnarled trees. Dimly, I recognize this place – the old Emerald Beach cemetery, on the edge of Beaumont Hills overlooking the bay, where the original families of Emerald Beach buried their dead.

Where someone tried to bury me.

Antony bursts from the trees onto a narrow road. His car is parked in the shadows. He opens the passenger door and settles me inside before diving behind the wheel and gunning the engine.

We tear off down the road. Antony rips around the deadly corners like he's on a racetrack. Steep cliffs and crumbling old mansions pass by in a blur.

"My parents…" I gasp out. "Where are my parents?"

"I'm sorry, Claws. I didn't get to them in time. I only found you."

I wait for this to sink in, for the fact I'm now an orphan to hit me in a rush of grief. But I'm numb. My body won't stop shaking, and I left my brain and my heart buried in the silence of that coffin.

"Who?" I ask, and I fancy I catch a hint of my dad's cold savagery in my voice. "Who did this?"

"I don't know yet, but if I had to guess, it was Brutus. I warned your dad that he was making alliances and building up to a challenge. I think he's just made his move."

I try to digest this information. Brutus – who was once my father's trusted friend, who'd eaten dinner at our house and played Chutes and Ladders with me – killed my parents and buried me alive. But it bounces off the edge of my skull and doesn't stick. The life I had before, my old life, it's gone, and as I twist and grasp for memories, all I grab is stale coffin air.

"What now?" I ask.

Antony tosses his phone into my lap. "Look at the headlines."

I read the news app he's got open, but the words and images blur together. "This… this doesn't make any sense…"

"They think you're dead, Claws," Antony says. "That means you have to *stay* dead until we're strong enough to move against him. Until then, you have to be a ghost. But don't worry, I'll protect you. I've got a plan. We'll hide you where they'll never think to look."

Read My Stolen Life now
http://books2read.com/mystolenlife

AGATHA CHRISTIE MEET BLACK
BOOKS

**What do you get when you cross a cursed bookshop, three hot
fictional men, and a punk rock heroine nursing a broken
heart?**

After being fired from her fashion internship in New York City,
Mina Wilde decides it's time to reevaluate her life. She returns to
the quaint English village where she grew up to take a job at the

local bookshop, hoping that being surrounded by great literature will help her heal from a devastating blow.

But Mina soon discovers her life is stranger than fiction – a mysterious curse on the bookshop brings fictional characters to life in lust-worthy bodies. Mina finds herself babysitting Poe's raven, making hot dogs for Heathcliff, and getting IT help from James Moriarty, all while trying not to fall for the three broken men who should only exist within her imagination.

When Mina's ex-best friend shows up dead with a knife in her back, she's the chief suspect. She'll have to solve the murder if she wants to clear her name. Will her fictional boyfriends be able to keep her out of prison?

Agatha Christie meets Black Books in this steamy paranormal romance collection. Join a brooding antihero, a master criminal, a cheeky raven, and a heroine with a big heart (and an even bigger book collection) for three zany supernatural murder mysteries by *USA Today* bestselling author Steffanie Holmes.

This collection includes books 1-3 in the Nevermore Bookshop series, plus Heathcliff's shop rules, and alternative POV scenes from Mina's heroes. Read on only if you believe one book boyfriend isn't enough.

READ NOW
books2read.com/nevermorebox

ABOUT THE AUTHOR

Steffanie Holmes is the *USA Today* bestselling author of the paranormal, gothic, dark, and fantastical. Her books feature clever, witty heroines, secret societies, creepy old mansions and alpha males who *always* get what they want.

Legally-blind since birth, Steffanie received the 2017 Attitude Award for Artistic Achievement. She was also a finalist for a 2018 Women of Influence award.

Steff is the creator of *Rage Against the Manuscript* – a resource of free content, books, and courses to help writers tell their story, find their readers, and build a badass writing career.

Steffanie lives in New Zealand with her husband, a horde of cantankerous cats, and their medieval sword collection.

STEFFANIE HOLMES NEWSLETTER

Grab a free copy of *Cabinet of Curiosities* – a Steffanie Holmes compendium of short stories and bonus scenes – when you sign up for updates with the Steffanie Holmes newsletter.

http://www.steffanieholmes.com/newsletter

Come hang with Steffanie
www.steffanieholmes.com
hello@steffanieholmes.com